BABE'S BIBLE

SISTER ACTS

KAREN JONES

DARTON · LONGMAN + TODD

I dedicate this book to my three sisters –
especially Ali over recent years –
women who fiercely face the edge of
darkness and continue to shine.

First published in 2013 by
Darton, Longman and Todd Ltd
1 Spencer Court
140 – 142 Wandsworth High Street
London SW18 4JJ

ISBN: 978-0-232-52980-7

A catalogue record for this book is available from the British Library.

All characters appearing in this work are fictitious. Any resemblance to
real persons, living or dead, is purely coincidental.

Printed and bound in Great Britain by Bell & Bain, Glasgow

CONTENTS

ACKNOWLEDGEMENTS

I want to thank my husband Si, who still has the ability to make me laugh, and my children Sophie and Sam for inspiring me to keep thinking of how to communicate an old story in fresh ways.

Thank you to the wonderful women at City Hearts: Karen, Lara, Helen, Sue, Tina, Eva, Queen and Amanda for all your stories and insights. Meeting each of you has changed me. Thank you.

My grateful thanks to Susie Bishop and Barbara Hughes for your insights, questions and corrections.

Finally thank you to all those who have contacted me after reading *Babe's Bible Gorgeous Grace* – I'm very grateful for all your encouragement and anticipation of this sequel. You keep me going in the long hours spent alone in the creative process.

1. CHANGE

Acts 2–5:11 The women of new beginnings

From the safe distance of the bench she watched the blonde, willowy woman pushing her son on a swing. His dark curls alternately covered his face then flew behind him like tendrils of smoke. He squealed with anticipation as he rushed towards his mother again and again. She watched each face pensively to see if either would tire of the repetitive game. Neither did. She marvelled.

She shifted in her seat, beginning to feel uncomfortably hot in the May sunshine. She slid across the bench into the shifting shadow cast by a chestnut tree and lit a cigarette.

Doesn't matter, she thought pressing her free hand against her belly. But through the smoke she continued to gaze hungrily at mother and child.

� ✖ ✖

Grace turned at the scent of cigarette smoke. Its seductive earthiness reminded her of heady adolescent days; missing lessons; lying hidden in long grassy fields surrounding her boarding school; gazing up through swaying stalks; watching clouds expand and change against endless blue through the forbidden, mysterious haze she exhaled through her mouth and nose.

She smiled at the young woman on the bench and then looked back to Zack who was shouting 'Mummy!' demanding that he alone have her attention.

'Yes, love, I'm here,' she replied patiently. The wind caught a corkscrew of her white-blonde hair, throwing it into her face. She scraped it away and tucked it behind her ear.

'I want to go on the slide now,' Zack kicked his legs, making the swing wobble and lose its rhythm.

'Okay – but just wait 'til I get you out.'

His little body was twisting now, one knee half out of the confines of the swing seat and harness. 'Wait, Zack!' Grace's voice rose, warning him of the danger he was in. He stopped struggling. Grace moved towards him and caught hold of the chains, slowing the swing safely. Then she helped him out and set him on the ground. No sooner had his feet touched down than he was off towards the slide.

Grace followed. *He's not even four but already he's so sure of himself.* She shook her head thinking of the pleasure this characteristic gave Peter. It disconcerted her, but she loved it too. She shoved her hands into her jeans pockets feeling her hipbones jutting out. She hadn't needed to stick to salads since Isaac had been born and hadn't wanted to either; she burnt calories just watching him. She liked not thinking about what she ate; she liked not thinking about herself. He really had fulfilled his name and surprised them both with laughter. Never in all her days had she hoped to be as happy as she'd been in becoming his mother.

※　※　※

The watching woman took a last drag and then stubbed out her cigarette on the side of the bench. She leaned across the gap between her and a rubbish bin and flicked the butt on top of the overflow of crisp packets, ice-lolly sticks and soft drink cans. She noticed a doll's head, one eye missing, lips pursed and pink, with a few tufts of blonde hair still intact lying on top of a crumpled newspaper. She shuddered involuntarily and got up, walking quickly away. Her eyes followed the boy as he hurtled down the slide into the waiting arms of his mother. The sound of their laughter hurt her.

※　※　※

Grace's eyes followed the woman as she walked away. She was holding Zack upside down, tickling his tummy, making him squeal with delight. She felt something, something that had become familiar over the last five years: like wind tugging at a kite. She stopped tickling Zack and concentrated hard on the diminishing figure.

'Mummy!' demanded Zack, slapping her thighs.

'Sorry, love,' she turned him right way up and plonked him on the rubber surface of the play area. He ran back to the slide's ladder. She followed, pondering the sense she had. She found she was praying in the language she often used when she didn't know how to pray.

'Wat'cha doing Mummy?' Zack pulled back from the shoulder he'd snuggled into after landing in her arms again. He touched her lips with his chubby fingers.

'Praying,' she smiled.

'Why?' he pulled at her lower lip.

'Not sure,' she caught his hands in hers and kissed them. 'Shall we go home for some lunch?'

He nodded vigorously.

※　※　※

The watching woman lay on the operating table in the impersonal clinic and stared hard at the ceiling.

The anaesthetist leaned over her with the gas mask in his hand, 'Please count from ten down to one for me,' he asked politely.

As he placed it over her mouth and nose she began to count in English but by the time she got to 'six' she was speaking in another language. She faded out at 'four'.

When she came round she was in a ward with others. She vomited on herself, wishing she were alone. Someone called a nurse, who huffed and sighed as she changed the top sheet and blanket. Dull throbbing pain oozed through the morphine barrier. She turned her head towards the wall, yearning not to exist.

When she next opened her eyes, someone was shaking her. Glass marble thoughts scattered on the stone floor of her brain. She squinted to focus on the face leaning over her. Dread fear sucked her down. Her whole body recoiled into the bed away from him.

'All done?' he asked brightly, his coarse voice mirroring his shaved head and the tattoo that wove its way up his neck and around the back of his left ear. She nodded, eyes down.

'Good girl. So – you be out today? Got to get back to work, you know; not lying around here – no money here.'

Overhearing him, the nurse came alongside, wondering what Eastern European country he was from. 'She's lost a lot of blood. She's going to need to stay in for a few days just until we've stabilised her.'

He looked annoyed, but then quickly cloaked his expression. He was now charming, accentuating his accent, surprised and concerned over the blood loss. The nurse looked anxious but left them.

He leaned down and stroked her hair, feigning affection and whispered into her ear, 'Three days – no more. Don't think about escape. I have eyes and ears everywhere. You are mine.' He pretended to kiss her forehead, pressing his teeth into her skin. As he pulled away he smirked down at her. When he was gone her body began to shake.

The nurse returned and took her temperature. As she waited at the bedside, their eyes met briefly. 'Is there anything I can do for you?' she asked, concern furrowing her brow.

Rescue me! The internal scream did not reach her eyes, which were well practised in the art of subterfuge. In broken English she replied, 'No – thanks you – I sleep now.' As the nurse walked away the watching woman's mind drifted back to the mother and son she'd seen in the park. She rolled onto her side, pulling her knees up to her chest as silent tears soaked through the frayed pillowcase edge and pooled on institutional plastic.

❉ ❉ ❉

After lunch Grace put Zack down for his afternoon nap. She read a Thomas the Tank Engine story to him as he held his favourite Thomas and Gordon toys in either hand, then she kissed his forehead. She could hear him telling Gordon to be good and go to sleep as she pulled the door, leaving it slightly ajar.

She cleared lunch away and then went to her computer. She clicked on her emails and saw that a search engine had sent two job vacancies to her. She opened the first one. She read through the details but felt no surge of interest. *What is the matter with me?* She downloaded the application form anyway, printed it off and lay it beside her laptop.

Folding her hands in her lap she looked up at the icon of Jesus that her grandmother had given her before she died. *What do you want me to do?*

She waited.

Nothing.

I can't go on like this much longer. Trevor told me last week that the diocese wants him to become a training incumbent and to take on a new curate in September. We'll have to get out of this house. I know you know all this ... but why aren't you speaking to me? Please tell me what to do – I don't just want to do a job for a job's sake. I want to do what you created me to do. Please speak to me this week.

She picked up her journal, which she'd written in early that morning. Maybe the answer lay somewhere among its pages? She flipped back through neat prose, poetry, sketches and quotes from books as well as Bible verses. She came to an early entry after arriving at St Matt's. Trevor had been the Associate Minister when she'd started her curacy. It was funny to think he was now the vicar. She flipped forward through the days she'd struggled to support Chloe in the aftermath of her affair with Tom, the previous vicar. She smiled as she came across an entry after Chloe and she had ended up kneeling and praying together on her living room floor – the first of several breakthroughs.

She flipped on to the amazing day when she and Peter had seen their first scan of Zack at fifteen weeks. The scan photos she'd stuck onto the page still moved her. She sighed and traced the image of Zack's tiny yet completely formed body with a finger.

He had been born halfway through her four year curacy. She'd taken extra maternity leave after giving birth to him. It had been hard to return to finish the last two years of her curacy, part time, but she'd done it. St Matt's parochial church council had gladly agreed to her proposal of staying on in a non-stipendiary capacity for another two years, as the diocese had said they couldn't have another curate until Trevor had got some experience under his belt. They'd allowed her and Peter to continue living in the house in exchange for a low rent. But time was running out now and she hadn't found anything in the diocese that grabbed her attention. She'd looked further afield, but hadn't really wanted to move out of the area, and anyway nothing had felt right.

Maybe I'm meant to focus on being a Mum? She waited.

No – there's something more, I know it, but what?

Please show me ...

The gold and blue Jesus stared serenely back at her.

It's okay for you – you know everything and can see what's ahead. No wonder you're so calm! She smiled at the image that represented her dearest friend. *Sorry, Lord – I do trust you – please help me wait for your leading. You are the way.* She spilled over into prayer out of reverence and creaturely awe. She exulted in friendship with her Creator. She didn't look at the second job vacancy.

It only seemed like minutes later that she heard Zack's feet landing on his bedroom floor and padding across to his door.

'Mummy?'

'Coming, love,' she went through the hallway and up the stairs as Zack came out of his room. He was still holding Thomas and Gordon in either hand as he smiled sleepily at her. She loved these moments halfway between waking and sleeping. He curled up in her lap as she sat down on the top of the stairs. She breathed in the smell of him, savouring the moment. It was broken by the doorbell. Grace carried Zack downstairs. It looked like Chloe through the marbled, stained glass. It was.

'Hi, Grace,' Chloe looked strained.

'Hi, Chloe.'

'Go 'way,' said Zack.

'Sorry,' Grace laughed, 'he's just woken up. He'll be all right in a minute. Do you want to come in?'

'Yes please – any chance of a cuppa?' Chloe looked hopefully at her friend.

'Sure,' Grace stepped back to let Chloe past.

'Noooo!' Zack wailed.

'Oh, Zack, it's only Chloe. Let's see if there's any of those yummy, chocolate-chip cookies we made the other day. Do you think she'd like one?'

Zack shook his curls stubbornly as they followed Chloe into the kitchen, who dropped her bag unceremoniously onto the table, dragged out a chair and flopped into it. 'I am *so* tired,' Chloe exclaimed. 'Who'd be a mother? Honestly, if they'd told me it was going to be like this when I was feeling broody, I would have gone and got sterilised!'

Grace settled Zack onto the work counter while she filled the kettle with water and turned it on. He stared crossly at their intruder. Chloe was oblivious.

Grace didn't respond to Chloe's comment. She felt slightly annoyed. She reached over Zack's head to the cupboard where the cookie tin lived. She lifted it down and opened it. Zack was finally distracted from his post-sleep grump. He tenderly put Gordon down beside him and chose a large one.

'Do you want coffee or tea?' Grace asked.

'Black coffee please,' Chloe replied, rummaging in her bag and pulling out a hairbrush. She dragged it through hair that looked like it hadn't been brushed since the day before.

Grace looked up from her pale blue mugs, 'The last time you had black coffee was ...'

'Yeah, I know, when I was in such a mess after the affair. Don't know why I've gone back to it now. Just suddenly hate the taste of milk,' she said as she gathered her dark hair into a sleek ponytail.

Grace lifted Zack down and settled him on his booster seat at the table. She placed his plastic cup of juice in front of him. 'Do you want a delicious homemade biscuit?' Grace held out the tin to Chloe.

'No thanks, haven't been feeling very hungry lately either.'

'Oh?' Grace brought the steaming mugs over to the table and settled herself next to Zack who was happily munching away.

'I'm finding it hard juggling everything,' Chloe cupped her mug in her small hands. She looked at her watch, 'I'll have to go and pick up Charlie soon, I've only got forty-five minutes. See this is what I mean – there's no time for me! I've been wanting to have a catch up with you for ages and haven't been able to find the time and when I do, it's gone before you know it.'

'We all knew being a mature student would be tough for you – with three kids and a house to run. Doesn't Mark help?'

'Yeah – sort of. They all do. Each of us has our chores, but it still feels like it's about scoring brownie points rather than anyone really doing it out of love. Don't you feel like that now with Zack and ministry and Peter? I mean, Peter doesn't even come to church – so you must know what I mean? It's like I'm looking after everyone else, but no one's looking after me.'

Grace's jaw muscles tightened. 'I can't say that I do feel like that. I actually feel like I'm the luckiest woman alive. I have everything I could possibly want in life – well, apart from knowing what I'm supposed to do next.'

Chloe's green eyes scanned her friend's face, 'I've annoyed you, haven't I?'

Grace fiddled with the handle of her coffee mug and then slowly looked up at Chloe, 'Sorry, yes – you have. I know you've had three children and they're all much older than Zack, but I never thought I'd even have him. I don't care what it costs me, I'm grateful to be a mother.'

'I'm sorry,' Chloe reached over to Grace's hand, 'I know ... but you wait 'til he's a teenager, then you'll understand. Don't get me wrong, I love my kids to bits, but it's just so exhausting. Melanie is absolutely foul these days and I am running out of ideas as to how to relate to her or help her,' she paused. 'Then with studying on top of everything else, I find myself crying for no reason sometimes when I'm driving to college. I've even noticed that my hair is falling out here,' she lifted up a long piece of fringe to reveal a thinning patch in her hairline.

Annoyance forgotten, Grace reached over and felt Chloe's scalp. 'You're right! You must be really stressed! Has Mark seen this?'

'Yeah – he just tells me to do less – stop worrying,' she rolled her eyes. 'He doesn't really engage with Mel and Charlie. It's only Josh he seems to bond with. If Charlie were sporty he'd probably pay him more attention, but he's more like me – more arty,' she smiled thinking of her youngest son, 'He's still innocent. But Melanie ... I know she's smoking now.'

'Really? Can you smell it on her?'

'No – she's pretty clever about that. But I found them in her bag last week. You should have heard that conversation,' Chloe grimaced.

Grace smiled, recalling a similar conversation she'd had with her mother many years ago.

They both took sips of their coffee.

'Can I get down now?' Zack asked.

'Yes love. Do you want to watch a Thomas DVD?'

He nodded vigorously flashing his tiny milk teeth in a big grin. Grace helped him down and together they went into the living room.

Chloe called after them, 'If only I could do that with Melanie!'

Grace came back and topped their mugs up. 'Hey, maybe you should drag her along to some of your psychology classes?'

Chloe laughed, 'Yeah, and guess what? It would all turn out to be my fault!'

Grace smiled remembering how she had blamed her mother for so many things for so many years. 'Maybe when she has her own children, she'll understand how you feel?'

'Oh God, no – not yet – not for years yet! I am not going to be a grandmother – not for a long time!' her expression changed as the next thought struck her, 'Do you think she's doing it already? She's only sixteen.'

'And legal,' Grace raised an eyebrow.

Chloe rubbed her forehead anxiously, 'See this is what I mean – it's too much. I'm struggling to cope with her and study and the boys and the house.'

'Hey – you raised her well, loved her a lot. She'll be all right in the end. They say they don't listen to a word you say but they do copy what you do.'

'That's what I'm worried about,' Chloe laughed dryly as Grace realised what she'd said.

'Not that! Sorry Chloe … but you know … the rest of your life. You guys have done so well since,' she climbed out of the hole she'd just dug.

'It's okay, Grace – I understand. I think we've done well?' it came out as a question.

'And you'll get your degree this summer.'

'Yeah – who'd have thought it? My Year 6 teacher would be amazed. She hated me – couldn't teach me. She always said on every report, "Could do better". But I never did – well, not until now,' Chloe smiled like a proud child.

'Any thoughts as to what you'll do with it?' Grace brushed some crumbs off the tabletop into her palm and then tipped them into her empty mug.

'That's what I wanted to talk to you about. I've thought about applying to Relate or trying to get work with a local surgery but what worries me is that I'd be hamstrung by political correctness. I wouldn't be able to bring the spiritual aspect of being human into the equation. I don't think I could work like that. I don't think I want to.'

'That's why I got ordained!' Grace smiled.

'No … that's definitely not for me,' Chloe laughed. 'They'd never have me anyway, not with my history.'

Grace smiled a little sadly, thinking of her own questionable history, but said nothing.

'Even if they didn't, it wouldn't be for me, Grace. I'd hate the restrictions – the public role. Can you imagine Melanie's reaction if I came home with a dog collar? That doesn't bear thinking about!' Chloe laughed. 'No – counselling is definitely the way for me. I think I want to set up some sort of psychosexual therapy practice. I was wondering if it might be something the church would consider as part of our ministry to the community?'

Grace chuckled, imagining a PCC discussion over a proposal like that. 'Now that would be interesting!' she tilted her head back and laughed. 'Can you imagine Doris Glenshaw's reaction or Giles Winter's?'

'But I'm serious, Grace. Don't you think it's a much-needed ministry? I mean – look at the two of us. We've both had to muddle our way through stuff, with no help from anyone – well, except each other, of course. And if we're anything to go by, don't you think the need must be pretty great out there?'

'I don't have a steady stream of people confessing their sexual brokenness to me,' Grace sighed, 'but I know you're right. I do wonder what's going on under the surface when I look out across the congregations some Sundays.'

'I don't mean just in the church – I mean out there in the community,' Chloe's smooth brow furrowed in concern. 'According to the social services they're only seeing the tip of the iceberg.'

'Really ... even out here in suburbia?'

'Apparently the leafy suburbs of London are the new hotbed of the sex trade.'

'What rubbish! There are no strip clubs or massage parlours here, are there?' Grace racked her brain, scanning her memory for all the streets she knew in their town.

'No. It's more an underworld of human trafficking; brothels running out of nice semi-detached houses in ordinary cul-de-sacs,' Chloe said.

'You mean Miss Smith next door could be a madam?' Grace joked.

'I'm serious Grace – it's no laughing matter.'

'How do you know all this?' Grace asked, still incredulous.

'Don't you read the papers any more?' Chloe asked, 'Or watch the news?'

'Yeah – well – that has been something I've been meaning to get back to. I've lost touch with the world somewhat. I think part of me hasn't wanted to know about all the bad stuff going on.'

'You'd never know you used to be a journalist!' Chloe laughed.

'That was a lifetime ago.' Grace sighed, 'I had no child to think of or to protect.'

'Yeah ... well ... we've got to think about what kind of world we're leaving for our kids. We're part of it – either part of the problem or part of the solution,' a fierce light lit her dark eyes.

'Are you sure you don't want to get ordained?' Grace asked.

Chloe drank the remainder of her coffee, looked at her watch and began reaching for her bag. 'Gotta go. Think about it – will you?' Chloe said, ignoring Grace's repeated question as she stood up.

'Yeah – sure,' Grace followed her ambivalently to the door.

❊   ❊   ❊

It was Whitsun. Trevor and Grace processed in to St Matt's morning service.

Come Holy Spirit, she prayed. Her eyes scanned the familiar faces, alighting on one as Trevor began the service with a welcome. *The watching woman from the park!* In that instant the woman looked up and their eyes met. Grace saw her raw pain – it tingled her skin and constricted her throat.

Eventually Grace stood to preach, ' "In the last days, God says, I will pour out my Spirit on all people. Your sons and daughters will prophesy, your young men will see visions, your old men will dream dreams. Even on my servants, both men and women, I will pour out my Spirit in those days, and they will prophesy ... And everyone who calls on the name of the Lord will be saved." ' Grace looked up from the Bible and smiled.

'Because of these words, I stand before you today. A woman. A preacher woman, prophesying – speaking forth God's thoughts.

'A few years ago it would have been unheard of for someone like me to be doing something like this. I know it took many of you some serious adjustments in your thinking to receive ministry from me. But you too were able to do this because of these words.

'God's Spirit has led us together to this time in history where both men and women prophesy because the Spirit of God is being poured out on all people.

'It's not just the good people either; the religious, devout or special people. Believe me, I am none of those. Since the day of Pentecost God has been pouring out his Spirit on all sorts of people; on everyone who calls on the name of Jesus.' Grace paused. The congregation waited. The watching woman held on.

'What makes someone call on the name of the Lord?' she asked. 'History teaches us that it is those who have come to the end of themselves; who have realised how much they are in need of a greater power; those who have discovered that the princes of this world have feet of clay and that they are in need of a true saviour.

'The prostitute who anointed Jesus' feet with perfume and dried them with her hair: she gatecrashed a dinner party to get to her saviour. She didn't care that the host knew what she was. Right there in front of everyone she poured the perfume she would have used to massage her clients, all over Jesus' feet. She knelt there, weeping over them and kissing them. She uncovered her head, undid her hair – her crowning glory, a symbol of her sexuality in that culture – and wiped his feet.

'Was this woman there at Pentecost among the waiting believers? I believe so. And if so, was the Holy Spirit poured out upon her? – Most certainly. She loved much because she had been forgiven much. I often wonder what she did with all that love once she was baptised in the Holy Spirit?'

She spoke on about the effects of the Holy Spirit's outpouring, about the cowardly Peter becoming a bold preacher; about three thousand people being added to the fellowship of believers that day; about the miraculous signs that were done by him and the other apostles and about how all the believers gathered together and had everything in common, selling their possessions and giving to anyone as they had need.

She saw Trevor fidgeting out of the corner of her eye and knew she was in danger of going over her allotted time. There was so much more she wanted to say to persuade and inspire her listeners out of their comfortable English middle-classness, but she knew she had to stop.

'There have been outpourings of God's Spirit in this place in the past. But we can't rest on our laurels. We need a new outpouring for now, for all those who are calling on the name of the Lord now – today!'

She stopped.

'Let's pray,' she said, closing her eyes and lifting her hands. She began to tremble slightly as she prayed, 'Come Holy Spirit. Fill us again. We need you ... oh, how we need you.' She stood there for what seemed ages as tremors ran through her body.

A stunned silence hung over the congregation. Someone nervously cleared their throat.

But then a sound of someone crying became audible; then a second ... and a third. Hushed whispery prayers began brushing together like angels' wings and then someone started singing, 'Oh, come let us adore him ...'

'More Holy Spirit – more of you!' Grace prayed as confidence grew and voices rose together, a mixture of lament, joy and yearning.

Grace opened her eyes. *Was it like this on that first Whitsun?* She looked wonderingly around her. Anyone walking in could have been forgiven for thinking a spell had been cast over the people. She looked over her shoulder for Trevor, but he was nowhere to be seen. Several people had made their way to the communion rail and were kneeling, heads bowed in intimate communion with the Great Unseen. Grace noticed that the watching woman was among them.

She raised her voice over the noise, speaking into her microphone, 'The Lord is here!' she laughed.

Some responded, 'His Spirit is with us.'

Grace felt euphoric, 'Lift up your hearts.'

More replied, 'We lift them to the Lord.'

'I know that's not where we normally say that bit of liturgy, but it seems fitting,' she beamed round the congregation. 'This is the end of our service. It's a bit messy, but we hope you don't mind. Quite fitting for Pentecost, don't you think?'

Someone said 'Amen'.

'If you have children in their groups then you need to go and collect them, but if you wish to stay and pray, worship or be prayed with, then please do stay. Go in peace to love and serve the Lord.'

'In the name of Christ, Amen,' came the frayed response.

The band came in strongly with the chorus of a song. The prayer team that Grace had been training over the last couple of years moved towards the communion rail. Others made their way to the front to receive prayer. Soon there wasn't any room left at the rail. They stood haphazardly around the front, some with hands outstretched and heads raised, others with heads bowed and hands folded. Wondering what had happened to Trevor, Grace moved towards the woman from the park. She turned her microphone off.

'What's your name?' she asked leaning down to speak into the woman's ear. There was no reply, just the sound of weeping. Grace reached into her alb pocket for a tissue and gently pushed it through the mass of bleached blond hair that hid the woman's face.

'Spirit of God – fill your child. Cleanse and heal her of pain, of the wrongs done to her. Wash her clean ...' Grace switched into her prayer language, babbling quietly – a collaboration of timeless river over stones, worn smooth by the flow of rushing water. She waited for the Holy Spirit to do his work. Slowly the woman stopped trembling and sobbing. Eventually she became still.

As the band put their instruments away she finally raised her head. The last band member was making his way out the door and only a few people remained at the rail when Grace asked, 'Are you okay? What's your name?'

The woman wiped her nose with the sodden tissue, 'Anja,' she said with a strong accent. She pushed her hair back off her face.

'Are you okay?' Grace asked again.

'I don't know – I think,' she paused and then said, 'I know you from park.'

'Yes,' Grace replied.

'I not think you were – a religious,' she faltered.

'A priest?'

'Mm, yes. Where I come – is Catholic – only mens.'

Grace nodded, 'Where are you from?'

'Croatia. I come here five year now,' Anja looked uncertain.

'How old are you?' Grace asked.

'I twenty.'

Grace hid her surprise. She looked much older. 'Do you want to sit down – can I get you a drink?'

'Please,' Anja nodded getting awkwardly up off her knees. As Grace turned and walked towards the vestry she saw Trevor's feet sticking out of the choir stalls. She leaned over and looked down at him. He was laying full length on the floor, eyes closed and lips curved in a smile. Laughing to herself, Grace went and got a glass of water for Anja.

When she returned Anja asked, 'He hurt?' looking at Trevor's feet.

'No – he's just resting. He'll be fine. But you – now tell me what made you come to the front?' she asked in her forthright manner.

'You speak to me – all time – speaking to me. I ... I ...' she pressed her hand to her chest, 'I have pain here and then hot – very hot.' Her hand moved to her belly, 'Then here ...' she started to cry again.

'What?' Grace asked gently.

'I kill,' Anja looked into Grace's face with a tortured expression, pressing her hand into her belly.

'Oh,' Grace understood, reaching out and touching Anja's arm.

'I – this woman – you say,' Anja looked forlorn.

Grace's eyes were blank for a moment and then realisation dawned.

'They take me. I four – no – fifteen they take me – they beat me, give me drug. I – we – others – we come here – work here for them. Today, I run – I fear – but I run – I ...' she touched her belly again with both hands. 'I want ...' her voice lost power as she began to cry again.

'I know,' Grace said simply.

'They come – look for me,' Anja said in an anxious voice.

Without a moment's thought Grace said, 'You can come home with me. You'll be safe there.'

❋   ❋   ❋

'Have you gone stark raving mad?' Peter exclaimed in a stage whisper as he leaned over the bath and poured water on Zack's head.

Grace was sitting on the toilet hugging herself. 'No,' she said sullenly.

'What if she's a con artist? What if she's played on your sympathies and now that she's in our house, we'll have trouble getting her out?'

'You weren't there. You didn't see her pain. It was real,' Grace said. 'And anyway, when the Holy Spirit works like that, he exposes the truth about people.'

'Well I don't know about that ... what if she's a drug addict? What if she steals everything we've got? She could stab us to death in our sleep! I can't believe you would put Zack in danger like this,' Grace had never seen Peter so angry.

'She was afraid – she had nowhere else to go. She needed rescuing!'

'You should have called the police or the social services – not brought her back here! How do we know these people she works for won't come here, kick down our door and beat us senseless?'

'Daddy – stop being cross with Mummy!' Zack ordered through a dollop of bubbles he'd put on his nose.

The two adults looked at their son and then back at each other.

'I'm sorry. I should have discussed it with you first before inviting her,' Grace conceded begrudgingly.

'Good Mummy,' Zack splashed her. She smiled at him pensively.

'Bloody right!' Peter reached down to lift Zack up. 'Time to get out of the bath, now Zack, before Mummy thinks you can walk on water or turn it into wine or something.' Grace felt hurt. 'God, I need a drink!' he growled as his son clapped his face between his dripping hands.

'For goodness sake, Peter – grow up!' she snapped as she made her way out of the bathroom door ahead of him.

I should never have married him! she fumed. *He'll never get this.*

Peter carried Zack to his bedroom and began the ritual of pyjamas, toys that were privileged to be in bed with him that night and a story. Grace went and stood outside the guest room door. She tapped lightly on its stripped surface.

'Anja – can I come in?' she called softly. She didn't get a reply but turned the handle slowly opening the door wide enough to look in. Anja was curled up in a foetal position under the cream duvet. There was no sign of her clothes so Grace assumed she must still have them on. Her frayed fabric plimsolls stood neatly at the foot of the bed. Grace's heart winced.

✳ ✳ ✳

She put the phone in its cradle as Peter came into the kitchen looking weary.

'I've just spoken to the police,' she said guardedly.

'Good,' he sighed running his fingers through his thick, greying hair and arched his back. 'Our boy is waiting up there for you to say goodnight.'

'Okay,' she pushed herself off the edge of the kitchen worktop and made her way past him. He reached out and took hold of her arm.

'Sorry,' he said. 'Do you want a drink?' he looked sheepish.

Her blue eyes welled up. She tried to smile through, but her chin wobbled. 'It's okay – I should have asked you first. Yeah – I'll have some of that red you opened last night,' she went upstairs.

Sorry – sorry – he's your son – even if he doesn't acknowledge it. Thank you for him. What a contradiction – preaching one minute and fighting the next. She shook her head as she snuggled Zack.

When she came back down Peter was sitting on the sofa nursing his drink. She sat down beside him as he handed her a glass, 'She'll be okay, won't she?' he asked. 'I was overreacting, wasn't I?'

'Well, no – I think you were thinking clearer than me,' Grace sipped her wine. 'But I do think I have to help her.'

Peter put his hand on her leg and squeezed gently, 'That's what I love about you. You're all about compassion and what's right. But we've got Zack now.'

'I know ...' Grace leant her head back and stared at the ceiling. *It was so different for Lila and Mary. They didn't have social workers, child protection policies or CRBs* she thought. They drank in silence for a little. 'The police are coming round tomorrow with a social worker. They have some kind of secure unit she can go to while they investigate her story. She'll only be here tonight.'

Peter said nothing.

'She's fast asleep you know,' Grace looked at him. 'She's curled up there like a baby, still in her clothes.'

Peter shrugged, 'Suppose she doesn't get much sleep in her line of work.'

Ignoring his dark humour she said, 'Chloe was telling me that the suburbs of London are now the hot bed of the sex trade. Human traffickers selling kidnapped girls from Eastern Europe and North Africa in semis down leafy cul-de-sacs. I didn't believe her.'

'Yeah – the *Guardian* did a big article on it a while ago. You should read the papers more,' he chuckled.

She leaned her head on his shoulder, 'Shut up.'

They were silent for a while. It was a comfortable silence, broken only when a thought suddenly struck Grace, 'Did I tell you what happened to Trevor this morning?'

'No,' Peter replied.

'Well after my sermon I got a bit carried away in prayer and there was this amazing moment of stillness. Then some people started crying, praying ... then singing. It was lovely. People came for prayer – that's when I met Anja – but I couldn't see Trevor anywhere.'

Peter listened, his face expressionless.

'When I found him he was flat out on his back in the choir stalls with this big smile on his face.'

'Do you think he'd fallen asleep in your sermon?'

Grace laughed, 'Or died?'

Peter smiled, 'Well, what happened to him?'

'I'm not sure. He got up much later – we locked the church up together. All I could get out of him was that he felt like he was a bit drunk and was going to seriously reflect on the experience.'

'How weird,' Peter said as he wrapped a strand of Grace's hair round his finger.

They hadn't made love in over a week. Sleep had taken precedence over sex since Zack had been born, and once a week was an exceptionally good week.

Whether it was the effect of Grace's new euphoria from that morning's service, the wine, the possible or imagined danger Grace had put them in, or the heightened emotion after arguing, neither knew or cared. Peter's first kiss was reconciliatory, but turned quickly to hunger. They tiptoed up the stairs, Peter struggling to undo his shirt buttons at the same time. On closing their bedroom door, Grace deftly undid his flies with one hand while pulling her vest dress over her head, leaving her blond ringlets looking even more tousled than ever. Hurrying wasn't sexy, but it was essential if they were going to get any before the next three-year-old demand.

'I've missed you,' she whispered into his hair. She thought ruefully of the days of lingering foreplay but gave herself quickly to arousal's current, stifling a cry of pleasure as she surprised herself. Peter came in her wake.

Later after changing into their dressing gowns, they returned to the sofa. 'Are you hungry?' Grace asked.

'I am after that,' Peter smiled.

'What do you fancy?'

'Apart from you?'

'Well, of course.'

'Bacon, eggs and toast?'

'Perfect,' Grace moved to get up.

'I'll do it,' Peter said.

'Even more perfect,' she replied trailing her fingers down his forearm as he stood.

Her eyes fell on her laptop after they followed him out of the room. She'd begun reading over the end of the old story she'd written about Lila and Mary. She hadn't done any creative writing since Zack – he had absorbed her completely. But recently she'd been feeling restless and only now recognised what it was. *I need to write again* she thought. She reached for the laptop feeling pleased with her epiphany, lifting the screen up and quickly opening a new Word document.

What happened after Pentecost to Lila and Jair? What about Anna and Joshua … and Mary and Stephen?

Warm affection flooded her as she recalled the characters she'd created in her pre-maternal days. In preparing her sermon this week, she had been thinking of them a lot – like long lost friends.

By the time Peter returned, laden tray in hand, Grace was absorbed in writing, her fingers dancing across the keyboard. Peter laid the tray down on the coffee table, reading over Grace's shoulder. 'Glad I was of assistance,' he smiled.

Grace looked up distractedly, 'What?'

'Getting your creative juices flowing,' he said smugly.

Grace laughed, 'Oh, really?'

Peter reached for the TV remote.

Grace smiled at him as she lifted a mug of tea to her lips. Her gaze slid to her laptop again. She read over the paragraphs she'd just written, made a few changes and then carried on writing as Peter settled into watching the news on low volume.

'Count down to the Olympics,' he said into his mug.

'Mmmmm …' Grace responded.

'Bet human traffickers will have a field day then.'

Grace looked up at the TV screen. Like a fish caught in shallow water, the growing sense of something – she wasn't sure what – thrashed round inside her. She returned to her writing:

Jair became aware of pain. He recoiled into unconsciousness.

'He's coming round,' Lila whispered, stroking his face.

Stephen, Mary and several others in the upper room continued their babbling prayers in the strange gift that had been given them that morning.

Jair lay still on the table.

Anna sucked her thumb as she pressed herself into her mother. She stared, wide-eyed at the blood soaked prayer shawl on her father's shoulder. Joshua had fallen into exhausted sleep where Mary had made a bed for him with her shawl.

They waited.

They heard footsteps in the stairwell. Peter and the other apostles were returning from a glorious day when three thousand people (someone had counted) had believed Peter's message about the resurrected Jesus Christ and had been baptised. It had been a day like no other.

The annual harvest festival, the Feast of Weeks, had swollen Jerusalem's population from around a hundred thousand to nearly a million Jews returning from their scattered locations around the Mediterranean. People were camped everywhere inside the city and out. When those gathered in the upper room had all begun speaking in languages they'd never learned, praising God loudly, a crowd had gathered outside John's family home. Peter had gone out to them, leading the others, singing, dancing and praising God in dialects familiar to many among the diverse crowd. He'd preached to them like his life depended on it.

Lila could hear them talking excitedly as they came up into the room. The words quickly died on their lips as all eyes fell on the bloodied body lying on the table. They gathered round and without any direction, all began to pray at once. Lila felt faith surge in her chest and tears tumble down her cheeks.

'Wake up, Jair – wake up darling,' she whispered.

Colour began to glow in his pale cheeks. His lips moved. Lila leaned closer, 'What my love?'

His head rolled to one side, breathing and frowning deeply.

Unbelievably he lifted his right arm and rubbed his eyes. As he lowered it the stained prayer shawl fell away from his wounded shoulder. Lila flinched, expecting to see a gush of blood from the gaping hole made by Aaron's spear. Her eyes took in the torn, blood-soaked fabric of his tunic, but could not see the wound in his flesh. She leaned forward and pulled the cloth away only to see a pink, uneven scar on his skin. Gasping, she looked up at Mary and Stephen, who were equally shocked.

Stephen reached down and touched the scar, a smile spreading across his broad features, 'Praise be!' he exclaimed.

At that moment Jair opened his eyes and looked bewildered as he took in the faces peering down at him.

'What happened?' he asked.

'Papa,' Anna cried, climbing up onto the table, throwing her arms round his neck.

'The Spirit of the Lord Almighty is among us!' Peter declared.

Jair sat up, holding Anna in the crook of his left arm, looking at the bloodied prayer shawl, which had fallen onto the table beside him. He picked it up with his right hand, staring at it. 'I remember running through Aaron's house, to the courtyard door,' he looked at Lila's happy face; she nodded. 'They were going to hurt you and Anna … you were trying to open the door …' his face contorted with remembered pain. He looked down frantically at his right shoulder, dropping the shawl, his fingers scrabbling through the hole in his tunic. He went still. Then he looked back at the crimson prayer shawl.

'We prayed in Jesus' name Papa, then you were better,' Anna told him.

'We thought you were going to die – you had lost so much blood. But the Holy Spirit has restored you,' Stephen hugged him and Anna together. 'Praise be!' he repeated, excitedly.

Jair swung his legs off the low table and stood up, still holding

Anna in his arms. He did a little jig with her, her curls bouncing round her excited face. 'And best of all we have you again my love,' Jair kissed his daughter several times. Lila watched them and cried. She had Joshua in her arms now, who had been startled awake by all the singing and dancing.

Lila eventually noticed Peter had sat down, his shoulders sagging. She went over to him, 'Are you all right, Peter?'

'I haven't eaten all day,' he looked suddenly spent and vacant.

Realisation hit Lila with force – none of them had eaten all day. 'Come to our house. Everyone come. I have food prepared.'

'For all of us?'

'It was to last for this coming week – a lentil stew. It should feed all of us,' she said looking around, 'Mary? Will you help me? We need to make bread and heat the food.'

Mary came forward and nodded eagerly.

'But we can't ask you to give up your week's food,' Peter frowned.

Jair put his hand on his shoulder, 'Brother, come home and celebrate with us. I have been brought back to life and what was lost has been found,' he stroked Anna's cheek. 'Come – the Lord will supply all our needs.'

'If you're sure?' Peter searched Jair's eyes.

'We're sure!' Lila's voice chimed with his.

Anna said, 'Come!'

❋   ❋   ❋

'This is very good, Lila,' Peter wiped his mouth on his sleeve.

Lila's already flushed cheeks flamed with pride, 'Thank you,' she smiled at the big fisherman.

'I can't believe you were able to feed us all,' he said as he handed her his empty wooden bowl.

'Nor can we,' she looked at Mary who was wiping her hot face with her headscarf.

'We just kept spooning out the stew and putting more dough in the oven,' Mary agreed. 'How many have we fed?' she asked Peter.

'There were about twenty five of us in the upper room when

you invited us. But then more joined us on the way. I think it's been about a hundred and twenty.'

Lila and Mary looked stunned. 'But ...' they both said in unison.

'But ... it's not possible,' Lila exclaimed, 'I was thinking it was just around twenty to twenty five – maybe thirty at a push.'

'A hundred and twenty people couldn't fit in here!' exclaimed Mary.

'Well no ... they came through really: in your front door and out into the back yard and round to the front again to pass their empty bowls on to those still waiting outside.

'I don't believe it! Jair,' Lila called, 'Jair!'

Jair appeared in the kitchen from the back yard.

'Do you think we've fed a hundred and twenty people?'

'Think? I know! I've been counting,' he laughed. 'I was wondering when the food would run out.'

'Have you eaten yet?' Lila asked.

'No – have you?' he suddenly looked concerned.

'No – I fed the children first and Mary put them to bed, but neither of us have eaten.'

'Well we must remedy that,' Peter interjected. 'Come sit down. Jair and I will serve you.'

Lila and Mary exchanged an even more surprised look. 'No need to look like that,' Peter said gruffly. 'Didn't Jesus himself wash our feet? He told us that he hadn't come to be served but to serve. Please,' he gestured, 'let us serve you.'

Mary giggled and pushed Lila past Jair and out into the courtyard. Lila resisted self-consciously at first but caught Jair's eye and started to laugh. It was good to be in the fresh night air after the stuffiness of the kitchen. There were still many people eating, talking and laughing together. Jair had lit lanterns and rolled out a few mats on the ground. Lila felt pleased as she took in the scene. A hundred and twenty people! She thought again in amazement as joy of finding Anna and of Jair's healing bubbled together with all the other euphoric emotions.

Mary pulled her down onto a mat that had been vacated for them. Peter brought out two bowls of stew and Jair carried a plate of bread. As they knelt down and placed it before the women Peter said, 'Thank you for what you have done for us this evening. It has been a perfect ending to the most glorious day. Your faith and generosity have been a blessing.'

The women glowed with pleasure. Jair winked at Lila.

'I thought there was none left?' Mary whispered to Lila. Lila shrugged, her mouth full.

'It tastes better than your normal cooking too,' Mary laughed as she bit into some bread.

Lila elbowed her good-naturedly but said to Jair, 'Please – go get some – you need it more than any of us, after all you've been through.'

'I feel surprisingly well, as a matter of fact,' he said as he rose to his feet.

※　※　※

'What are you thinking?' Jair whispered.

Lila turned, the shadow of her nose cast by lamplight, stretched long across the pillow between them. She smiled, 'How good it is that you are alive and here with us.' She rested her hand lightly on his and their fingers slid together as she stroked the scar on his shoulder.

'I thought I was going to lose you,' her face was solemn.

He didn't reply; his eyes drank in every detail of her face. He pulled her to him, kissing her slowly. She stayed still, sensing he didn't want her to interrupt. She couldn't help stretching however, as he moved down her neck to her breasts. He cupped them in his hands and kissed them tenderly.

Unable to resist any longer, Lila rolled on top of him, pressing herself against him, enjoying the feel of his coarse chest hair against her smooth skin. She was aching for him now, yearning to enfold him. They both savoured the accelerated rush of blood through their veins. Lila looked down at Jair and saw that he was smiling. She laughed, her hair falling around them.

They made love twice that night.

❋ ❋ ❋

She awoke to the sound of Anna and Joshua's laughter. She knew immediately what she wanted to do. She slid out from under Jair's arm, being careful not to wake him and pulling her long chemise over her head, she then wrapped her shawl over its transparent folds. She tiptoed to the children's room and watched them playing together through the door that she had left ajar.

Her cup was full to overflowing. She could feel it spilling over inside her. She was praying in that strange language again.

She pushed the door open to squeals of delight from Joshua and a joyous 'Mama!' from Anna. She knelt down on the floor and leaned her elbows on Anna's low bed, where both children lay.

'Good morning, beautiful ones,' she laughed as they launched themselves at her, planting wet kisses all over her face. 'Oh, I love you!' she declared.

'Is Papa awake?' Anna asked.

'Not yet sweetheart; let's leave him for a while.'

'Is he bleeding again?' Anna asked anxiously.

'No, my love; he's fine – just very tired.'

Joshua was hungrily trying to get to her breast. Lila caught him up in her arms and hugged him. 'Let's go downstairs and have breakfast, shall we?'

'Yes!' shouted Anna.

'Shhh!' Lila put a finger to her lips, 'Let Papa sleep.'

They made their way as quietly down the wooden stairs as possible.

Jair rolled onto his back smiling as he listened to his family, but quickly drifted off into contented sleep again.

'We're going to the Temple this morning to give thanks for your safe return and for Papa's healing. My grandmamma used to take me there when I was a little girl, you know.'

Anna was chewing a mouthful of bread thoughtfully. When she'd finished she turned her oval face up to her mother's and asked, 'What was her name?'

Lila smiled, 'The same as you – we named you after her.'

'I wish Anna-grandmamma was still here,' Anna said seriously.

'Me too,' Lila changed Joshua over to her other breast and then lifted her half-eaten piece of bread to her mouth. 'I'll make us some oatmeal in a moment. I just want Shua to be happy first.'

※   ※   ※

Breakfast had taken much longer than Lila had hoped, but it had meant that Jair had woken and been able to have Joshua.

Lila and Anna climbed the Temple steps as the sun neared its zenith. They made their way through the Court of the Women and Lila found the place where her grandmamma had always taken her. They settled themselves there and Lila began telling Anna about her great grandmother who had been a prophetess.

They ate their midday meal in Solomon's Colonnade, as it was too hot to sit in the sun by then. Anna fell asleep on her mother's lap in the lull before the daily afternoon time of prayer. Lila exulted in the time to focus her thoughts. Motherhood made it a near impossibility. She slipped her sandals off and enjoyed the cool of smooth stone on hot skin. She gave thanks for Anna, stroking her curly head. She praised God for her rescue and for Jair's recovery. She confessed her unbelief – her fear – asking for healing from the effects of anxiety. She reaffirmed her trust.

She could feel the tingly sensation of peace permeating her nervous system; her skin; her muscles. She soaked in clarity and hope. She noticed her prayers drifted from the unintelligible to the intelligible. She wondered if she were interpreting? It was all lyrical, rhythmical praise and worship.

She remembered that she had agreed with Jair that she would return so he could come to the afternoon time of prayer, and she could feed Joshua. She leaned down to wake Anna up. After having a drink they made their way back out through the Beautiful Gate and down the Temple steps. A man disabled from birth, whom they'd often seen begging at the temple gates was being carried between two teenagers, a boy and girl. They looked alike. Lila didn't know if it was due to them both having equally unkempt hair and dirty clothes, or whether they were related. She felt sorry for them. She knew they were aiming to get him up to the Beautiful Gate in time for the afternoon crowds.

The girl stumbled just as they were passing Lila and Anna. She lost her grip of the piece of wood the disabled man was sitting on. He tumbled over to one side, his shoulder touching earth first and then his head. A cry escaped his lips. The girl fell in front of him, one foot trapped under his torso. She struggled to pull it free.

Anna ran to the man. He had been knocked unconscious. She used her tunic to wipe the dust from his face tenderly. The crowds continued moving round them, oblivious of this sad little drama. Lila helped the boy lift the man's body, releasing the girl's foot, who jumped up quickly looking distraught. Lila made sure the young boy had a firm hold of the unconscious man before she addressed the girl.

'Are you all right?' she asked.

'Yes – thank you,' the girl replied self-consciously. She knelt in front of the man and was checking his head and shoulder for bleeding.

'Stupid girl!' the boy said.

'Shut up,' she retorted.

'If he's broken any bones, what will we do?' he glared at her.

Angry tears were in her eyes, 'He's not bleeding. There's no swelling ...' she searched the man's scalp for wounds.

'Mama, make him better like you did for Papa,' Anna's high voice cut through the tension between the teenagers. They looked at her momentarily surprised.

'Come on. Pick Uncle up again or we won't make it to the gate in time for the afternoon crowds.'

The girl obediently leaned down to take up her heavy burden again, but before she could her uncle groaned, rolling his head and opening his eyes. 'What happened?' he asked, looking confused.

'I fell, Uncle. Sorry. So did you – you hit your head. Are you in pain?'

He looked dazed and gingerly touched his head as he shook it. 'It's not too bad – a bit of a bump – but nothing to worry about.

Have we missed afternoon prayers?' He looked anxiously from one to the other.

'No – not yet,' said the boy, glaring at his sister.

The man saw and touched his nephew's arm, 'Don't blame her. It was an accident that could have happened to you.'

'But it didn't,' scowled the boy.

The man reached over and patted his niece on the back. 'Don't mind him. There's been no harm done. Are you all right? Have you hurt yourself?' he looked concerned. Her eyes filled with tears again. She reached down to her left knee. 'Let me see,' he said.

She lifted up her skirt to expose a bloody knee. The man pulled her gently down into his lap, rubbing her back. She didn't resist, but buried her head in his chest. The boy looked sorry. Lila felt a growing affection for them. She reached over and prayed silently for the girl. This fragile family seemed to have enough troubles without more being added to them.

'Jesus will make you better,' Anna said.

The man and his nephew looked enquiringly at her. The girl lifted her tear-stained face and focused on Anna. 'Who?' she asked in a subdued voice.

'Jesus of Nazareth,' Lila smiled.

'He's the Messiah,' Anna added importantly.

'I saw him at a distance a few times, but never met him. I heard he was executed,' the man looked confused.

'He was ...' Lila replied.

'But he came alive again!' Anna interjected. 'Papa was healed when we prayed in his name.'

Lila saw that this was too much information for them, 'Come, Anna. We must go and let these good people get on. We hope you have many blessings today,' she smiled and got up from her crouched position beside them.

'But Mama ...' Anna insisted.

'Come my love. Say goodbye,' Lila was firm.

Anna's brow furrowed, but she obeyed.

As they walked away Anna looked up at her mother, 'Why didn't you pray – like with Papa?' she asked.

'I did – I just didn't use words. They were too upset to take in what we were saying. We did what we were supposed to do, darling.'

'But I want their uncle to be able to walk,' Anna said stubbornly.

'I know – so do I. Maybe he will later?'

This new thought captured Anna's imagination and seemed to content her.

※　※　※

Jair made his way up the temple steps with Peter and John. A strong sense of camaraderie bonded them together as they strode towards the Beautiful Gate.

Jair noticed a disabled man being carefully placed down on the ground by two teenagers. He recognised Lila's description of them and began praying for him as they made to pass by.

'Alms for the poor,' called the man. The children sat either side of him, wet with perspiration.

Peter stopped and looked straight at him, as did John. Jair walked on a few steps before realising he'd left the other two behind. He turned back and immediately sensed the intense focus Peter and John were giving the beggar. He found himself softly babbling incoherently in prayer.

The beggar's eyes flitted hopefully back and forth between each face. Then Peter said, 'Look at us!' Surprised, he gave them his full attention, an expectant expression on his thin face.

Then Peter said, 'Silver or gold I do not have, but what I do have I give you. In the name of Jesus Christ of Nazareth, walk.'

Taking him by the right hand, he helped him up, and instantly the man's feet and ankles became strong. The children were on their feet as he jumped to his. They were astounded, clutching at him, fearful he might fall.

Together they went with Peter into the temple courts. The man was now walking and jumping and praising God. People were staring. When they recognised him as the same man who used to sit begging at the Beautiful Gate, a crowd gathered, filled with wonder and amazement at what had happened to him.

While the man held on to Peter and John, the children danced round him, hugging and kissing him and each other, their differences forgotten. All the people were astonished and came running to them.

Seeing the opportunity Peter raised his voice and said to them, 'Fellow Israelites, why does this surprise you? Why do you stare at us as if by our own power or godliness we had made this man walk? The God of Abraham, Isaac and Jacob, the God of our fathers, has glorified his servant Jesus. You handed him over to be killed, and you disowned him before Pilate, though he had decided to let him go. You disowned the Holy and Righteous One and asked that a murderer be released to you. You killed the author of life, but God raised him from the dead. We are witnesses of this. By faith in the name of Jesus, this man whom you see and know was made strong. It is Jesus' name and the faith that comes through him that has completely healed him, as you can see.'

As Peter continued to speak, a few priests, the captain of the temple guard and some Sadducees, pushed their way through the crowd. It was clear they were disturbed by Peter's assertion that in Jesus there was resurrection of the dead. They seized Peter and John, and because evening was approaching, they put them in the temple jail until the next day. Jair ran back to John's house to tell the others what had happened.

'About two thousand more have believed today because of Peter's preaching,' he gasped, 'but because of it the temple guard are holding them in jail tonight.'

James solemnly rose from his place at the table and said, 'We must pray for them.'

※　※　※

The next day a meeting was called in the Sanhedrin of all the rulers, elders and teachers of the law in Jerusalem. Aaron was among them. They had the man who had been healed and Peter and John brought before them.

Peter, filled with the Holy Spirit, said to them, 'Rulers and elders of the people. If we are being called to account today for an act of kindness shown to a man who was lame and are being asked how he was healed, then know this, you and all the people of Israel: It is by the name of Jesus Christ of Nazareth, whom you crucified but whom God raised from the dead, that this man stands before you healed.'

As they listened, Aaron was astonished by his courage, knowing Peter was an unschooled, ordinary man. He also knew the beggar, a leech on society, standing before them; knew he had been lame from birth; had passed him many times over the years at the temple gates.

'These men have performed a notable sign,' he said diplomatically in reply to Caiaphas' question, after they ordered them to withdraw from the Sanhedrin. 'Everyone living in Jerusalem will know about it by now. We cannot deny it. But to stop this thing from spreading any further among the people, we must warn them to no longer speak to anyone in this name.' A shiver ran down his scalp and neck thinking of the confusion and weakness that had descended upon him when Lila had spoken to him in that name.

When they were brought back in, Caiaphas fixed them with his hooded eyes and commanded them not to speak or teach in the name of Jesus.

Peter and John exchanged a look and then Peter said, 'Which is right in God's eyes: to listen to you, or to him? You be the judges. As for us, we cannot help speaking about what we have seen and heard.'

Aaron rose to his feet in a venomous rage, 'If we hear you have been speaking in that name again, we will have done to you what was done to your friend Jair.'

Peter looked at him steadily, 'So be it,' he replied. 'But know this,' a smile spread across his weathered features, 'Jair is fit and well today. There is no weapon you can fashion against the will of the Almighty that will prosper.'

Aaron's mouth fell open. He knew Jair had been mortally wounded. Why was this man not afraid? Others rose and added their own threats to Aaron's. The Sanhedrin dissolved in chaos and Peter and John were released.

They returned to John's house immediately to tell the others what had happened. Lila and the children had joined Jair in the upper room. There with many other believers, they raised their voices in prayer, saying, 'Sovereign Lord, you made the heavens and the earth and the sea, and everything in them … Now, Lord, consider their threats and enable your servants to speak your word with great boldness. Stretch out your hand to heal and perform signs and wonders through the name of your holy servant Jesus.'

Jair became aware of the ground moving beneath his feet. He instinctively wrapped his arms round Lila and the children, thinking it was an earthquake. But as the tremors grew stronger the walls did not crack and no timber fell. Then realisation dawned that it must be the effect of prayer. It was Emmanuel, God with them – in them – shouting a resounding, 'Yes and Amen'. The whole place shook and they were filled with the Holy Spirit and boldness.

2. ATTACK

Acts 5:12–7:60
The women caught in the crossfire

It was Friday afternoon of Whitsun weekend. Melanie raised her head, tipping it back and sniffed hard. The powder hit the back of her throat as she closed her eyes with relief. Slowly she lowered her head. A faint trace of a line was still visible on her small mirror. She bent down and vacuumed it up with a rolled ten pound note. Then she grabbed some tissue paper and dusted the surface clean. She got up from the toilet seat, wiping her nose with the back of her hand. She was buzzing. She tucked her bank card, mirror, tissue and money away in the inside pocket of her blazer.

Coming out of her cubicle she went to the sink and washed her hands thoroughly, wiping them on her skirt. She looked in the mirror and straightened her school tie and rumpled shirt, avoiding eye contact with herself. She wiped her nose one more time and gave herself a bright, brittle smile, chewing on the insides of her cheeks.

I should have waited, but to hell with it, it's Friday!

She'd resisted the longing to escape all morning, but feelings of isolation, anxiety and insecurity had swamped her like oozing pus from a festering wound. She'd caved in. As she checked herself in the mirror, she was reassured that she looked no different.

Before she got to the door it opened, banging against the wall with force as a crowd of Year 11 girls pushed their way in. She pressed herself up against the wall keeping her smile fixed in place. 'All right?' said one broad shouldered girl, eyes sliding up but not quite meeting Melanie's gaze.

'Yeah – fine,' her voice was too high. 'Gotta go,' she grabbed the door before it slammed shut. 'Bye,' Melanie called over her shoulder.

'Bye, bitch,' muttered the girl coolly. A few of the girls giggled. 'That's the one whose mum was shagging our vicar – you know at the end of Year 5?' The other girls looked blank.

'Oh come on, don't you remember?' She leaned towards the mirror as she stroked her gelled hair as if by doing so she could make it any flatter.

'No. You're the only one who didn't come here from St Stephen's,' said a pale-faced girl, examining her nose for blackheads.

'Yeah, you came from St Matt's, didn't you?'

'Oh yeah, you're right,' she looked mildly surprised at her poor memory. But then a sly smile curved her lips, 'Bloody hell, that was a wild time. You should have been there,' her eyes sparkled with pleasure at having a captive audience. She hesitated, drawing out the suspense.

'You gonna tell us or not, Lottie? Come on,' demanded a blonde girl wearing pink playboy bunny earrings.

Lottie leaned back against the mirror, folding her arms across her ample bosom. 'Well, it was me who heard them talking about it in the school office. Some kid had caught them at it in the church office – the church! Yeah – well – she was the youth worker and he was the new vicar. They used to come in to do school assemblies and stuff. Man, it was hot gossip. It was all over the school by break time. You should have seen Melanie's face when I told her,' she jerked her head in the direction of the door and laughed.

'They moved house; her mum lost her job; the vicar lost his too. It was cra-zy!' she scrunched her eyes shut as her mouth made a wide Cheshire-cat grin.

'You love a bit of gossip don't cha?' the blonde girl said as she pouted and applied pink lipgloss.

'Better than chocolate,' Lottie smiled.

'Better than sex?' the blonde girl arched her eyebrows and looked pointedly at Lottie. The others' interest sparked again as all eyes fixed on her.

'Oh yeah!' Lottie's worldly-wise look was too contrived.

'Like you'd know?' the girl turned and focused on Lottie who had now lost her position of power.

'We all know *you* know, slut,' Lottie cupped her hands under a running tap and hurled water at her inquisitor. There was one loud shriek followed by many more as a water fight ensued.

Meanwhile Melanie managed to make it across the school campus to her next class in very good time. She loved running when she was high. It felt like flying.

※　※　※

'Are you all right, Melanie?' asked her teacher halfway through the lesson.

'Yes, Miss,' Melanie stopped drumming her fingers on her desk.

'You seem agitated. Can you stay after class, please? I know it's the weekend, but I want to speak with you just for a minute.'

Melanie frowned but didn't argue. She bent her head over her notebook and furiously scrawled out the first lines of the poem they were studying for GCSE English Literature.

When the classroom was empty the teacher propped herself up on the edge of her desk and folded her arms across her chest, 'Well? What's going on?' she asked.

'Nothing,' Melanie lied.

'I've been worried about you for a while now. Your behaviour is quite erratic. Is everything okay at home?'

'Yep – I mean, yes, Miss,' Melanie's eyes darted to the window and back.

'You're a bright girl, Melanie. You've got everything going for you. Don't mess it up by hanging out with the wrong people.'

Melanie jumped up, 'Are you being prejudiced, Miss?' she started to shove her books into her bag.

'No, of course not, Melanie,' the teacher said defensively. 'It's nothing to do with race or religion or anything like that. I'm worried about their age and life experience versus yours and wondering why you aren't hanging out with people more your own age?'

'You don't know anything!' Melanie glared at her, 'You don't understand!'

The teacher reached out and touched Melanie's arm. Her school shirt rode up and the teacher glimpsed pink cut marks across the soft, white skin. 'Melanie ... I just want to help.'

The schoolgirl shrugged off her teacher's touch and made to leave, 'No one understands,' she threw the words over her shoulder.

'Melanie ... ' the teacher's shoulders sagged as the girl continued to walk out the door.

✖   ✖   ✖

'You coming out tonight?' he asked casually, his arm around her shoulders.

'It'll be later. I've got to finish an English essay.' She looked up at him checking to see if this annoyed him. His face remained placid, his eyes hooded, as usual.

'Cool. I'll wait for you in the park,' he tugged a strand of her dark hair playfully. 'Don't keep me waiting too long,' he leaned down and found her mouth, pushing in his eel-like tongue. As he pulled away they passed Lottie, leaning up against the school railings. Melanie caught a glimpse of envy in her eyes and pushed her chest out that little bit more.

'Will Sony and the others be there too?'

'Depends ... '

'On what?'

'On what you wanna do tonight,' he stuck a cigarette into the corner of his mouth that he'd fished out of his shirt pocket and looked slyly at her from the sides of his eyes. Melanie felt a mixture of anxiety and excitement grip her stomach. She didn't reply, but just smiled as he lit up, inhaled deeply and then blew out a long swirl of blue smoke.

'Have you got any more stuff?' she asked too casually, 'I used the last lot today.' He offered her a cigarette, but she shook her head, 'Too near school.'

'Didn't I say?' he paused to take another deep drag. She waited. He looked down at her and smiled that smile that churned her stomach, 'Yeah, I got more stuff. You got money?'

The smile faded from her lips, 'I thought ...'

'You thought it would always be free, did you, babe?' his voice was teasing.

'Well ...' her young eyes were confused, 'I thought it was what we did together – you and me – you know ...'

'I guess it could be again this time if ...'

'If what?'

'You know.'

Melanie knew. She'd always known. It was only a matter of time. She changed the subject.

✳ ✳ ✳

'Are you going to "Youth Alpha"?' Chloe called up the stairs. The slam of a bedroom door was her reply. 'Melanie?' she persisted. Loud music began blaring. Chloe ran up the stairs and knocked on Melanie's door. 'Melanie,' she shouted over heavy drum and bass. She didn't give up – still kept knocking.

Eventually the door opened revealing a bored looking teenager, 'What?'

'Are you going to "Youth Alpha" tonight?' Chloe kept her voice calm but firm.

'No – got too much work to do.'

'But it's the Whitsun weekend – the Holy Spirit weekend tonight and tomorrow. That's the best bit. You've been every other week. Why are you backing out now?'

A nonchalant shrug with no eye contact was her only reply.

'It's that guy you've been seeing, isn't it?' Chloe felt herself losing control.

A stony stare ensued. Then, 'You mean Yusuf? He has a name.'

Chloe breathed deeply, 'Can you turn the music down so we can talk?'

Jaw muscles clenched; hands balled into fists. She reached over to her desk and turned the volume down on her stereo.

'Thank you,' Chloe reached out to her daughter's hand, only to feel it pull away from her. 'Look, Melanie, why don't you bring Yusuf to the Alpha weekend? You never know, he might like it.'

'I've decided I'm not a Christian Mum,' Melanie said in a low voice. 'I know that'll upset you, but there it is. I'm not coming to church any more or the youth group.'

'Oh ...' was all Chloe could say, the wind knocked out of her. They stood facing each other in an uncomfortable silence, the wood of the door standing ajar between them. Chloe noticed Melanie inching it closed, signalling the end of their conversation. 'Wait ... maybe you're just stressed with all the GCSE work you've got on? You shouldn't make big decisions at times of high stress you know? Maybe you should talk to the youth worker about how you feel?'

'Mum – just leave it. I'm sixteen now – I've made up my mind,' the door was now only two inches ajar.

'Melanie, please, darling, don't shut me out. Let's talk about this.'

'It's all crap ... you're all full of crap!' and with that the door slammed again.

Chloe was shocked by the rage reverberating in Melanie's voice, eyes and the force she used on the door. She stood there for what felt an age, at a loss to know what to do. Eventually she made her way down the stairs into the kitchen where Mark was sitting at the table helping Josh with his homework.

'That went well, then?' Mark said dryly.

The tears Chloe had been fighting choked her, 'I think she really hates me,' she whispered.

Mark replied coolly, 'No she doesn't. She's just being a teenager. She's probably got her period.'

Josh laughed with his dad. Chloe felt control even further out of reach, 'She says she's not a Christian and isn't coming to church anymore,' her voice broke in a sob.

'Oh don't listen to her. She's just being melodramatic. You know what she's like – she knows just where it hurts with you and she's gone for it big time tonight.' Mark looked at Josh and shrugged his shoulders as if to say '*Women!*'

On seeing that, Chloe turned on her heels, grabbed her keys on the hall table and stormed out of the house. 'I'm going to get Charlie,' she shouted as the front door slammed behind her.

※　※　※

She cried all the way to Charlie's friend's house.

Pull yourself together Chloe. Maybe Mark's right; maybe she is just being a drama queen? But then why am I so upset? She waited at some lights, sniffing hard and wiping her cheeks with the back of her hand. *It's because of me – of what I've done. It's my fault.* A fresh surge of tears flooded her vision as she pulled away and turned right. She braked suddenly because the car in front had slowed.

It was too late; she'd hit it.

'Oh, damn it!' She sat there for a moment, her mind in chaos. *Get a grip!* She silently shouted at herself.

She put her hazard lights on and got out of the car. Hesitantly approaching the car in front, she looked for damage. But as much as she looked she could see none. The other driver was now out of her car – a slow moving, elderly lady. 'I'm terribly sorry,' she said in a cultured voice, 'are you all right?'

Chloe was surprised and relieved all at once. 'Yes – I'm okay. How about you?'

The elderly woman smiled a watery smile, 'I'm a bit shaken, but no harm's been done, I think,' her eyes scanned both cars at interface.

'No – surprisingly it doesn't look like there has been any damage. It wasn't a big bump – I was braking.'

'It was a squirrel,' the elderly lady gestured elegantly to the road ahead of them.

Chloe stared at her, 'Oh.'

'I didn't want to crush one of God's creatures,' she tilted her head and smiled at Chloe.

'No – of course not,' Chloe became the consoling counsellor and was in control again. 'Well, as long as we're all all right, I best be getting on.'

'Goodbye then, dear,' the old woman watched as Chloe got back into her car.

It was only on arrival to pick Charlie up that she realised she'd driven the rest of the short distance in second gear and without her seat belt on.

I need a holiday, she thought. 'Hi, Charlie,' she called brightly out of her car window. She waved to the boy's mum, whom she'd chatted to a few times at the school gate. She was giving Charlie his party bag. 'Thanks for having him.'

'It's been a pleasure,' came the reply with rolled eyeballs and an over-exaggerated look of exhaustion.

'Hi, Mum,' Charlie put his bag at his feet and strapped himself in. 'What's wrong?'

Damn – he's so sensitive! 'Nothing. How was the party?'

'Yeah it was cool. Ben had a magician – he was awesome!'

'That's great. Did you have good food?'

'Yeah, a barbeque. I had two lamb kebabs.'

'Have you got any homework for the weekend? Do you want to do it when you get home or wait 'til Sunday afternoon?'

'I haven't got any. The teacher said we could have a free weekend.'

'That was nice of her.' *Thank God for that! I can get on with my essay.* 'Why did they have it on a Friday after school – seems a bit of a weird time to me.'

'Oh – 'cuz Ben's going to Legoland tomorrow.'

'Lucky him!'

'You sure you're okay, Mum? Have you been crying?'

Why didn't I wear my shades? 'Oh, it was just Melanie – we had a bit of a run in before I came to get you.'

'She's so rude to you, Mum. She shouldn't speak to you like that.'

Chloe smiled and patted his knee, 'Thanks, Charlie. She's just being a teenager, I guess, or at least that's what Dad says.' Chloe felt the shift in her son's attitude. She glanced at his profile. There was that look again. 'What?' she asked.

'Nothing.'

'Sweetie – what?' Chloe persisted.

Charlie held his breath and then in a very grown up voice said, 'I don't think Dad understands.'

They were pulling into their drive and Charlie jumped out as soon as the car stopped, ending the conversation. Chloe sat staring after him as he ran round the side of the house to go in via the back door, with a gloomy sense of foreboding creeping upon her.

※　※　※

Melanie put the CD on repeat on a low volume, locked her bedroom door and grabbed her phone. She went to the sash window and raised it fully. It was nearly dark. She swung her leg over the windowsill and found a foothold on the jutting brickwork that encircled the house above the ground floor windows. She was well practised at this escape and was on the ground in minutes. The side of the house had one big kitchen window and then a marbled bathroom window. She saw her mother's reflection in the mirror that hung by the kitchen table, tapping away at her laptop and glancing occasionally at the piles of opened books surrounding her.

She'll be there for hours. Josh and Dad will be in the living room watching World's Strongest Man *or some other crap, until Dad realises the time and sends him to bed. Charlie went an hour ago. I'm free!*

She edged her way along the shadow of the hedge that divided their home from next door and then headed for the park.

'Hello, babe,' Yusuf wrapped his arms around her, found her mouth and kissed her hard. She could hear the others talking and laughing beyond the large clump of bushes that sheltered them. The smell of weed lingered sweet and strong on the still, warm air.

'I'm ready,' she said, kissing him back equally hard.

'Right here?' he laughed.

'No,' she felt herself go red and was glad it was dark.

He hugged her small body to his wiry one. 'Oi, Sony – I'll see you later, bruv. I'm off to the pad.'

'About time – enjoy!' came the reply followed by lewd laughter.

'Where are we going?' Melanie asked, quelling the nervousness in her stomach and hooking her finger through a belt loop of his jeans that hung impossibly low on his hips.

'It's not far. It's a place we share. It's nice – you'll like it,' he kissed her hair.

The flat was situated above a row of shops. The smell of curry wafted through the open windows from the Indian takeaway that plied its trade below. Everything was black and white: black leather sofas and lamps, white walls and rugs. Melanie took it all in quickly, feeling she was stepping into another world. Yusuf threw his keys into a black bowl on a table in the hallway.

'Well, babe,' he held out his arms. 'What do you think?'

'It's nice,' she said as she peered round a doorway into a small black and white kitchen. It didn't look like it got used much. 'How do you guys afford this place?'

'Oh, we have our ways and means,' he smiled and reached out, pulling her to him.

'But you haven't got a job?'

'Do you want more stuff?' he asked dropping his hands down to the small of her back, pressing her into his hips.

Questions forgotten, Melanie eagerly nodded, her eyes glittering with anticipation. They went into the small living room and Yusuf dropped a clear plastic bag of white powder on the glass coffee table. He started unbuttoning his shirt. 'First you gotta take your top off,' he smiled that smile.

Melanie shed her conscience, a skin that no longer fit, as she pulled her T-shirt over her head, exposing the red and black bra she'd bought in town the previous Saturday. Yusuf reached over and stroked the swell of her small breasts with a finger.

She caught his finger, twisting it playfully, 'First give me what *I* want,' her hazel eyes teased him through her heavily laden lashes.

He laughed, tore open the bag pouring some onto the table. He took his time chopping it up again and again, then lined it up with his credit card on the glass surface. She had already rolled her ten pound note and knelt down, greedily sucking up the first line. She closed her eyes, shook her head and sniffed hard.

'Now get your jeans off,' he said, grinning.

She felt fantastic as she stood up to undo her jeans, her red and black thong leaving little to the imagination. She threw her jeans in his face and he laughed, burying his nose in the crotch.

He knelt down and snorted the second line, leaning back and pinching his nose between finger and thumb. He pulled her down beside him, reaching round behind her and undoing her bra. She smiled at him, loving the feeling of being so alive. He cupped her breasts in his hands and began kissing them. 'You got protection?' he murmured. She nodded, closing her eyes and pointing vaguely to her jeans. He reached for them and fished out a packet of condoms. 'Good girl,' he whispered, 'you brought more than one. Now, let's go into the other room and you can put this on me.'

He helped her to her feet and led her into the bedroom. Melanie was vaguely surprised that everything was black in there: black sheets, walls, carpet and curtains. He took off his jeans and she stared at him. She'd never seen a naked man before. All she knew of the male anatomy was what she could vaguely remember from sharing a bath with Josh when they were kids and what she'd learnt in sex education classes.

Yusuf pulled her onto the bed with him, 'I'll treat you right, babe. I won't hurt you ...'

She felt mild panic rise through her high, but fought it.

He did hurt her.

Melanie didn't get into her own bedroom until the small hours of Saturday morning. Only when she pulled her pink duvet over her head did the tears come.

❋　❋　❋

'Do you want another cup of tea?' Grace asked the social worker and policewoman who sat opposite Anja in her living room on the grey Monday morning after Whitsun.

'No, thank you,' they both replied simultaneously.

'So what happens next?' Grace looked at them in turn. They'd taken their notes, listening carefully to Anja's halting story.

It was clear that Anja was in pain and also going through some kind of withdrawal. Her hands shook and tremors ran through her body uncontrollably. Her skin was ashen, with dark rings under her eyes. The social worker addressed her answer to Anja, 'Well, we will take you to a secure unit for assessment with the psychiatric team and then, depending on what decision they make we will hopefully get you into a women's refuge.'

'I go home soon?' she asked hopefully.

'You are free to call home now, if you like,' said the social worker.

'By all means, Anja – please feel free to use my phone,' Grace said, annoyed at herself that she hadn't thought of this before now.

Anja looked forlorn, 'In home – no phone – only publics.' She clutched her stomach as a cramp seized her.

'Oh ...' there was a pause while they all thought.

Then the policewoman said, 'If you tell us the name of where you come from we can try to locate your family and contact them.'

'Donji Javorang – close to Dvor,' she let out a stifled groan of pain.

'Are you all right, Anja?' Grace asked leaning forward.

The social worker cleared her throat. Grace looked at her as she mouthed the word 'heroin'.

The policewoman went on, keeping the conversation light, 'We'll get onto multimap and see if we can find, what did you say – Dvor? Right ... are you ready to come with us? Do you want to get your things?'

'This – all,' said Anja gesturing to her self.

'I'll follow you in my car Anja, and I'll stay with you until they make their decision,' Grace stood and patted her on the back.

As they walked out to the police van, her body language became furtive. Grace watched and felt that tug on her internal kite string again. As she followed in her car she prayed a mantra, 'Lord, help us make her safe.'

When she parked at the secure unit she texted Trevor telling him where she was and that she would keep him posted. It took all day to get Anja assessed, most of which was spent waiting to be seen by the psych team. It was a good thing it was Zack's day with his grandmother.

Anja's torment increased as the day wore on. She was like a caged animal, pacing the small holding room they'd been put in. When it seemed more than she could bear, Grace found herself praying out loud in tongues. The pain seemed to subside then and Anja would curl up in the only other chair in the room and sleep fitfully. Grace thought about one of the books she'd read early on in her Christian life about a woman called Jackie Pullinger, who ministered in Hong Kong, praying in tongues over heroin addicts in the walled city as they came through cold turkey. She hoped her prayers were helping in a similar way.

The psych team withdrew after a brief interview to discuss their findings. When they returned they said they would keep her in until they found her a bed in a safe house. They said they would make her more comfortable with methadone.

Grace hugged Anja, blessing her silently in Jesus' name, signing her with the sign of the cross on her back.

She sat in her car for a while afterwards, praying. She eventually looked at the time. *No wonder I feel so hungry* – she thought. She texted Trevor again and told him she was on her way back, asking if they could meet for a debrief. She was about to turn the key in the ignition but felt a check in her spirit; the kite string tugged again. She closed her eyes and rested her hands, palms up, in her lap.

The Spirit of the Sovereign Lord is on me, because the Lord has anointed me to preach good news to the poor. He has sent me to bind up the broken-hearted, to proclaim freedom for the captives, and release from darkness for the prisoners, to proclaim the year of the Lord's favour and the day of vengeance of our God ... Her skin goosepimpled in awe at the words. She waited, barely breathing. Across the screen of her imagination she saw the words 'My Sister's House' emblazoned in red. She read it out loud, wonderingly.

Isaiah 61? She reached into her bag and rummaged through its contents until she'd located her pale blue leather bound bible. She found the passage and read on beyond the words that had come to her '... *to comfort all those who mourn and provide for those who grieve in Zion – to bestow on them a crown of beauty instead of ashes, the oil of gladness instead of mourning, and a garment of praise instead of a spirit of despair. They will be called oaks of righteousness, a planting of the Lord for the display of his splendour.'*

Then Matthew 12:48 came into her mind. She flipped over to the New Testament and read out loud: *'Who is my mother, and who are my brothers?' Pointing to his disciples, he said, 'Here are my mother and brothers. For whoever does the will of my Father in heaven is my brother and sister and mother.'*

She leaned back in her seat and closed her eyes. She remembered throwing grass seed over a patch of earth in her garden. *Let these words fall where they may on the earth of my mind,* she prayed.

Eventually she looked down at her bible again. She scanned the opened pages. She read other verses that she'd underlined.

'A bruised reed he will not break, and a smouldering wick he will not snuff out, till he leads justice to victory.'

'He who has ears to hear, let him hear.'

'For this people's heart has become calloused; they hardly hear with their ears, and they have closed their eyes. Otherwise they might see with their eyes, hear with their ears, understand with their hearts and turn, and I would heal them.'

Thank you for speaking to me. Help me hear, see and understand with my heart what it is you want me to do.

She stuck Hildegard von Bingen's *Canticles of Ecstasy* into the CD player. As she listened to the lilting harmonies, layer by layer the tension eased within her and understanding settled like sediment on a river bed.

※　※　※

Grace picked Zack up from her mother's. She was later than she'd said.

'That's okay, dear,' her mother smiled graciously. 'We've had such fun, haven't we?' she stroked her only grandchild's curly head.

He nodded, his mouth full of biscuit.

'Thanks, Mum – so sorry I'm late,' Grace was still uncertain of her mother, even though they had been reconciled for nearly four years.

'The traffic can be terrible between here and yours at this time of day. I thought you were being a little optimistic when you said four,' her expensive scent wrapped round Grace like a luxurious pashmina.

'You know me – never good with time,' Grace admitted.

'No, but you can't be good at everything. Here, Zack, don't forget the kite we bought,' she leaned down and picked up a brown paper bag, holding it out to Zack.

Grace watched her, feeling pleased at the inferred compliment, 'Thanks, Mum,' she reiterated. She leaned in and hugged her lightly. Then on impulse, 'Do you want to come for Sunday lunch? It'll be late – like one-ish by the time I've got back from church?'

'That would be lovely,' she replied looking pleased. 'Do you want me to bring anything? Dessert?'

'Yeah … that would be great. Nothing fancy now, just something easy. I think Peter said he's going to cook lamb this week. He's going to do it with garlic and rosemary.'

'Sounds divine! I'll bring a nice red.'

'Okay… say thank you and goodbye to Grandma, Zack.'

'Bye,' he said, waving the brown paper bag, ' … and thank you,' he smiled his best smile.

'Such a charmer … oh, the girls will love him,' she clasped her hands, lavishing him with an adoring smile.

※   ※   ※

Grace returned the next day to the secure unit after dropping Zack off at pre-school. Eventually they let her in after much to-ing and fro-ing. She presumed they had to make sure she was who she said she was.

She found Anja in a room at the end of a long ward, which had a reinforced window. Instead of looking out at the large swaying pine tree beyond it, she was staring vacantly at the wall. Her eyes moved slowly as they focused on Grace.

'Park-religious,' she mumbled, half smiling.

'Hi, Anja ... how are you?' Grace sat gingerly on the edge of the plastic seat beside her bed.

'I – good – they give me ...' she gestured with her hand in a slow, swirling motion.

'Methadone?'

'Mmmmm – is nice you come – thanks you ...'

'Have they said how long you can stay here?' Grace asked, speaking deliberately slowly.

Anja rolled her head from side to side.

'Do you know the name of the doctor who's looking after you?'

Again she rolled her head.

'I brought you some grapes and chocolate. I also brought you some other clothes and shoes. I don't know if they're the right size, but I guessed you were an 8 and a size 4 shoe.' Grace realised as she spoke that Anja wouldn't know what she was saying. She reached into her bag and brought out the gifts.

'Aah ... thanks you,' Anja's lips curved slightly.

It wasn't long before Anja had eaten half the chocolate bar. 'You hungry?' Grace smiled as she watched her.

Anja nodded, asking through sticky lips, 'I stay you?' She looked hopeful.

Heat rose up Grace's neck, 'I don't think so, Anja. I need to ask the doctor what the next step is for you. It's going to be okay – I promise you – you're safe now.' She saw the disappointment and rushed on, 'Do you want to go home or stay in England?'

'I go home. My mama ... my sister ...' a tear trickled out of one eye and rolled through straw-like hair.

'Okay. We'll aim for that. I'm sure there's a way to sort it all out. So tell me about home,' Grace wanted to keep it light, keep her from thinking about the life she'd just escaped.

'Is good – no much – but have food, house. In ...' she moved her hand up and down, drawing mountains in the air.

'Mountains?' Grace asked helpfully.

The girl nodded. She looked out the window and pointed to the tree.

'Pine trees?'

Anja nodded.

'Sounds nice.'

They talked like this for some time. Grace marvelled that she could understand so much of what Anja was trying to convey through signs and sounds and facial expressions. It didn't seem long before there was a knock at the door. A doctor in a white coat accompanied by two others came in and stood round Anja's bed. They spoke to her briefly, checking her chart.

Finally the doctor in charge asked, 'Anja, would it be okay to speak with this lady here about you?' he gestured to Grace.

The girl seemed to understand and nodded.

'Hello,' Grace reached out to shake his hand, 'I'm Reverend Hutchinson. Anja came to my church. I called the police and the social services and then we came here.'

'So I believe,' he smiled. He had kind, tired eyes, 'Dr Holmes.'

'I just want to know what will happen to Anja next? She can't go back out there. They will kill her or just put her right back to work.'

Dr Holmes nodded gravely. He seemed too young. *What things has he seen in his short life?* Grace wondered.

'We're waiting to hear from the police if they've found her a bed in a safe house. If they can find her one she'll have forty-five days to be repatriated or to seek asylum as Croatia is outside the EU.'

'She doesn't want to stay. She wants to go home.'

'That's good then, isn't it?' he smiled at Anja who stared back at him.

'If they can't find her a bed, then I'm not sure. The government's provision for victims of human trafficking is in its infancy really. We're all learning as we go along.'

Grace was mildly surprised at this, 'So what provision is there?'

'I'm not entirely sure myself,' he looked apologetic. 'We have had a few cases like this, but not enough to send me researching. I think the police are your best bet for info ... or in your line of work, the Sally Army.'

'Oh?' one of Grace's eyebrows rose.

'Yes. They run safe houses for human traffic victims – for women ... and men more recently,' he added.

'Really?'

'Men get trafficked for sex or labour or fraud. Human trafficking has become one of the world's biggest businesses.'

Grace felt very small and foolish. She wanted to crawl back into the comfort of oblivion that motherhood had brought her. She stared out the window at the swaying tree. A verse danced along with it, pirouetting on her shame ... *All creation strains on tiptoe to see the sons and daughters of God come into their own ...*

'I'll ... I'll speak to them then ...' her voice sounded like she felt.

'Anja will be here until we've heard from the police.'

'Can I come and visit her again? Only it was quite hard getting through reception today.'

Dr Holmes smiled tiredly, 'I hope you understand why that is. But yes ... now we know who you are, that should be no problem. It will be good for her to have a visitor.'

'Thank you. I'll talk to the police and the Sally Army and see what part we can play in all of this.'

'We?' the doctor looked puzzled.

'The local parish church,' Grace smiled.

'What could the church possibly do, apart from pray, of course,' Dr Holmes barely disguised his cynicism.

'I don't know, but I'm damned well going to find out!' Grace stood up, trying to shake off the slime of shame.

❈   ❈   ❈

Days went by. Grace visited Anja every morning Zack was in pre-school.

She met with Trevor and as they talked Grace became aware that their levels of interest in Anja's predicament differed. Eventually Trevor changed the subject.

'I need to talk to you about your role here at St Matt's, Grace.'

'I know,' she felt irritated by the inevitability of it.

'I think you need to meet with the Bishop and have a chat about what's next for you.'

'Yes,' she agreed. There was no point in arguing. She'd been in her curacy for far too long.

'So if any ministry does develop through your contact with Anja, it can't be rooted here at St Matt's.'

'I see,' she gazed at him, feeling slightly sick.

'You know as well as I do, that for your own sake, you need to move on,

Grace. You don't want to go on being a curate, do you?'

She sighed and looked away, 'No. Sorry … I guess I just feel a little vulnerable at the minute. I've been looking, but nothing's grabbed me and I don't really want to have to move out of the diocese. I've been praying … but nothing is clear … except …' she paused and then told him about what had happened to her in the car park after leaving Anja.

Trevor was thoughtful. He scratched behind his ear, dislodging several flakes of dandruff, which fell onto his shoulder, 'These inbetween times are hard. I do understand. But the Lord has not called you for nothing. He will make it all clear to you when you need to know.'

'But I'd really like to know now,' Grace frowned at the dandruff.

'So would I. I've been praying for you,' he smiled.

'Thanks,' Grace said half-heartedly.

'Look – you've been a great asset here. The prayer ministry team you've developed is such a bonus to the life of the church and Whitsun was amazing! I've never experienced anything like that before. So please hear me – you're not being rejected. It's just time …'

Grace raised her eyes to his and smiled a small reconciliatory smile. 'I know. Thanks.'

※　※　※

Bishop Duncan listened quietly to Wendy. Now and then when she drew breath he refocused, concentrating hard. He spread butter on his toast methodically and watched with satisfaction as it melted into the coarse surface of the latest healthy offering Wendy had ordered from the bakery.

'Well, my love, I really didn't know what to say to that. I mean – it beggars belief that she could treat him that way, don't you think?' she didn't wait for a reply and Bishop Duncan didn't hesitate in his morning ritual to even formulate one. 'I mean, really! How could she be so self-absorbed not to see that he needs his cricket. It's what keeps him going in the week. He works hard in the city – for what? For her and the children. Lord knows we don't get enough sunny days in the summer any more and the one good Saturday we've had, she kicks up such a fuss.' Wendy shook her head and raised her china mug to her lips.

Bishop Duncan took the opportunity offered him by Earl Grey tea scalding her mouth, 'Not all women are as supportive of their husband's work as you, dear.'

She swallowed and smiled with pleasure.

It takes so little ... he felt a pang of guilt as he reached out and lifted her hand to his lips, kissing her fingers affectionately. 'Would you be so kind as to pour me some of that tea and, if it's okay with you, I'll take it into my study.' He watched her face fall, adding quickly, 'What time did you say you'd like us to go?'

'I thought ten would be good. That way we'll get to theirs by about twelve in good time to help with lunch.'

'That's perfect. I'll only be an hour – just need to look over some things for tomorrow,' he leaned forward and kissed her plump cheek.

She raised her hand to his face and patted it, 'Don't worry about me,' she smiled a little too brightly, 'I've got some tidying to do,' she indicated the perfectly laid kitchen table with her other hand, 'You carry on, my love.'

Bishop Duncan picked up his cup and saucer and gratefully escaped to his study. As he closed the door behind him he breathed in the peaceful atmosphere. *If only she were more like Julian of Norwich* ... he sighed, lifting the book he'd been reading about the mystic, scanning the cover. He set his tea down on the worn leather top of his desk along with the book and settled himself into his chair. The smell of old leather engulfed him. *Oh Lord, forgive me ... thank you for your mercy in giving me Wendy ... bless her as she waits for me ... meet with her in the kitchen, I pray. May she know you ... your nearness ... the joy of being yours, not mine.*

He continued in prayer, intermittently sipping his tea. Eventually he reached for his diary and opened it to the following day's appointments that his secretary had neatly noted on the crisp page. *Revd Grace Hutchinson – 10.30 ... Now let me see ... Ordained deacon by the Bishop of London at St Paul's ... I priested her. She's the one who successfully enabled that marriage to survive at St Matthew's after Tom ... Goodness – she's been there far too long – what has it been? Oh, yes ... she had a child ... took extended maternity leave, now finishing her part-time curacy ... she's coming to see me about what's next, no doubt. She and her husband came to a dinner-party once ... yes, tall, thoughtful, forthright ... her husband? Yes ... I liked him ... yes ... we had a conversation about Degas ...*

Bishop Duncan returned to prayer ... *Father, thank you for Grace, for all* the gifts and skills you've given her. Thank you for giving her to your church. Give me wisdom as we meet tomorrow ... help me discern your voice as I listen to her. Tell me what I need to know to enable and direct her.

He waited, his spirit keenly straining to hear the familiar promptings.

... She is my servant. I will use her to lead many to myself; to bind up the broken hearted and to proclaim the time of my favour.

... You must put on the full armour of God so that you can take your stand against the devil's schemes and enable her to serve me. For your struggle is not against flesh and blood, but against the rulers, against the authorities, against the powers of this dark world and against the spiritual forces of evil in the heavenly realms ...

Surprised, he reached for his Bible and turned to Ephesians 6 to read the whole passage. He read through the verses that had come to mind, checking that he had remembered them correctly and then read verse 13 out loud, "'Therefore put on the full armour of God, so that when the day of evil comes, you may be able to stand your ground, and after you have done everything, to stand.'"

He leaned back into his chair again, the surface of his consciousness rippling from the stone thrown and still falling through its depths. The comfort his chair usually afforded, now eluded him. *What? What do you mean?*

Silence.

He looked at the rest of the appointments for the next day, not really taking any of them in, or being able to pray about them. He knew it was no use, he knew God's love of afflicting the comfortable and comforting the afflicted; he'd preached about it enough times. But it was always a surprise when it happened to oneself.

To his dismay he realised his time was nearly up and that he must change gear and prepare for a day of chaotic meals, grandchildren, dogs and guinea pigs.

Sighing deeply, he prayed, *Father in heaven ... reveal to me the full meaning of your word ... of its implications for me, for your daughter Grace, for your church, your flock, of whom you have made me a shepherd. Good Shepherd, I wait on you ... you are the way ... I will walk in you.*

�֍ ✖ ✖

Grace and the secretary exchanged a polite smile as she was ushered into the Bishop's office. He rose from his ordered desk to greet her.

'Good morning, Grace. How good to see you,' he said moving towards her with a smile.

She remembered her interview with him after she'd got through selection; that he'd spoken at her ordination retreat, administered communion at her ordination to the diaconate in St Paul's Cathedral, priested her in St Matthew's and led confirmation services there too. She knew his face well from the diocesan website, which she used to pray for him, but nothing prepared her for her reaction to him now. He stretched his hand out to her and as she took it in hers she felt as if she'd come home.

They looked at each other until Bishop Duncan broke eye contact and let go her hand. A line she'd written came to mind – *He isn't even good looking*, blindsided her. She fumbled in her bag for her diary and phone. 'I'll just turn this off,' she said trying to find the button to press.

'Please,' he gestured 'have a seat. Would you like a cup of tea or coffee?' the timbre of his voice reminded her of something wonderful, but she couldn't recall what.

'Thank you,' she sat down, suddenly acutely aware of her legs, crossing them at the ankle and tucking them under the chair.

'I'll just get Julia to bring it in,' he walked to the door and spoke briefly to the secretary.

When he returned she detected a change. *His eyes ... they're guarded ...*

He sat opposite her and folded his hands in his lap, 'So how are you and how is it going at St Matthew's?' he asked.

'I'm well, Bishop Duncan,' the reminder of his role strengthened her. 'St Matthew's is going really well – Trevor is doing a wonderful job.' She found she didn't know what to do with her hands. She decided to rest them on her diary and keep them there.

'Yes, I hear good things – the church has doubled in size in the last five years, when most Anglican churches are in decline. You must be doing something right,' he smiled.

She observed how this little praise gave her an inordinate amount of pleasure, and felt annoyed, but couldn't help saying, 'Well we have been learning how to allow God's Spirit to lead us within the framework of our liturgy.'

'A powerful combination,' he smiled. There was a pause, then, 'Word and Spirit, Spirit and truth ...' he mused, the guarded look dropping momentarily.

'Yes,' she replied, feeling almost breathless. Their eyes met and again she felt as if she'd known him all her life.

The secretary entered with the tea tray, placing it on the table between them. After a few pleasantries she withdrew, leaving Grace with a distinct feeling she had been warned.

They drank their tea and chatted casually about ministry at St Matthew's. The conversation covered all the expected subject matter until it turned to the events involving Chloe and the previous vicar. 'You have done an excellent job in pastoring Chloe and her husband, is it Mark?'

Grace nodded.

'Adultery is a difficult thing to recover from in a marriage – not impossible – but very few marriages I've known make it through such a breach of trust,' Bishop Duncan put his cup and saucer down on the table and folded his hands in his lap again.

'Yes ... but with God nothing is impossible,' Grace smiled, ' and it seems that He has enabled them to be gracious to one another. I only hope the same can be said for Tom and his wife.'

'Indeed,' he replied, giving her no more information, the guarded look in his eyes again.

'How is Tom doing?' she ventured the question cautiously.

'He's doing well. He has had a wonderful spiritual director. I believe it may well have been the making of him.'

'That's good to hear. I heard that he moved out of the diocese?'

'Yes,' he said simply.

Grace moved on, 'I wanted to thank you for the wonderful handwritten letter you sent Chloe. It meant a great deal to her, you know.'

He smiled self-effacingly, 'She said so in her reply,' he was now looking at his hands.

They were beautiful hands, Grace thought. The veins raised clearly like Michaelangelo's David. She suddenly realized she was thinking of him naked. She was shocked and raised her cup to her mouth to hide behind it.

'So I'm guessing you have come to talk to me about what might be next for you?' He raised his clear grey eyes to her face.

'Yes ... I've been praying for some time now for guidance.'

He smiled. 'Have you a mentor or a spiritual director?'

'Yes,' Grace responded, visualising her mentor's face. It helped to calm her feelings, which were becoming unmanageable. 'She's been very helpful in the process.'

'What have your thoughts been so far?' he asked, raising his folded hands to his chin, touching his steepled forefingers to his lips.

As Grace began to talk about meeting Anja she forgot about herself and her unwanted and incomprehensible feelings. She told him all about the sense she'd had when she'd first seen Anja in the park and then how she'd turned up at a church service and had come forward for prayer afterwards. She laughed when telling him about Peter's reaction to her bringing the girl home and about the meeting with the police the following day.

Grace noted that Bishop Duncan was caught up in her description of sensing the Holy Spirit's leading, despite remaining hidden behind his hands. As she finished her story the look in his eyes affected her ability to breathe again. There was a long silence.

Eventually Bishop Duncan seemed to rally and organise himself. He shifted in his seat and lightly ran a hand over his thinning hair. 'So Grace ... what might this all mean?'

'I'm not sure yet,' she replied. 'When I've been praying recently I have repeatedly seen the words, "My Sister's House" emblazoned on the screen of my imagination.' She hesitated and then bluntly came out with it, 'I think I am to run a ministry of some sort to women caught in human trafficking and the sex trade.'

Bishop Duncan didn't flinch. Grace sensed he was praying. She silently joined him, closing her eyes. She felt so in tune with him, so at one. On the screen of her imagination she saw their spirits rising together and entwining in mid-air. Surprised at the image, her eyes flew open.

His were still closed.

What is going on?

Every sense was heightened, it was almost like sexual arousal, which, when the thought struck her, sent her into a panic.

After a minute he opened his eyes and looked steadily at her, 'Could you leave this with me for a while?'

'Yes,' Grace replied, at a loss for anything else to say. 'Thank you.'

'You're welcome – it's been a pleasure to meet with you. I'm sorry it's taken so long,' his eyes were guarded.

'Well ... I'd better go. I'm sure you've got a full day ahead of you.'

'Yes,' he replied looking at his watch and raising his eyebrows. He stood up and walked ahead of her to the door.

'I'll wait to hear from you?'

'Yes,' he said again. He held out his hand to shake hers. She took it lightly. She didn't know how long she held it and then, as if in a scene deleted from a film and left on the editorial suite floor, she leaned forward, kissing him on the cheek, very near his mouth. Neither breathed.

He opened the door and she walked out not looking back. As she got into her car, horror descended upon her.

※　　※　　※

She lay in Peter's arms wondering how to confess to him. She tried several versions of events in her head, but her passion for truth pinned her down with each attempt. Eventually she turned on her side, his ear inches from her lips.

'I need to tell you something that happened today.'

'Mmmmm?' Peter replied sleepily.

'I went to see Bishop Duncan this morning for a ministerial review.'

'Exciting,' she could hear the smile in his voice.

'It was actually ...' she held her breath.

She heard his head turn on the pillow; felt his breath on her cheek.

'Really?'

'It's never happened before ... I knew it would at some point ... but you've been the only one I've ever ...'

'Wanted?' again the smile in his voice.

She nodded her head silently, knowing he'd feel the movement on his arm.

'A Bishop! Well I never thought that would be where my competition would come from.' In the silence that followed she knew he was processing the disclosure. 'So tell me, what was it like?'

'It was ...' she searched for an adjective, 'so weird!' They both laughed. 'He's not even good looking ...' there was that line again. 'But it felt like coming home; like I'd known him all my life.'

'And do you think he noticed?'

'That's what made it worse. I think he felt the same way.'

'That's not good.'

'No. No it's not, and what's even worse is that I kissed him goodbye.'

'On the mouth?' she heard the alarm change the tenor of his voice.

'On the cheek ... but quite close to his mouth,' she said sheepishly.

Silence.

'What possessed you to do that?' the barb of annoyance stung her.

'I don't know ... I really don't. I'm so sorry. It's never happened to me before.'

There was a silence in which she could almost feel Peter's brain going through several gear shifts. 'You gonna leave me for a Bishop?' he said rolling onto his side, sliding his other arm around her. He had chosen humour again.

Relieved, she pushed him away from her, 'Oh shut up, you idiot. Of course not.'

'Come here, you wild woman,' he reached for her again, tickling her.

She stifled a shriek into her pillow.

Later as she drifted off into sleep, he whispered, 'Thank you for telling me.'

She smiled secure in his trust of her. The peaceful sleep of confession quickly overtook her.

❋   ❋   ❋

'So ... how are you coping? Not something you're that familiar with,' smiled the old nun.

'I'm not sure I am,' he looked confused, 'I've not been sleeping.'

'Is it just lust or something more?' The stillness that surrounded her, permeated through his confusion.

'I think it's both and ... I mean ... Wendy reminds me more and more of my great aunt Lorna these days,' he smiled apologetically, 'I know I'm no Adonis myself ... but ... since we became grandparents ... '

'The marital bed has grown cold?' she offered.

'It was never that warm,' he sighed, 'I thought that was just the way it would have to be. We've made the best of it. It's been a good marriage,' he gazed sadly at his hands.

'Have you thought of making love to her?'

There was a long pause and then in a low voice, 'Grace?'

The nun nodded.

'I have thought of nothing else. That's why I am here.'

'The warning you had before meeting Grace,' she spoke hesitantly, 'suggests to me that an attack is being launched via your human frailty. This encourages me to believe that the Almighty has purposes he wants to fulfil through you both, which the enemy wants to thwart. When anything that raises itself up against the knowledge of God and obedience to his Christ, alarm bells should start ringing,' she quoted St Paul.

'It feels like love – like love I've never known; never thought existed – for me anyway,' he frowned.

'Duncan, from what you have told me and from looking at her photo on her church's website, she is a remarkably striking woman. I'm sure many have struggled as you are now on meeting her.'

There was silence. A shaft of light came through the small gothic window high in the convent wall. It radiated down between them onto the smooth stone floor.

'On meeting her before I never had this reaction. Perhaps because she was not as spiritually open as she is now? Or perhaps because I am getting older and am having a mid-life crisis?' he paused in thought, smiling a little. Then he looked at the nun, 'If I were blind, I would have felt the same way about her this time. I felt we were kindred spirits. When we prayed …' he stopped.

'Like foreplay?' she mused quietly.

He smiled, 'You know far too much of these things to be a nun!'

'I'm a woman – I know.'

'So what do I do?'

'You could move her out of your diocese – remove the temptation. After all it is time she moves on to pastures new.'

'But that would be wrong – she would be forced to move as consequence of my weakness, not as a directive from the Lord,' he unfolded his hands in his lap, spreading them slightly.

'It would, but that's generally what happens.'

Bishop Duncan shook his head, 'Wee men,' he put on a Scottish accent and they both smiled sadly at the joke.

After a pause she said, 'Or you could look at your frailty, nail it with

Christ to his cross and continue to enable her to serve God, ensuring that the powers of your flesh and this dark world do not hinder what God wants to do through her.'

Tears welled up in his eyes as he gazed at his mentor, 'Thank you, sister. That is what I needed to hear.'

She accepted his thanks with a nod. 'So what is the nature of your frailty?'

He didn't answer right away. 'I think I am lonely.'

The nun waited.

'Despite reminding me more and more of great aunt Lorna, Wendy is a wonderful wife and mother, but I think it is that she is so different than me.'

'Most marriages are made up of opposites.'

'Yes … She does not share my spirituality. She is very practical, very present, very now,' he paused for thought. 'I, however, live elsewhere … in another dimension. I would never say this outside of these four walls, but I often think I live in eternity, in communion with heaven … a mystic … like you?' Their eyes met in understanding. 'I thought marriage would bring us closer, enable us to be more in tune with each other, but instead, after all these years I find we are poles apart.'

'Are you saying your spirituality is superior to hers?'

There was another long silence. 'I don't mean to … we just don't connect on that level at all. I have always assumed that it just wasn't a possibility … but with Grace I sensed that it was … I still haven't recovered from the shock and dismay of realising it. I cannot still the thoughts of jealousy that another man has what I have always longed for.'

'But does he?' the nun raised her eyebrows, causing her habit to shift slightly on her brow.

'Perhaps not … perhaps that is why … I think she felt the same towards me, which makes it all so much worse.'

'Yes,' she said quietly. Then changing tack, 'What about your ego?'

Bishop Duncan shifted in his seat uncomfortably.

'Feeling a reciprocal response from someone with physical and spiritual beauty such as Grace possesses, must be a heady concoction?' she continued.

He stared at his hands for some time. 'There it is,' he sighed. He raised his eyes to hers, 'It's triggered childhood memories of connection.

My identity was so enmeshed with Mother's. We knew what each other were thinking and feeling without speaking,' the yearning in his voice was palpable. 'Once I went to boarding school that was it. Amputation – a ruthless severing of the tie that bound us. I have been lonely all my life, possibly out of choice? Possibly pride ... misplaced loyalty ... has kept me this way?'

The nun nodded slowly.

'Poor Wendy ... she has been lonely all this time too ...'

'Let's not get into self-recrimination, shall we?' she broke into his reverie pragmatically. 'Bringing it to the cross will suffice. Let redemption's power work on these things. Resurrection will follow, in one way or another.'

Bishop Duncan nodded, 'The breastplate of righteousness and the belt of truth.'

'Yes,' she replied.

They sat quietly for a time. Then without further conversation they both moved simultaneously to the prayer stools that faced the window and a simple wooden cross that hung beneath it. They went to the hard work of prayer together, wrestling flesh to rough-hewn wood.

As they made connection with the nurturing presence of God, Bishop Duncan placed his hands on his abdomen.

This is where I feel it ... the loneliness ... Father ... please come and fill this void. You live in me by your Holy Spirit. I am in the eternal circle of your love.

I confess my sin of wanting to fill this emptiness with what is not mine. I confess my self-indulgence and self-pity.

Forgive me for hiding this part of myself from your love, from keeping this loneliness from you. I have sought to be comforted apart from you.

Please take the effects of my sin away from me.

Help me open my heart to receive your forgiveness and grace.

He waited in the stillness, aware that the nun was praying for him fiercely.

She surprised him when she broke into his silent prayer, 'You may need to forgive your mother, Duncan, from your deep heart, from when it all went wrong.'

'I love my mother. I bear no grudge towards her.'

'You as an adult may well fully understand her reasons for leaving you in boarding school. But you the child … he still lives within you. It is from that deep place that you may need to forgive her.'

Bishop Duncan did not turn towards her as she spoke. He remained with his eyes closed, concentrating on the unseen. As he listened something within him concurred with what she was saying. 'Could you lead me, sister? I am in unfamiliar territory.'

She nodded silently and then began, 'Father, I forgive my mother for not being there in the ways I needed …' she waited, leaving space for Duncan to silently repeat the words and make them his own.

'I confess where I have nurtured unforgiveness towards her and I now release her to you …

'I confess where I closed down and refused what love she did have to offer …

'I forgive her for all her failures, her absences and abandonment of me …

'I forgive her for not ever having me as the focus of her maternal love …

'I turn to you to comfort me, heal me from the grief I feel at the loss of nurture and touch …

'Meet me in my longing for attachment I pray … Amen.'

Tears streamed down Duncan's face.

※　※　※

Grace met Dr Holmes in the corridor as she was returning from the bathroom to Anja's room

'Oh, I'm glad I've seen you. Anja's being moved to a safe house tomorrow. The police are coming to escort her. It's taken this long because there are so few safe houses with available beds,' he explained.

'Can you let me know where?'

'I'm afraid not,' he smiled apologetically. 'Perhaps if you speak to the police they might be able to help? They should be here by midday tomorrow.'

'Okay. Thanks, doctor. I'll see you tomorrow,' she hitched her bag further up on her shoulder, 'I'll just go say bye to Anja.'

'Hopefully they'll be able to offer her some counselling to deal with PTSD,' he said collecting a pile of files off the counter at the nurses station.

'PTSD? What's that?'

'Post Traumatic Stress Disorder. That's what most trafficked victims need help with, along with everything else,' he waved a free hand in a wide arch.

'Haven't you started any kind of therapy with her here?' Grace was surprised.

'Oh no – we have no funding for that. We've just given her methadone to keep her stable and given her a bed to sleep in. Sorry to disappoint you,' his shoulders were stooped.

Grace looked at him amazed at both the lack of provision and her own ignorance of what was available for the most vulnerable. 'Oh no – you've been great! Where would she have gone if you hadn't taken her in?'

'Your house?' he laughed mirthlessly.

My Sister's House ... the thought glowed in red on the screen of her mind again as she walked down the corridor to Anja's room.

'Hi, Anja,' she said warmly.

Anja turned from facing the wall to look at Grace. Her eyes were swollen and red. With no reply she returned her gaze back to the wall, her back to Grace.

Grace came and sat beside her on the bed, resting her hand on Anja's arm. She didn't speak for a while, just gently patted it, like she would have done with Zack if he'd had a nightmare. 'I'm going to ask the police to let me come and see where they take you.'

Anja turned again slowly to look up at her, bloodshot eyes full of pain. 'Yes?'

'Yes ... I promise ... I'll make sure you're being looked after properly.'

'Thanks you,' she reached up and held on to Grace's hand. Grace thought about Lila and Mary.

※   ※   ※

'If her pimp has been looking for her, as he will have, he may well have you under surveillance. If that's the case then he will follow you straight to the safe house, if you were to visit,' the policewoman explained.

'I understand all that,' Grace said patiently, 'but I'm the only person she knows other than those sick monsters.' Grace noted the surprise in the officer's eyes at the extent of her rage. 'Don't you think she needs some sense of connection to someone as she makes this transition?'

'I'll talk to my supervisor, but it's unlikely, so don't get your hopes up,' she shifted her police vest on her shoulders uncomfortably.

Grace waited in the hospital hallway while the officer stepped outside to speak to her superior on her radio. *For your name's sake – for Anja's sake – please open the way for me –* she prayed, scrutinising her painted toe nails, noticing that two of them were chipped. The automatic doors slid open, ushering the officer back into the hallway.

'It's your lucky day today. The Super's in a good mood and says you can come with us – but not in your car.'

'Great!' Grace smiled broadly, almost raising a reciprocal smile from the officer.

They drove in an unmarked car in relative silence on the M25, apart from the police radio intermittently crackling into their thoughts. Grace texted her mum asking her to pick Zack up from pre-school as she wasn't sure what time she'd be back. She got an instant reply in the affirmative.

Anja sat hunched staring out the darkened window vacantly. Grace was trying to keep her eyes on landmarks so as to remember the way as they turned off into the Kent countryside; it was unfamiliar territory to her. They eventually came to a halt outside an ordinary looking detached house, down a leafy lane in a nondescript village.

A pear-shaped, middle-aged woman greeted them at the door. She was pleasant, practical and quietly spoken. She was especially kind to Anja, which gave Grace confidence. Grace was wearing her dog collar in a light blue shirt. The woman whose name was Barbara addressed much of what she said to Grace. It became clear that clergy authority was of more significance to Barbara than the Queen's constabulary's authority.

Eventually Grace asked, 'Are you a faith-based charity?'

'Yes we are. We're a new project of the local parish church. Our vicar's been with us for three years, bringing all sorts of wonderful changes with him. Not everyone's happy about it in the village, of course, but I for one think it's fantastic!' smiled Barbara.

'How long did it take you to do the preparation work before you started offering a service?'

'About a year – we've been running for eighteen months.'

'So your vicar didn't hang about?' Grace smiled.

Barbara laughed, 'No. He's a force to be reckoned with. Our PCC didn't know what had hit them.'

'Have you access to interpreters?' the officer interjected.

'We've been building up contacts slowly. We've got Albanian, Nigerian, Turkish and Lithuanian translators. She showed Anja a cabinet, which held toiletries, white towels, pink pyjamas and a pair of slip-on slippers.

'For me?' Anja asked.

Barbara nodded.

The girl's eyes welled up. Grace could sense a battle going on inside Anja: to trust or not to trust? She wondered how many times she had been given things only to lull her into a false sense of security by her traffickers. A fresh surge of anger burned Grace's throat as she watched Anja struggle.

'It's okay, Anja. You're going to be safe here. This is a good woman. She's here to protect you and help you. These things really are for you,' she gestured to the cabinet.

'We'll get you some clothes tomorrow too,' Barbara added continuing to talk slowly and succinctly. Anja sat on the bed listening but comprehending little.

❋ ❋ ❋

'Milk?' Chloe lifted the small jug.

'Yes, thanks,' Grace held up her mug.

She enjoyed watching the light and dark swirl together as she stirred the liquid with her spoon. Here they were sitting at *the* table of reconciliation in Chloe's kitchen. She smiled at the thought.

'What?' Chloe asked.

'This table,' Grace patted it humorously.

Chloe looked blank and then on realising Grace's meaning let out a short, dry laugh, curling a glossy lock of dark hair behind her ear, 'Wish it could set the scene for reconciliation again with Mark … with Melanie too,' she sighed.

'Why, what's wrong? Are you and Mark not getting on?'

'Oh, we're fine … I guess … bumping along … probably like every other couple who've been married as long as us.'

'Mmmm … and Melanie?'

'Oh, she's a piece of work!'

'Maybe this table will be the scene of reconciliation between you. You know God can't resist a praying mother and that tables are pretty significant symbols of provision and reconciliation in scripture.'

Chloe made a face mimicking Grace's sermonising.

Grace laughed, 'Well – it's true!'

'I know – but you don't have to live with them. It can't go on much longer, or I'll be adding murder to my list of sins,' Chloe sipped her black coffee. 'Melanie's become so nasty. She's taken to locking her bedroom door too – I haven't seen inside it for weeks. For all I know she could be harbouring ex-convicts in there, along with every germ known to man,' she shook her head and sighed. 'I'm at my wit's end and Mark's no help at all.'

'Do you think she'd talk to me?' Grace asked.

'It's worth a try – anything's worth a try. Anyway, let's not talk about Melanie anymore. I get so down just thinking about her. What did you want to talk to me about?'

'You know, about what you said the other week,' Grace watched Chloe's eyes refocus. 'Something's happened which has made me really think and pray.'

'Oh?'

Grace told her about meeting Anja, about the safe house she'd visited, her interaction with the police and the doctor at the mental health unit. Then she told her about her conversation with Bishop Duncan, being careful not to give away any of the emotional turmoil that had accompanied it.

'Wow,' Chloe sat back, processing everything. 'Have you heard back from the bish yet?'

'No not yet,' she ignored the warm feeling she had just thinking of him.

'Would the diocese back a project like this? I thought they were skint?'

'They are,' Grace affirmed, 'but he seemed genuinely interested in the idea – so we'll just have to wait and see if they'll be willing for their charity status to cover the project or whether we need to set up our own and whether there's any funding available to get a safe house ready and furnished. So would you be interested in helping me?'

'One of my tutors has just agreed to supervise me when I leave college – maybe she could help me in the process of setting up the psychotheraputic side of things?' the tired expression was gone and Chloe looked younger by the minute.

'I take that as a yes then?' Grace smiled.

'Oh, yes!' Chloe laughed. 'It matches everything I've been thinking about. It's like I've been preparing for it these last three years.'

'It's not going to be a viable St Matt's project. I have to move on. How would you feel about that?'

'That's neither here nor there for me. Hey, maybe we could take a team of us down to this safe house you've been to already – see how it works? Maybe we could go to the Sally Army head quarters to get an understanding of how to apply to be one of their safe houses?'

'Let's walk before we can run, eh?' Grace said pensively.

'Grace – I feel like I've been waiting for this all my life! This is what I've been preparing for!'

'Shall we pray about it then? If it *is* what God wants us to do, it's gonna get serious.'

And so as Grace closed her eyes, she silently took captive her feelings for Bishop Duncan and forced them to be obedient.

Chloe brought her anxieties about Melanie and her anger at Mark, praying for help to be a good mum and wife, as well as the ability to fulfil her life's calling.

❋   ❋   ❋

'Hello, Grace?'

She instantly recognised his voice, 'Hello, Bishop Duncan,' she couldn't help smiling.

'How are you?'

'I'm fine thank you. How are you?'

'Good … good,' there was a pause. Grace waited. 'I'm just coming back to you on the matter we discussed recently.'

'Yes?' she held on to her excitement.

'I've been in conversation with our head of finance and our strategy team. You'll be glad to know the initial sounds are positive.'

'Oh?' she didn't breathe.

'What we'd like you to do is to write a proposal for the project and submit it to the strategy team as soon as possible. It looks like you'll have to set it up as a charity in its own right, but there are diocesan funds that could go towards start up costs,' he paused briefly to let this sink in.

'Okay … that's great,' Grace's mind shifted several gears.

He continued, 'I also wanted to ask you to consider something else.'

'Yes?' she breathed.

'The next parish to St Matt's, St Stephen's, has been vacant for two years now.'

'I know – but it's an Anglo-Catholic tradition. They're looking for a male priest aren't they?'

'Well they have been, but success has eluded them in finding one. Their PCC has been challenged to reconsider their previous decision to pass resolution B and to accept female applicants. To my delight, last week they decided to revoke it.'

Grace was stunned. Then she laughed, 'There is a God!'

She revelled in his deep corresponding chuckle.

'You'll still have to apply and be interviewed for the post and it is only half a stipend.'

'What about a vicarage?'

'Yes – there is a very substantial vicarage.'

'So if I got it, I could work part time in the parish and part time developing "My Sister's House"?'

'Theoretically,' he hesitated. 'If they offered you the post, you would need to discuss your vision for a ministry to human traffic victims with them. But something tells me they may well be open to such a project.'

'Really? What?' she realised how blunt she'd been, 'Sorry, Bishop Duncan … I didn't mean to be rude.'

'That's all right Grace. I thought you'd be interested,' she heard him smile. 'As I've been praying I have sensed that this may well be the ground from which salvation will spring. It often springs up where we have not perceived it.'

'Thank you, Bishop Duncan, thanks very much.'

'You're welcome. Now is there anything else you'd like to ask me?'

She paused and thought, 'Oh, yes – when I write the proposal what do I need to include in it?'

'I'll get Julia to send you some bullet points via email.'

At the mention of the secretary's name Grace felt herself come down with a bump. This was ministry – work – professional stuff – not just a cosy chat. She guiltily thought of Peter.

If only he was spiritually alive like Duncan ... Duncan? She reprimanded herself fiercely. 'Okay – that would be great,' she said out loud.

'Goodbye, Grace. All the best.'

'Bye, Bishop Duncan,' she put the phone back into its dock feeling bereft. She stared at her blue and gold Jesus knowing full well she couldn't hide what she was really thinking from him.

She went upstairs and changed into tracksuit bottoms and a T-shirt. *Pre-school pick up in an hour. Just got time for forty minutes.* She felt better as she began to sweat on the cross trainer.

❈　❈　❈

On the way to get Zack, she stuck a CD of the audio book of Acts into her car stereo. She managed to listen to chapters five through seven before having to change gear into mummy mode.

Zack wanted his friend Harry to come home to play, so after some discussion, Grace sorted it out with his mum and strapped both boys into the back of the car, having borrowed Harry's car seat.

Grace watched them in her rear view mirror. She laughed quietly to herself listening to their inane chatter. When they got back they had a snacky lunch round the kitchen table and then the boys ran upstairs to set up Zack's wooden train set. Hours of endless fun, Grace thought.

She made herself a coffee, settled herself with her laptop at the table, opening her bible to the book of Acts. She read over the chapters she'd listened to in the car.

Why did I react to Bishop Duncan that way? It must be attack? Must have the devil scared by the prospect of St Stephen's and 'My Sister's House'. Gotta guard myself. Lord ... if I were to give into this weakness ... the repercussions would be devastating! Please help me.

She thought of the conundrum of God working His will out on earth, despite the attacks the early believers endured as they ushered His Kingdom in. Inspired she opened her story file and started tapping on her computer keyboard:

Aaron was in daily discussion with the high priest and the Sanhedrin, strategising a way to quell the 'Jesus movement', as they had begun calling it. A young Pharisee named Saul of Tarsus, one of Gamaliel's disciples, had been very persuasive in his zeal for the law and the honour of God, despite the fact that he was too young to be a member of the Sanhedrin. Aaron liked him, fast tracking him to becoming one of the youngest members. Together they advocated a ruthless persecution of the movement; zero tolerance. However, Gamaliel held his council. He was the grandson of Hillel, for whom an entire school of thought was named within Pharisaism, and honoured among the people for his teaching of the law.

Aaron and Saul convinced them to arrest not just a few, but all the apostles this time and put them in the Sanhedrin jail. It didn't take long – the apostles did not put up a fight. In fact they didn't seem that surprised or concerned. The temple guard were bemused by them singing Psalm 40 in unison as they were led through Jerusalem's streets.

> 'I waited patiently for the Lord
> He turned and heard my cry
> He lifted me up out of the slimy pit
> Out of the mud and mire
> He set my feet upon a rock
> And gave me a firm place to stand
> He put a new song in my mouth
> A hymn of praise to our God
> Many will see and fear
> And put their trust in the Lord.'

John had come up with the tune some months before and it had become a favourite chant among the community. His sensitive nature and creativity were lit on fire at Pentecost and since then he had led many moving times of worship among the apostles and the growing number of disciples. He turned to the guard who walked beside him and said, 'Will you join us?' It seemed such a strange thing to ask, given his circumstances.

The guard searched John's young eyes for any sign of madness, but found none. He did not reply, but many weeks later he did join them.

Long after the door of the jail had been locked and the night had worn on, the apostles worshipped and prayed together. Peter was the first to eventually doze off, slumped against the wall. He was woken with a start by a flash of light. Confused he covered his eyes and cowered against the cold stone. The other apostles were on their feet. He struggled to his, realising that the source of light was a person … a person with wings. He rubbed his eyes hard and looked again, awe dawning upon him. The door of the jail stood open and the angel led them out into the night.

'Go, stand in the temple courts and tell the people the full message of this new life,' said the radiant being in a voice that reminded Peter of crashing waves on pebbled shores. They didn't hesitate, making their way in silent reverence directly back to the temple courts. Day was breaking as the first worshippers began to arrive and they obediently taught them about Jesus.

※　※　※

The guards returned with the news that they'd found the jail securely locked and the sentries standing at the doors, but when they'd opened them, they found no one inside. Aaron was furious.

A messenger arrived from the temple with the news that the apostles were standing in the temple courts teaching the people. Aaron caught the eye of Saul and recognised there a kindred fury. He moved round the room as they waited for the apostles to be brought before them again, positioning himself next to Saul. When the apostles were brought in Aaron whispered to Saul, 'I have had enough of these unschooled men.'

Saul turned his head slightly to acknowledge his mentor but before he could respond the high priest began speaking.

'We gave you strict orders not to teach in this name, yet you have filled Jerusalem with your teaching and are determined to make us guilty of this man's blood.'

Peter replied, 'We must obey God rather than men! The God of our fathers raised Jesus from the dead – whom you had killed by hanging him on a tree.' His voice did not waver nor did his gaze, which was directed at the high priest. 'God exalted him to his own right hand as Prince and Saviour that he might give repentance and forgiveness of sins to Israel. We are witnesses of these things, and so is the Holy Spirit, whom God has given to those who obey him.'

'Put them to death!' Aaron's voice was the first of many to cut through the air.

Gamaliel motioned with his hands for silence. He ordered the apostles to be removed for a little while. When they had gone he addressed the Sanhedrin, 'Men of Israel, consider carefully what you intend to do to these men. Some time ago Theudas appeared, claiming to be somebody, and about four hundred men rallied to him. He was killed, all his followers were dispersed, and it all came to nothing. After him, Judas the Galilean appeared in the days of Quirinius the Roman governor of Syria during the census and led a band of people in revolt against Roman rule. He too was killed, and all his Zealot followers were scattered. Therefore, in the present case I advise you: Leave these men alone! Let them go! For if their purpose or activity is of human origin, it will fail. But if it is from God, you will not be able to stop these men; you will only find yourselves fighting against God.'

The majority of the Sanhedrin were persuaded, but Aaron insisted, 'They must be punished. Flog them before you release them.'

Saul shared sadistic satisfaction with him as the public executioner was brought in and each apostle had his back flayed. But it didn't seem to deter them.

Peter, the natural leader among them, cried out with each stripe on his back, but it was what he cried that baffled and frustrated Aaron. 'Ah Lord ... like you ... thank you ... disgrace ... for you ... for your name ...'

❋ ❋ ❋

The message was brief and read: Mary, will you come immediately? Bring your oils with you. Lila.

Mary looked up from the scrap of parchment in her hand at the sweating messenger, 'What has happened?'

'The apostles have been flogged in the Sanhedrin,' he gasped

'All of them?' she asked.

'Yes.'

'I'll return with you now,' she said quickly, shock tingling across her chest and down into her arms and hands.

Martha came out into the courtyard, taking in the exhausted state of the messenger and the look on her sister's face, 'What has happened?' she asked.

'It's the apostles – they've been flogged – by the Sanhedrin,' Mary held out the note sent by Lila. Martha took it and scanned it.

'I'll come with you,' she said instantly.

'What about everything here? All the preparations ...' Mary's mind flitted in a panic over everything she and her sister had been preoccupied with for weeks.

Martha looked at her in that matter of fact way of hers, 'Mary ... each day has enough trouble of its own. Let's focus on this now and trust that everything will fall into place.'

Mary reached out and squeezed her sister's hand, crumpling the note. 'Yes ... let me get my things ...'

'Come,' Martha said to the messenger, 'would you like a drink and some food?' She led him towards the kitchen.

On hearing what had happened, Lazarus came with them, and together they made the journey from Bethany to Jerusalem as the afternoon sun cast long shadows behind them. They went straight to John's house and were met by Lila, who had been watching for them. Mary gave each of them a bottle of oil as they climbed the stairs.

They were appalled by the thick, sweet smell of blood that hit their nostrils on entering John's house. It made Mary want to retch, but she swallowed hard and willed her stomach to be still.

Already Mary Magdalene, Jesus' mother, Stephen, Jair, Joanna and Susanna were washing the wounds of the apostles who lay face down on tables and benches.

When Stephen saw Mary his eyes welled with tears.

They held one another's anguished gaze and then Mary went to work. Stephen came alongside her, praying in tongues over Thomas's back as she anointed his wounds with oil. The skin was hanging in strips from gashes so deep that Mary could see the white of his ribs through the blood. Stephen gently lifted each strip of skin and placed it carefully back into its place, praying all the time. A muffled groan escaped from Thomas, whose face was half buried in a pillow.

Mary was about to move on to Matthew who lay next to him, when Stephen caught her arm exclaiming, 'Look!'

She returned her gaze from Matthew's lacerations to Thomas's. They looked different. It took her a moment to assimilate the information her eyes were giving her. She leaned in closer and saw that each wound had knit itself together and was quickly forming scar tissue. She watched one wound actually heal completely before her eyes.

'Praise be!' Stephen whispered and proceeded praying louder in tongues, interspersed with delighted laughter. The others gathered round to see what the cause of celebration was. By this time Thomas had rolled onto his side and was sitting up.

'Power is surging through my body!' Thomas's voice shook as he looked at his trembling hands in amazement. He reached round to his back, 'The pain is gone – I'm healed!' he jumped up and immediately began praying for the others with Stephen, continuing to anoint them all with oil.

※　※　※

'What do you think Philip?' Stephen asked across the table.

Philip pulled his eyes away from the door to the kitchen to focus on Stephen. 'Sorry, Stephen, say that again.'

Stephen quelled impatience with the younger man and repeated himself, 'What if we split the city up between the seven of us,' he stabbed the map of Jerusalem again which lay on the table, 'and made a list of the young men from each sector who will assist us with distribution of food for our widows. We could do it tomorrow at the gathering in Solomon's Colonnade?'

Lazarus leaned forward looking at the map, 'Seven sectors – pretty perfect really,' he smiled.

Stephen had asked if they could meet in Bethany to plan a strategy for the food distribution. It meant he could see Mary one more time before their wedding. No one was in any doubt as to why the location had been chosen.

'I think it's a workable plan. It means each of us can focus on the widows in a smaller area, that way ensuring that no one gets left out.' Philip turned his head towards the kitchen door again as he spoke.

'Are you that hungry?' Stephen asked irritably.

'Sorry,' Philip looked embarrassed and then concentrated his attention hard on the map.

'Right. Who will have which sector?' Stephen wanted the meeting to be over now. He wanted just a little time alone with Mary, if Lazarus would allow it.

As they began discussing the details, Mary and Martha came into the room with bowls of olives and flat breads. As Mary placed her plates carefully beside the map, she smiled shyly at Stephen. It should have warmed his heart, but he caught sight of Philip looking at her with a moonstruck expression on his face, which annoyed him intensely.

He looked back at his betrothed and focused on her. She was his and always would be. Those soft lips; those almond eyes; that golden skin ... We should have set the wedding date sooner. He ran his fingers through his dark curls, taking in a deep breath and began silently praying. The tension slowly eased within him.

By the time the women brought in the meal, decisions had been made and everyone seemed clear of their responsibilities. They stood to pray together, breaking bread and passing the cup between them in remembrance of Jesus, as he had taught them. This had become a precious ritual, which they savoured and lingered over.

It was late before they all departed. Stephen waited until everyone had left the courtyard, looking hopefully at Lazarus. He gave his permission with one nod of his head and gently took Martha's arm, withdrawing into their home. An owl hooted in the tree above them. The night sky was veiled in low hanging cloud with the threat of a storm in the air. 'Not long now, my love,' he said looking down into Mary's upturned face. The lantern that hung from the tree cast warm light on one side of her face, leaving the other in darkness.

She smiled and then shivered involuntarily, though the night was warm. A fleeting anxious expression crossed her features.

'What is it?' he asked.

'I don't know – just when you said "not long now" I felt something, I don't know what.'

He cupped her chin in his hand, drawing her to him. It was to be their first and last kiss.

※　※　※

'Oh, Lila, it was wonderful!' Mary dragged the brush through her hair.

'In what way?' Lila was amused by Mary's animation.

'It was like no other kiss I have ever known. It was tender at first – then it grew in intensity – it felt like my whole body was coming alive – I mean really alive. I think I have always connected arousal with guilt and shame before,' she looked for understanding from her friend.

Lila smiled her affirmation, flicking a fly away from Joshua's sleeping face. He lay sprawled out on the couch beside her. Anna was playing with a friend next door.

Mary began plaiting her thick hair. She pulled the glossy mane round her shoulder and continued to weave it together until it reached her waist. Then she tied the end with a white ribbon and flung it over her shoulder. It thudded softly against her small back. She'd come to stay for the last few days before the wedding, to complete her beauty treatments with Lila and not get under

Martha's feet as she had little interest in beauty regimes.

'Have you heard anything more of how Stephen is getting on with the synagogue?'

Mary felt anxiety grip her stomach again. 'Do we have to talk about that now?' she asked.

'Sorry, Mary – but Jair was telling me about it last night and it doesn't sound good.'

'It's a few men who hate losing an argument. They've been debating with Stephen for weeks even though they can't stand up against his wisdom or the Holy Spirit in him.'

'I know Mary, but Jair told me that now they're spreading rumours that Stephen has been blaspheming against Moses and the temple.'

'That's ridiculous. Anyone who knows him would know he would never do such a thing,' shock sharpened Mary's voice.

'Well, let's hope it all comes to nothing ...' Both women were thinking of the flogging the apostles had received from the Sanhedrin.

'I wish he would just be quiet,' Mary felt ashamed as she said it.

There was a pause as Lila absorbed this sentiment. 'Really?' she asked softly.

'Yes ... no ... I mean ... I don't know,' Mary said unhappily, fiddling with her fingernails.

'How can we be quiet about what we have seen and heard – about what we know – what he did for us – for you – for me?' Lila leaned forward to try and make eye contact with Mary.

'But what if they do something to him before ...'

'Before what? Before you get a chance at happiness?' Lila guessed.

There was another silence and then Mary nodded her head.

'Don't you remember what Jesus said?' Lila asked gently reaching out and resting her hand on Mary's knee. ' "Unless you deny yourself, take up your cross and follow me, you cannot be my disciple."'

There was another silence.

'Don't you think Stephen is tempted to be quiet for an easy life – a life with you and everything he's hoped for?'

Mary lifted her young head and looked sadly at Lila.

'But he cannot. He is a man of integrity. His love for God and his people compel him.'

'I know,' Mary said in a small voice. 'That's one of the things I love about him.'

Lila smiled softly, 'Shall we pray and then let me give you that massage you taught me.'

Mary sighed and nodded again, turning the palms of her hands upwards in her lap and closing her eyes. The anxiety over the ominous feeling she'd had the last time she'd seen Stephen slithered inside her.

'Come Holy Spirit – fill us afresh with courage for whatever is ahead,' Lila whispered.

'Father forgive me for wishing he would be quiet. Thank you that he loves you so deeply. Please give him ... and me ... courage to continue to speak your son's name with boldness.' Strength rose within her as she prayed and the anxiety loosened its grip.

❋ ❋ ❋

'This fellow never stops speaking against this holy place and against the law. For we have heard him say that Jesus of Nazareth will destroy the temple and change the customs Moses handed down to us.'

Stephen stood alone surrounded by an angry mob of men before the Sanhedrin.

I will give you the words to speak ... the gentle voice floated through his jumbled thoughts as he listened to further accusations of blasphemy.

Thank you, Lord, he prayed silently, grasping the promise firmly and embracing it to the core of his being.

Today you will be with me ... continued the voice, like a feather floating on a gentle breeze.

He began praying in tongues as a joy so sweet that he could hardly bear it came over him. He felt as if the air around him would be pulled back like a curtain, revealing the face he loved so dearly. Excitement mounted in him at the thought and then, like a dagger to the heart, Mary's face rose before him. Tears sprang to his eyes.

Lord Jesus ... she's known so much sorrow ... so much hardship ... I want to stay and care for her ... bring her happiness ... I don't want her to be caught in the crossfire of this spiritual battle ...

Trust me, came the reply.

One of his accusers was speaking at length, gesticulating passionately as other angry voices rose in agreement.

I trust you, Stephen affirmed. Another surge of joy engulfed and overwhelmed him as he let go and let God.

You can drink this cup ... came the strong affirmation. He smiled in response. A scent captured his attention. At first it reminded him of one of Mary's perfumed oils, but as it grew stronger he knew that he had never smelt anything as beautiful as this in his whole life. It captivated him and stirred deep longings within him. Into his mind came the words from Psalm 23:

'Even though I walk through the valley of the shadow of death
I will fear no evil
For you are with me
Your rod and your staff, they comfort me ...'

He realised that silence had fallen around him and everyone was staring at him intently.

※　※　※

His face is like the face of an angel, Aaron grudgingly allowed the observation to form in his mind. He speaks well ... he mused, eyeing his prey speculatively ... perhaps he has been schooled in the art of rhetoric – perhaps in Rome? Perhaps Jair has been training him? He's subtle ... very clever ... yet forceful ... indirect insinuation ... recounting our history in such a way as to convince us that our rejection of the Nazarene equates to our ancestors' rejection of Joseph and Moses ... Ah, yes ... of course ... and God has not limited the manifestation of his presence and glory to one man-made location. Very clever ... Abraham, Joseph, Moses ... quoting Isaiah ... always a good ploy ...

Aaron watched with hooded eyes, his hand half covering his mouth as Stephen reached the climax of his speech. 'You stiff-necked people, with uncircumcised hearts and ears! You are just like your fathers: You always resist the Holy Spirit! Was there ever a prophet your fathers did not persecute?'

'That's it – he's finished now,' Aaron muttered to Saul who was standing next to him, who nodded in agreement.

'They even killed those who predicted the coming of the Righteous One. And now you have betrayed and murdered him – you who have received the law that was put into effect through angels but have not obeyed it.'

The reaction was violent.

Everything went into slow motion. A fist came from the left into Stephen's peripheral vision, connecting with his cheekbone. Delicate sinus gave way beneath solid knuckle. He staggered to withstand the blow. Another came from behind, just beneath his ribs, causing him to throw his head back, an agonised cry escaping his lips. His eyes followed an insect in flight above him. As he watched, light began to appear in its wake, like morning sunlight as curtains are drawn. He stared enraptured as glory poured down upon him, a solid force of sheer love.

Lord Jesus! 'Look,' he cried in awe, 'I see heaven open and the Son of Man standing at the right hand of God!' Why are you standing? he asked the burning, radiant one. For me?

Welcome good and faithful servant ... came the joyful reply.

❈   ❈   ❈

All hell broke loose. The teachers of the law sat and watched as Stephen disappeared momentarily beneath a maelstrom of fists. The high priest said nothing as they dragged their victim from his presence. Among the Pharisees that followed, as they kicked and beat Stephen through Jerusalem's streets and out of the city, were

Aaron and Saul. They well knew that a Roman provincial law was being violated, but stood and watched as the witnesses began to stone him.

Saul casually gathered up the cloaks that many had discarded at his feet as the blood oozed down Stephen's face from a deep gash across his brow. 'Nearly done,' he said pragmatically to Aaron.

'Lord Jesus, receive my spirit,' they heard Stephen pray as he fell to his knees. 'Lord ...' he gasped, 'do not hold this sin against them.'

Saul looked at Aaron and raised a sardonic eyebrow, 'Sin? We have done the work of God here today.' He picked up the last cloak, shaking the dust off it and folding it across his arm.

Aaron gazed at Stephen's mutilated body, waiting for him to breathe his last. An image of Lila crumpled at Jesus' feet in the temple courts came to mind. It rattled him.

3. SCATTER

Acts 8 The suffering, surviving women

The discussion between Peter and Grace went back and forth for several weeks about what was next. He was happy to move, but not too much further from work; he liked the idea of a part-time post for Grace, but then was flummoxed by Grace's vision for the other half of her time being spent developing a project to help women like Anja. Eventually he said he'd agree to it as long as her work didn't impinge upon their family life. Grace promised it wouldn't, and prayed fervently that she would be able to keep her promise.

When she told her mother about the potential post and her vision for the safe house project, she was surprised at her supportive response. St Stephen's was that bit closer to her – close enough to just drop by occasionally, rather than having to stick to agreed dates and times and waiting for invitations to meals. Grace began to realise that her mother actually wanted more involvement, something she had previously found hard to believe.

Writing the proposal took longer than Grace hoped. She reworked and reworked it in keeping with the guidelines Julia had sent her, hoping and praying the diocese would support and provide some funding to get it off the ground. Eventually she submitted it.

She applied for her first incumbency at St Stephen's, and to her amazement was shortlisted and was invited for interview with two others, both women.

It wasn't an exciting parish. Not many young families or students. The demographic was largely middle-aged professionals and elderly retired folk. People moved there once they'd earned large salaries in the city. The congregations were small, made up mainly of the retired. Care for the poor was non-existent and there was no missional outreach. They did financially support two mission societies working overseas, but that was it.

The church building itself smelt of mould. Grace tried hard to ignore it and focused on the beautiful wooden statue of Madonna and child that stood in a side aisle. She sat before it for some time, her eyes following the smooth lines carved in the rich, dark wood. It wasn't something she'd been used to in the evangelical circles she'd moved in since becoming a Christian. As she enjoyed it, she wondered why there was such a distrust of the Catholic tradition of honouring Jesus' mother. She reached out and stroked the faces of both mother and child as she stood up. She smiled. *Sister*, she thought. She moved on to explore the ornate candle stands, the elaborately embroidered alter cloths and banners and the stunning stained glass windows.

When she came to the place where the reserved sacrament was kept, a candle burning constantly above it, she felt ambivalent. *Could I embrace this too?* – she asked herself. She moved on, deciding that it would need further reflection.

Despite the gloomy parish statistics, she found she loved St Stephen's. She hoped and prayed they would offer her the job.

The vicarage was amazing. It must have been one of the last remaining old buildings that had survived the downsizing of the Anglican Church's property portfolio in recent decades. It was high ceilinged and rambling, with six bedrooms and three reception rooms, as well as a huge kitchen-diner that opened out onto a massive, if unruly, garden. She was informed by one of the church wardens that refurbishment would be carried out by the diocese in collaboration with the new incumbent's requests. Grace hid her excitement as she thought of 'My Sister's House'.

Two days later she got a phone call offering her the post of Vicar at St Stephen's, starting in the autumn. She gladly accepted.

❋   ❋   ❋

Peter and Grace slowly began packing up St Matt's curate's house. It had been their home for nearly six years. Grace was amazed at the amount of clutter they had managed to collect. Over the summer Peter ruthlessly made regular visits to the tip.

Grace had been in intermittent contact with Barbara in Kent, and had visited Anja whenever she could. Chloe had even travelled down twice with her; Val and Mo had been once. Barbara and her team had not been able to repatriate Anja and had applied for asylum in the UK instead. No living members of Anja's family could be found; no property in her family's name; nothing, nowhere and no one for her to go back to. Her funded time had run out long ago at the safe house, yet she still remained, waiting for whatever the powers-that-be would decide.

Grace couldn't imagine the devastation and isolation in Anja's world. She prayed for her daily. 'It's like a bomb went off in her life, blasting all recognisable landmarks into a barren wasteland.'

'I know,' Chloe replied over a bowl of pasta in their favourite spot in the pub. 'I wonder what happened?'

'Maybe the whole family got trafficked?' Grace mused, dipping a chip into some mayonnaise.

'I wonder if the vicar down there is doing anything to help Anja's case?' Chloe twirled a ribbon of pasta round her fork.

'I'm sure he is. It would be good to meet him now that I know I'm going to be a vicar at St Stephen's. It would be good to hear things from his point of view – you know running a parish and getting the safe house going?' Grace wiped up the remaining mayo with her last chip.

'Yeah – I'd be interested in meeting him too,' Choe said. 'He must be quite a visionary.'

'I'll talk to Barbara and see if we can set up a meeting. Anyway … how are things with you and Melanie? Any better?' Grace asked.

'No change there. Mark's keeping his distance – idiot – and Sean, seeing as he is her youth worker, has tried to meet up with her, but she isn't playing ball with him. I'm just hoping this horrible phase will soon pass and then we'll have our lovely daughter back again. Planning for "My Sister's House" is what's keeping me going really.'

Grace felt concerned, 'How's your hair?' she smiled.

'I don't think any more has fallen out,' she felt her temples with her fingertips. 'I'm glad I've finished studying. I think my body is slowly recovering from the stress of it all.'

'You've done an amazing thing,' Grace's eyes were filled with affectionate admiration.

'Thanks, Grace, that means a lot,' Chloe smiled back at her friend.

'I would hate to study now that I've got Zack. My memory is shot to bits – I blame it on hormones and constant demands for attention.'

'And that's just Peter,' Chloe laughed.

Grace giggled, 'So you're still frustrated with Mark?'

'He annoys me so much. Maybe I'm just a horrible wife?'

'I don't know, are you?'

'Well – when I'm stressed I'm not great. I get so angry at him. Like the other day he said something about Mel being on her period and rolled his eyes. I couldn't bear it! I just feel he has no real empathy, respect or compassion for her or for me. As long as he's getting everything he wants, he's fine. It just makes me worry that not much has changed in him. Like he views women as being there to supply his needs. He doesn't want to have to look after or care for them! I wonder if he's secretly the same as before … just hiding it.'

'Do you mean with porn?'

'Well – yeah. I mean if I found out he was still looking at porn, I don't know what I'd do. Has Peter ever talked to you about it?'

Grace laughed, 'Yes. He was drawn in by it after his first wife died. But it doesn't seem to be an issue for him. He said it wasn't much comfort. He just wants me.'

'That's nice,' Chloe looked sad, 'I wish I could be sure Mark wants me. I guess that's what seduced me with Tom. I thought he really wanted me … stupid woman!'

'I'm so sorry you're still not sure about Mark. I thought things were good between you.'

'They're way better than they were – sure – maybe it's stress warping my perception?'

'Mmmm – maybe. Do you guys pray together much?' Grace thought of Peter and wished they could, her mind flitting to Bishop Duncan.

Chloe laughed, 'No! We did for a bit after we renewed our marriage vows, but that soon faded out.'

'Maybe that would help?'

'Maybe,' Chloe ended the conversation as she looked for the waitress and called her over to get the bill.

❄ ❄ ❄

A few weeks later they arrived in Kent after stopping for lunch at motorway services. The vicarage was next to the quaint village church. They pulled up into the wide, gravelled drive as a chocolate Labrador rose from the porch and ambled slowly towards them.

'Hello …' Chloe said stretching out a hand as she got out of the car. He came up close to her, sniffed her fingers and then rubbed his head against her knees. 'What a sweetie!' she smiled, scratching behind his ears. The front door opened and Chloe's head snapped up at Grace's sharp intake of breath.

It was Tom.

The three of them stood rooted to the spot, staring at each other in horror.

Tom broke the silence first, 'Well … this *is* a surprise!'

Chloe's first impulse was to run. Her second was to burst into tears. Her third was …

'Hello, Chloe,' he said walking towards her, 'Grace,' he nodded, 'Barbara gave me your name, but not that of your travelling companion,' his eyes moved from Grace's face back to Chloe's anxiously.

'Barbara called you Father Thomas … I didn't think to ask your surname or look you up in Crockfords … I've had so much going on … I'm so sorry …' Grace's eyes darted from one to the other.

The colour was beginning to drain from Chloe's cheeks. Grace realised too late that she was about to faint. She crumpled. Grace lunged forward and managed to catch her just in time to stop her head from hitting the gravel.

'Let's get her inside,' Tom said pragmatically, bending down to pick her up. Between them they carried her into his vicarage.

'Where's Kate?' Grace asked tensely.

'At work,' he replied, laying Chloe out on a worn sofa. He put a cushion under her feet and then disappeared through the living room door. 'I'll just get some water,' he called over his shoulder.

Grace sat down on a footstool that was near Chloe's head. 'Chloe … Chloe … can you hear me?' her mind was reeling.

Tom came back with a pint size glass of water. Grace observed that he looked older, balder and fatter. *Good,* she thought, but then remembered the Bishop – looks didn't matter.

'It's good to see you, Grace,' Tom said putting the glass down on a chunky, oak coffee table.

'I'm a little shocked to see you, myself,' she replied. 'I wish I'd known it was you. I would never have brought Chloe with me.'

'I'm sorry, I wasn't sure how you would have reacted if you'd known. Would you still have come?'

Grace gazed at him thoughtfully, 'I think I would have,' she said eventually. He looked relieved, 'Thanks.'

Chloe's head rolled to one side, she opened her eyes and focused on Grace first. 'What happened?' she asked. Then she stared at Tom as delayed shock brought it all flooding back.

'I'm so sorry to have upset you this badly, Chloe,' he said shakily. 'I'm spinning a little myself.'

'Here … drink some water,' Grace reached for the glass as Chloe struggled to sit up. She took a few sips, then handed it back to Grace, tucking her hair behind her ears self-consciously. She swung her legs off the sofa and looked poised to get up.

'Don't leave, Chloe. Stay – it's okay, isn't it? We can do this, can't we?' his eyes darted between Chloe and Grace.

Eyes down, Chloe sat motionless. Grace waited for her to decide. Eventually she lifted her gaze to Tom's face. She didn't speak straight away but when she did her voice was calmer than Grace expected, 'We can do this,' she agreed.

Tom flopped back into his chair. Grace breathed deeply.

'Where's Kate?' Chloe asked.

'She's at work.'

'What does she do?' she tilted her head slightly to one side.

'After … after we left …' he faltered, 'she retrained as a midwife. She works in Pembury hospital.'

'That's good … does she like it?' Grace watched with growing pride as Chloe manoeuvred her way forward through the minefield.

'She loves it. She's really happy now,' Tom's lips curved in a wobbly smile.

'That's good. I've prayed for her a lot.'

Tom's eyes glistened. He cleared his throat, 'How's Mark?'

'He's okay …'

'I'm glad … and the children?'

'Josh and Charlie are fine, but Melanie is … well, Mark says she's just being a teenager … but I'm not so sure. How are your boys?'

'They're doing well. It took a while for us all to process everything. There'll probably be more to come at some stage. We're saving up for their therapy,' he laughed dryly.

Grace joined Chloe in a tension-releasing half-laugh. She could feel her shoulders drain and her heart unknot a little.

'So …' Tom spread his hands. 'Would you like a cup of coffee or tea?'

Grace and Chloe looked at each other, 'Coffee,' they said in unison.

When he'd left the room Grace leaned forward and whispered, 'Are you okay with this? We can go now if you want.'

'No – I'm recovering. In fact I'm wondering whatever possessed me in the first place?'

'Really?' Grace hugged herself.

'Yeah – I mean, he really hasn't got much going for him, has he?'

They giggled.

'No old longings?' Grace asked.

'No … not really … maybe it was the idea of him more than the reality?'

The sound of him clearing his throat as he returned cut them off.

'Where do we start?' Tom asked as they all cradled their mugs.

Grace felt like a chat show host, 'Well, we came here wanting to know how you got the safe house project off the ground. I'd still like to hear about that.'

'So would I,' Chloe added. Grace smiled at her, pride swelling her chest.

'Well it all came about as a direct result of … what happened … between us.'

Chloe looked away briefly, then back at him.

'I can't believe this is happening …' he rubbed his face with his hand.

'It's a bit of beautiful ugly,' Grace said in a far-away voice.

Chloe and Tom looked at her, uncertain of her meaning. She didn't elaborate.

Distracted, Tom took a moment to rally before he continued, 'After we left … it was hell. The kids were all over the place, insecure and frightened.

Kate was angry … and hurt … so hurt. We went for counselling for about a year together. I had counselling on my own too – carried that on for another year after that. The Bishop recommended this nun. She was amazing. Who'd have thought a nun could help a broken man and marriage?' his features still held surprise at the idea.

'Kate took me back after a year … around the time we saw you at that farmers' market.'

Chloe's eyes widened at the memory, but she said nothing.

'Your face …' compassion furrowed his forehead and bald scalp as he remembered.

'It was good for me to see you together,' Chloe said. 'It was what I needed.'

They stared at each other in the silence that followed and then simultaneously they both started to speak, 'I'm so sorry …'

'Please forgive me …' Tom blundered on. 'I have prayed you would forgive me so many times. I never thought I'd be able to ask you face to face.'

Chloe smiled, 'Only if you'll forgive me,' she responded quietly.

Grace revelled in the beauty unfolding before her. A line from a U2 song ran through her head … *Grace makes beauty out of ugly things* …

Silence hung lightly between them as the work of giving and receiving forgiveness continued.

Tom's voice had more power in it when he spoke again, 'We came here about three years ago. I knew the minute I saw the job that it was for me, and I knew what I had to do. I'd seen a film called *Nefarious* about stopping global sex trafficking and how Christians could get involved. I was pretty raw on the back of all the soul searching I'd done with my counsellor … with the nun. It got to me … you know?'

They nodded.

'I couldn't stop thinking about how us men treat women around the world and about my part in it. As I prayed I knew God was calling me to stand up, to make amends … to get involved in the solution.' He looked from one to the other.

Grace said, 'So what did you do when you started here?'

'Well I contacted another organisation who'd won a bid from the government.'

'Yes.'

'And I spoke spoke to the police and to the PCC – they were the hardest ones. Barbara and three others came forward pretty much straight away and we started to pray and plan. An elderly widow who'd wanted to be involved from the start, died a year after I arrived here and bequeathed her house to the project. She had no living relatives, so there was no contesting of the will. The diocese were happy …'

'I bet,' Grace interjected.

'We've learnt as we've gone along,' Tom shrugged. 'I can give you all the paperwork we've got on the bid we put together for funding – you know policies and safety procedures – risk assessments and strategies. That'll certainly save you a lot of time and effort. No point reinventing the wheel.'

'That would be great,' Grace replied. 'You don't happen to have a copy of that film, what was it called?'

'*Nefarious*? Sure – in the end it was what swung it with the PCC.'

'That's what I was thinking,' Grace smiled.

Aware of Chloe's silence, Tom turned to her, 'What happened to you after …'

Chloe smiled and looked at the floor, 'Do you need to know?'

'No … I guess not … but I always wondered what happened with your youth work? You were so good.'

Chloe shook her head, still looking at the floor, 'I lost my job … spent a couple of years assessing everything. I'm a psychotherapist now. I'll be developing that side of the project,' she met his gaze, seeming suddenly much older.

'Can I ask you something else, Tom?' Grace broke in.

He looked back at her, 'Sure.'

'Have you been able to do anything to help Anja's case?'

'Well, being a member of the clergy helps a bit when you're talking to civil servants. I think we are regarded as distant cousins,' he smiled. 'We're just waiting to hear from immigration now. I ring them every week to check on the progress of her case. I'll keep you posted.'

'What about any form of therapy? The doctor at the mental health unit said most victims of human trafficking need help with Post Traumatic Stress Disorder.'

'Yeah … we learnt that pretty early on. We got two voluntary counsellors at first through a contact I had. We've just raised the money from within the church to employ them both part time. Pretty pleased about that one!'

'That's great,' Chloe said.

'Yes – it is. We still send those that are severely traumatised for quiet days at a local retreat house, where they receive intensive care. The ones who had terrible family backgrounds don't survive as well as the ones that came from stable backgrounds.'

Tom pushed himself out of his chair. 'Let me go and print off all the paperwork I think you'll need. I won't be long.'

After Tom returned from his office, a folder of warm paper fresh off the photocopier in hand, there didn't seem much reason to linger. Saying goodbye was awkward. Grace shook his hand and Chloe just said it with a little smile as she turned towards the car. He stood in the drive, hands shoved deep in his pockets, watching them as they drove away.

When Chloe could no longer see him in her side mirror, she exhaled deeply. 'I can't believe it!' she exclaimed.

'I know,' Grace replied, shaking her head, 'I'm so sorry I didn't do my homework before we came. It's just been so hectic with getting ready to move and everything.'

'It's okay … I could have easily gone on the internet and looked up the church. Just didn't think!' After that they hardly spoke all the way home. Layers of understanding settled between them like sediment forming rock strata.

'I feel exhausted,' Chloe said when they eventually pulled up outside her house.

'Me too,' Grace replied.

'I'll call you tomorrow.'

'Yep,' Grace squeezed her left shoulder, trying to loosen the knot that had developed again while driving. She smiled wearily at her friend as the passenger door swung shut. She was glad she'd asked Peter to pick Zack up from her mum's. It had meant him leaving work early, but he hadn't minded, and it wasn't often she asked him to do it.

※　※　※

'How are you today?' Grace asked Chloe on the phone the next morning.

'All right, I think,' Chloe replied.

'What did Mark say?'

'I didn't tell him.'

'Why not?'

Chloe didn't respond.

'Chloe?'

'I'm just letting it sink in and brew for a bit.'

'Okay … but I do think you should tell him eventually.'

'I know.'

'So what are your thoughts so far?'

'I guess I feel quite overwhelmed at how that meeting was orchestrated. I would never have come with you if I'd known.'

'No … I wouldn't have brought you,' Grace smiled.

'I feel good – I feel I've really moved on – grown up – whatever you want to call it. I was thinking last night how weird it is for me to be okay with having seen Tom.'

'Yes – I think you did so well. I was proud of how you handled the whole thing.'

'Were you? Thanks. I felt proud of me too. It almost felt like passing some kind of test.'

'Mmm … hadn't thought of it that way, but now that you say it, it makes sense. I guess what lies ahead with "My Sister's House" is going to require a lot from both of us. It's not just what we do, but it's who we are – our characters,' Grace replied.

'Yeah. All this time, unbeknownst to me, things have been turned around and used for good in Tom's life, like they've been for me. It made me think that we haven't a clue really – we just see from our small vantage point. We don't see the whole picture.'

'Yes … it requires simple trust and obedience doesn't it?'

'Yeah,' Chloe sighed, 'easier said than done.'

※　※　※

Emotions were all over the place at St Matt's farewell for Grace. The love that had bound them together over the years was palpable in the bring-

and-share food, the old lady flowers, the child-scrawled, ragged decorations, the speeches and the thank you gifts.

She almost lost her composure when she unwrapped a beautifully framed print of William Holman Hunt's 'The Light of the World'. She'd sat in front of the original in Oxford after her conversion, allowing the painting to answer many of her early, embryonic questions. She'd told Chloe about it – it must have been she who had suggested it.

※ ※ ※

They say moving is one of the most stressful things you can do. The last time Grace had done it, it had just been her and Peter: newly married; travelling light. They'd hired a medium sized van and moved in themselves, with no professional help. Now six years of Christmas and birthday presents later and a family of three, they filled the removal lorry. Grace was grateful that the diocese paid for it.

Grace's mum came and Chloe, Val and Mo turned up the next day to help them unpack boxes. As it was a Saturday, Charlie had come too and kept Zack entertained playing space ships in several emptied packing boxes, even though he really was too old for such things. The house seemed hollow even after they'd put everything in its place. Their semi-detached curate's house had felt almost overstuffed by comparison. Grace didn't like the way her voice echoed through the spaces in between things. She comforted herself with thoughts of sectioning it off for My Sister's House.

※ ※ ※

Barbara rang when Anja was granted asylum. A council flat had been secured in Tunbridge Wells. The church in Kent gathered up a collection for her and with their generous gift Barbara had helped her furnish the one bedroom first floor flat with the basics. They were helping her apply for a hairdressing course at the local tech.

Grace rang Anja on her new mobile number.

'Is it good?' she asked, trying to keep it simple.

'Yes – good,' came the small voice on the other end of the line.

'If you get into the course, when will it start? This month?'

'Uh … next month,' Anja replied.

'Can I come and see you?'

'Please,' Grace heard desperation in the reply.

'Next week? Tuesday?' Grace had her finger on the blank day in her diary.

'Yes … thanks you,' she sniffed hard.

'Don't cry Anja. It's going to be okay, everything is going to be okay now,' Grace soothed.

'I go now,' Anja said abruptly. 'Bye,' and hung up.

❋　❋　❋

As it turned out, Grace couldn't go on Tuesday. Over the weekend the flower ladies of St Stephen's had banded together and cornered her after the morning service. Two years of interregnum had not been good and a lot of the proverbial was hitting the fan. The only day everyone could make for a meeting was Tuesday. It wasn't until Monday evening that Grace got round to texting Anja to let her know. Being in charge of a church was a big step up from being curate. Grace was already scouring the congregations for a willing volunteer to help her with admin.

She didn't get a text back. She tried ringing each day after that and by Friday she was feeling anxious and called Chloe to ask her opinion.

'Have you called Barbara?' Chloe asked.

'Yesterday. She said she'd pop in on her over the weekend, but I can't shake this niggling feeling … I want to go down there tomorrow if I can.'

'Do you think you've got too attached to her?' Chloe asked, sounding very much like a psychotherapist.

Grace felt annoyed, 'She has no one – nothing!' she said too sharply.

'Grace, she's not your responsibility now. You've done everything you can for her and more. But if you want to go down tomorrow for your own peace of mind, I'll come with you. But I'll need to check with Mark first to make sure he's okay with holding the fort alone on a Saturday.'

'Yeah – sorry. I just don't have any peace about it. I need to check with Peter too. I'll text you later.'

'Okay. Don't worry.'
But Grace did worry.

※ ※ ※

They had some trouble finding the flat as it was buried in a warren of new-builds. The twisting, oddly named roads seemed to have no logical sequence of door numbering and the satnav was completely confused. After stopping to ask directions twice they found it. They rang the doorbell several times, with mounting anxiety. Eventually Chloe pressed all the buttons, receiving several irate responses through the tannoy. But at least one person released the lock and let them in. They ran up the flight of stairs and Grace knocked loudly on the door. The noise bounced back and forth off the bare walls of the stairwell. She dialled Anja's number for the umpteenth time, but neither the knocking or the phone calls illicited a response.

Grace started banging on the cheap plywood with her fists as a neighbour opened his door a fraction, keeping it chained, to see what was going on.

Chloe turned to him, 'Have you seen anyone come or go from this flat in the last couple of days?'

'Nope,' he replied, 'I saw them move her in, but that's been it.'

Chloe put a hand on Grace's shoulder to stop her, 'Let's call Barbara.' She dialled as she spoke. 'Hi – Barbara? Have you been able to get in touch with Anja? – We're down at her flat now – yep – yep – I know – she's not answering the phone or the door. What? – no, the neighbour hasn't seen her either – yes – I think so – okay. See you in a bit,' she hung up.

Grace stared at her as she dialled another number.

'Police please …' she told them the address, who she was and what she suspected. As Grace listened her face went ashen. Before Chloe had finished the call, Grace was kicking the door with all her might. Chloe quickly hung up. 'Grace! Stop! *STOP!*' she shouted, pulling at her friend's shoulders. She had no idea Grace was so strong.

'If she's dead, you breaking the door down ain't gonna help,' came the neighbour's voice, who was now standing in the hallway in a pair of loose fitting, striped pyjamas and string vest. The fly of the pyjamas was unbuttoned, leaving a gap which left little to the imagination. Several days growth of stubble covered his puffy face. His presence shocked Grace out of her panic. She looked at him for several moments, panting for breath, her fists hard-balled at her sides.

'*Aaargh!*' she gave the door one last kick and hurled herself against the wall in frustration. She sunk to the floor, her hands in her hair.

'It won't be long, Grace, they'll be here in a minute,' Chloe stroked her friend's white blonde curls. Grace didn't reply.

The neighbour shifted his weight from left to right, undecided as to what his next move should be. There was more drama to come, but 'the filth' never came when you wanted them, and there didn't seem to be much going on now. He decided to shuffle back into his flat, leaving the door chained and ajar.

It was half an hour before the police arrived. Three officers crowded the hallway, moving Grace and Chloe out of their way. With a loud crack the door gave way to their weight and crowbar. As Grace stood up it was the smell that hit her first.

'Oh, God,' Grace whimpered, covering her nose. She was ahead of Chloe, pressing herself up against the last officer, straining to see over his shoulder.

The first officer turned on reaching the kitchen door and shouted, 'Keep them out.'

But it was too late – Grace saw and screamed, 'No!'

It took two officers to push her out and hold her down. She fought them like a cat. Eventually she submitted out of exhaustion. They made her sit on the floor again and Chloe took her into her arms. Then the tears came hard and fast.

※　※　※

Grace cried the whole way home. Chloe had never seen her friend so distressed.

'I should have come down on Tuesday like I said I would,' she wept.

'It's not your fault, Grace, that you couldn't look after her,' Chloe said softly.

'Why did I let the stupid flower ladies distract me? So trivial! I was trying to impress them as the new vicar … trying to win them over … when she really needed me! Oh, God …' she sobbed.

'Grace – please listen to me … it's not your fault. It was Anja's choice. Even if you'd gone down on Tuesday, she would still probably have done it.'

'Choice?' Grace exploded, 'Choice? What choice did she have in life? It had all been taken from her!' she blew her nose loudly.

'I know … I know …' Chloe tried to soothe her. 'It's gonna take us a while to recover … but remember what you said to me about attack? The devil really mustn't want us to do this work … all we can do is pray that God will somehow make Anja's life count … that he'll bring good out of this … somehow …'

Relentless sobbing was her only reply.

※　　※　　※

Tom and Grace discussed the funeral together on the phone. They agreed they wanted to do everything to honour Anja's body in death as it had been so dishonoured in life. Tom arranged for a plot in the extended church grave yard, located on the edge of the village. He would do the graveside rites. Grace didn't think she could cope with that.

She went to the funeral parlour the week before, wanting to see Anja one last time, hoping it would erase the last image she had of her.

Her body lay in a coffin made of the same cheap plywood her front door had been made of. Her small frame had shrunk. Grace's eyes were inexorably drawn to the red rings around her neck, partially hidden by a white scarf. They'd put her in an ill-fitting red dress. It was too bright. It seemed all wrong. Her eyes moved down to Anja's hands and she noticed that the fingers of the right hand were bruised; discoloured; swollen. *Did you have second thoughts and try to stop it? Oh sweetheart …* she started to cry again, reaching out to touch them, but jerked her hand back: they were cold and stiff. Her eyes travelled up to Anja's face. Thick make up covered it. It didn't look like her at all. Grace realised the make up was there to disguise burst blood vessels and bruising. She suddenly felt sick and knew she had to leave.

Back in the safety of her car she sat waiting for the nausea to subside. Despair crept up on her.

※　　※　　※

Grace and Chloe asked Barbara if they could club together with her and her team of volunteers, covering the cost of the grave plot and a simple headstone which would be erected later, once the earth had settled.

It was a grey September day. Soft mizzle quickly drenched the small group of mourners. Grace dropped her bouquet of yellow rosebuds into the grave and then a handful of soil, feeling each clod of earth thud against the wood with every fibre of her being. The others followed. Grace had no tears left.

※   ※   ※

'Can you pray – Melanie didn't come home last night,' Chloe's voice was staccato down the phone.

'Have you rung all her friends?' Grace asked stupidly, dreading more trauma.

'Yep. Mark and I have taken turns driving round town looking for her through the night. We're calling the police now.'

'What else can I do? Shall I come round?'

'Don't you have things on today?' Chloe asked flatly.

'Unusually – no. I'll be over in ten,' Grace was dressed only in tracksuit bottoms and a T-shirt but she jumped up from snuggling Zack on the sofa with Peter and reached for her bag. 'Is it okay with you if I go over to Chloe's, Peter? Melanie didn't come home last night – they're about to call the police.'

'Sure, babe,' his eyebrows drew together in concern. 'We'll hold the fort here.' He hugged Zack to him whose eyes were glued to Saturday breakfast TV and whose mouth was full of cereal.

Zack dragged his eyes from the TV screen, swallowed his mouthful and looked up at his mum, 'The angel's there,' he said.

'What, love?' she asked distractedly, checking her bag for her car keys.

'The angel's there,' he repeated patiently.

She stopped rummaging and looked at him, a swell of emotion constricting her throat.

Peter looked down at his son too and began stroking his curls, 'You've been watching too much TV young man,' he smiled.

Zack looked up at his dad, his mouth slightly open. He turned back to Grace, 'You know, Mummy,' he was intensely serious.

Grace knew Peter didn't want her to encourage Zack in what he called 'nonsense', but that invisible kite string was tugging hard in the opposite direction.

'I understand, love. Thank you. I'll tell Chloe.' She bent down and kissed the top of his head and then brushed her lips lightly against Peter's cheek.

He muttered, 'He'll be hearing voices next!'

'He's fine,' she retorted. 'He sees and hears much better than either of us.'

Things had been strained between them since Anja's death.

※　※　※

By the time Grace pulled up outside Chloe's house, a police car had arrived. Two officers were slamming their doors as she parked on the opposite side of the street. Her armpits and hands tingled – *Does an angel mean she's alive or dead? Oh God ... oh God ...* she began praying unintelligibly. It was too soon after her last encounter with the police. Her mind recoiled from the images she could not erase of Anja hanging from her kitchen ceiling.

She followed them into Chloe's house focusing hard on Chloe, Mark and the boys. Once she was there she couldn't really leave. The day dragged on interminably. She made cups of tea and distracted Charlie with stories about Zack's latest escapades. Josh stayed near his dad, following him about like a semi-detached shadow. In answer to Grace's suggestion, Peter brought Zack over in the afternoon. She knew Peter's calming presence would do Mark good and Zack would preoccupy Charlie.

By three Mark was so agitated that Peter suggested they go out looking again. Josh went with them. They returned at six, exhausted. They brought fish and chips with them, but neither Chloe nor Grace could eat. It was eight when Chloe stood up and said she was going out to look. Grace went with her while Peter took Zack back home.

'Oh God, oh God, oh God ...' Chloe breathed, leaning forward over the steering wheel as she peered into the autumn evening cloaking the town.

Grace had forgotten to tell her about Zack's angel. She debated whether to now and decided to risk it, 'Zack said a strange thing to me this morning. He said an angel was with Melanie.'

Chloe didn't respond at first. Then she whispered, 'What does that mean?'

'I don't know ... I was thinking maybe it would be good to pray and ask God to show us what it means?'

Chloe continued to stare out the windscreen as the car crawled slowly along the road causing other drivers to flash their lights and honk their horns. She was oblivious.

'Maybe put your blinkers on?' Grace suggested.

'Yeah ... right ...' Chloe put them on obediently. 'You pray ... I can't,' she whispered.

Grace didn't know if she could either, but from somewhere within her came enough energy to formulate a prayer, 'Lord, what does the angel mean? What should we be looking for? Please show us.'

They lapsed into silence as they continued peering out of their windows and Grace tried to stay open to interpretation. They were both looking in opposite directions down a particularly dark street. Neither was focused on what was ahead. The next thing they simultaneously heard a loud bang and lurched forward against their seat belts. Neither had seen the car in front.

Shaking, Chloe got out at the same time as the other driver. Grace got out more slowly rubbing her neck.

'It's you again,' Chloe said in surprise.

'So it is,' replied the elderly woman. Grace noted that she was taller than herself, a rarity in women. 'How have we fared this time?' she asked, her aristocratic voice seeming to be at odds with that part of town at that time of night. They both were looking at their respective cars.

'Not as well,' Chloe replied shakily.

'Oh dear, dear, dear. You mustn't cry. It's only a car. Easily fixed,' the woman reached out an elegant hand and patted Chloe on the shoulder.

'I'm fine ... really ... I'm fine. I'm just looking for my daughter, she's been missing for over thirty six hours.' Chloe scraped her hair back off her forehead and tried to breath deeply to stop herself crying.

'Oh, that's terrible. You must be worried sick. The last thing you need is to bump into me again,' soothed the woman. 'It was probably my fault as well ...'

Grace had collected her wits by this stage and suggested they exchange insurance details.

'Could we go into that place over there? I can't see out here,' the woman asked. Chloe and Grace looked up and across the road to see a dimly lit Indian takeaway restaurant.

'Good idea,' Grace agreed, still massaging her neck.

Strong spicy smells hit them as they pushed open the door of the shop. They explained to the man behind the counter that they just needed to exchange details as they'd had an accident. Grace watched his face and realised that he was nervous. She observed him looking furtively to a door over to his left.

'Everything all right?' she asked, feeling the invisible kite string tugging.

He jerked his attention to her and quickly arranged his features into a magnanimous grin. Grace felt even more uncomfortable. Chloe and the woman were busy writing on paper napkins. Feelings of revulsion toward the man grew until she knew she had to get away from him. 'I'm gonna wait outside,' she said to Chloe who nodded without looking up.

The man seemed even more anxious, 'You don't want to order?' he asked.

'No,' Grace said her suspicions rising. For a split second, as she passed the elderly woman, their eyes met. The thought whipped through her mind faster than her consciousness could catch it that she'd seen eyes like that somewhere before. She stood on the pavement slightly perplexed and looked through the shop window.

Why did I feel like that about that man? And why do I feel weird about that old woman?

She raised her eyes to the window of the flat above the shop. Venetian blinds slanted up to the ceiling enabling her to see in. There was a lamp on, probably on the far side of the room, as it was quite dim. On the ceiling she could see the shadow of someone moving about. She was trying to process her feelings when suddenly something heavy hit the window, crushing the flimsy blinds against the glass. She heard a faint scream. Adrenalin propelled her into action. She ran down the alleyway beside the shop looking for the flat's door. Phone in hand she dialled 999 as she tried to open the black pvc door. It was locked. She started banging on it.

'Hello ... Police, please ... someone is being beaten ... I think it's a woman ...'

'What are you doing?' Chloe asked breathlessly, running round the corner to find her.

'I saw someone get thrown up against the window of that flat and I heard a scream,' she replied '... Yes ... yes ...' she said into her phone still pressed to her ear. She continued to tell the police who she was and where she was.

The elderly lady was making her way slowly towards them when suddenly the shopkeeper came round the corner shouting, 'What are you doing? This is private property! Leave now!'

As he pushed past the older woman, Grace ran at him. She grabbed him by the shirt collar and threw him up against the wall. With her full weight pinning him there and an inch from his face she hissed, 'Open that door now, do you hear me? Open it now!'

Blue eyes pierced into black. He reacted, punching her in the diaphragm, winding her. She staggered back into Chloe.

Street light glinted on a sliver of steel he'd drawn from a pocket. Chloe cried out in terror.

'I don't think you want to be doing that,' the elderly woman stepped between them calmly.

'Out of the way,' he wielded the knife wildly.

'I'm afraid not,' she smiled. 'Now put that away.'

He stood tensed, ready to spring. His phone went off in his pocket. With his free hand he reached for it, 'What?' he barked.

There followed a short explosive conversation.

Then the door behind him opened and another slight, Asian man appeared.

Chloe vaguely recognised him. Where had she seen him? Suddenly she remembered. 'Yusuf? Where's Melanie?' she shouted.

Shocked he peered at Chloe through the gloom of the alleyway.

Grace seized the moment of distraction and lunged past the knife-wielding shop owner and knocked Yusuf aside. Easily taking the stairs two at a time, she was into the flat in an instant. The men weren't far behind her. The elderly woman reached out and restrained Chloe, 'Wait,' she said, 'It's going to be okay.'

Chloe didn't know why, but she obeyed.

Grace went into the living room, passing the black and white kitchen on her right. There in a corner was a skimpily clad, blood stained girl. She cowered in a foetal position, behind a black leather sofa. Grace was on her knees in front of her when the men came into the room behind her.

'Get away from her!' Yusuf shouted.

At that the girl looked up. It was Melanie.

'Oh God …' Grace burst out, reaching for her.

With a wordless howl Melanie threw her arms round her neck and clung, trembling to her.

At the same time Yusuf viciously grabbed Grace by the hair, pulling her backwards. Melanie went with her, falling on top of her.

Then Grace heard the sweetest words cutting through the air. 'Freeze! Police!'

※　※　※

One of the officers carried Melanie down the stairs to the police car.

When Chloe realised who it was she wailed, half running, half falling towards her daughter. Grace held Chloe, walking her to the police car through the small thrill-seeking crowd that had begun to gather on the pavement. Once inside she looked out the window, wanting to thank the elderly lady, but couldn't see her.

Chloe had Melanie in her arms, kissing and stroking her hair back off her face. Mascara and lipstick smeared and mingled with blood. 'My baby … my baby … what have they done to you? Oh God … oh God …' Chloe sobbed.

Grace had no words. She had her arm round them both. She didn't care when it started going numb. She watched as Chloe examined her child's arms and legs, looking for the wounds from which the blood had come. Whenever she found one, Melanie wimpered pitifully.

Several phone calls to Mark and Peter, hours in Accident and Emergency, an excruciating examination for Melanie, three police statements and several cups of very hot, sweet tea later, Grace was returned home in the small hours of the morning in a taxi.

Melanie was sedated.

Chloe sat beside her hospital bed grieving.

Having had no sleep, Grace and Peter returned to Chloe's an hour later to stay with the boys. Grace called her mum to come over and stay with Zack; she also phoned Trevor, telling him the basics of what had happened and asking him if he could send one of his Readers over to St Stephen's to do the Sunday services.

The police returned Chloe's car, which looked surprisingly unscathed in the light of day. Grace ran her hand over the front bumper, distinctly remembering it had been dented. There were three scratches where she guessed the older woman's number plate had made contact. A police officer explained, with a smile, that he'd been a car mechanic in his previous working life and knew that if banged with a fist in the right spot, some bumpers would pop out, and it had. She waved them off as they drove Mark to the hospital.

It was only when they all sat down in the lounge to help the boys grasp the essentials of what had happened, that Grace's body began to go into shock. She was sitting with her arm around Charlie, whose emotions were far more evident than Josh's. As she explained how she had found their sister, she could feel her head getting lighter and lighter. When she got to the part where she had Melanie in her arms, her whole body began to shake.

'Let's get you upstairs,' Peter said reaching over and taking hold of his wife's hand. 'The main thing, boys,' he continued in a calm voice, as he stood and helped her up, slinging one of her arms round his shoulder, 'is Melanie's safe now. We found her. She's going to be okay. I'll just get Grace into the spare bed ... could you put the kettle on for me and maybe put some bread in the toaster? I haven't had any breakfast.' He took her up to the spare room and put her to bed like a child. He leaned against the door for a while, staring at the shape of her curled up under the duvet. He hadn't signed up for this.

✳ ✳ ✳

Chloe and Mark sat opposite each other, their daughter mercifully asleep in the bed between them.

'Don't,' Chloe couldn't help herself as Mark reached out to trace a gash on Melanie's forehead, stuck together with paper stitches.

Startled he looked up, a baffled expression in his greeny-blue eyes.

'Sorry …' she faltered, a wave of shame crashing over her first instinctive defence.

'What?' he asked, looking back at Melanie and tenderly stroking her hair.

Angrily Chloe brushed the tears away, sniffing hard. He looked at her again waiting for an explanation. Eventually Chloe said, her eyes everywhere but on his face, 'You're a man …'

Mark stared at her uncomprehendingly. Then slowly understanding dawned, followed quickly by a matching anger, 'I'm her father!' he exploded in a forced whisper.

'I said I'm sorry,' Chloe looked at the floor.

'How could you even think like that?' he shook his head in dismay.

Chloe didn't reply.

'If it had been me there instead of you last night, I would've bloody well killed them!'

'It's a good thing you weren't then … and please keep your voice down.'

Mark frowned, 'Sorry,' he raised Melanie's hand to his lips and kissed it. Chloe noticed that there was still blood under her nails. They'd taken samples from them for DNA testing last night. Why hadn't they cleaned them? Agitated she reached into the bedside cabinet and dragged a wetwipe out of a pack left there by a nurse. She started on the hand nearest her and then reached over to take the other from Mark.

He watched her trying to make everything better.

'This is all our fault,' Chloe sobbed, no longer able to hold back, as she desperately tried to erase any trace of the trauma.

'Chloe …'

'It is … I know it is … yeah, she's a teenager … but it's been more than that. I know it. She's never been the same since … since,' she was finding it hard to get the words out, she was crying so hard now, '… and then she meets these guys … and I don't even notice how old they are … or what they're really after … I mean, how could I not have seen it? What kind of mother am I that I didn't suspect anything?'

'She was only eleven when …' Mark was reaching for her hand, 'she was too young to really understand what went on.'

Chloe moved out of his reach.

'Don't you think it's just been high school and puberty that's changed her? She's made some bad choices, got in with the wrong people ... how were we to know? She's been so secretive anyway?' he frowned.

Sobbing was his only reply.

Eventually Chloe raised a swollen, red face to his, 'I wish I could believe you, but I don't. In my guts I know that what I ... what we did ... has something to do with where we found her.'

Mark had nothing to say in response.

A nurse came in and checked Melanie's temperature. Awkward professional silence hung between them. She checked the other wounds of which there were three: one on her ribs, one on her thigh and one on her knee. Chloe's mind shied away from thinking how she'd got them.

Bruising was beginning to show round each of them, telling of the impact that had been inflicted. It was when Mark saw the other wounds that he broke down and cried.

✳   ✳   ✳

The church did what it did best. Val organised a rota of people to cook meals for them. Mo and Sean, whom Grace noted were getting quite close, took the boys out several times over the weeks that followed and organised the youth group to do their gardening once a week. Trevor visited them regularly, spending time with Mark and Chloe together and individually. Everyone accepted that Melanie didn't want him to visit her, but Chloe was relieved when she said she would like to see Grace.

Grace knelt in her cavernous study before visiting Melanie. She'd hung the Holman Hunt print over to the right of her desk. She studied it now. *No handle on the door ... she's got to open it from the inside ...* she went to prayer. Quickly she became aware of Jesus, not just depicted there in the print but substantially there with her. She knew she would not see him with her physical eyes if she opened them, but his presence was so strong, it felt as if she would. *Oh, Jesus ... I love you ... the good shepherd ... you don't steal or destroy ... you heal and bind up ... please use me ...*

I will use you ... came the reply

Please help her trust me ... trust you ...

Tell her what I have done for you, came the command. Grace bowed her head to the floor and stayed like that for a time, lost in worship.

Then slowly she got to her feet, went to the downstairs toilet to wash her face and reapply mascara. She looked at herself in the mirror … *whoever the Son sets free, is free indeed* … she smiled an exhausted little smile.

❋   ❋   ❋

Chloe met her at the door, 'She's in her room. Do you want a coffee brought up?'

'That'd be great,' Grace took her coat off and hung it on the banister. She went up the stairs slowly, praying as she went. She knocked once and waited.

'Come in,' came Melanie's voice over radio music playing softly.

Grace pushed the door open. 'Hi,' she smiled.

'Hi,' Melanie was sitting cross-legged on her bed, surrounded by paper cuttings.

'What are you doing?' she asked, stepping into the room and pushing the door behind her.

'Making paper doll clothes.'

'Can I sit here?' she asked, indicating the chair at her desk.

'Sure,' Melanie looked up from what she was doing.

Grace noted that the bruising around the small scar on her forehead was yellowing. Without make-up she looked much younger. 'Thanks,' Grace sat down, leaning forward to look at Melanie's paper dolls. 'They're great. I like that one,' she pointed to a dark haired beauty. 'She looks like you.'

Melanie winced, 'No she doesn't.'

Grace didn't argue. 'I didn't realise you were so artistic, Mel,' she smiled. The teenager shrugged, 'It's relaxing.'

'Looks like you're taking after your mum. She taught me how to do embroidery, you know. She's very artistic.'

Melanie didn't reply to this, just kept cutting carefully round a purple skirt.

Chloe knocked, 'Coffee,' she called. Grace opened the door and took the steaming mug from her friend. Chloe looked past her into the room, 'Do you want anything, darling?'

'No thanks, mum, I'm fine,' Melanie didn't look up.

Chloe and Grace exchanged a heartfelt look.

Grace returned to her seat and settled back into it, cradling her mug in both hands. *Show me how to do this* ... she prayed, waiting for wisdom. She breathed in deeply and relaxed her shoulders. There was no rush. Melanie had wanted to see her ... she'd say something when she was ready.

They sat in companionable silence for some time, listening to the radio. An Adele song soared over the airwaves, telling of broken dreams and hearts. The sense she'd had of Jesus in her study, returned, evoking tenderness and a deep compassion that expanded her heart. It grew and grew until Grace thought she could not contain it ... *the love of God* ... she thought. The song ended with the anti-climax of the DJ's trivia.

Melanie looked up and studied Grace, 'You're praying aren't you?'

'Yes,' there was no use in denying it, she thought. 'How do you know?'

'I can feel it,' she said simply.

Grace was surprised. 'How does it feel?' she asked tentatively.

'Warm,' Melanie replied.

Grace smiled and nodded, 'Yes ... that's a good word.'

'I used to feel it when you baby sat for us years ago. Same thing – like being wrapped in a soft blanket.'

'I never knew ...' Grace's throat constricted.

'You were our favourite babysitter,' Melanie folded the tabs of the purple skirt round the hips of the two-dimensional, brunette doll.

'That looks great. Do you wear purple much?'

Melanie shook her head.

'You should, you know, it would suit you. Maybe with some sap-green?'

Melanie scrunched her nose in disgust at the thought.

Grace leant forward and picked up the right colour felt-tip. She scribbled on the corner of a blank sheet, then held it up to the purple skirt. 'See?'

Melanie studied it, then gave a non-committal shrug. After a pause she said, 'I'm glad you're my mum's friend.'

'I'm glad she's my friend, Mel. She's a wonderful woman.'

Melanie shrugged again, 'Thank you for looking for me ... and finding me,' she stared at the scissors in her hands.

'Did your mum tell you what Zack said to me when I heard you were missing?'

'Yes …'

'I think the old lady that we bumped into was the angel … she led us right to you.'

'What old lady?' she made eye contact at last.

Grace told her about the accident with the elderly lady and how she'd reminded her of the man she'd once met in a graveyard long before Zack was born. She knew it sounded crazy as she said it.

Melanie looked thoughtful.

'It says in the bible somewhere,' Grace smiled ruefully at her inability to remember chapter and verse, 'that many of us have entertained angels unawares. It also says that angels are ministering spirits sent to serve those who are being saved. I really believe that if we hadn't bumped into that wonderful old woman, we would never have found you.'

'I know …' Melanie whispered.

'What happened, Mel? How did you get there in the first place?'

'Hasn't mum told you?' she asked.

'No,' Grace shook her curls.

Melanie looked pleased. In a more confident voice she told Grace how it had all come about; about the loneliness and isolation; the cocaine; the pressure to repay with sex. 'Then he wanted to share me with his friend Sony. I said no, but he kept on. Then that night they were both there at the flat,' she stopped.

'You don't need to …' Grace held up a hand.

There was a long silence which Grace eventually broke, 'Why do you think you got involved with him?'

Melanie frowned, 'At first it was like, this older guy wants me, I mean … wow … he noticed me. But when it was for real and he asked me out, it was like, well, mum did it with the vicar. I thought, why shouldn't I?'

Grace studied her young face, 'You were very hurt by what happened, weren't you?'

Melanie's eyes welled up, 'That cow, Lottie Stanton, told me in front of everyone in Year 5. We'd had our first sex education classes that term. "It" was all we talked about. The boys especially had gone overboard. It was bad enough knowing your mum and dad did it, let alone finding out your mum was also doing it with the vicar! School was a nightmare. It followed me to my new school too, 'cuz Lottie came to St Stephen's in Year 7. I know they still laugh about it now behind my back,' she wiped her eyes with both hands.

Grace passed her a tissue from a pink box on the desk.

After she'd calmed down she continued, 'Dad's never been close … I mean he's a good guy and all that … but we've never bonded really. He's never seemed that interested in me. It's always been mum. But then she was taken up with the vicar and for ages after was shut down with depression. I felt like I lost both parents.

'The cocaine was it for me … I could escape, forget, be happy, even if it was just for a little while. Yusuf was so nice to me at first … he hooked and reeled me in. I was such a freaking idiot.'

'No you weren't, Mel. You were easy prey. He'd have had his radar out for any lonely, unhappy girl. In fact I'm sure he's done this before and it won't be his last either.'

Surprised by this Melanie's mouth dropped open slightly, 'But he'll go to prison, won't he?'

'Yes, he will. But these kind of men don't ever seem to learn … or care …' sadness overwhelmed her, thinking of Anja.

'Mum's told me about what you and her are going to do … you know, My Sister's House?'

It was Grace's turn to be surprised, 'Oh?'

'I'd like to help … to get involved … when I'm, you know, better?'

'I'm not sure about that Mel. You're going to need time to recover from this trauma and putting yourself in situations where memories of it could be triggered wouldn't be good.'

'But I want to do something … I want to help girls like me, who've been treated worse than me.'

Grace searched her face, 'You're so young, Mel … you've got your whole life ahead of you. Finish school, get your A-levels, go to university, have fun. You could study fashion or something?' she gestured to the paper clothes all over the bed.

'Why are *you* doing it then? I get why mum is, but why you? You went to Cambridge, you had the career in London. Now you're the vicar of St Stephen's … but you wanna rescue girls from the sex trade?'

Grace was stumped. She looked at Melanie and knew the time had come.

'I believe it's part of my calling. I think He wants me to give what I have received ...' Grace paused, searching for words. 'Melanie, I've not always been like I am now. I didn't have a good relationship with my mum and dad. I cut myself off from them when I went to uni and to pay my way I did some modelling. From there I got some escort work,' she watched Melanie's reaction. The young girl's mouth dropped open.

'Yes – me. Some really bad stuff happened and I eventually got out of it and started life again as a journalist in London. When I became a Christian, I think I thought I'd left the past behind. It was wonderful knowing I was forgiven and free to be my true self. When I felt the call to ordination it was like God was giving me a whole new identity. I was flying high.

'Marrying Peter was the icing on the cake and then we moved to St Matt's for my curacy. But as time went by I realised that there was a whole load of stuff that needed dealing with. I had to forgive my mum and my dad for some things. I had to forgive myself and some other people too. I hadn't realised that I needed to be so specific in my prayers.

'It was while babysitting for you once that I had an amazing encounter with God sitting on your sofa. I was able to let go of the hatred, hurt and anger ...' Grace looked down at her hands and then back up at Melanie.

'I need that ... what happened to you on our sofa ... I'm so full of hated right now, for myself most of all,' Melanie whispered, 'and for those ... those sick freaks,' she began to cry.

'I know,' Grace soothed.

'Look – I used to cut myself before ... before Yusuf,' she showed Grace her wrists.

'Mel! Oh, love,' Grace exclaimed reaching out and touching the raised scars.

'I hated mum and dad and ... and everyone ... but most of all, myself. I think that's why I could feel you praying – it was so opposite to what's inside me, you know?' she asked haltingly.

Grace nodded, 'Do you want us to pray now?'

'Yeah ... okay,' Melanie said half-heartedly.

Grace gathered herself into the presence of Jesus and began to pray quietly, a hand resting on Melanie's scarred arm. 'Lord, thank you so much for leading us to Mel; for helping us. You are the Good Shepherd and you don't give up until you find your sheep and carry them home on your shoulders. Thank you that you are the one who heals us and sets us free from things that tie us up in knots, keeping us from being our true selves. As Mel opens this door, would you come in … and fill her with your love. Hatred is the absence of love. It's nothingness can't stand up against love's solidness.'

Melanie had stopped crying. Head raised, eyelids closed and fluttering, lips parted she met the Jesus she'd heard about in church.

Grace thought about the invisible symbol of the cross that marked all those who were baptised. *It must be like a homing beacon to the Holy Spirit,* she smiled. *He's fulfilling his vow to her, he has found her and claimed her for his own.*

The mixture of joy for Melanie and grief for Anja, who had never had the chance to know such love, burned fiercely in Grace's chest. *Make it count Lord, … make Anja's life count … don't waste her sorrows … they cost her too much to waste… take what's happened to Anja and Mel and explode it … scatter light everywhere. One way or another – come what may – My Sister's House will be.*

When Grace got home she went straight to her bible and laptop to write, before inspiration evaporated. She turned to Acts chapter eight and the notes she'd taken a couple of days previously and began to write:

Lila worked on Mary's back, firmly pressing into the muscles beside her right shoulder blade. The smell of perfumed oil filled the room. Mary was thinking of Jesus, thanking him for giving her a hope and a future, for giving her Stephen. She was startled out of her reverie when Jair burst in through the door. Joshua woke and instantly began to cry.

'Jair – why did you do that? Look what you've done now!' Lila scolded reaching over for their son. She looked reproachfully at her breathless husband as she soothed Joshua, patting his back and kissing him. As she looked back up at Jair she realised that something was very wrong, 'What is it?' she asked in alarm.

Mary quickly pulled her tunic down her back and sat up staring wide-eyed at Jair. Dread crept stealthily upon her as Jair looked from one to the other, a tortured expression in his eyes.

'What ... what is it? Tell us,' Lila demanded.

Jair focused on Mary as he came and knelt in front of her. He took her hands in his.

Mary's stomach went cold. She knew, just as she'd known before she'd lost each of her babies, what was coming.

'It's Stephen,' he said quietly. 'He's ... they took him outside the city and ...' his voice failed him.

'Take me to him,' Mary said calmly, reaching for her shawl and headscarf.

Jair looked at Lila imploringly. Fighting tears Lila reached over to Mary, at a loss for words.

'Where is he?' Mary said in that strange, calm voice.

'They are bringing him to John's house. They have sent runners to his mother and aunt ... and to Bethany.'

Mary stood, wrapping her small body tightly in her shawl. Lila stared up at her.

'We are all in grave danger now,' Jair rose from his knees. He looked down at Lila, 'You must get Anna and pack as much as you can. I will purchase a donkey and cart. We need to get as far away from Jerusalem as possible. I suggest we go north, to Damascus. I have family there – my father's brother – a godly man. He will surely take us in.'

The magnitude of their situation dawned on Lila in tingling waves. Anxiety for Anna suddenly clutched her chest as she struggled to her feet, making her way to the backyard as she called her daughter's name.

'Come ...' Jair took Mary's elbow and drew her to the door.

'Wait ...' Mary pulled away from him.

'What? We haven't much time,' Jair urged.

She went to the couch picking up the alabaster jar of oil that Lila had been using, placed the stopper firmly into the neck and held it tightly to her.

Tears glistened in Jair's eyes.

When they got to John's house they found Stephen's body laid out on the same table on which they had laid Jair, not so long ago. Mary took in the bruises and wounds, the blood soaked clothing to which dust had stuck. The skin of his lips had been torn off and they were ruby red. No one spoke; the only sound was the raw grief of men crying.

She approached slowly, her mind a blank. When she reached him she touched his face with a finger. The skin was still warm, the blood still sticky. 'Get me a towel and a bowl of water,' she was surprised at the evenness of her tone. Jair left her side, quickly returning with them. She went to work, beginning with his face. As she tenderly wiped the blood and dust away, she felt a swollen and spongy part of his skull. She realised that it was completely crushed on one side. What size of stone did they use for this?

She wrung the cloth out over it, watching the water trickle through his thick hair and form pink pools on the table. She finished wiping his face and examined her handiwork. One eye was grossly swollen, but other than that, it was still the face she loved. He looks peaceful … almost happy. She bent and kissed his forehead as she began to shake.

His mother and aunt entered the room in silence. They approached slowly until his mother stood beside Mary. Then she broke, howling as she fell across his chest, clutching him to her, 'My son … my son … what have they done to you?'

The anguish was unrelenting; hope crushed like a rose.

Oh God, if you want to raise him to life, give me the chutzpah, the faith I need to pray it into being … Jair stood beside the women praying. He looked at Peter and John who stood on the other side of the table, their faces ashen with grief. These men had been used of God to heal so many sicknesses and diseases. Surely God would give them the gift that was needed now? But as he searched their faces he saw no sign of it.

There is a season and a time for every purpose under heaven … came the familiar words of Ecclesiastes. Jair shook his head. What possible purpose does this serve?

Silence.

The chutzpah never came.

Stephen's body grew cold slowly, looking less and less like him as the evening drew on. The women stripped the torn and stained clothes from him and gently washed his precious body. Then they anointed it with Mary's oil, wrapping it in grave cloths.

I never thought it would be like this; seeing you and holding you ... like this ...

She knew it was time to let him go, but couldn't. As the men went to lift his body she held on. A strange tug of war ensued until Stephen's mother gently took her in her arms and loosened her grip on him.

'He's gone now ... we must trust and let him go ...'

Mary buried her face in the older woman's chest and wailed brokenly as the men carried Stephen's body from the room.

⁂

Saul leaned back into the cushions of Aaron's couch, 'We must round up all the followers of the Nazarene.'

'You will be pleased to know that I have been keeping a record of where they live,' Aaron threw a scroll onto the expensive fabric between them. Needing time to clear their heads, to think and strategise, he'd invited Saul back to his home. 'We must act swiftly and without mercy,' he continued.

'I agree, brother. This blasphemous movement will soon stop with the threat of imprisonment and death.'

Aaron nodded, stroking his beard, 'The Sanhedrin will not openly condone stonings, but neither will they lift a finger to hinder them, as we saw today.'

'I know,' Saul smiled. 'It was a few zealous witnesses who got out of hand. Very unfortunate.'

'But so convenient,' Aaron smiled and lifted an ornate goblet to his lips.

'Yes,' replied Saul. There was a pause and then he cleared his throat, 'I need assistance to carry out the plan we have been discussing.'

'All my resources are at your disposal,' Aaron replied without hesitation, bowing his head slightly. 'I will speak with others sympathetic to our cause in the Sanhedrin. There will be ample finance and manpower to accomplish the decimation of this movement.'

'For the glory of Yahweh and Israel,' Saul said raising his cup, a triumphant look in his eyes.

'Amen!' Aaron raised his.

Saul began destroying the church the next day. Going from house to house he dragged men, women and children off to prison. The scroll that Aaron had given him proved very useful, however some of the homes were abandoned, as if they'd had warning of his coming. Aaron seemed piqued when he heard this. He asked about a particular house and was even more disturbed when Saul informed him that he had found it empty with the front door left open.

� ✻ ✻ ✻

They had travelled through the night and had only stopped briefly to eat and drink and rest the donkeys. Sychar was about 30 miles north of Jerusalem and they reached it the following day in the afternoon. The weary group of travellers consisted of Mary and Martha, Lazarus, Philip, Lila, Jair and the children. Jair had invited Philip to come with them as they'd returned from burying Stephen. Being young and recently arrived in Jerusalem from Rome, he had no ties to bind him to the city and had eagerly agreed. Jair felt more secure with another younger man travelling with them.

'Do you know anyone in Sychar?' Philip asked doubtfully.

'Yes – we know a woman whom we met once with Jesus,' Jair replied. 'We must pray God leads us to her quickly.'

As they approached the town, Lila prayed fervently that they would find her before it got dark. Nervous of being in enemy territory she feared for her children more than for herself and she feared for Mary, exhausted by grief as well as travel.

They made their way into the town centre, aware of staring eyes and whispered words hidden behind raised hands. As they were tethering the donkey to an old tree, Lila heard a coarse voice shouting, 'Shalom ... remember me? Shalom!' She turned her head in the direction it came from and squinted against the rays of the setting sun. 'It is you! I knew it! Didn't I say it was them? Shalom!' Lila could see a woman striding towards them, backlit by the sun.

'It's her ... I'd know that voice anywhere!' Lila exclaimed to Jair.

'Shalom!' she declared again spreading her arms wide. 'What brings you here again?' She embraced Lila and then Mary. 'You look exhausted,' she held Mary at arm's length scrutinising the face that had aged years in so short a space of time. Mary said nothing; could say nothing.

'Who are all these?' she asked bluntly, turning to look at the others.

'Do you remember Jair, my husband?' The woman frowned and shook her head, but bowed politely. Lila turned and introduced the others, 'This is Mary's brother and sister, Lazarus and Martha, and this is Philip – he came recently from Rome and joined the community who follow Jesus, our Messiah.'

'Persecution has broken out against us,' Philip blurted out. 'Our brother was stoned to death yesterday. We fled for our lives – that's why we're here.'

Jair was unsure as to the wisdom of this disclosure, but said nothing.

Lila darted a look at Mary's face only to see a tear trickling down her cheek. 'Philip!' Lila chided him.

He looked from Lila to Mary's face and his expression changed to one of horror. 'Sorry, Mary ... I didn't mean to ... I mean ...'

Martha came and stood beside Mary, wrapping her arm around her small shoulders. 'It's all right, Philip. Let's find somewhere to stay first before we tell our story. We are all very tired and need to rest.'

Mary found she loved her sister's sensible, pragmatic voice, which had irritated her so often in the past. It was now a comfort.

'You can stay with us – my husband and I,' the woman said proudly. Gesturing dramatically she continued, 'Come, come ...'

'But do you have enough room for all of us?' Lila queried.

'Oh, yes,' the woman replied, 'I am now the proud manageress of Sychar's best guest house! Lucky for you business is not so good and it is empty.'

And so they spent the next days with the 'well woman' as they had come to know her since first they had met. Interestingly enough, she had named her guesthouse 'The Well'.

Each day she took Philip into the centre, eager for him to teach the people about Jesus. Many had believed in him when she had first met them at the well, but she wanted more people to hear and to understand that the Messiah had come at last. They stood under the old tree proclaiming Jesus as the Messiah. Lazarus went with them, but Jair stayed with the women and children, unable to bring himself to risk further danger.

Filled with compassion and uninhibited by fear, Philip went up to those who used crutches or sticks to walk and offered to pray for them in Jesus' name. Some allowed him to and were instantly healed, throwing their walking aids away. When a crowd began gathering because they'd seen him perform miraculous signs, they began to pay close attention to what he said. With shrieks, evil spirits came out of many, and many paralytics and cripples were healed. For those few days there was great rejoicing in Sychar.

Philip sent word to the apostles who had chosen to stay in Jerusalem, not fearing death. He told them that Samaria had accepted the word of God. This was shocking news – for the Samaritans were not properly Jewish nor Gentile, but detestable half-breeds.

So far the apostles had only focused on preaching the good news of Jesus to their own people, but hearing that the Samaritans were embracing Jesus as Messiah and entering the community of believers through baptism, they sent Peter and John to investigate Philip's claims. The repercussions were unthinkable, were the Sanhedrin and the synagogues to hear of it.

'Let's stay until Peter and John come,' Jair said to Lila. 'It will be good to see them again and to hear news from Jerusalem.'

Lila was worried about Mary. She had slipped into a dark despair where she could not be reached. She wasn't eating or sleeping. Lila and Martha held her and prayed daily for her, to no immediate effect. The grief was so deep.

'Don't you think it would be better to move on and get to Damascus – settle down – build a new life? The longer we are in limbo, the longer Mary may stay in this valley of the shadow, don't you think?'

Jair listened quietly and then later discussed it with Lazarus and Martha. They agreed to stay until the apostles came and then they would move on. Philip however felt he must stay in Samaria and continue to spread the word. It was clear that his preaching and prophetic gifting were growing stronger with each day that he stood preaching on the streets of Sychar. Jair thought that he had the same radiance about him that Stephen had. After all, they had both been chosen to wait on tables because they were recognised to be full of the Holy Spirit. He was younger and a little rash, but experience would teach him.

❋   ❋   ❋

It was a wonderful reunion for Jair and Philip when they met Peter and John at the gates of Sychar in the late afternoon. Jair found it hard to get a word in edgeways, as Philip overflowed with story after story of those he had led to faith in Jesus and baptised. Lila, Martha and Lazarus welcomed them at 'The Well' and introduced them to their host once again.

Lila observed that they seemed somewhat out of their depth. She sensed they were feeling their way, trying to discern if Samaritans could truly be followers of Christ and therefore be part of the new community of faith. She remembered how Peter had been so protective and defensive of Jesus when their host brought people from the town out to meet Him at the well, the first time they had met.

Mary didn't come out to greet them. It was John who persisted in asking to see her until she hesitantly came into the courtyard. He embraced her in a brotherly hug and wept with her for the loss of Stephen. He spent that first evening talking quietly with her, slightly apart from the others. Lila was glad that finally someone seemed to be able to break into her darkness.

❇ ❇ ❇

Peter and John returned to Jerusalem, assured that the Spirit of God was being poured out on Samaritan believers too. It was the night after they left that Philip spent in prayer on the roof of 'The Well'.

Go south to the road – the desert road – that goes down from Jerusalem to Gaza. The radiant being's mouth did not move, but Philip knew what he said in his mind, as if thought had somehow been transferred there. He had begun his prayers with his feelings for Mary, but as he laid them down before God, he was soon caught up in worship, praise and thanksgiving as the Holy Spirit led him. He had only become aware of the being's presence because he could hear the brushing of feathers, which had caused him to look over to his right. There in the space between the guest house and the next building hovered what Philip could only assume was an angel. He glowed with a white light, shot with blue and purple fire, flickering through transparencies of his body, or clothing, Philip wasn't sure which. His feathered wings moved like that of a hummingbird, so fast that it was almost impossible to see them other than the glint of golden, peacock blue.

Philip's body reacted with shivering convulsions – never had he seen anything so beautifully powerful or awe-inspiring. He wished Peter and John were still there so he could run and get them, that is, if his legs would have worked.

It was just before dawn. As the eastern sky lightened, the angel faded from view, cloaking himself with layers of time and space. Philip's body slowly came back under control, the convulsions subsiding bit by bit. The rim of the sun was breaking the horizon as he climbed down the stairwell with weak knees to wake the others.

On hearing of his experience, Lazarus and Martha responded immediately, 'You must go now.' Jair and Lila agreed and they all prayed blessings on him. He collected his few belongings, glancing furtively in the direction of Mary's room. Then as the sun rose in the clear morning sky he bid his friends goodbye, all except Mary, and set out from Sychar heading south.

4. CHOOSE

Acts 9–11 The women who choose life

'Oh, I like that!' Melanie said.

'Thanks,' Charlie smiled proudly, folding the tabs of an outfit he'd made round the paper doll in his hands.

'You're really good – I mean it,' she persisted.

Charlie looked up at her uncertainly, 'I've got loads more drawings in my room. Do you want to see?'

'I'd love to,' she replied, leaning back on her pillows watching him run from the room.

They'd been in her bedroom all afternoon drawing and cutting. It didn't take long for him to return with three black A4 sketchbooks in his arms. He sat down on the bed and handed them to her, looking tense.

She opened the first one.

He watched her face pensively.

As she turned the pages a smile grew on her drawn, pale face, 'Charlie … these are excellent! Have Mum and Dad seen them?'

'Mum has … Dad wouldn't be interested,' Charlie doodled in a space beside a pink outfit, yet to be cut out.

'You don't know that …'

'Him and Josh are into *Die Hard* and *Die Harder* … blokes' stuff … he'd laugh.'

Melanie shrugged as she turned the pages, 'Well I think you're really talented. What about school – do they know?'

'No. I just do this at home.'

'Well, I think you should start letting them know. You should do GCSE

Art and then go on to do the A-level too. You've got such an eye for colour and design. I mean look at this one – that's good enough to be in a fashion show. Hey – you could be the next Gok Wan!'

Charlie pursed his lips and went to grab the sketch books off her.

'What? Why are you being like that?' Melanie wouldn't let go of the last book.

'Give it to me!' he said angrily.

'Charlie … what did I say?'

She let go and Charlie fell back on the bed, the three books landing on his chest. When he sat up she could see tears in his eyes. 'Because that's what Dad will say … and Josh!'

'Oh …' Melanie said in a small voice.

Silence blanketed round the moment as Charlie looked miserable.

Eventually Melanie reached out and held one of his hands. She squeezed it kindly and said nothing more.

He got up and left, leaving her staring after him.

'Kids … dinner!' came Chloe's voice up the stairs. Melanie still didn't feel hungry. It had been several weeks now and she'd lost quite a bit of weight. She knew her mum was worried about her, even though she had said nothing about it. Meal times were becoming tense. Dreading it, Melanie swung her legs over the side of the bed and slowly stood up. Even so, she had a head-rush and grabbed onto her study chair to steady herself. Once her vision had cleared she made her way slowly downstairs to the kitchen. She sat down in her seat, her stomach turning over at the smell of cauliflower cheese steaming in the centre of the table.

Charlie was the last to sit down. Melanie could tell he'd been crying. Mum and Dad didn't seem to notice. Melanie caught his eye and winked at him. It seemed to strengthen him.

※ ※ ※

Chloe looked across the table at Mark. It was like he wasn't really there; like he was pretending. She pursed her lips and speared a piece of cauliflower with her fork. Only Josh seemed to be enjoying the meal she'd cooked. He was chatting about football practice and how he'd scored a goal. She smiled at him. She couldn't catch Charlie or Melanie's eye. They were both pushing their food round their plates. At least Charlie was putting some of it in his mouth, but not Melanie. Chloe hated the anxious feeling that was growing in her chest, glancing at her daughter's plate for the third time. *Don't say anything. It's just a phase ... it'll pass. Don't make a fuss. She's been through a lot. Hunger will win in the end. I need to see the doctor, get Prozac again. I can't take much more of this.*

She watched Mark, imagining herself shouting at him, *Be a father!*

※   ※   ※

Grace gathered up the paperwork from her desk for the PCC meeting. She picked up the DVD last, and placed it on top. *Here we go...* she looked at the Holman Hunt painting. *Help them open up to this ...*

'Right boys, I'm off,' she called as she went to grab her coat in the hallway.

Zack came running out of the living room, 'Don't go, Mummy. Stay! I want you to read to me. Daddy doesn't do the voices right,' he pulled her coat.

She picked him up and kissed him firmly on the cheek, 'I promise I'll read to you tomorrow night.'

He pulled a ringlet of her hair and put it in his mouth, looking sullen. He shook his head stubbornly, 'I want you.'

Peter came to the living room door and leaned up against the door frame, folding his arms across his chest. 'I want you too,' he mouthed the words.

Conflicted, Grace didn't reply, but bent down, putting Zack on his feet and gently loosening his grip on her hair. 'I'll only be an hour-and-a-half. I'll come up and see if you're still awake when I get back,' she said, hoping this would convince her son not to throw a tantrum. It seemed to do the trick.

Peter wearily uncrossed his arms and moved into the hallway, resting a hand on Zack's dark curls. 'Come on son, let mummy go to her meeting. We'll have fun here. I bet she wishes she didn't have to go,' his eyes held hers in a steely stare over the boy's head.

Sparks of anger firing in her eyes, Grace turned quickly to open the front door, before she said something she'd regret. She still wasn't used to its heaviness and had to pull hard to swing it open. *If this is Your will, why is it such a strain?*

She heard the door slam shut behind her as she walked past the old church, dreading the smell of mould that awaited her in the old hall. She perfunctorily turned on the lights, set out the chairs, putting papers on each one. *Please don't let Donald Chadwick come tonight,* she pleaded. Her arms felt as heavy as the door. She sat down behind a tea-stained table and closed her eyes.

I worship you, Lord. Let your Kingdom come, let your will be done ... help me be gracious ... sorry for getting angry ... I know he loves me ... wants to be with me ... help him want what you want ... your Kingdom come ... Fleetingly an image of Bishop Duncan's face came into her mind. She swatted it like a fly.

※　※　※

'I for one do not want the police, pimps and social workers sniffing round our church buildings,' Donald Chadwick was in full flow, his double chin bouncing off his collar. Several others were nodding vigorously. 'Whoever heard of such a thing? This is a house of prayer – a respectable community of the faithful. We don't want to be associated with the dregs of society. We're here to raise the standard, not lower it!'

'With respect,' interrupted a stooped, elderly lady, rising unsteadily to her feet. 'Surely the church is exactly the place for the "dregs of society", as you put it Donald?' A school mistress in her day, her voice, although wispy in parts, still carried an ominous note.

Donald frowned but didn't sit down, 'Look, Gwen, we've got the social services now to do this kind of work. Our society has been built on Christian values, ensuring that we provide for the poor and care for the marginalised. Let the local council deal with this issue,' public school pomposity oozed out of him as he sat down, squeezing himself into his seat with some discomfort.

'But I thought you said, Grace, that the council cannot deal with the issue alone; that there aren't enough safe houses and that the money made available by the government is there for any organisation to bid for?'

'Yes, that's right, Gwen. The time has come when we can't just sit back and leave it to someone else to sort out, because the problem is too big. We, the church, need to be partnering with other agencies,' Grace scanned the PCC, her conviction ebbing slightly as she looked into many passive faces.

'Well …' Gwen pierced Donald with a beady eye, 'I for one think it's a wonderful idea and would like to give my full support to the venture.' She sat down, pulling her plaid skirt down over her knees.

'Thank you, Gwen …' Grace paused, her conviction refired, 'Perhaps I haven't made my proposal clear enough? May I reiterate that this will not be a St Stephen's project. It will be an independent project in the diocese, set up by myself and my colleagues, supported by the Bishop and his strategy team. I will be involved in its development outside of my St Stephen's time. The reason this is being brought before you is simply to ensure transparency because I am your incumbent. I am sure that in the future there may be some overlap, and I wanted you to be aware of this from the start. We would very much like your support, because we, I, value it – I value you,' her open gaze disarmed some.

'You haven't specifically said where the safe house will be?' Donald's neighbour piped up.

'I'm afraid I can't divulge that information,' Grace felt like a broken record.

'But in order to make an informed decision, we need to be informed,' Donald said sarcastically.

'You've seen the DVD – this is a global issue. You've heard the facts and listened to the proposal I have put together as to what I think I am called to do with the other half of my time. It's nearly nine-thirty, so I suggest you show your support, or lack of it now,' Grace forced a smile. She felt slightly sick. She wasn't sure she liked being in charge.

The secretary of the PCC said, 'All in support?'

Eight hands went up.

'All against?'

Five hands rose.

'All abstentions?'

Two.

'We have a majority in support,' the sparrow-like secretary smiled at Grace admiringly.

'Thank you, everyone,' Grace stood, speaking over rippling conversation. 'Shall we close with a prayer?'

Slowly everyone stood and obediently bowed their heads. Grace raised hers, looking at each person as she finished the prayer. Donald's glare sent a heatwave through her.

It was ten before she had said goodbye to everyone, cleared the chairs and tables away and collected up all the forgotten papers.

As she put her key in the door she thought of Zack's face. Guilt stabbed her. She looked into the living room before taking off her coat. Peter was reading the paper with the sound turned low on the TV. 'Hi, love. Sorry I'm so late,' she said shrugging out of her coat.

Peter looked up, 'An hour and a half?'

'Oh, don't be like that Peter,' she said as she hung her coat up. Standing in the doorway she waited for a reply.

'Sorry,' he looked back at his paper.

'Do you want a drink? A whiskey maybe?'

She watched him. He looked up at her again – he was struggling. She smiled, hoping to win him over. Eventually he gave in and smiled back, skin crinkling round eyes and cheeks. She breathed.

'What do you want? Red or white or Jack?'

'I'll go for Jack on the rocks,' he put the paper down beside him. 'Let me get it …' he rose to his feet.

As he came alongside her in the doorway, she caught the fading scent of his aftershave, warm and earthy, mixed with the scent of his skin. She reached out and hooked a finger through a belt loop. 'I really am sorry – I made it end at nine-thirty, but they all stayed and chatted. I did try!'

'I know,' he replied, facing her. He sighed as he put his hands on her hips. 'I'm just not sure I signed up for all this … I mean, what's it going to be like when you start the "Sister's House"? Will we ever see you?'

'I'm not sure I signed up for all this either,' she tugged him towards her. 'I'm just trying to be obedient. I wish you could understand that.'

He searched her blue eyes, 'I know that's what you think you're trying to do … I'm just not sure there's anyone out there to obey.'

'What if I'm right and there is?' she leaned back against the door frame.

'You'll have invested well. But what if you're wrong?'

She looked at him, loving the way his thick, dark eyelashes edged his eyes. 'I'll have lived well – done some good.'

'But missed precious moments with Zack, with me …' his hands dropped to cup the cheeks of her bottom. He pulled her in and pressed into her.

'Living – really living – isn't about instant gratification, Peter. It's about …' he nudged through her curls and kissed her neck,' … it's about acting justly …' he caressed the small of her back with the tips of his fingers, as he took her earlobe between his lips … 'about loving mercy …' he moved to kiss her cheek. She felt the day's growth rough against her skin,'… about walking humbly with …'

'With me!' Peter laughed, and kissed her mouth.

Her arms went round his neck.

As they pulled apart she whispered, 'I love you so much, Peter. Don't make me choose between you and God.'

'I'm sure I'd lose if I did,' he laughed ruefully, disentangling himself from her.

She didn't reply, but let her hands fall limp to her sides. 'I'm just going to check on Zack,' she said as she made her way to the stairs, watching him walk towards the kitchen.

'Anyway … if there is a God, how can you be so sure he'd want you to spend hours in PCC meetings?' he threw this parting shot over his shoulder as she climbed the stairs.

He was right there, she thought, shrugging and smiling a little. She couldn't imagine Jesus enduring long PCC meetings. She quite fancied the thought of him throwing some tables around like he'd done in Jerusalem's Temple.

She knelt beside her son's bed. Zack lay with his arms up either side of his head. The night light softened his features so that he looked utterly innocent, except for the naughty dark curl stuck to his forehead with sleep sweat. She resisted the desire to hug him tightly to her, and just gently moved the curl back off his forehead, kissing the place where it had lain.

❋　❋　❋

'Why are you being so weird?' Chloe propped herself up on one elbow, studying Mark's face. He lay on his back staring between the two pools of light made by their bedside lamps on the ceiling.

'Am I?' he asked dully.

'Yes.'

'In what way?' he asked turning to look at her.

'I don't know ... like you're pretending to be something you're not,' Chloe wasn't sure what she meant.

'Are you analysing me again?' he looked back at the ceiling.

Perturbed Chloe shifted her head on her hand, 'I don't know ... maybe?'

'Well don't. It's Melanie who needs an analyst, not me,' Mark said abruptly.

'She's seeing Grace every week. I know that's helping ...'

'Yeah – but she's still not eating!'

'You're angry ...' Chloe reached over to touch him.

'Don't,' he said turning his head away.

'Look Mark, if we're not careful this thing will drive us apart again. We've got to face it together; no running away to find comfort elsewhere.'

Mark turned and looked at her oddly.

'What?' she asked.

He didn't reply, just looked back up at the ceiling.

'We don't know what we're doing – we've never faced this sort of situation before – but we've got to find a way forward. I hope we will,' she paused, then said, 'I've been to see the doctor. I'm back on Prozac ... my anxiety levels were just getting too high ... I haven't been sleeping for weeks now.'

'I noticed,' Mark said. After a long silence he turned to her, torment in his beautiful eyes, 'I can't stop thinking about what they did to her.'

'I know,' Chloe said.

'It's doing my head in,' he closed his eyes, rubbing a hand over his face.

'Maybe you should go see the doctor too? Do you want us to pray together about it?'

He opened his eyes again and looked at her, 'Why should I talk to a god who let this happen to our daughter?'

Chloe felt a lump in her throat. She had no reply.

'And why would God want to listen to a guy like me who let this happen to his daughter?' He rolled away from her, reached out and turned off his bedside lamp.

Chloe stared at his back for a time, and then turned off her own light. She lay awake for ages in the dark, her thoughts chasing anxiously after each other.

※　※　※

The builders began work on sectioning off the vicarage. Grace and Peter would be left with two reception rooms, the kitchen, four bedrooms and two bathrooms. 'My Sister's House' would have an office in the front of the house, with the back room being converted into a kitchen-diner, two large bedrooms converted into four and two bathrooms. The estimated time for the works was two months, but Grace was sceptical as she watched the builders arrive at seven-thirty in the morning and, after many cups of tea and coffee, leave at three in the afternoon. She wasn't going to complain though – the diocese was paying.

She received a grant from the diocese for furnishings and so began her tempestuous affair with Ikea. Chloe took responsibility for applying to the Charities Commission, having much help from the diocese with the process. It was several months later that she came round to the vicarage, waving their charitable status ecstatically. They went to the pub to celebrate.

'Here's to My Sister's House!' Grace held up her wine. They clinked glasses and drank deeply. She felt the alcohol hit almost straight away, not being used to drinking during the day, 'Lovely,' she smiled at Chloe.

'Mmmm … it's a smooth one …' Chloe looked into her glass and sniffed appreciatively.

'So we've got Gwen, Val and Trevor on our board of trustees. We need a couple more – a business man would be good, someone who understands money … and maybe a legal person?'

'Yep,' Chloe replied. 'But we've got enough to start with. We'll find the others as we go along. Gwen's a good woman, isn't she?'

Grace nodded, swallowing her wine, 'She's from another world, but as sharp as a pin and no push over.'

'I know – I'd have hated to have her as my headmistress!' Chloe laughed. 'She'd have definitely expelled me.'

Grace smiled. 'Talking of schools, what's happening with Melanie's schooling?'

'She doesn't want to go back – she wants to sit her GCSEs by correspondence. The school have been great, really understanding, but it scares me – the thought of Melanie being at home all the time. She's got to engage with the real world again at some stage, hasn't she?' Chloe looked to Grace for confirmation.

'She'll be okay, Chloe. Give her time. She's always hated school anyway. It's partly why she ended up in such a mess.'

'I know – I had no idea. I feel dreadful that I was so ignorant. Wrapped up in my own little world, finding my identity,' she grimaced into her glass.

'Don't be so hard on yourself, Chloe,' Grace frowned, tucking ringlets behind her ears.

'So she's not been blaming me for everything then?' Chloe asked.

Grace smiled, 'You know I can't tell you anything that Melanie says to me.'

'I know,' Chloe shrugged, 'I thought I'd try though.'

'You are all going to be okay,' Grace assured her friend.

'I hope so,' Chloe's dark eyes were troubled. 'She's still not eating much – she just picks at her food.'

'You know that's a symptom, not the real problem,' Grace turned the stem of her glass between her finger and thumb.

'I know – but she's so painfully thin, it's scaring me. The atmosphere round meal times is unbearable. Charlie's particularly affected by her. He seems so unhappy at the minute. Nothing I do or say seems to lift him.'

'Has Mark been able to talk to him?'

Chloe's mouth turned down at the corners. She shook her head. 'They don't get on. You know he's always been a mummy's boy.'

Grace nodded.

'I kind of thought that by now he would be bonding with Mark – you know, making the transition from childhood into manhood. But it's like Charlie doesn't trust his dad at all, like he doesn't want to be near him or do anything with him. And Mark just accepts it. I mean, him and Josh are great buddies. I've tried talking to Mark about it, but he just shrugs it off and says he can't help it if I've mollycoddled him.'

Grace thought of Zack and wondered if she mollycoddled him.

'I guess I did get a lot of comfort from Charlie when he was younger – when my world was falling apart. But I didn't think I did anything wrong in that, did I?'

'You're very close, Chloe. There's nothing wrong with that. Charlie needed you just as much back then. I guess this latest trauma may have triggered old responses in him. He just needs time to sort through his feelings. As long as you and Mark remain stable and there for them all, they'll be okay in the end.'

Chloe frowned, 'What if we can't? Mark's really angry about what's happened to Melanie. He's acting very weird and I'm not much better. I'm back on Prozac … just to keep me level. Why is life so difficult?' Chloe asked emptying her glass.

Grace smiled, 'I was asking God that the other day – He wants His will to be done, but why then is it such a struggle?'

'Let me know when you get an answer,' Chloe pushed her glass away and reached for her bag.

Grace drank the last of her wine. 'After Anja died I really wanted to just give up. But I came to the point where I knew I had to choose to keep on trusting and hoping. It's like you said to me – I'm praying that God brings good out of evil.' She pushed her chair back and stood up, 'I've felt better since then. Come on, let's get back to Tom's paperwork.'

Chloe nodded, 'Yep … keep on keeping on …'

'Have you told Mark about seeing Tom yet?' she asked.

Chloe looked at her, 'No.'

'Why not?'

'I don't know really … didn't want to stress him out any more.'

Grace shook her head, 'You should tell him.'

'Yeah …'

❉　❉　❉

'Are you all right to chat for a minute?' Trevor asked down the phone.

'Yes. What's up?' Grace queried, putting down her pen. She'd been writing notes on Acts chapters nine through eleven.

'Couple of things: first did you know that several members of St Stephen's have been coming to St Matt's for the last couple of weeks?'

'I knew we were low on numbers at the nine o'clock service, but thought people were away on holiday or something.'

'No, they've been coming here.'

'Let me guess … Donald Chadwick and crew?'

'That's right. They've asked to have a meeting with me. I just thought you should know.'

'Good luck,' Grace laughed.

'So they haven't spoken to you about leaving?'

'No, not a word. Tell them not to be so rude!' she covered her hurt pride with humour.

'Don't worry – I will!' Trevor said. 'The other thing is a little more encouraging,' he continued.

'Oh?' Grace waited.

'James Martin – you remember him?'

'Yes,' Grace realised she was gripped the phone too tightly at the mention of the name. She consciously loosened her fingers.

'Well he's been to see me with a rather odd request.'

'Really? What?'

'Well, it's clear to me that God must be doing something in his life, because he wants to give his money away.'

'Good for him,' Grace frowned realising her grip had tightened again.

'He specifically asked me if I knew of any projects helping women get out of the sex trade.'

Grace was silent.

'He couldn't have known about My Sister's House, so other than divine inspiration, I don't know what led him to me?'

'Maybe he heard about it through Donald?'

'Well, he hasn't been coming to church that much – once a month maybe, with his wife. So I don't think he'd have met any of the St Stephen's lot yet.'

'Mmmm …' Grace didn't know what to say.

'I said I'd have a think and get back to him.'

'Good. Did he say how much he wanted to give?'

'Yes … yes he did …'

'Well, how much?' Grace asked impatiently.

'So you are interested?'

'Well, if we could give Chloe a salary and maybe pay a part-time administrator from the start, that would be wonderful!'

'Yes … I agree.'

'So how much?'

Trevor laughed and Grace thought she heard him scratching his head. She pictured the dandruff falling onto his black dog-collar shirt.

'He wants to give £10,000 per year for three years ... to start with.'

'To start with?'

'Well I supose he wants to be involved in some way and see where it goes.'

'Mmmm ...' Grace was lost for words. Then, 'Did he say why?'

'As a matter of fact he didn't need to.'

'What do you mean?' Grace asked.

Trevor cleared his throat, making Grace hold the receiver away from her ear. She remembered James coming into the church to make his confession – how she'd called Trevor to hear it ... *he must have told him everything ...*

'I see. Well – let's sleep on it, shall we?' Grace made her voice matter of fact.

'And the St Stephen's crew?'

'You're welcome to them ... hope you have more success with communicating the gospel to them than I've had,' Grace smiled.

'Any advice?' Trevor asked.

'Don't give them any power.'

'Right,' she heard him smile.

'Okay ... I better go. Speak to you soon. Bye, Trevor.'

She put the phone down and stared at her journal. She'd drawn a swirling circle in the margin.

❈　❈　❈

Chloe was pleased with the prospect of a possible small starter salary.

Val was speechless at being offered the same to be the part-time administrator.

Grace was uncomfortable.

James Martin had asked Trevor if he could volunteer with the project. Trevor had redirected him, suggesting training as a Street Pastor with a project that was running in another part of the diocese. James had jumped at the suggestion and had already submitted his application.

Grace had thought she'd never have to meet the man again once she'd left St Matt's. It looked like the trustees were going to go for the idea of developing a Street Pastor's team for the project. They put out an advert in both St Matt's and St Stephen's churches and several others, including Sean, St Matt's youth worker, signed up and applied for the training. Grace could think of no good argument against the idea. She resigned herself to having to meet James Martin again.

When she told Peter, he shook his head. 'You're playing with fire, Grace – I hope you know what you're doing?' Grace uncertainly twisted a white-blonde ringlet round a finger. She couldn't hold her husband's gaze.

The building work came to its end a month later than the date stated, of course. They'd decided on keeping the front of the house as it had always been and using the back door as the entrance. So St Stephen's vicarage didn't look any different from the outside. All the church knew was that the vicarage was being refurbished in accordance with diocesan policy on the arrival of a new incumbent.

Val had the admin for 'My Sister's House' well in hand and all procedures were in place. Mo was to be their first voluntary case worker. Because she worked as a council youth worker she understood much of what was required, so the training was nothing new to her. The bid had been accepted, all CRBs were through and a risk assessment had been completed by the diocesan vulnerable adults advisor. Gwen volunteered to be available in the house during the day along with Melanie and the nights were to be shared between the others.

Grace didn't feel ready, but she guessed she probably never would. *Just got to start* she thought.

Their first girl came via the police. They'd raided a brothel in central London and needed a safe house for a trafficked Nigerian. It was all systems go.

The team gathered together to pray before she arrived. Grace looked round each beloved face, her heart warming with the sincerity and grit she saw.

'Lord, we lift Rose before you as she comes here. Please calm her fears. Please help us connect with her and enable her to ... to ... recover ... to feel valued and respected,' Val prayed hesitantly.

'Yes, Lord, please help us get her – you know, Lord – understand where she's at, God. Father, you know this girl. Share your understanding of her with us, Father God,' Mo prayed in a way that Grace thought she could only have learned off the God Channel on TV.

'Dear Heavenly Father,' prayed Gwen, 'We thank Thee for Thy great compassion towards Rose. We thank Thee for the police finding her. We ask Thee to use us as Thy hands and Thy feet, that we may be as Jesus to her.'

Grace smiled at the vastly different traditions represented in their little group. She prayed silently, a smile playing round her mouth.

They all jumped when the doorbell rang. 'Here we go …' Grace said hitching her jeans up on her hips as she walked to the door.

❊ ❊ ❊

Rose was tall and slender; an Amazon. Her eyes were wide set in a heart-shaped face. They were hard; defended; fifty year old's eyes in a sixteen year old face. She handed her phone to Gwen when instructed by the plain-clothes police officer and watched impassively as they gave Gwen a plastic bag of other items they had already taken from her – mainly anything that might be used to harm herself.

Grace thought of Anja, wincing internally as a bubble of grief surfaced and burst again.

She spoke good English and agreed to the house rules, signing her name at the bottom of the sheet. Once the officer left through the back door, Mo and Gwen took her up to her room. Chloe, Grace and Val exchanged wordless glances.

I hope you know what you're doing? Peter's voice echoed in Grace's head.

❊ ❊ ❊

Chloe had been having sessions with Rose twice a week, during the forty five days they had to process her case. Initially she had said nothing. Chloe had accepted this. She prayed for God's love to fill the room as they sat in silence.

In the fourth session Rose spoke, 'Why are you doing this?' she asked boring holes into Chloe's skull with her black, almond eyes.

Chloe did not allow surprise to show on her face, 'Because I want to help you,' she replied.

'What good is it to sit here?' she asked scornfully.

'I'm hoping you might realise that I want nothing from you and that perhaps you might begin to trust me.'

Rose sniffed, raising her chin and closing her eyes. Her look seemed haughty and it felt like rejection, but Chloe didn't react. She listened to the creaking of the central heating chugging through the radiators of the old vicarage. She savoured a trace of her perfume, rising from between her breasts as she moved her hands from a clasped position on her knee, to resting them palms down in her lap.

'If I trusted you, what could you do for me?' Rose was staring out the window that overlooked the back garden. Gwen and Val were in the process of clearing it.

'I could hear your story. I could help you cope with the traumas you've been through. You would know that someone understands and cares how you feel.'

Rose continued to stare out the window.

Eventually she spoke again in such a quiet voice that Chloe had to focus hard to hear, 'I was a virgin when they brought me here. I thought I was going to work in a restaurant. I was going to send money back to my mother.'

Chloe held her breath.

In a monotone she continued, face turned towards daylight, 'My friend told me her uncle could give me a job. He said I would be met by his sister when I arrived in England. She would take me to the restaurant and show me what to do. But there was no woman waiting for me, only a man. He said he was sorry that the woman could not come. I trusted him.'

The sun broke through the clouds outside, heightening the contrast of her profile against the sky. 'He took me to a house where there were seven other men. They told me why I had been brought here. They said I had to have sex with all of them to get me ready for my new job.' She raised a hand to her cane-rowed hair, running her fingers along a plait which curved behind her ear. Chloe noticed the tremor in her long fingers.

'I told them I was a virgin and that I would not do such work. I begged them to give me any other work.'

'What did they say?' Chloe asked.

'They said I was worth more as a virgin. They could get £10,000 for me.'

Shock made Chloe's stomach go cold.

'I said I would never do that work. So the man who had brought me there locked me in a room and gave me nothing to eat for three days. After that he told me that they would get the witch doctor in our village to make me sick if I did not do what they said. When I became ill—'

'What do you mean by ill?'

'Vomiting,' she paused and then resumed her line of thought, 'he told me the witch doctor had done this and it would kill me and the same would happen to my mother. After two weeks I gave in. I had to give the men oral sex.'

'All of them?'

'One after another,' she nodded her perfectly shaped head, no expression on her noble face, still turned towards the sky.

Chloe swallowed bile rising in her throat. She reached for a glass of water on the table beside her and took a sip, keeping her face expressionless.

'Then they sold me to another man. I did not see any money, but I know it was a lot. They argued about it for a long time.' She raised her hand to her chin this time, the tremor more marked than before.

'So he was a wealthy man?'

Rose shrugged. A tear trickled down her shadowed cheek, catching sunlight within it as it rolled under her chin and down her neck. Her lips trembled and her fingers shook as she covered her mouth. 'He had me for a whole night, even though I was crying, he did not stop.'

Chloe reached for a tissue and passed it across the space between them. Rose took it, raising it to her eyes. 'After that the man who met me at the airport told me every day where I had to go. I worked all the time.'

'What do you mean?'

'I had to pay him rent for the house he'd brought me to, but I never stayed there. I was in one brothel or another, always he'd phone me and tell me where to go next.'

'When did you sleep?'

'If a man had me for an hour, sometimes afterwards he would sleep. I would sleep then.'

Chloe shook her head in disbelief, no longer able to keep from reacting, 'Why didn't you run away?'

'They told me I owed my friend's uncle £40,000 for bringing me here. I had to pay that off by working for them and pay my rent ... he only gave me enough money to keep my phone and to eat a little every day ... and I was afraid the witch doctor would kill my mother.'

'When did they bring you to England, Rose?'

'Last September,' she folded her tissue into smaller and smaller rectangles.

'When did the police find you?'

'Two days before I came here. They kept me in a cell for one night, then brought me here.'

'How were the appointments Mo took you to with the doctor?'

'I'm waiting for test results.'

'Rose …' the girl looked up and their eyes met, '…why did you feel you had to earn money to send to your mother? You are so young. Shouldn't you still be at school?'

'My father threw my mother out. His other wife didn't want her around. So me and my brothers and sisters had to go with her. I left school and started looking for work. I got a job in a kitchen washing dishes at night and in the day I got a job sweeping the floor in a hairdressers. I went from one to the other. Then my friend told me about her uncle.'

Chloe nodded.

'What kind of school did you go to?'

'It was a Christian school.'

'Did they teach you that the love of Jesus is more powerful than evil?'

Rose looked at her oddly, 'Why do you ask this?'

'Well,' Chloe hesitated, 'If they had taught you that, then you needn't have feared the witch doctor. Maybe you wouldn't have believed what those men told you – maybe you would have been able to run away?'

'In my school we were all Christians – but still we feared the power of the witch doctor.'

'Maybe it's something to think about … Jesus can protect you from any curse of the witch doctor.'

'You do not know what you are talking about,' Rose said, shaking her head. 'You have not seen what they can do. But I sing to him – the songs we learnt in school. When it was a bad man … a cruel man … I would sing to Jesus.'

Chloe's eyes welled with tears.

※　※　※

'I don't know how God can endure it all,' Chloe shook her head sitting at her kitchen table with Grace.

'I know. I've been struggling with the same thing. Why does he answer some prayers and not others? Why did he let Anja die and then rescue Melanie? Don't get me wrong, I'm glad he did, we did,' she reached out and squeezed Chloe's hand, 'but it does seem so unfair. And Rose ... you know about her singing while ...?'

Chloe nodded, 'If He could hear her singing to Him, why didn't He rescue her sooner?'

They both sat in bewildered silence. Then Chloe said, 'Maybe He's not as nice as we thought He was?'

Grace looked at her friend trying to gauge if she was serious. 'Chloe – we've got to stick with the Jesus revealed to us in the gospels. He and the Father are one. When we look at him then we see what God is like. You can't say Jesus isn't as nice as you thought he was ... He's way better than we could ever imagine.'

'Yeah – but look at the evil we're uncovering. We're only seeing a glimpse of it. God sees all of it all the time. How does he bear it?'

'Because he's the only one who's able?'

Chloe shook her head, overwhelmed, 'It's too much, Grace. What's happened to Mel ... and how Charlie's not coping ... and Mark and I so distant from each other ... I want to be a strong supportive counsellor, but right now I feel like a wreck.' She stared at her coffee, watching the steam swirl upwards from it's dark surface.

'Have you seen your supervisor recently?'

'I'm seeing her tonight.'

'That's good.'

'Yeah.'

❋   ❋   ❋

Lord, I don't understand, Grace wrote in her journal.

It seems so wrong that some of your children suffer so little and some suffer so much. Yet you say you love us all equally. It doesn't make sense.

What's happened to Melanie is terrible – the knock on effect is devastating on Charlie, Josh, Chloe and Mark. Yet Chloe's here serving you on the front line.

Why won't you protect, honour and provide for her? She's giving herself for your gospel.

Lord, even if I never understand, help me to trust you and obey you no matter what. Help me to stay faithful to ministering your gospel come what may. Help Chloe do the same. Help her know your presence and choose you. Please ... help her.

�֍ ✖ ✖

Chloe sat in her car for a long time after seeing her supervisor.

Can you hear me? Do you care? Does prayer work? What am I doing? Maybe you don't mean me to do this work? Maybe it's just been my idea ... maybe I've gone where angels fear to tread? The fall-out is too much, if that's what it is. The cost is too high. I just want my kids to be safe and happy. I want to feel secure and ... peaceful, not exhausted and anxious all the time, like I do now. I don't even earn much ... I'm such a fool.

She looked out the car window up at the stars.

Are you out there somewhere or are we all alone in the universe? I thought it was what I'd been waiting for all my life. Thought somehow I'd feel fulfilled – that everything would make sense, I'd know who I am and what I'm for. But my marriage is in the gutter and I don't know how to fix it ... Charlie is who-knows-where in his head and Melanie? Oh, God ... I can't bear the pain. If this attack is because of what I'm doing, it's not worth it, it's really not. I'd rather choose to have safe kids and no ministry.

✖ ✖ ✖

Winter came and went in a grey fog, Grace discovering the rich liturgy and symbolism of her first Anglo-Catholic Christmas. It was Spring before the Street Pastors had finished their training and the time had come for a meeting with the trustees of My Sister's House.

'I'm really not happy about this,' Peter said over Zack's head as they sat round the kitchen table eating boiled eggs and toast. Zack had his toast cut into fingers and was carefully dipping them into his egg yolk.

'Nor am I,' Grace replied, 'but it's got to be done. He's funding Chloe and Val's jobs and he may give us more. Just think what we could do?'

'It's guilt money,' Peter said, taking a sip from his pale blue mug.

'Maybe,' Grace agreed, 'but it's not our place to judge his motives. God will use anyone with all sorts of motives to get His will done. I've got to leave the judging to Him. Please don't go on about it.'

'But what if he does finally remember who you are? What then?'

'Daddy, why are you cross?' Zack asked.

Peter's lips disappeared into a thin line, his jaw muscles clenching.

'Daddy's just worried for mummy, because he loves her,' Grace explained, scooping the last of her egg out of its shell. The edges cracked and caved in as she withdrew the spoon.

'That's right!' Peter said.

'Look if the worst comes to the worst, I can always text you and you can come in and do your thing.'

'My thing?' Peter raised his eyebrows enquiringly.

'You know – what men do – strut their stuff, beat up the bad guy – rescue the damsel in distress.'

'I wouldn't describe you as a damsel in distress,' Peter laughed.

'Glad you're laughing,' Grace smiled.

'What's a damp-cell-in-a-dress?' Zack asked.

※　　※　　※

They met in St Matthew's Church hall, mainly because Grace thought it smelt a lot better than St Stephen's. She really needed to get their PCC to agree a refurb of the church rooms.

Trevor called the meeting to order and opened with the collect of the day. Grace valued the sense of boundaries it gave. It made her feel safer than she knew she really was.

'So,' Trevor began, 'My Sister's House is up and running. Good relations have been established with the police and social services. St Stephen's are supportive of the project, although it is separate. No one knows where the safe house is, but those involved in the project … and so far everyone has stuck to their confidentiality agreement.'

'Yes – it has been a lot of hard work,' Val said, 'but once we started it wasn't as difficult as I thought it might be.'

'Val has been incredible with the admin,' Grace said, smiling at her friend. 'And it's thanks to you, Mr Martin, that we are able to pay her something … and Chloe.'

'Please, call me James,' James Martin said, his tanned skin crinkling round his eyes. His smile was lost on Grace.

'Yes,' Chloe echoed, 'we are indebted to you.'

'No you're not,' James Martin raised his manicured hands. 'It's been something I've wanted to do for a long time, and believe me, it's a privilege.'

'So James, tell us what your proposal is for Street Pastors in the area?' Trevor asked.

'Well, as you know, we've all been through our training,' he looked at Sean, present heart-throb of Mo, who nodded his head, 'It's been really good. We want to start as soon as possible now. We've been walking round our town, looking for the trouble spots and we've found a few. I guess we wanted to partner with you, seeing as you specialise in rescuing women from the sex trade. We would like to think that we could possibly be the first point of contact on the streets for girls caught up in it and even for the clients and traffickers.'

'Sorry,' Grace cut across him, 'did you say the clients and traffickers?'

James Martin leaned his elbows on the table between them, folding his hands in front of his face, 'Yes. As a woman of the cloth, surely you believe that no one is beyond redemption?'

His mid-Atlantic accent annoyed her intensely. Grace felt heat rising up her neck and was glad she had a pashmina around it to hide the red rash that would surely be blotching her skin. 'We are focused on the victims of trafficking, Mr Martin. It would be a conflict of interests for us to have anything to do with those who use them. But if you want to do that, then be our guest,' she leaned back, breathing deeply.

Trevor broke the silence that followed, 'Of course we believe that no one is beyond redemption. That's the whole point of the gospel,' he scratched behind his ear causing several clumps of skin to fall. 'The clients and traffickers aside, James, I think it would be a very good thing to partner with you and your team. What My Sister's House does is behind the scenes and must stay as such. But to have a presence on the street, which would enable us to know what is going on in our own back yard, would be invaluable.'

Mo spoke up, 'Yeah – I agree mate, even about the clients and traffickers.

We're so focused on rescuing the victims, but who's ministering to the a-holes, sorry,' she nodded in Trevor and Grace's direction, 'who use them? If we could help them change, then trafficking wouldn't be such a lucrative business.'

'Exactly,' James said. 'We need to help these men see themselves and see women differently. Our culture is steeped in misogyny ... we've got to address it from every angle.'

Grace was dumbstruck as the conversation flowed around her like treacle. *I hope you know what your getting yourself into?* Peter's voice echoed through her brain again.

It was agreed that the Street Pastors would partner with My Sister's House when they needed help with a sex worker. Any work with clients and traffickers would solely be the Street Pastors' domain, but both churches would support them in prayer.

Grace's head was spinning by the time the meeting ended. She couldn't think straight. In a panic, she emailed Bishop Duncan on her iPhone, asking if she could come and discuss developments with him. She later regretted sending it.

✖ ✖ ✖

'Hello, Grace,' Bishop Duncan smiled. The tenor of his voice soothed her. She wanted to fall into his arms.

'Hi, Bishop Duncan,' she shook his hand leaving it there a little longer than was necessary. She heard Julia cough behind her and walked on into his office, glad of the closing door that separated them.

'Have a seat,' he motioned to a chair. She sat down. He sat opposite her, folding his hands in his lap, 'how are you?'

'I'm okay,' she smiled, feeling foolish. She was having second thoughts, 'When I emailed you I was in a bit of a panic. I'm sorry ... I shouldn't really be wasting your time,' she leaned forward and caught hold of the shoulder strap of her bag that she had just let go of, as if she was about to leave.

'You're here now, Grace. I've set the time aside. So let's talk. Why were you in a panic? Is everything all right at St Stephen's?'

'Yes, everything is going very well at St Stephen's. It's more than a part-time job, as I'm sure you were aware when you suggested it, but I'm coping.

I've even got two people volunteering to do the church admin now … so that's good.'

'I don't think any clergy job could ever be described honestly as part time,' he said. 'So if it's not St Stephen's, is it My Sister's House?'

'Yes … well it's an issue related to it,' she looked down at her hands, suddenly feeling her mouth go dry.

Bishop Duncan waited, his eyes travelling over her from the top of her golden head down to her long, tapering legs. She was wearing a knee length skirt, revealing the toned muscles of her calves. Her ankles were slender and her feet were fine-boned, barely covered by the flat pumps she wore. He raised his folded hands to his chin, steepling his forefingers to his lips.

'We're grateful for the investment the diocese have put into developing and furnishing half of the vicarage.'

He nodded, smiling slightly.

'I don't know whether you are aware, but we have had an influx of more income via a businessman from St Matt's. It's quite substantial – we've been able to pay Chloe something as our counsellor and Val as our part-time administrator.'

'That's good news isn't it?'

'Yes. This man has trained to be a Street Pastor and is heading up a team, which will partner with My Sister's House as our liaison on the streets.'

'Excellent,' Bishop Duncan said.

'The thing is he has suggested that the Street Pastors' team also work with those who use sex workers, both clients and traffickers. He wants to address the issue from more than one angle.'

'What did the trustees make of the suggestion?'

'They were in favour of it.'

'But you're not?'

'No,' Grace looked down at her hands. 'I emailed you in a panic during the meeting.'

'I see. Do you feel it is a conflict of interests?'

'I do,' she said hesitantly.

'I understand that, but I sense there is more to this?' His grey eyes penetrated hers. She was aware she had flattered him with her request to see him so urgently. A red light began to flash on the dashboard of her conscience.

'I ... I ...' she stammered uncharacteristically, 'I don't want to fight him on the issue, seeing as the trustees are in favour. I also don't want to rock the boat in case he withdraws his financial support. I feel responsible for Val and Chloe now. It's not just about what I want – it's their income – their families. But I really feel strongly that users of sex workers and traffickers are a completely different mission field, in which I have very little or no interest at all,' she ended the sentence with some feeling.

Bishop Duncan looked surprised as he verbalised a sudden revelation, 'You've been deeply hurt in the past, haven't you?'

Grace's mouth fell open a fraction. She closed it quickly and looked down at her hands.

Before she could reply he spoke again, 'I'm so sorry Grace ... I shouldn't have asked you that. The thought caught me off guard.'

She shifted in her seat, biting her lip to keep her emotions in check. She wrestled silently, wondering why she felt like a child. He got up, crossed the room and sat next to her, handing her his monogrammed handkerchief. It smelt of lavender and leather. She ran her fingernail along the straight line of the embroidered letter 'D'. 'I'm so sorry Bishop Duncan ...'

'Call me Duncan,' he said gently.

She looked up, faintly aware of the internal flashing red light. The kindness in his eyes was laced with something else she could not read. She raised the handkerchief to her cheek and soaked up the tear that had trickled halfway down it. As she inhaled his scent from the soft fabric, she felt the invisible kite string pull insistently inside her. She ignored it.

He was leaning forward and she could feel the chemistry between them pulling them together. Yearning overpowered self control – she went with it. Their heads were inches apart. Their eyes met. He reached over and took her hand, caressing her palm with his thumb. She looked down at it but didn't withdraw it. When she raised her eyes to his again she understood the thing she hadn't previously been able to read.

Disappointed she gently, but firmly withdrew her hand and began folding the handkerchief. She offered it back to him.

'You keep it,' he said.

'No,' she replied still holding it out to him.

'You might need it.'

'Exactly,' she smiled a little.

When he took it their fingers brushed against each other.

'I shouldn't have come. I'm so sorry for wasting your time,' Grace said.

He leaned back in his chair, raised his hands and lightly ran them over his head. He breathed deeply. When their eyes met again they were candid, both acknowledging what had transpired between them.

She leaned down and picked up her bag. 'I'm going to go now,' she said firmly.

'Yes,' resignation saturated his voice.

She stood up. He rose slowly with her, pushing himself up off the scrolled arms of the chair. She turned and walked to the door, put her hand on the door handle, but turned back to him one last time. 'I won't bother you again,' she said firmly.

'Oh, but you will,' he smiled sadly, 'in here,' he tapped the side of his head.

'Our spiritual directors are in for a treat,' Grace began turning the handle.

'Yes indeed ...' he sighed. 'Goodbye, Grace,' finality ringing in each syllable.

'Goodbye,' she opened the door and faced Julia.

❋ ❋ ❋

'We take every thought captive and make it obedient to Christ.'

'I don't know how, not with this. I have never dealt with this before. I am tormented!' Bishop Duncan exclaimed pressing his fingers into the corners of his closed eyes.

'Now you know how the rest of us mortals feel most of the time,' said the nun with a wry smile.

'Why have I never struggled with this before now?'

'Perhaps the stakes have never been so high,' she said, rolling a Rosary bead between her finger and thumb.

'What do you mean?' he asked, exasperation ploughing furrows between his eyebrows.

'Do you not remember those verses that came to you some time ago? You were warned that you are in the middle of a spiritual battle. The powers of this world, your flesh and the devil are working together against the accomplishment of the will of God.'

'Yes … yes … I remember,' he leaned his head back and looked up at the gothic window. The sky was grey outside. 'So you think I am a casualty of war?'

'I do,' she nodded, moving to the next Rosary bead. 'I think the work that Grace is embarking on is a great threat to the kingdom of darkness. If either of you fails to surrender your unmet needs to Christ, darkness will win the day.'

'Teach me how to take these thoughts captive, Sister,' he pleaded.

'You must take each one to the cross in prayer. You must see yourself come to the cross, bringing each weakness, each longing, each unmet need. See yourself rise up and take your place on the cross with him. Let the nails be driven into your flesh with him. Die with him there and then be laid in a tomb with him. Then, and only on his leading, rise with him and live by his Spirit the new life he gives you,' her face shone as she spoke.

Bishop Duncan's face did not reflect it. He looked depressed. 'I know these things, sister, but I have no desire to let these thoughts and feelings die. I want to keep them alive because they make *me* feel alive! She is everything I never knew was possible.' As he spoke his features became animated, 'Love has been aroused and has woken … desire has found me and will not let me go …'

The nun shook her head, 'Quoting scripture doesn't make it all right … you really do have it bad,' she smiled affectionately at him.

He looked bleak, 'I know.'

'You must be ruthless with yourself, Duncan, or you will fall as so many have before you. And if you fall you will take many with you. The impact will be devastating. The enemy will strike and scatter the flock. You must die to yourself.'

He nodded grimly.

※　※　※

On returning home, Bishop Duncan took a small nail and hammered it through the handkerchief into wood. It took only three blows of the hammer. He picked up the crucifix and hung it back up on the wall opposite his desk. *That will do for a start …* he thought.

Then he knelt before it and began to pray, *Father, renew my mind. Where I have made unhealthy connections to Grace, come and rewire me. Eliminate all negative and unhealthy thoughts and replace them with your truth.*

Untangle my emotions. Enlarge my capacity to receive love from you.

Help me love Wendy.

He knelt in silence until Julia disturbed him for an afternoon cup of tea.

❋ ❋ ❋

Charlie's computer had frozen. He didn't want to wait any more for it, so ran down the stairs to his dad's study, shouting, 'Is it okay if I use your computer, Dad? Mine's frozen.'

Mark was in the living room playing a Playstation game with Josh. Chloe was on duty that evening at My Sister's House and Melanie was in her room studying.

Charlie wasn't perturbed by the lack of response from his dad. It wasn't unusual. He sat down at the desk and turned on the computer. He went to Google and typed in the name of the designer he wanted. Up came websites with images of his designs. Charlie clicked on one site and scrolled through. He went back and clicked on another website, and another until he found the image he wanted. He printed it off.

Then he went to history to delete the websites that he didn't want his dad to know he had been on. Charlie looked in surprise at the list his dad had visited that day. Out of curiosity he clicked on one site. Instantly the screen was filled with a shocking image. Charlie could hear his heartbeat thudding in his ears. He stared at the screen, a cacophony of feelings assailing him. He reached out and shut down the website, blinking several times. He left the study in a daze.

He didn't tell anyone what he'd seen.

❋ ❋ ❋

Grace couldn't tell Peter, not until she had a better handle on what had happened herself. After putting Zack to bed and loading the dishwasher she retreated to her study. Peter was out at a business dinner in London. He would be home late.

She sent her mentor an email asking to meet with her as soon as possible. She then opened her bible to the book of Acts and placed her hands on it, closing her eyes. 'Please speak to me through your word, Lord. I need to see things as you see them. Please give me understanding, Holy Spirit.' She was silent for a while and then read chapters nine through eleven again.

She looked up at her blue-gold icon.

Saul, Ananias, Tabitha, Cornelius and Peter – they all chose to live – Tabitha especially. To really live, rather than accept things as they were.

Saul let go his past world view for a diametrically opposed one. So did Ananias … he risked his life and as a result brought life to Saul.

Peter didn't accept the finality of death, he chose to risk looking like a fool and prayed for a dead body to come alive. Tabitha must have agreed to live too?

Cornelius chose to trust a vision and to hope against custom and tradition. His whole family received life as a result. And Peter? He had to choose between the old way of doing things and trust the vision he'd had and the understanding he was being given, risking everything he held dear.

Lord, I don't want to go on being hijacked by things from my past. Please help me access your life … help me understand what happened today. Why did I … we …?

Into the silence came an image of her father in his three piece, pinstriped suit. Despite the emotional reaction it evoked, she stayed with it. She studied her memory of him and allowed the emotions to wash over her in waves. She realised the feelings were coming from a younger and younger self. As she waited she seemed to settle at about two or three as she looked at him. Such a strong yearning for his attention overwhelmed her. She saw him playing with her brothers, laughing in rough-and-tumble on the floor. But when he looked at her he was serious, aloof … uncertain? She recognised the yearning … the need to please him … it was how she had felt today. It was so strong – a two year old's longing to be noticed, loved and wanted by daddy.

Then she was moving forward in age and seeing the developing relationship between them. He had not known how to relate to a girl other than in a sexualised way. The intimacy that formed was warped by him but also by her deep yearning for his attention, and her attempts to gain it by trying to please him.

That's it ... my part, Lord ... forgive me ... cleanse me of this driving need to please. Heal me of my yearning ... for the corruption it allows to come in like a sluice-gate! I choose your love for me instead. You have always had eyes for me; you are my perfect father; you don't relate to me in a sexualised way ... heal me of this, Lord ... satisfy me with good things ... forgive me for looking to Bishop Duncan. I turn to you ... I choose you ... your life in all its fullness.

She sat in silence for a time, eyes closed, heart thudding in her chest. Then into her mind came an image of Peter. She began giving thanks for him and blessing him.

Forgive me for comparing them ... you knew what you were doing when you gave him to me ... he will never be a father figure to me ... you made sure of that ... he is my equal ... my partner ... I can't look to him for these needs to be met ... I have to look to you. You are a jealous God ... thank you for him, for who he is, for where he's at with you. Thank you that despite his lack of faith, he is so supportive of mine. I honour him for that ... for never thinking he could compete with you ... where as Bishop Duncan was ... the sin of presumption ... of ego ... oh, God ... have mercy ...

After a while she went and made herself a cup of coffee and then opened her laptop and began writing:

They arrived in Damascus after several days' journey along the trade route that connected Jerusalem with the far east. The cypress trees that lined the paved road cast long shadows in front of them as they approached the Djabiya Gate on the western side of the city. The Barada river flowed smoothly to their left. Mary watched enviously as a group of women with their children collected water in earthen jars. She was so absorbed in longing that she stumbled over an uneven paving, only stopping herself from falling by catching hold of Lila.

'Mary!' Lila reacted crossly, 'I nearly dropped Joshua.'

'Sorry, Lila,' Mary gasped, 'I tripped.'

'We're all tired. Let's not take it out on each other,' Jair said, taking Joshua into his arms. 'We're nearly there now.'

Lila fixed her head scarf, giving herself time to regain her good humour, then looked at Mary and asked, 'Are you hurt?'

'No,' Mary replied, a faint smile hovering somewhere near her lips. 'You saved me from that.'

It was the first time Lila had seen Mary come close to smiling since they'd left Jerusalem. Annoyance forgotten, she hugged her.

Mary could feel herself about to burst into tears. She bowed her head and fought the wave of grief.

Jair put Joshua on the cart beside Anna, amongst their belongings.

'I think the Jewish sector is beyond the theatre, further into the centre of the city,' Lazarus said.

'Yes, off to the right from Straight Street. It shouldn't be too hard to find,' Jair took the donkey's reins in hand and led the way.

They went past the theatre on their right, with many surrounding stalls selling carvings of the gods, sweetmeats, fruit, jewellery and other bric-a-brac. Artemis, Athena and Dionysus were among the gods that Jair recognised. He wondered as he had done many times, how people could worship such things. How did they possibly satisfy the human heart?

They eventually found the Jewish quarter and after asking several people for directions, found Jair's uncle's house which was situated next door to a synagogue. Jair knocked on the door, trying to remember what his uncle looked like. It had been many years since he had seen him.

A man with a snowy white beard that reached down to the middle of his chest opened the door. 'Can I help you?' he asked.

'Uncle Ananias?' Jair asked in reply.

'Who are you?' the elderly man squinted his eyes, searching Jair's face.

'I'm Jair, your brother Nathaniel's eldest son. We last met after his death.'

'Jair? Is it really you?' He opened his arms and embraced him, kissing him on both cheeks. He held him at arm's length and then hugged him again, 'What brings you all this way? And who are all these?' he peered over his shoulder. 'Ah, don't answer yet ... come ...' he gestured to the women, 'come in and rest while I show the men where to tether the donkey.'

He led Jair and Lazarus down a side alley and round to the

back of the house. He opened a small door in the wall with a large, heavy key. It swung into a courtyard, one wall of which was covered in purple bougainvillea. Together they unloaded and then unhitched the cart from the donkey's back. Ananias brought some vegetable peelings from his kitchen for the weary beast who was already drinking from the water trough where his own donkey stood. Then slowly, one by one they carried bundles of their possessions indoors.

'Just leave them there for now,' Ananias ordered excitedly. 'First let me wash your feet,' he scurried into the kitchen and quickly returned with a bowl, towel and a jug of water. He washed the children and women's feet first and then Jair and Lazarus's. Everyone sat silently as this ritual was carried out. Ananias eventually stood up beaming at them. 'How wonderful to have family here!' he declared.

'Where is my aunt?' Jair asked tentatively.

'She went to her rest three years ago now,' sadness cast a shadow across Ananias' features.

'I am so sorry,' Jair bowed his head.

'It is the way of all things,' sighed the old man. 'But let me complete your welcome ...' he chased the sadness away with a wave of his hand as he disappeared into the kitchen again returning with a jar of olive oil. He poured a little on all their heads. They humbly received his blessing.

'I have little in the way of food – some figs, olives and bread ...' he looked worried.

'Please don't worry about that,' Lila interrupted him. 'We have provisions too. We have hummus and dried peppers and grapes. We'll have a feast!' she smiled, already liking him.

'This is Lila, my wife,' Jair introduced her and the others after her. He left the children until the end. 'This is Anna – Anna, this is your great uncle.'

Anna smiled at him, 'Your name sounds like mine,' she tucked her chin down and peered up at him shyly.

'So it does,' he replied kindly.

'And this is Joshua.'

'What an excellent name! He looks like you,' Ananias cupped the boy's chin in his hand.

'Yes ...' Jair exchanged glances with Lila and said no more.

❊ ❊ ❊

Ananias had three bedrooms. Lila and Jair took the largest on the top floor, which led out onto the flat roof. The children were glad to share it with them. Mary and Martha shared a room and Lazarus shared Ananias's room, where there were two beds. Over the next few days, they told Ananias of all that had happened in Jerusalem. He had heard of Jesus, but not very much. Damascus was a long way away. The trouble surrounding that name had not touched the sizeable community of Jews there as yet.

They talked into the night and as he listened the Holy Spirit came upon him. He quickly embraced the good news they brought. Lazarus and Jair baptised him in the river the next morning and after they had laid their hands on him, he was filled with the Holy Spirit and spoke in a language that made Anna giggle. She had never known any grandparents or relatives ... she quickly formed an attachment to her great uncle and followed him wherever he went.

Ananias introduced Jair and Lazarus to the synagogue and invited them to speak. Lazarus's story had them spellbound. Jair continued to show them, through the scriptures, that Jesus fulfilled all the prophecies foretelling the long awaited Messiah. Many believed and were baptised in the Barada river. It was not long before news reached Jerusalem that the new 'Jesus Movement' had spread as far as Damascus.

Back in Jerusalem, Saul was still breathing out murderous threats against the followers of Jesus. Backed by Aaron, he went to the high priest and asked for letters to the synagogues in Damascus, so that if he found any there who belonged to the Way, as many had begun calling it, whether men or women, he might take them as prisoners to Jerusalem.

As Saul was nearing Damascus, he suddenly stopped in his tracks, his hands flying to his eyes. He cried out and fell to his knees.

Surprised, the guards travelling with him reached out to him asking him what was wrong. Then they heard a sound, that could only be described as a thunderclap, but there wasn't a cloud in sight. They all fell to their knees in terror.

❋ ❋ ❋

Blinding light flashed around Saul as he knelt on the ground. He heard a voice say to him, 'Saul, Saul, why do you persecute me?'

Terrified Saul asked, 'Who are you?'

'I am Jesus, whom you are persecuting,' replied the voice. 'Now get up and go into the city, and you will be told what you must do.'

The men travelling with Saul were speechless; they'd heard the noise but hadn't seen anything. Saul was trembling as he got up from the ground, but when he opened his eyes he could see nothing. Terrified, he was led by hand into Damascus by the guards that were with him. For three days he was blind, and did not eat or drink anything.

The news travelled fast through the city's synagogues that Saul had come to hunt down followers of the Way.

❋ ❋ ❋

Ananias was meditating on a passage from the prophet Isaiah, sitting in the shade afforded by his bougainvillea ... *Fear not for I have redeemed you, I have summoned you by name, you are mine ...*

Lila and the children were taking an afternoon nap upstairs. Lazarus had convinced a reluctant Mary to come with him, Jair and Martha to the market to buy food. The house was quiet again, like it had been before they had come. He'd been so glad of the company at first, but had found in the last few days that he missed the solitude. He savoured this rare moment of quiet. Eyes closed, hands resting in his lap, palms up. He thrilled again and again knowing now that the Spirit of God indwelt him. He could hardly believe it ... yet somehow he did. He worshipped in the new tongue he had received. Consciousness of the Lord's presence grew to the point that he wasn't sure he could bear the beauty of it.

Ananias ... Ananias!

'Yes, Lord,' he answered. He wasn't sure if he'd heard an audible voice or not.

The voice continued, *Go to the house of Judas on Straight Street and ask for the man from Tarsus named Saul, for he is praying. In a vision he has seen a man named Ananias come and place his hands on him to restore his sight.*

'Lord,' Ananias faltered, 'I have heard many reports about this man and all the harm he has done to your saints in Jerusalem. He has come here with authority from the chief priests to arrest all who call on your name.'

But the voice said to him, *Go! This man is my chosen instrument to carry my name before the Gentiles and their kings and before the people of Israel. I will show him how much he must suffer for my name.*

The key rattled in the courtyard door, bringing him back into the present. He opened his eyes in time to see Jair walk through the low door, head bowed, carrying a basket of vegetables. The others filed in behind him, each with their purchases.

'Are you all right, uncle?' Jair dropped the basket and ran the few paces to his side, anxiety making one eyebrow over his sharp nose.

'Yes ... I'm fine ... I think ...'

'You've gone as pale as your beard!' declared his nephew.

'The Lord spoke to me ... in a vision,' his old voice broke in awe.

'What did he say?' Lazarus knelt down beside him with Martha and Mary close behind him.

Ananias scanned their faces slowly, returning to rest on Mary's.

'He told me that I am to go and lay hands on Saul ... yes,' he breathed seeing her pupils dilate with shock, 'the same man who approved your Stephen's death.'

Stunned silence followed.

'Are you sure?' Jair asked, feeling guilty for casting doubt on his uncle's account.

'I told Him!' he expostulated, 'I told Him that I'd heard the reports about Saul and that I knew he'd come here to harm us.'

Mary backed up against the wall of the courtyard. 'You will lead him to us ... he will kill us all! We must leave ... now!' Panic lit the touchpaper of her grief. Martha could see it spreading quickly into every fibre of her sister's being.

'Mary,' Lazarus said, 'if it truly is the Lord who has spoken to Ananias, then all will be well.'

'No,' Mary replied clutching at her throat; her breathing escalating; her eyes growing wide. 'I can't breathe,' she gasped.

Martha was beside her, holding her. 'She's suffered too much trauma, Lazarus. Let's get her to her bed. Jair, bring her up some wine.'

'You must do what the Lord has told you, no matter what,' Jair returned his attention to Ananias after they had gone.

'I know,' said the old man. 'I will go now, before conviction and courage leave me.'

'The Lord is with you,' Jair embraced him as they stood together.

※　※　※

He knew only one Judas who lived on Straight Street, overlooking the fifty foot wide colonnaded thoroughfare. He was a strict adherent to the school of Pharisees and was a synagogue ruler; not the synagogue Ananias attended, for it was too liberal.

He made his way through the Jewish quarter, greeting those he knew. He arrived at the house and on entering was led to the room Saul occupied.

Judas did not hide his surprise at Ananias's arrival. He knew he had become a follower of the Way. He knew that many Jews in several synagogues across the city had believed the testimony of Ananias's nephew and Lazarus, the man claiming to have been raised from the dead. His story had spread like wildfire from synagogue to synagogue. Judas had been very firm with his congregations, that they would not be inviting these men to speak.

Ananias stood at the bedroom door staring at the back of the man he assumed must be Saul. His slight frame was bent in prayer, his hands raised in the customary way. Judas cleared his throat, 'Excuse me, Saul, there is someone here to see you.'

'Is it Ananias?' Saul asked turning slightly in their direction.

'Yes ... yes it is. How did you know?' Judas was puzzled.

'The Lord told me he was coming,' Saul said.

Ananias took courage in tremulous hands and stepped into the room. He placed them on Saul's head, 'Brother Saul, the Lord – Jesus – who appeared to you on the road as you were coming here – has sent me so that you may see again and be filled with the Holy Spirit.'

Before Judas had time to react, Saul exclaimed, 'My eyes ... I can see!' In his hands lay something like scales that had fallen from his eyes. He scrutinised them momentarily then stood and turned to Ananias, desperation in his voice. 'What must I do?' he asked.

'Repent and be baptised,' Ananias answered.

'I have been repenting these three days,' Saul said.

'He has not touched food or water,' agreed Judas. 'He has done nothing but pray in this room.'

Judas watched as Ananias baptised Saul in the bath. It was such a strange sight, so contrary to what Judas had expected. When Saul came out of the water and Ananias prayed a blessing upon him, the Holy Spirit descended in so powerful a way, that Judas ran from the room.

It was midnight before Ananias returned home, praising God.

※   ※   ※

Martha and Lazarus spoke at length with Jair and Lila. 'We cannot stay here. Ananias said himself that Saul wants to come and learn from Jair. Mary is far too distraught,' Martha said, 'she would not cope knowing he was here.'

And so it was that the friends parted company. The sisters and their brother gathered up their few possessions and, accepting Jair's donkey and cart as a gift, they left Damascus that morning.

'Where will you go?' Lila asked sadly, watching Martha tie things into bundles.

'I'm not sure,' Martha replied. 'Lazarus is talking of Caesarea. We have distant relatives there on our mother's side.'

'That's three or four days' journey, Martha.' It seemed like the other side of the world to Lila.

'I know. On the way we will stay with Peter's family again, in Galilee, I think.'

'Is she in any fit state to travel?' Lila wrestled the sense of loss already gripping her at their imminent departure.

'I don't know ... but we have to try. She cannot stay here. She will go out of her mind if she sees that man.'

Lila nodded, accepting there was nothing she could do to stop her friends from leaving.

Mary was not herself at all as she said goodbye. It seemed that with the death of Stephen, all the other traumas of her young life had become too much to sustain. Darkness had swamped the love-light she'd found in Jesus; in restored relationships; even the gift of the Spirit bestowed on her at Pentecost. Her mind seemed broken beyond repair.

Lila held Mary in her arms, rocking ever so gently. Mary rested there as if she were in a semi-conscious stupor. Bring her back to us Lord Jesus. Heal her mind. Bring us together again, Lila prayed as she continued to hold her dearest friend.

Lila watched them go. They are my sisters ... my true family ... Lila spent the rest of the day in tears. Saul came to the house that evening, but Lila did not come down from her room.

He spent several days in Damascus, discussing the scriptures with Jair and Ananias. Others crept out of the woodwork, seeing he did not put them in chains. Gatherings grew at their house and in the synagogue that met next door.

Eventually Lila plucked up the courage to meet him. She expected him to be like Aaron and was surprised to find that he was not. He was a short man, with an unassuming manner. She immediately sensed in him a tenderness that surprised her. It was incongruous with the stories she had heard about him.

Listening to him she realised that, fresh from encounter with Jesus, his heart was cut wide open. The shame and grief he expressed for the persecution he had inflicted on followers of Jesus was genuine. 'I can never forget ... never erase from my mind the terror I have seen in my fellow brothers' and sisters' eyes,' he said one night. 'Worse are the memories of those who praised the Lord even while I watched them being beaten, stoned and imprisoned. I mocked them ... mocked Him,' his voice dropped to a whisper.

'Do you remember Stephen?' Lila couldn't stop herself.

Saul looked at her, screwing up his eyes. She had noticed he often did this. She wondered if it was an after-effect of having been blinded for a time. 'Stephen – from the Greek speaking synagogue?'

'Yes,' Lila replied, the back of her throat burning.

Alarmed, Jair cleared his throat and was about to speak, but Saul held up a hand. 'Yes, I remember him,' he admitted quietly. 'His face was like the face of an angel. I will never forget it.'

There was a pregnant silence, then Lila cried, 'How could you?'

Saul sat very still, his eyes down.

'Lila – you mustn't ...'

'No, Jair, let her speak. Do not defend me,' Saul raised his eyes to Lila's.

'Nothing I say to you will ever make amends for the pain I have caused. Was he a relative?' his eyes glistened.

'No,' replied Lila. 'My friend, Mary – my sister – is a broken woman. She was betrothed to him. They were to be married,' she struggled to control her voice.

'Is she here? Would she speak with me?'

'No. She has gone. She is out of her mind with grief. Her family could not risk her meeting you.'

Saul buried his head in his hands and wept.

Lila watched.

Slowly something changed inside her. She later told Jair it was like catching the smell of freshly baked bread on fresh air. It was mercy. She stepped into Saul's sandals; felt how he must have felt; saw through his eyes; thought what he must have thought. She understood why he'd done it, how zealous he'd been to prove he was a true Hebrew. It was a Divine work ... she told Jair later... she could never have experienced those things of her own volition.

'I will pray for her. What is her name?' Saul asked eventually.

'Mary,' Lila felt she was giving him something precious, as

precious as the worship Mary had poured out on Jesus' feet all that time ago.

'Mary,' he repeated quietly. He nodded his head slowly. Then he turned to Jair, 'I want to return to Jerusalem and share with a friend what has happened to me. I want him to know the love of God that has been shed abroad in my heart and mind,' he sniffed and wiped his face with both hands. 'Perhaps Aaron will listen to me. If he were to turn to the Lord, the Sanhedrin might be influenced,' Saul wiped his hands on his prayer shawl.

'Aaron?' Jair and Lila echoed in unison.

'Yes ... he was my mentor, my sponsor ... a member of the Sanhedrin. It was he who enabled me to have the influence I had.' Saul looked from one to the other, still wiping his eyes intermittently.

'You need to know that we have a history with Aaron.' Jair said.

And so Jair began to tell him their story, with Lila interjecting details here and there. When they had finished Saul was silent. Eventually he asked if they might pray together for Aaron and for Mary.

※　※　※

Saul began to preach in the synagogues of Damascus that Jesus is the Son of God. All those who heard him were astonished and asked, 'Isn't he the man who raised havoc in Jerusalem among those who call on this name? And hasn't he come here to take them as prisoners to the chief priests?' Yet Saul grew more and more powerful and baffled the Jews living in Damascus by proving that Jesus was the Messiah from the scriptures.

After many days had gone by, there was a conspiracy among the Jews to kill him, but Saul learnt of their plan. Day and night members of Judas's synagogue kept close watch on the city gates in order to kill him. But Jair and the other believers took him by night and lowered him in a basket through an opening in the city wall.

Then he headed for Jerusalem.

※　※　※

Lazarus and his sisters settled in Caesarea with their relatives. Starting all over again, building up their business from scratch, was hard at first. It was made harder by Mary's inability to engage with life. She became a recluse who seldom spoke. They prayed with and for her regularly but to no apparent avail.

Mary spent her days trapped in a dark spiral of thoughts that revolved around Stephen's dead body. In utter despair, she could not break free from the bleak place she found herself in. All the sadness and disappointments of the past seemed to be manifest in that one image of his beaten and bloodied body. It was as though she was caught in a current and was being carried along into an ever decreasing, spiralling whirlpool. Times of worship with the believers who soon began gathering in their home, walks by the sea, outings to Caesarea's exotic markets – none of these things seemed to be able to pull her out of it.

One Friday evening a tanner named Simon came up from Joppa to share news from the community of believers who lived there. He shared with them how he had come to faith through kindness shown his newly widowed mother by a disciple named Tabitha. He went on to tell how many had come to faith through this woman. She was always doing good and helping the poor, especially widows. The number of believers in Joppa had grown significantly because of her ministry. She was a young, single woman, who had devoted her life to serving the Lord. Contrary to cultural norms she had chosen celibacy rather than marriage in order to focus completely on the Lord's work.

But she'd become sick suddenly. He asked the fellowship of believers in Caesarea to pray for her. He also told them that the apostle Peter was in Lydda and that he'd been used by God to heal a paralytic who had been bedridden for eight years. Many were turning to the Lord there as a result.

After earnest prayers of intercession and praise, the meeting came to an end. Martha leaned over and whispered to Lazarus, 'Let's take Mary to Joppa. Maybe, even on her sick bed, this Tabitha could help her overcome her grief? Maybe we could see Peter too? We could stay with the believers in Joppa tomorrow and then travel on to Lydda the next day. If not through Tabitha, perhaps the Lord will give the gift of healing she so desperately needs through him?'

Lazarus looked at his sister appreciatively, 'Yes ... It would be so good to see Mary happy again. It would be good to see Peter too after all this time. What has it been, two years?' he asked, stroking his silver beard. Martha had noticed he was getting more forgetful in his old age.

'More, I think,' Martha replied, graciously sweeping over the detail.

'It is wonderful to hear how the Lord is using Peter so powerfully to heal the sick,' Lazarus was thoughtful. 'Our brother Simon might appreciate our company on the return journey too?' Lazarus's eyes were bright.

Martha didn't reply. She went to talk with Mary, while Lazarus went to talk with Simon.

They left early the next morning.

※　※　※

As they approached the house, they heard wailing coming from an upstairs room. Mary grew agitated at the sound. Simon excused himself and ran up the outside stairwell that led to the roof and the room situated there. They followed him.

There placed on the low bed was the body of a young woman. Her skin was pale; Mary could see the blue veins through it. Her lips were grey as were the dark rings under her eyes. Her hair was swept back onto the pillow. It was clear that someone had painstakingly arranged it in that way. It looked damp, as if it had just been washed. There were eight or nine widows, dressed in black, kneeling round the bed weeping and praying. It slowly dawned on Mary that this was not just a sick person – it was a dead body. Panic began to constrict her throat.

'When did she ...?' their travelling companion could not say the word.

An elderly woman broke off her crying long enough to say, 'This morning ... she left us this morning ... we begged her not to go, but she couldn't hear us. The sickness took her,' she began to sob again.

Mary wanted to run from the room. Martha sensed it and held her firmly by the hand.

'We must call Peter ... he's in Lydda ...' Simon began turning toward the door.

'We've already sent two men to fetch him,' said another younger woman kneeling on the other side of the bed. 'We've been waiting for him. He should be here soon.'

As she spoke a young boy ran into the room, 'He's here ... he's coming up now.'

Simon and Lazarus went out onto the roof to meet him.

'Lazarus! What brings you here?' Peter cried on seeing his old friend. He embraced him in a bear hug.

'We heard you were near. We wanted you to pray for Mary. She has been destroyed by grief since Stephen's death and nothing we do or say seems to break through her despair,' Lazarus said all this quietly in Peter's ear while still embracing him. He didn't want to distract his grieving hosts with his own family's concerns.

'Is she here?' Peter asked drawing back and looking over Lazarus' shoulder.

'Yes, with Martha, but you must see to Tabitha first,' Lazarus said, barely hiding the anticipation he felt.

Peter turned to Simon, 'Do you know that Jesus raised this man from the dead?'

Simon stared at Lazarus and then Peter, 'No ... he never said ...'

'Yes ... he'd been dead four days! Came out in his grave clothes and face cloth still in place!' Peter chuckled. 'What a day that was!' Peter clapped Lazarus on the back, making him cough.

'It's true, Simon. Ask my sisters,' Lazarus smiled broadly.

They led Peter into the room. The widows rose to their feet; several ran to him. Others showed him robes and other clothing that Tabitha had made while she was still with them. After listening to them and consoling them as best he could, he sent them out. 'Leave me with her for a time,' he asked. 'Not you,' he said to Mary, Martha and Lazarus. 'You stay with me and pray.'

When the room was quiet, he knelt down beside the bed and

began to pray. Lazarus followed suit; Martha pulled Mary down with her. Mary gazed dumbly at Tabitha's body as memories of Stephen's lacerated, bruised and beaten body superimposed themselves over the present reality. Horror and despair choked her; death had won; she'd been a fool to ever believe in life.

Then suddenly the memory of her brother coming out of his grave flooded her mind. She had not thought of it for so long, it shocked her. Following it came the memory of standing in dawn light, watching Mary Magdalene grieving outside the empty tomb. Then Jesus there ... between them ... calling her by name ... Mary ... Mary ... Mary ...

Peter turned towards the dead woman and said, 'Tabitha, get up.'

Mary looked from Peter's face to the pale face on the bed, holding her breath. Get up ... get up ... leave death behind you ... choose life ... life ... life ...

A flush crept up Tabitha's neck, turning her cheeks rosy. Her eyes fluttered open, settling on Peter's face, her lips turned pink as a smile began curving them. She sat up.

Mary dragged air into her lungs, as if she too were coming alive. She was starving for life, suddenly desperate for it.

Peter took Tabitha by the hand and helped her to her feet. Mary and her siblings rose to theirs with her.

'Simon!' called Peter, 'Come and see.'

Simon came to the door with two distraught widows, a pensive expression in their eyes. The women screamed at what they saw and ran into the room, leaving Simon standing dumbfounded at the door.

'Tabitha! Tabitha!' they shrieked throwing their arms round her and kissing her.

Simon – astonished – joyful – speechless, turned and ran out to the wall that edged the roof shouting down to the others below. 'She's alive! She's alive! Praise the Lord, she's alive!'

There was a stampede up the stairwell.

※ ※ ※

Colours seemed brighter, sounds seemed clearer, sun on skin seemed warmer. Mary kept stopping to pick wild flowers as they made their way back to Caesarea. Martha and Lazarus didn't mind that it slowed their progress. They were only glad to have her back from the grip of dark despair. She showed them each flower she picked, joyfully poring over detail of petal and scent. It was as if she had never seen them before.

As they were nearing Caesarea another traveller came alongside them. Lazarus realised who it was first, 'Philip!' he exclaimed. The sun was sinking low in the sky as they reunited with their old friend. They had little time to make it home before dark. 'You must come and stay with us!' Martha insisted, 'Or have you already got plans?'

'No ... I have been travelling slowly up the coast these past few years, preaching the gospel in every town since we parted company. Recently I sensed God calling me to settle in Caesarea, but I had no idea where. I have been praying as I've been walking that he would lead me ... and he has!' he beamed.

'Praise the Lord,' declared Lazarus.

'Where are you coming from?' he asked, glancing Mary's way.

Martha answered, 'We've been in Joppa, with Peter. The Lord used him so powerfully ...'

'Yes,' interrupted Lazarus excitedly, 'We were there when he raised a woman from the dead!'

'Lazarus! I wanted to tell him!' Martha looked at her brother with a mixture of affection and annoyance for stealing her thunder.

'Sorry, Martha, I couldn't help it. Resurrection life is still pumping furiously through my veins!' Lazarus smiled apologetically.

'What happened?' Philip asked, intrigued.

As they walked into the town they told him their story, in turn. It was dark when they reached home. Philip was acutely aware that Mary had not spoken once. When they entered the courtyard, she quietly went to fetch water with which to wash their feet. When she took his right foot in her hands and began washing away the dust of the journey, she looked up. Their eyes met for the first time and she smiled.

※　※　※

Mary woke the next morning, thrilled at the absence of dread. She sat up in bed, glad to be alive.

She surprised Martha by appearing in the kitchen just as the sun was coming up. Normally she didn't appear until mid-morning. Martha smiled and said nothing.

They carried out the morning chores together in companionable silence. Somehow the smell of baking bread was more wonderful than Mary could remember. Her mouth was watering by the time they sat to eat breakfast together with Lazarus and Philip. She had forgotten what it was like to enjoy food.

The conversation flowed easily between them as Philip regaled them with stories of his ministry along the coast. Martha and Lazarus rejoiced at the change in their sister. Philip wanted to know what shared secret they were smiling about.

'Things have been very different for us,' Martha spoke first. 'Since we saw you in Damascus, Mary had not been able to shake off the effects of trauma and grief.'

Mary looked at her sister, 'I'm so sorry,' she said.

'It was out of your control, Mary – out of our control, wasn't it?' Martha looked to Lazarus.

'Yes ... we don't really understand ... but it seems to me that the many traumas Mary had experienced in her young life overwhelmed her on the death of Stephen. It has taken these years resting here in Caesarea to recover. There is a time for everything, and a season for every activity under heaven,' he quoted from Ecclesiastes. '... It was Mary's time to mourn. Perhaps it is now her time to dance?' he said with a twinkle in his eye.

Mary looked down self-consciously as Philip turned his gaze upon her.

He had dreamed of her often over the years, unable to forget her beautiful face and passionate nature. Several times in different places the fellowship of believers had tried to matchmake him with women from among them, but always something had held him back. He knew now it had been hope: hope that the Lord would give Mary to him someday, somehow, somewhere.

✳ ✳ ✳

Mary observed Philip over the next months from a friendly, but polite distance. She had no desire to become emotionally entangled again with anyone. She knew he had feelings for her, had known since before Stephen had died, but she felt no reciprocal interest.

She visited Tabitha in Joppa several times, considering joining her and the growing number of celibate sisters who had gathered to her since her resurrection. They had extended their good works to rescuing women from the sex trade, plied openly in the main seaport, which served Jerusalem and all of Judea.

As she met some of these women, she was reminded of her former self, and felt fresh gratitude for Lila and Jair taking her in. Caesarea had a similar problem with the sex trade. She discussed with Tabitha whether they might partner together, sending some of the sisters up to live in Caesarea to start a similar work. Most were widows. Mary considered herself a widow in many ways and felt a deep bond with them.

She spent much time in prayer and in studying the scriptures with Lazarus. This also meant that she saw a lot more of Philip than she cared for. He had grown so much in character and in his understanding of scripture that although Lazarus was his senior, he sought Philip's counsel often.

Reluctantly Mary had to admit to herself that Philip was a fine teacher and evangelist. A fine man in fact – compassionate, wise, incisive. The years had knocked the rough edges off him. Any woman would be blessed to have him as a husband. The church that met in their home had doubled in size since his arrival. To her annoyance she sometimes found herself wondering what it would be like to kiss him.

She discussed her idea about developing a work among the trafficked women in Caesarea with Martha, Lazarus and Philip. They were unanimous in their support. Mary and Martha began to visit the area down near the harbour where the trade was plied.

Martha was disturbed by what she saw. Ignorance had kept a veil drawn over her understanding of her sister's horrific past. However now Martha knew for herself what Mary must have been through. She spent many days in tearful prayer.

The whole church got behind the idea and soon Mary was placing young girls, who had responded to the gospel, with families. She oversaw the practicalities of helping them adjust to normal life, and spent hours teaching them and praying with them.

Eventually Tabitha sent several of the sisters up from Joppa to help them. One of them was a six year old named Junia. Tabitha had taken her in when her mother died in childbirth. She had taught her about Jesus and loved her as a daughter. However in response to a vision Tabitha sent her with the others to Mary. She wrote saying she believed God wanted Junia to be trained by Mary, asking if she would seek God for confirmation. If Mary thought it seemed right, she asked that she adopt her into her family.

As they joined Mary in prayer with the rescued girls, delivering them from tormenting, unclean spirits and healing their minds, emotions and bodies of the effects of abuse and slavery, Mary prayerfully observed Junia. Even though she was so young, the Holy Spirit seemed to move powerfully through her when she prayed for the girls. It wasn't long before, after prayer and discussion with the others of her household, Junia became part of their family.

Eventually the church bought a beautiful limestone villa down near the harbour, where the sisters established their community. This became the centre of operations for the ministry. There were several rooms for girls to live in temporarily, until they could place them with a family of believers. There was a large room that they used for holding teaching sessions and times of worship. Clothing, food and medicine were distributed from there along with the good news of Jesus.

As the church and the ministry grew, Mary grew closer to Philip unawares. It was only when he returned south to Azotus for several months, to strengthen the church he had planted there, that she realised she had missed him.

※　※　※

As he returned on the coastal road from Azotus he prayed, Lord, I cannot go on as I have done. You know I cannot bear to be so near to her and yet so far. I pray you will have worked in her heart in my absence, that is, if it be your will to give her to me to look after for you, he smiled humbly as he prayed, sitting atop his donkey.

If there is no change I will accept it is not in your will. I will move on. I pray you would show me where, he squinted into the afternoon sun, straining to catch his first glimpse of Caesarea.

It had been a good trip. The church in Azotus had grown both in faith and in numbers. Despite the many encouragements he'd had each day, he had wrestled with the underlying sadness that plagued him because Mary did not reciprocate his love. He had felt frustrated with himself for not being able to focus completely on the believers there and had frequently prayed for forgiveness.

※　※　※

'Where is he? I thought you said he was coming back today?' Mary asked Lazarus, as she looked down the road for the fourth time that day, shading her eyes against the afternoon sunshine.

'What does it matter if it's today or tomorrow?' Lazarus couldn't help smiling, standing behind her in the courtyard doorway.

Mary looked round at her brother crossly, 'It matters because a man of his word should be there when he said he would.'

'Really? Is that why it matters?'

Mary could hear the teasing smile in his voice and couldn't stop a self-conscious giggle from pushing through her frown, 'Oh, stop it!' she declared.

'You've missed him haven't you?'

She didn't reply.

'Oh, come on, little sister, we all know you're in love with him. You're the only one who doesn't know.'

'Am I? Am I really?' she slammed the wooden door shut and pushed past him. She busied herself with hanging the washing out to dry.

❋ ❋ ❋

The sun was setting when he knocked on the outer door. It opened instantly.

'Mary!' he exclaimed.

'I feared you weren't going to make it before dark,' she said, her whole face lit with an internal glow.

As he studied her eyes he saw the answer he'd been praying and longing for. He wanted to take her in his arms there and then, but custom forbade such rash behaviour. 'I've thought of you every day,' he said holding her gaze.

'I've missed you every day,' she laughed.

'Is that Philip?' they heard Martha's voice calling from the kitchen door.

'Yes, he's back!' Mary exclaimed.

'Well let him in then!' Martha ordered.

They stood looking into each other's eyes as dusk fell fast upon them.

'Mary ...' Martha came up behind her, 'Whatever are you both doing standing like that in the doorway? Come in, come in, Philip. You must be exhausted! Here give me the donkey's harness. Mary get water for his feet.'

Mary turned and ran for the bowl and towel she'd already prepared. When she took his foot in her hand, the story of Ruth and Boaz came into her mind. She looked up and like her ancestor before her, offered herself to him.

Philip saw.

When she anointed him with oil, it was with one of her own infusions.

Do not arouse or awaken love until it so desires ... came a line from The Song of Songs into his mind.

Let him kiss me with the kisses of his mouth ... Mary thought.

❋ ❋ ❋

Warm, golden candlelight flickered all around them in their courtyard. The stars shone in a silvery-bright canopy above them. Friends and family were crowded around them as they faced each other.

'With this ring, you are made holy to me, for I love you as my own soul. You are now my wife,' said Philip, as he slid the band of gold onto her finger.

Mary looked up into eyes that burned so fiercely that it made her blink. She looked back down at the ring reflecting the flickering candlelight. Tears welled up and spilled down her cheeks. Philip took her in his arms and held her, praising God for His goodness and kindness.

Martha could wait no longer. She threw her arms around them both, laughing and crying all at once. Lazarus engulfed the three of them in his wedding finery and his glistening silver beard and ringlets.

Junia was the first to start the time of dancing.

5. WHY

*Acts 12 The women living in the now,
hoping for the not-yet*

Bishop Duncan refocused his eyes on his archdeacon. It was an effort. He knew he shouldn't think uncharitable thoughts, but … *he really is the most pompous little man!* He watched him as he progressed through the meeting's minutes meticulously. The bishop stifled a yawn and shifted in his chair, recrossing his ankles under the coffee table.

Julia was taking notes in shorthand, her notepad perched on her knee. He noticed that her light brown hair was parted on the other side of her head than normal. It was cut in a short bob and tucked behind her ears. Her designer glasses stylishly framed her unremarkable eyes, a welcome distraction. Her knees were dimpled. Bishop Duncan imagined she must have been a formidable force on the hockey field in her day. He wondered what she thought of the archdeacon. He returned his gaze to his colleague's officious face, only to see something else there in his expression. The man's beady eye was fixed on the minute gap between Julia's knees and her tweed skirt. Bishop Duncan felt revulsion and sat up slightly.

With the movement Colin averted his eyes, licking his lips, 'And so we come to the last item on the agenda, St Stephen's vicarage development.'

Bishop Duncan's thoughts immediately flew to the last time he'd seen Grace. Her long bare legs, her elegant ankles and beautiful feet. With a shock he recognised in himself the very thing he'd just found repugnant in Colin. Wrestling with the ensuing emotions, like he'd often done with his stubborn dog, Rufus, and forcing his mind to the details of the moment, he managed to get through the meeting.

After he'd seen Colin to the door, he walked back through Julia's office towards his study. As he reached for the door handle, he turned to her and asked, 'What do you think of Colin?'

Julia looked surprised, 'He's a good archdeacon, very precise … efficient. Why?'

'I mean – off the record – what do you think of him? Do you like him?'

Julia frowned and did a button up on her lemon-yellow cardigan, 'I thought he was married?'

Bishop Duncan laughed, 'Oh, he is, don't worry. I wasn't trying to set you up or anything.'

'I should hope not!' she blushed.

'Do you think he has an issue … with … um …'

'Bishop Duncan, you are being very indiscreet. All I'll say is I wouldn't want to be left alone with him.'

'No … no … you're right … Sorry, Julia,' he fumbled to open the door and beat a hasty retreat to the safety of his study.

Dear Lord, what is happening to me? Is this a mid-life crisis? If it is please let it be over soon.

He went straight over to the cross where he'd nailed the handkerchief and knelt down before it.

I give you this need, this craving for her. Oh, God … lust … ego … forgive me, Father … you know what I am made of … search me and try me and cleanse me … help me resist … satisfy my soul with good things … I shall not want … you are my shepherd … He began to recite Psalm 23 … *I don't want to be like Colin!*

※ ※ ※

Grace dried her hair with the towel as she perched on the end of their bed. Peter was sitting up reading a book on Klimt. It was late. She'd had a long day: led two services in the morning, hosted a lunch for the over sixty-fives, taken home communion to a cancer patient and finally finished Sunday with Evensong. She didn't like being away from Peter and Zack, but it had just been one of those days. She was tired; Peter was withdrawn.

She'd bathed Zack and put him to bed, giving Peter some much needed downtime of his own. She knew Peter wanted her to spend some time with him, but the yearning for time on her own was too strong, so she'd gone on the cross trainer and had a shower.

'Are you sulking?'

Peter looked up from his book, with an eyebrow raised, 'No, why?'

'It's been a long day … sorry I haven't been around much.'

'That's okay – it's your job – it's not normally as bad as this,' he turned a glossy page, 'The Kiss' spreading to the edges.

'Really? You're not upset with me?'

'You can't always get what you want, can you?' he replied pragmatically, scanning the golden image.

'No …' Grace agreed her eyes dropping from his face to the picture.

'Life's not all about snuggling up in an embrace with your lover in a golden patchwork blanket,' he smiled as he raised his eyes to hers.

She smiled back, a surge of love for him defusing her anxiety. She dropped the damp towel onto the bedroom floor and crawled across the duvet towards him, her white towelling dressing gown loosening as she moved. She tucked her bare feet under the duvet and leaned up against him.

'So how was your day?' he asked.

'It was mad! I don't know if I'm imagining it, but there seems to be lots of new people about. By lunch I was all talked out, but had to muster up the strength to play host. What did you guys do for lunch?'

'We went to McDonald's.'

'Peter!'

'It's not like we go there every week,' he lifted his arm and put it round her shoulders. 'Zack likes getting the toys.'

'I know,' she smiled, tucking her shoulder under his arm. 'Then I went to see Joan at home – took her communion. Don't think she's got long now.'

Peter said nothing.

'Then home to see you guys briefly before going out again to do Evensong. There was quite a crowd there too!'

'Really? Do they all know what to do – you know – when to sit and stand and what tune to sing?'

'Not particularly … it's a bit of a disaster. Joan's been teaching me the tunes when I visit her, but I'm not confident enough to lead strongly. They don't seem to mind. Numbers have doubled in the last couple of months, so I must be doing something right?'

'Just being yourself, no doubt,' she could hear the smile in his voice and turned to look up at him. 'I am proud of you, you know,' Peter said.

She didn't reply.

'You're doing a tough thing – a woman in what until recently, has been an exclusively male role. And you're a fantastic mother – *and* you're my gorgeous wife. I don't know how you do it all!'

She turning her body to his and kissed him. He slid his hand inside her dressing gown and cupped her breast, gently fondling her upturned, hardening nipple. Klimt dropped to the floor as Grace rolled on top of him, unwrapping herself. Peter's face was surrounded by her white-blonde curls as her lips hovered over his. He leaned up to kiss them, but she played with him, pulling just out of reach, 'Tease,' he whispered. She smiled mischievously. She was glad she'd given herself the time alone she'd needed, rather than dutifully coming to him earlier. Her energy levels would have been low and she would have been much less fun.

Peter ran a finger along her collar bone, and then reached up and brushed his lips along it. She arched into him as he moved over her skin.

'Thank you, God,' Peter said reverently as she disentangled herself from her robe and threw it on the floor.

Grace laughed, 'So you're a praying man now?' she ran her hands through his salt and pepper hair.

'You have no idea!' he grinned.

※　※　※

'Do you think I'm ready now to start volunteering at My Sister's House?' Melanie asked.

'Have you spoken to your doctor about the idea?' Grace studied her young face. It was still very thin; still carrying traces of trauma around the eyes.

'She's concerned about my eating. I'm just not hungry,' Melanie pressed her hands into her loose fitting T-shirt that served as a nightie. She was sitting cross-legged on her bed, with Grace in her study chair at the desk.

Into Grace's mind came a picture of Jesus hanging on the cross praying, 'Father forgive them, for they know not what they do.' She allowed the image and words to settle in her mind as she continued to stay focused on Melanie.

'Have you had any thoughts about why you're not hungry?' Grace asked.

'Yeah ... I've been reading a book called *Puppet on a String*, about a girl who nearly died from anorexia. Don't tell mum!'

Grace smiled, 'Melanie – I never discuss anything we talk about with your mum. How many times do I have to assure you of that?'

'Lots?' Melanie tucked her lifeless hair behind an ear.

'Okay ... but what's struck you as you've been reading?'

'Mainly all the things that happened to her that were outside her control. Food became the focus of her determination to have some control in life.'

'Do you think that's relevant to you?'

'I don't know ... I mean, I guess I had no control over what mum did with the vicar and then the misery I suffered at school because of it. But I was in control of things with ... with Yusuf ... at first. It was what I wanted ... the coke kind of took over though, I suppose ...' she paused, twiddling a strand of hair between finger and thumb, '... but when he brought Sony in and I had no say ... yes ... I had no control,' her eyes welled with tears.

Grace nodded.

'Do you think that's why I can't eat? Because I'm trying to control something so I'll make myself feel better?'

'I don't know Mel ... it could be a bit of that ... what do you think?'

Melanie stared at the strand of hair, 'Maybe ...'

'What feelings do you have when you're faced with food?'

Melanie looked up, 'Fear mainly ... my stomach goes into sort of knots.'

'Fear of what?'

'... I ... I ... don't know ...'

'Why don't we pray and ask God to show you what you're afraid of?'

'Now?'

'Yes – why not. He knows – he can show you if you want,' Grace smiled encouragingly.

'What do I do?' Melanie looked strained.

'Just close your eyes, ask God to show you what you're scared of and then tell me whatever comes into your head.'

'What if it's rubbish?'

'It may well seem to be rubbish, but it's a bit like panning for gold in a river. Your thoughts are like a river of consciousness, and when we ask God to speak to us, He usually does – in our own thoughts – but you've gotta pan for them – for the golden thoughts. I'll help you … it takes a while to learn what His voice sounds like to you. You need to know His character …' Grace leaned forward intently.

'How can you know someone who's invisible?' Melanie asked.

Grace smiled, 'Through this …' she held up her pale blue leather-bound bible. 'Read it enough, asking the Holy Spirit to speak to you, and you'll get to know what He's like … then it's easier to recognise His thoughts when they come.'

'I only know the bible stories from when I was young. I started trying to read it in Alpha, but got distracted by … him,' she rolled her eyes scornfully.

'Isn't it interesting that just when you were making strides in your faith all this stuff began to happen?' Grace mused.

'I hadn't thought about it that way before,' Melanie frowned.

Grace waited for Melanie to process the thought. Eventually she said, 'Do you want to ask God to show you what you're scared of?'

'Yeah … okay …' she closed her eyes. Grace watched her face, praying silently and hoping furiously that Melanie would be able to spot God's thoughts in her own.

After a while Melanie spoke, keeping her eyes shut, 'They came inside me – they invaded me …' she gasped out a sob.

Grace felt the trauma reverberate through her, echoes of her own past.

'When I look at food it feels the same – like it's going to invade me. I have to let it into me and I don't want to … I don't want to …' she broke down.

Grace reached out and took hold of Melanie's hand. 'Oh, Mel, I know … I've felt the same in the past. But can you sense beyond the feeling? Can you sense Jesus here with us now?'

Melanie wiped her nose with the back of her free hand. Tears trickling down her sunken cheeks; dropping onto her tracksuit bottoms. 'All I can see is a picture of him on the cross – He's saying "Father – forgive them."'

Grace was surprised and grateful. She squeezed her hand.

'I don't want to forgive them. They don't deserve to ever be forgiven for what they did to me.'

'I know …' Grace said nothing more. There was a long silence. Melanie became very still, her eyes still closed, the tears slowing in their flow.

'What's happening?' Grace asked eventually.

Melanie replied in a whisper, 'He took my place ... I ... it was like Jesus pushed me out of my body ... I was watching them abuse him ... in my body ... and he was saying, "Father forgive them, they don't know what they're doing" ...'

Grace's eyesight blurred.

'He took this for me ... with me ... I wasn't alone ...'

Grace opened her bible and flicked through it until she found the verses that had come to her mind. '"Christ in you the hope of glory," Mel – look.'

Melanie opened her eyes and looked as Grace held out the page, pointing out the verse for her to read. Then she turned to another part of the Bible and opened to Psalm 23 and showed her, ' "Even though I walk through the valley of the shadow of death, I will fear no evil, for you are with me ..." He'll never leave you. He suffers everything we suffer with us, and if we let Him, He'll carry our burdens for us, He'll take evil ... become sin ... so we can go free.'

'I think ... I'm not sure ... but I think I feel different ... seeing Him take my place ... I feel different.'

'Let Him be the judge of these men. It's too heavy a thing for you to carry – this justified anger that's defending you so ruthlessly – it could destroy you. Let Him have the responsibility of anger and judgement. Do you think you can let go?'

'I don't know,' Melanie looked at Grace, grappling with emotion. 'If I don't protect myself, I could ... they could ...'

'Yes ... you would be making yourself vulnerable. But if you trusted Jesus to be your protector and defender ...'

'But He didn't protect me from them.'

Grace had no reply.

'I – I was so unsafe,' Melanie frowned.

Grace flicked to another part of the bible and read it out quietly, ' "What do you think? If a man owns a hundred sheep, and one of them wanders away, will he not leave the ninety nine on the hills and go to look for the one that wandered off? And if he finds it, I tell you the truth, he is happier about that one sheep than about the ninety nine that did not wander off. In the same way your Father in Heaven is not willing that any of these little ones should be lost."

'Do you really think that old lady that mum crashed into was an angel?'

'Maybe,' Grace smiled.

'Do you really think God sends his angels after us?'

'Yeah … I do … when we need them. I think we'll be surprised when we get to heaven to see battle-weary angels who have fought for us throughout our lives,' she laughed softly at the thought and then grew serious again, 'I think they often protect us from the worst … but sometimes evil wins … I think it helps the angels, you know – gives them strength, when God's people pray. We were all praying for you – to find you.'

'But what about people like Madeleine McCann?' Melanie asked.

Grace nodded, her mouth turning down at the corners, 'So many people have prayed and are still praying for her to be found … I don't know, Mel. It's horrible … it seems it hasn't been enough … that evil has won. I really don't know … I wish I did … it's one of the things I'll ask God when I meet him along with a long list of others.'

Melanie said, 'Do you think you'll still have questions when you see Him?'

'Maybe not … maybe seeing him will be enough … our questions answered.'

They lapsed into silence. Grace became aware of the Ed Sheeran song playing softly in the background on the radio. It was a ballad to a baby who had died.

'I don't know what would have happened if you hadn't found me … I think they were going to sell me … they were talking about some Turkish guys … I was so scared,' Melanie shivered.

'Don't think about that any more, Mel,' Grace took her hand again.

'Yeah … I want to be free … can I pray?'

'Of course,' Grace replied.

'God …' Melanie started as only a teenager could, 'I'm so mad at myself for getting so unsafe. I know you want to … help me forgive myself.' She was quiet for a while, then nodded slowly and began again, 'I hate them … it's doing me no good … please help me trust you to judge them … I want to let you carry this horrible anger… I want to trust you to defend me.' Again she waited quietly. Then, with fresh tears rolling down her face she went on, 'I've really hated Mum, God. I guess I wanted to hurt her … I don't know … I don't want to judge her any more … I'm sorry for that.

You understand why she did what she did and you forgive her.'

Melanie cried and cried.

When it seemed she'd run out of tears she whispered, 'I forgive her … help me with eating.'

They sat for ages holding hands and listening to the radio.

✻ ✻ ✻

Melanie got all her GCSEs via correspondence. She'd turned a corner with food as well and had begun eating, albeit very oddly: food had to be separated on her plate, nothing could be mixed up. She couldn't have sauces or noodles or anything messy … but at least she was eating and gaining a little weight. Chloe was beyond relieved.

Summer had come round again and the longer hours of daylight seemed to help with her mood. Melanie started volunteering at My Sister's House twice a week. At the time there were four girls staying in the house.

Val had developed a programme for each day, to keep the girls occupied and to help them begin to pick up the threads of normal life again. Each had daily chores to do round the house. They had sessions of craftwork and journal writing; weekly outings to the cinema or bowling; they had a beauty session together each week and every Friday evening they had dinner together, making it a special occasion with flowers and candles. There was a recovery program which Grace, Mo and Chloe delivered, dealing with issues of self esteem and coping strategies for anxiety. All had to attend this. They were also offered sessions with Grace, teaching them about Jesus and the work of His Holy Spirit. Some of them accessed these sessions which they began to call the Life Program, but not all.

Mo was rushed off her feet handling four case loads. She had suggested they advertise for another volunteer trained in social work. So they had. When Melanie heard, she was excited, 'I've been thinking I want to study social work at university! I want to do Sociology, Psychology and English for A-levels. I could do all my placement work here, couldn't I?' she asked Mo.

'Well, luv,' Mo sucked air through her teeth, 'I guess by the time you go to uni, we'll be a much more solid organisation. I should fink – yeah – it would be a good place to cut your teef,' her cockney accent sliced up the air. She no longer had her hair in cane rows, but it hung in a wavey mass around her shoulders. She'd been looking more feminine recently and everyone suspected that things must be hotting up with Sean, St Matt's youth worker.

Chloe came into the office, having finished a counselling session with one of the girls. She looked wrung out. 'You all right, Mum?' Melanie asked.

'Yes … it's just so unbelievable what people are capable of …' she stared out the window at the newly landscaped garden. The lawn curved at the edges into flower beds crammed full of riotous colour. 'I need a cup of coffee. Anyone else?' she looked from Melanie, to Mo and Val.

Everyone said yes, so she went into the kitchen, filled and turned on the kettle, then leaned up against the work top crossing her arms under her breasts. She noticed the slight bulge of her belly between her forearms and her jeans – it annoyed her. She consciously pulled it in. Melanie had followed her into the kitchen and stood next to her. 'Is it very hard hearing everything?' she asked.

'It is. It's a good thing I'm seeing my supervisor tonight, or I might go a bit loopy myself,' Chloe smiled affectionately at her daughter.

'Do you think it was as hard for Grace to listen to me?'

'Probably …' Chloe turned as the kettle came to the boil. 'You've been doing so well, Mel,' Chloe said as she poured a steaming stream over the pile of dark granules in the cafetiere.

'Yeah – it's really helped. It's great that you do the same thing for the girls here.'

Chloe looked up in surprise at the rare praise, 'Thanks, love. That means a lot coming from you.'

'I know we haven't been close for a long time … I wanted to say … um … sorry for that.'

Chloe froze with her hand on the cafetiere plunger. It began to sink slowly, pushing through the gritty brown liquid. She swallowed hard and looked at Melanie, 'Darling … you have nothing to say sorry for … it's me that needs forgiving …'

'But that's it, Mum, I hadn't forgiven you … I'm sorry … for that.'

Chloe couldn't push emotion down any longer. Her torso heaved with a silent sob, her hands flew to cover her mouth, but not fast enough. She suddenly came undone, her mouth breaking open letting out repressed grief and guilt. Mother and daughter held each other, surrounded in the beautiful scent of fresh coffee. Needless to say the others soon came and joined in.

※　※　※

'That's amazing!' Grace marvelled.

'I know, isn't it?' Chloe cradled her coffee mug against her chest. They were in their favourite alcove of the pub, having finished a lunch of freshly made lasagne.

'That girl is something else,' Grace smiled. 'She's a chip off the old block, isn't she?'

Chloe laughed, 'When she was little we were so close, being our first and a girl. I can still remember those new feelings of love I had for her. They were so fierce, they frightened me. I would have killed for her!'

Grace agreed, 'Maternal instinct is a powerful thing.'

'Yeah … she's doing so well … still eating strangely, but hopefully she'll grow out of it as she learns to deal better with anxiety.'

'I was thinking, it would be good to get her into some kind of therapy to help her with that. I'm no counsellor – as you know – I think apart from being there for her and helping her along whenever it's needed, I've done my bit. She needs some professional help with anxiety.'

'Okay … I'll talk to her and look into it, if she wants.'

'Good,' Grace sipped her coffee.

'She's got very close to Rose, hasn't she?'

'Are you worried about that?'

'No, not really.' Chloe replied, 'I guess I'm just thinking Rose is going to have to move on soon – we've had her far longer than we should have, way longer than we're funded for, but it's been a nightmare getting her asylum.'

'I know … but maybe she needed this time … she's changed so much.'

'She has. I have absolutely loved working with her. You know she wants to do a business course?' Chloe said.

'Yes, she was telling me the other day about her ideas for jewellery. She's got some beautiful designs. Did she show you her drawings for that big silver rose necklace? I'd buy that!'

'Bit chunky for me – you know I like my small, understated diamonds.'

'We all know!' Grace smiled, eyeing the diamond studs Mark had given her for their tenth wedding aniversary. 'What have you asked for your twentieth? An eternity ring?'

'We may never get there,' Chloe looked out the window. 'He's withdrawn completely from me. Maybe he feels like a failure as a man and a dad because he couldn't protect her. He won't talk about it, so I can only guess.'

'Why won't he talk?'

'I don't know … God knows I've tried.'

'How are the boys doing?' Grace moved on, not sure what else to say.

'Josh is fine – skimming along the surface like Mark. As long as he's got his football and Playstation he's okay. Charlie's hitting puberty like there's no tomorrow. I think what happened to Mel has really affected him. We're still close, but I sense there's something that he's not telling me. I'm not sure what. I wish he and Mark were closer.'

Grace listened, thinking fondly of Charlie.

'How about Peter and Zack?' Chloe turned the conversation away from herself, 'How're they getting on? Do they complain that they don't see as much of you as they used to?' Chloe sipped her coffee.

'Peter's been pretty amazing, actually. I know he wants more time with me, but he's been so supportive and great with Zack. I feel guilty about not being there as much. My Mum's been wonderful too, when neither of us can be there. But Granny's not the same as Mum, is she?'

'No. The dilemma of the working mother!' Chloe said ruefully.

'Mmmm,' Grace drank the remainder of her coffee. 'I was never close to my Mum. Having her around to help has been really good for me. I guess I've been doing a bit of what Melanie did with you the other day.'

※　※　※

'I can't come,' Mark was saying for the second time on the phone. Chloe continued reading at the kitchen table. 'No … work's pretty full on at the minute … so … sorry mate,' he cradled his mobile between his chin and shoulder.

'Who was that?' Chloe asked, trying to sound nonchalant after he'd hung up.

'Rob,' Mark said not looking at her as he stuffed his phone into his jeans pocket.

'What did he want?'

'Wanted me to come to the prayer triplet tonight,' Mark rummaged in the 'messy' drawer, 'Where's my calculator?'

'Should be in there … you working tonight?' Chloe put her book down.

'Yep … got a list of things to do that didn't get done today and need doing by tomorrow.'

'Oh? That's unusual …'

'No it's not. You've been so preoccupied with Mel and that "Sister's House" of yours that you haven't noticed. I told you a while ago that I might be up for a promotion. It's not a cert … I've gotta dazzle them.'

'Sorry, I didn't realise,' she pushed her chair away from the table to stand up.

'Yep,' he said again in a clipped tone.

She walked over to him, reaching for his hand, 'Things have been pretty crazy recently … I'm sorry.' As she looked into his bluey-green eyes, she saw his guard was up. *So defended,* she thought fleetingly.

His hand lay limply in hers; disengaged. She let it go and took a step back.

'You haven't seen Rob and the guys for a while … I guess maybe they're just a bit worried about you?'

'Yeah, well … that's life isn't it?' his eyes slid from hers to the clock on the wall.

'Mark … is everything okay?' she had a growing sense of unease.

'I've just got a lot on, Chloe. I can do without the guilt trip …' he said moving away from her towards the hallway which led to his study.

'Fine …' Chloe said, shrugging her shoulders, 'be like that.'

With that he turned his back on her and headed down the hall.

She stood gazing after him for a while, trying to read between the lines. Eventually she returned to the table and her book. *Crisis in masculinity? Oh sure …* she rolled her eyes in the direction Mark had gone and picked it up to find her lost place. *Idiot! I'm not your mother … just grow up, you self-absorbed …* She stopped the internal tirade, reprimanding herself for being equally immature. *I'm too tired to face more drama.* She looked at the clock. It was seven-thirty. *Wine time!* She went to the fridge.

Charlie and his friend Jules sauntered into the kitchen. Jules was tall and slender, with blond floppy hair and big doe eyes. 'Can we have some ice-cream, Mum?' Charlie asked.

'Sure, sweetie,' she opened the freezer. 'What flavour do you want?'

'Chocolate, please,' said Jules.

'Yeah, chocolate – thanks Mum,' Charlie said.

She brought the tub over to the table along with her bottle of Pinot, while Charlie got out the bowls and spoons. 'Can you get me a wine glass – no not that one – one of the big ones,' she directed as she scooped thick creamy chocolate into their bowls.

Charlie looked small standing next to Jules, even though he was an average height for his age. His dark hair needed a cut, it was hanging down into his eyes. Chloe went to sweep it away with a finger and was surprised by Charlie's reaction. He flung his head back, out of her reach, his eyes spitting fire at her.

'Sorry,' she said lamely. Jules stared at her with his big, dark eyes, as if to say, *How could you?* Charlie didn't respond, but focused on Jules completely as if his mother did not exist.

'Let's take this upstairs,' he said.

'Cool,' the tall boy said and followed Charlie out of the room.

I'm surrounded by pubescent boys ... thank God for this, she sighed unscrewing the top and tipping the neck of the bottle into the balloon glass. It only took a few gulps to get that first hit. She closed her eyes and breathed deeply, closing the book.

Don't think I can read any more of this anyway ... just can't get there. You're straight or you're gay ... whether it's passed down in your genes, the effect of events in your early years or your relationship with your respective parents. People are people and sex is sex ... she took another few sips of wine. *The main thing is to love and be loved, which ever way you like it ... I mean, Rose has only had orgasms with women, even if she doesn't think she's gay. The things men have done to her ... I'm not surprised! I wouldn't be upset if Melanie decided she never wanted to be with a man again ... and Charlie? Oh, sweet Charlie ...*

Feeling unsettled, she got up and walked into the living room. Josh was playing Playstation with two friends. 'I thought Charlie was coming in here?' she asked.

'Nope,' Josh answered without turning his head from the screen.

She walked into the hall again, 'Charlie?' she called up the stairs.

'Yeah?' Charlie's voice immediately responded. She heard his bedroom door open on the landing.

'What are you doing?' she sipped her wine.

'We're playing Scrabble,' he came to the top of the stairs, 'why?'

'Just wondering. What time does Jules have to go home?'

'Nine,' he replied. 'His mum's coming to get him.'

'Okay,' she smiled up at him. He returned down the hallway. Chloe nursed her drink for a while, then decided to find Mark. *He can't be that busy* ... she thought. The office door was closed. She turned the handle silently and pushed the door ajar, putting her head round to check it was okay to come in. Mark's desk faced the window that looked out onto their drive and tall hedge. The computer screen was at an angle in one corner of the desk and what she saw there made her stomach somersault.

A young, nubile woman lay naked, save the S & M gear strapped tightly to her flesh, her legs spread-eagled. She instantly withdrew her head, pulling the door shut. She stood frozen listening to her heart thudding in her ears.

Not again ... She felt sick and on hearing Mark moving on the other side of the door, ran for the stairs, to the safety of their en-suite, locking the door.

She sat down on the toilet and drained her glass in three big gulps. She kept looking at the door, anticipating Mark's knock. It eventually came. She didn't respond.

'Chloe, can I come in? Please ... we need to talk ...' Silence. 'Please, Chloe ... I can explain ...' Silence. 'Chloe ...' she heard him slump to the floor outside the door. 'You'll have to come out some time and talk to me.'

Chloe stayed there until eight-fifty. Then she stood up, went to the door and said, 'I'm coming out now.' She heard him moving out of the way hurriedly. She turned the lock and opened the door, coming face to face with him.

'I had to ... I couldn't stop it ... I'm so lonely now you've got your career and mission in life all rolled into one ...'

She gazed at him, 'You're making no sense to me,' she said as she moved passed him through the bedroom.

'Where are you going? We need to talk ...'

'Now you want to talk?' she said, visualising herself smashing his face in as she made her way to Charlie's bedroom. She knocked on the door and waited for a response.

'Charlie, it's time for Jules to go. His mum will be here any minute,' she said.

'Yeah, okay … be down in a sec,' Charlie replied.

Chloe went back downstairs and straight to the bottle of wine she'd left on the table, pouring a third of it into her glass with a shaking hand. It had lost some of its chill, but she didn't care. She drank deeply. The doorbell went. She headed for the front door as Charlie and Jules came down the stairs.

'Bye … see you Monday …' Charlie waved as Jules got into his mum's waiting car.

'Thanks for having him,' his mum called through the open window.'

'You're welcome,' Chloe waved and smiled, the perfect hostess, mother and housewife. 'He's a good friend,' Chloe said.

'He's my best friend,' Charlie replied.

'Is he in any of your sets at school?' Chloe asked.

'He's in Year 9.'

'What? I thought he was in your year?'

'We share an advanced computer class on Tuesdays.'

'Oh …'

'Why are you sounding all weird?'

'Am I? Sorry sweetie. That explains why he's so much taller than you,' she forced a smile. 'Doesn't he get teased for having a best friend in Year 7?' she regretted saying it the minute it was out of her mouth.

'No!' he glared at her, then turned and went up the stairs. 'I'm going to bed – night!'

'Night,' Chloe hung limp as a sail in the eye of a storm. Then she moved numbly to the living room door and opened it, 'Josh, what time are your friends going home?'

'Soon … Jack only lives round the corner.'

'Yeah, I do …' the spotty teenager tore his eyes briefly from the TV screen.

'And Ollie lives five minutes' walk from here.'

'Over on Edward Street,' Ollie pointed with his chin to the front window.

'Yes, I'm aware of where you live, boys. I just think it's getting late and you should be going home soon.'

Josh looked at his mum irritably, 'Okay – ten more minutes?'

'Okay – ten more minutes.'

Chloe returned to the bottle of wine in the kitchen and poured the last third into her glass. She was relieved to be feeling slightly tipsy. She sat down heavily and opened her book again. She opened the index. *Is there a chapter on S&M, internet sex or sex addiction?* A wave of anger roared through her, leaving a dull grey wash in its wake. She heard Josh seeing his friends to the door and then going upstairs, calling goodnight to her as he went. Then she heard Mark coming down the stairs. She squared her shoulders and took another big gulp of wine.

Mark sat down opposite her, folding his hands in front of him, keeping his eyes focused on them. Chloe studied his face. She had thought she knew him, but he'd done it again ... kept himself hidden from her ... she didn't know him at all. She wondered what all the years of marriage had been about. She wondered how she could have been so stupid to think everything could be okay after the first time.

'I'm really sorry, Chloe ... I don't know what else to say to you.'

'How long have you been looking at that stuff?' Chloe pierced him with her dark eyes.

'I ... I don't know ...' Mark stammered.

'What if the boys had seen what I just saw? What if Melanie had? It would destroy them, after all they've been through. I can't believe that you would risk your own children for such pathetic self-gratification.'

Mark looked down at his hands again. 'I'm powerless Chloe ... I have no control.'

'I think you'll find you do have control. You just don't want it,' Chloe swallowed the rage that bellowed up her oesophagus. 'How could you after what your own daughter's been through?' she glared at him.

There was no reply.

'Is it just porn or are you involved with someone else too?'

Still no reply.

'Right ...' Chloe breathed deeply. She suddenly felt there wasn't enough oxygen in the room. 'I want you out of our bed,' she said emphatically.

Mark gazed blankly at her.

Chloe could feel panic clambering up her ribcage. Her breathing escalating, 'I need air ... can't breathe ...' she stood up, swaying a little, went and opened the back door. She stood there propped up against the door frame, gulping in oxygen.

She heard Mark push back his chair and stand up.

She said nothing.

'Chloe ... '

She whirled round, fury and shock entwining into a doubleheaded snake, 'I cannot bear to have you near me ... In your study? ... When your own daughter has been at the mercy of misogynistic, sadistic, dehumanising narcissists ... who it turns out are just like you? I can't bear to think of it ... just go!' her voice was rising dangerously. She shut her mouth tightly and turned away from him her face white, forcing her emotions into submission.

He left the kitchen without another word. She went to the fridge, got another bottle of wine and poured again. She listened to him moving around upstairs as the wine anaesthetised her.

Grace dropped Melanie off at midnight after her shift at My Sister's House. Melanie was surprised to find her mother asleep on the kitchen table, two empty wine bottles beside her. She helped her to bed, wondering where her father was. Neither said a word.

※　※　※

The phone rang. Grace squinted at the luminescent screen of her phone – it was 4 a.m.

'Hello?' Grace said, her voice groggy with sleep.

'He's done it again, Grace.'

'Who's done what again?'

'Mark ... he's been looking at porn again ... oh, God ... and I think he's seeing someone else too.'

'What?' Grace sat up, pushing her hair off her face.

Peter woke up, 'What's wrong?'

'It's Chloe ... I'll go downstairs.'

She found her dressing gown on the floor and dragged it on, listening to Chloe as she did.

'I found him tonight, while the boys were in the next room. I mean, what was he thinking?'

'Sorry, Chloe, say that again?' Grace tied her robe belt round her, clamping the phone to her ear with her shoulder while Chloe continued to speak.

'Where is he now?' Grace asked as she entered the kitchen.

'In the spare room,' Chloe replied.

'Do the kids know?'

'No … not yet … what do I tell them? That their dad's a perv?'

'Chloe …' Grace hesitated, 'don't …'

'Haven't you been listening to me?'

'Yeah … but … sorry, Chloe … just want to keep you calm.'

'Calm? How can I be calm when the man I thought I knew, whom I've lived with for seventeen years, has been living a double life? My whole world is crumbling, Grace!'

'I know … oh, love,' she felt desperate for her.

Silence.

'You know … I think I knew … but didn't want to believe it. All the signs were there. It's over … I really think it's over now.'

❋ ❋ ❋

Grace sat at her desk several nights later, longing … longing to rest her head and listen to the sound of an older and wiser heart beating in her ear. Peter had fallen asleep several hours ago, but she had lain awake beside him trying to bring coherence to her thoughts. In the end she'd gone downstairs.

She opened her bible. *Lord, speak to me … help me. How can so much good and so much evil all happen at once? How come you can rescue Melanie and Rose but yet Mark is still held a secret captive to addiction? Why do you answer one prayer and not another? How will Chloe be able to carry on?*

She felt herself sinking under the heaviness of her questions. She turned the thin, gilt edged pages to where she'd last left off: Acts chapter twelve. She forced herself to focus, running her finger under each line as she read, sometimes reading over the same line several times.

She sat back in her seat when she'd finished the chapter. *That makes no sense God … I don't understand your ways …*

There was no answer. She opened her laptop and opened her story file. She read over the last bit of what she'd written and lost herself in writing a new chapter:

❀   ❀   ❀

'Anything you can do, your highness, to aid us in crushing this outrageous sect, will increase the love and esteem your people have for you,' Aaron smiled his most ingratiating smile.

King Herod looked at him from the sides of his eyes as he turned one of his many rings round and round on his fat finger. A young servant girl leaned in between them and offered them a plate of roasted lamb shanks. Herod picked one up by the bone and tore the meat from it, chewing noisily as meat juices dribbled into his beard.

Aaron hid his disdain at the oafish and foolish puppet king. He turned his attention to the servant girl, eyeing her small cleavage that showed as she leaned down to him. He raised his goblet of wine to his lips, touching it with his tongue first. His eyes idled on her rosebud lips and then eventually rose to her eyes. Something about them reminded him of Lila, increasing his lust. He made a note of the outfit she was wearing, storing it in his mind for later, when the wine would have done its work. He declined the lamb but asked her to return.

He gave his attention back to the King who was speaking with his mouth full, 'You're right. The people need a strong lead on this. The leadership of the Sanhedrin is not enough, I fear. I will see to it. Who are their leaders?'

'Would it surprise you to know that I have a list of them with me?' smiled Aaron.

The King wiped the back of his hand across his mouth as he grinned, 'You are indeed a most resourceful man, Aaron. I believe you may be very useful to me.'

'I am at your command,' Aaron bowed his head.

❊   ❊   ❊

Rhoda feigned sickness so brilliantly that she convinced Chuza, the manager of the King's household to let her go home early. She'd seen the look in the Pharisee's eye. She'd seen it too many times before at parties in the palace and knew she needed to move fast.

As soon as she was out of sight of the palace she discarded her act, straightened up and ran as fast as she could. She made it to the home where she knew a group of her neighbours were meeting that night. She rapped her knuckles on the door in the secret rhythm known only to believers.

Lila opened the door, 'Rhoda! We weren't expecting you! Aren't you supposed to be working tonight?' She hugged her, glad to see her young friend. She reminded her so much of Mary. Mary, her dearest friend; her sister whom she had not seen in years.

'I was, but I excused myself ... there was a man there who had plans for me that I could not agree with,' her big eyes seemed luminous in the dimly lit doorway.

'Come in, come in ...' Lila pulled her in through the door, remembering how Mary used to dance at the Hasmonean Palace, and shuddering at the thought, locked it quickly behind her.

'Are James and John here?' she asked.

'Yes ... and Matthew and Thomas,' Lila led her into their main living room, which was crammed with people. They were listening to John who was teaching them a new song he had written.

Lila and Jair had been back in Jerusalem for nearly a year. Anna was thirteen. They'd celebrated her Bat-Mitzveh on their return. Joshua was coming up to his tenth birthday. After Ananias had died, a happy man, full of years, they had decided to return to Jerusalem. Animosity towards the Jewish population, followers of The Way or otherwise, had escalated in Damascus. It had been hard to leave the fellowship of believers there, but the urge to return to Jerusalem had been strong. When they returned it had not taken long for them to reconnect with believers in the city. Daily, people gathered in their home for teaching and fellowship.

Rhoda stood at the door and waited for John's song to end. He sang a line at a time, while everyone echoed it back to him.

Eventually they sang the whole thing together. It was a beautiful, lilting meditation around a prayer that Jesus had taught them.

When the last voice died away, Rhoda spoke up, 'Cousin, may I speak?' she asked John.

'Speak, Rhoda,' John smiled. James leaned forward to see her past Thomas who sat next to him.

'I have just come from the palace. I overheard a conversation between a guest, who I think was a member of the Sanhedrin, and the King. They were planning to harm the leaders of the church, hoping to destroy us.'

James looked at his brother John. Jair leaned forward at John's side, 'You have all shown great courage and perseverance in staying in Jerusalem. Perhaps now is the time to disperse?'

'This is our home, Jair. I for one will not be frightened away by the schemes of men. Unless the Lord tells us to go – we stay,' James said forcefully.

'What is the point of staying, if our own countrymen turn against us?' Jair continued, 'My family and I left Jerusalem for Damascus after the death of Stephen. We returned here because the threat to our lives grew daily in Damascus too. From what we'd heard, it seemed a time of peace for the church had arrived in Jerusalem. But now this? I feel torn – for our children's sake. We have seriously been thinking of travelling further – perhaps to Greece. Perhaps we may assist Paul in his missionary work there?' his eyes met Lila's across the room. 'It seems from what we hear from him that the Gentiles are more receptive to the gospel than our own people.'

'We must seek the Lord,' James insisted.

'I am ready to go to the farthest nations,' Thomas said. 'I have always wanted to know what lies in the East.'

John looked at him and smiled, remembering how strong his doubts had been. 'It seems those who doubted most among us, now believe so sincerely that they may travel the farthest with the gospel?'

Thomas smiled, 'I touched his wounds.'

'How can we forget?' John responded.

'It may well be that we travel to the farthest nations,' James sighed, 'but my heart will always be in Jerusalem,' he paused. 'If we are to drink from the same cup as the Lord, then so be it.'

John nodded agreement with his brother, remembering Jesus' words to them when they'd argued over who would sit at his right and his left in his Kingdom. He shook his head ruefully thinking back to their impetuous naivity. Then he turned to his cousin, 'Thank you, Rhoda ... we will use the information you have brought us to aid our prayers.'

As they turned to prayer, Lila clasped Rhoda's hands as they both proceeded to pour out heartfelt intercession.

※　※　※

'They have taken James!'

'Who has?' John asked.

'The King's guard,' Rhoda gasped, having run all the way from the Hasmonean Palace to John's house.

'When?' John asked, horror filling his eyes.

'I saw them drag him in this evening, while we were preparing the food for the banquet. They chained him and locked him in a cell.'

'No!' John's hands went to his face, his mouth open. Eventually he closed it, drawing his hands over his face and down his beard. 'Send out messengers to the church. We must gather to pray.'

Throughout the night runners were sent to the seven sectors of the city. The next morning the church gathered in homes across the city to pray for James.

Rhoda returned to the royal kitchens, apprehensive of what might have happened in the night. The day wore on without event. As evening drew in all the servants were summoned to the great hall. No one knew why. Anxious tension hung in the atmosphere as they gathered uncertainly.

King Herod Agrippa the First, entered and sat down on his throne with a flourish of his purple robe. Before him was what looked like a footstool, but it was a simple block of wood. Rhoda wondered why it was there. It was incongruous with the other ornate furniture.

The King fastidiously straightened all his rings on his fingers before speaking, 'You have been gathered here to witness the authority and power of your King. You are to take the news of what you are about to see throughout Jerusalem. Tell the people that as a direct decendent of Herod the Great, a Hasmonean through my mother's line, I live continually in Jerusalem and am exactly careful in the observance of the laws of Israel. I keep myself entirely pure and there is not a day that passes me by without the appointed sacrifice. Today you will know that like my grandfather, I do not tolerate divisive sects. Guard, bring in the prisoner.'

Rhoda's heart was pounding as she watched her cousin dragged in, shuffling between two soldiers. Despite his chains, he held his head high, looking boldly at the King.

'This is one of the leaders of "The Way". It is a sect that has grown up among our people in recent years, deceiving many. Just like my grandfather, I ruthlessly oppose it.' He nodded at one of the guards who drew his sword, 'Kneel,' commanded the King.

James did not. Horrified, Rhoda suddenly knew what the block of wood was for. The other guard pushed him down forcefully, cursing him under his breath. He pressed his neck down onto the rough, wooden surface.

Without skipping a beat the other soldier raised his sword and brought it down in a flash. It happened so fast, without ceremony. There was a united sharp intake of breath from the watching crowd of servants at the sickening thud of metal cleaving flesh and bone. Rhoda screamed as blood exploded into the air. James's head was severed clean from his torso. It rolled several times, and came to a rocking halt a few feet from the throne.

Rhoda covered her face with her hands, gasping for air. She ran from the hall, only to feel her stomach heave. Stopping at the top of the grand staircase that led down into the large entrance courtyard, she vomited violently. She watched the bile flow like lava down several steps before becoming aware that others were running past her from the scene. Her head was reeling as she tore her scarf off and wiped her mouth. In a daze she started running again, skirting the mess she had made.

She ran to the nearest home she knew of where believers were meeting. She was gasping for air, shivering with trauma as she incoherently tried to tell Mary, the mother of John-Mark, what she had just witnessed.

Mary sent word to Lila to come quickly.

When she arrived she found Rhoda curled up on one of Mary's expensive couches, still shivering from the shock of what she'd seen. Lila comforted her as best she could. She thought of Mary leaving Damascus in a strange, detached state. She wondered if Rhoda would be the same as she held her and prayed for her with John-Mark's mother.

❋ ❋ ❋

The news rocked the church. Stephen's death had sent many scattering, but the first of the apostles to die for the cause of Christ sent them to prayer in a way that they had not known before.

The news had a different effect on the Sanhedrin, which spurred Herod Agrippa on in his violent intentions towards the church. He had Peter seized during the Feast of Unleavened Bread and imprisoned in a cell in the Fortress of Antonia, located at the northwest corner of the temple.

The seven day feast followed on from the great pilgrim festival of Passover, causing Jerusalem's population to explode. Herod Agrippa knew what he was doing. His message would reach the largest number of his people in the shortest amount of time: Israel's King was a devout adherent to Judaism; divisive sects would not be tolerated.

❋ ❋ ❋

Ten years Lord ... ten years since you faced the farce of your trial at Passover. I denied you then. Please give me courage now. Oh, God ... he wept for James, shuddering at the thought that the same fate awaited him. He touched his neck with his fingertips and swallowed hard. At least it will be quick, he thought. His chains clinked together as he lowered his hands. This is the last night ...

The soldiers either side of him both stirred in their sleep. Peter closed his eyes, visualising the Roman squad outside the prison door. A fresh squad took over every three hours. He wondered how many changes had occurred; how much longer before the end?

Thank you Lord for releasing me from prison in the past. My times are in your hands. If it be your will, let me live and declare your works. But if it be your will that, like James, I depart this life, then so be it. For the glory of your Name ... your Kingdom come ... He shivered involuntarily. He slipped into fitful sleep.

The next thing he knew someone struck him hard on his side. He opened his eyes with a start, only to close them again against blinding light. He lifted one hand as a shield; his chains rattled. He squinted through his fingers into the light, realising that the source of light was, yet again, a person. He thought he was dreaming about his previous escape from prison.

'Quick, get up!' the angel said. Instantly the chains fell off his wrists. 'Put on your clothes and sandals.'

Peter obeyed.

'Wrap your cloak around you and follow me,' the angel instructed him.

Peter followed him out of the cell in a trance-like state. He had no idea that what the angel was doing was really happening. They passed the first and second guards and came to the iron gate leading to the city. It opened by itself, and they went through it. When they had walked the length of one street, suddenly the angel left him.

Peter came to his senses, like a sleepwalker. He looked around him at the empty street in bewilderment. Was it real? ... Not a dream? ... Am I really free? You sent your angel to rescue me again ... why not James? Oh, God ... why not James? ... This makes no sense ... Ah, Lord ... forgive me ... blessed are those who trust when they do not understand ... I trust you, I trust you ...

Gathering himself together and getting his bearings he began walking in the direction of the nearest place where the believers were meeting. A wealthy woman had opened her home to be used for prayer after James's death. Peter knew a number of believers had been praying there day and night. It was only a few streets away from the temple. When he found it he rapped the secret knock on the outer door and waited pensively.

✳ ✳ ✳

Rhoda had fallen asleep on Mary's couch in the living room where believers had gathered to pray. She hadn't returned to work, but stayed huddled in a truamatised state since James's death. People had taken it in turns to pray with her, never leaving her alone for a minute. They ministered to her all through the Passover and the feast of unleavened bread. She had finally been able to sleep through the last few nights, but only when surrounded by people.

She woke with a start. There it was again – the secret knock only believers knew. She looked around her, but no one else seemed to have heard it. They were absorbed in earnest prayer. She slowly stood up, steadying herself against the wall. She felt less anxious than she had done for some time. She breathed in deeply and opened the door beside her, making her way to the outer courtyard and entrance. She stopped at the door and waited. There it was again.

She opened a shutter covering a small peep-hole at the centre of the thick wood. She gasped and slammed it shut. It couldn't be!

She ran back and burst into the living room shouting, 'Peter is at the door!'

'Oh, Rhoda, come rest … your mind is overwrought with grief,' Mary said hurrying to her side and putting her arms around her. 'John-Mark, get a wet cloth for her head.'

'I swear to you, he is standing outside the outer entrance. I heard the secret knock and looked through the hatch. It's Peter!'

'Perhaps it's his angel?' someone said.

'No – it's just him – go and see!'

As Mary and John-Mark hurried down into their courtyard they heard the knocking on the outer door. 'She's right – there is someone there,' Mary said to her son. Everyone else followed them out under the stardusted night sky. John-Mark opened the hatch and looked through. He then motioned for his mother to look.

On seeing Peter, she opened the locks as fast as she could and flung the door open, 'Peter!' she exclaimed.

Once they had all gathered in the living room again, Peter motioned with his hands for them to be quiet. He described to them how the Lord had brought him out of prison, 'Tell John, Jesus' brother, and the other apostles about this.'

'The most pressing concern for us now is that you escape to a place where Herod cannot harm you,' John-Mark said. A discussion ensued as to where Peter should go.

As he was leaving, Rhoda stopped him at the door. With anguished eyes she asked him, 'Why did the Lord not do the same for James?'

Peter bowed his big head, shaking it sadly from side to side, 'I don't know, Rhoda. All I do know is that while I have breath I must proclaim that the Kingdom of Heaven is near. When breath is taken from me, I will enter into his Kingdom fully. Your cousin has the joy of being with Christ now, of seeing him face to face, while we live on here through sufferings of many kinds, holding dear to our hearts the promise of what is to come.'

Rhoda's young face was wet with tears, 'It doesn't make any sense ...'

'No child, it doesn't. Not from this side.'

He lifted her small chin gently with a big hand. Her red eyes raised to his, searching for something to hold on to.

'Your name ... Rhoda ... it means rose, doesn't it?' asked the weathered fisherman.

'Yes ...' she looked bewildered.

'Bloom no matter what,' he said, 'and when you cannot bloom because you have been crushed, then let your fragrance rise from your crushed petals as a pleasing incense before the Lord.' Rhoda began to cry again.

❋   ❋   ❋

'That is beautiful,' Lila said.

'I know ... it has sustained me,' Rhoda's young face had some hope in it now.

John wiped his eyes, 'Like a rose,' he whispered, 'he was crushed like a rose.'

Rhoda nodded, 'May our prayers, rising from our sufferings, be like incense before the Lord.'

John stood up, raising his hands and began to pray, 'Make his life count, Lord, may my brother's life be a fragrant offering before you. Bring good out of evil, do not waste it.'

The others stood, joining him in prayer.

6. FREE

Acts 16:11–40 *The liberated women*

'I don't think Alpha would be right for St Stephen's,' Grace said to Trevor over a lukewarm cup of tea and a past-its-use-by-date digestive biscuit at their monthly Deanery meeting.

'Perhaps if you ran it for the church only, they might gain some confidence in it first?' Trevor replied, dunking his biscuit too far into his mug and losing half of it.

'Maybe,' Grace grimaced as she watched him fish around in his tea for what he'd lost. 'How's the course going at St Matt's?'

'Really well. We've got the Holy Spirit weekend coming up. James and Marie Martin have been to every session and have signed up for the weekend. We've got about thirty people coming away all together. Marvellous!' he beamed, his skin cracking round his mouth and eyes as he spooned biscuity-sludge into his mouth.

Grace had to look away, 'Let me know how it goes.'

The Area Dean was calling the meeting back to order so they returned to their seats. A message came through on her phone. When she saw it was from Chloe she opened it.

Help! Mel wants to know why Mark's sleeping in the spare room. What do I say? OMG!

Grace read it twice, keeping one ear on what was being discussed in the meeting. Then she replied, *Snoring? Farting? And that's just you. Speak to you in a bit.* She added a smiley face, desperate to keep it light even though the situation Chloe faced was so awful. How would the kids cope if they knew things were bad between their parents? Maybe they already knew.

They weren't stupid.

Grace noticed that her heart rate had accelerated just thinking of the chaos in her friend's life. She sent a prayer heavenward for each of them and then tried hard to concentrate on the matters at hand.

Chloe texted back, *lol*.

※ ※ ※

The next morning she drove down to Kent to visit Anja's grave. She could hardly believe it had been a year since her death. Her eyes wandered over the small headstone that Tom and his team had erected over her plot. She liked the inscription: *Anja, just as your angel has stood before the face of God day and night, now so do you.*

She went and filled the old jam jar she'd brought with water from the nearby tap and placed the bunch of roses in it. She set them down on the dark stone, liking the contrast of yellow on black. Her mind flitted to the remembrance service she had been planning for the following week. *I'll light a candle … Lord, could you tell Anja … tell her I'm making her life count … tell her thank you for coming into my life, even if it was for such a short time.*

Her eyes welled up, making her blink several times. She took in a deep breath, held it and then released it slowly. It was a damp autumn day. The air hung heavy with moisture around her. She knew it would send her hair into a chaos of curls. She touched it and frowned.

She looked at her watch, stepping away from the grave.

Zack had started going to school in the mornings at the beginning of the year and was now going full time. She made her way back along the M25, glad she had until three o'clock. She planned on finishing her sermon for Sunday and the service sheet for All Saints' Day next week after meeting up with Chloe. It was eleven-thirty when she arrived, half an hour later than planned.

'Sorry I'm late,' she hugged Chloe in the doorway.

'Look at your hair,' Chloe observed.

'I know – it's the moisture in the air.'

'Where have you been, a sauna?'

'No, I went to Anja's grave.'

'Oh yes … it's been a year hasn't it? I forgot. You're such a good friend! Will you do that for me when I'm gone?'

'You're not thinking of going any time soon, are you?' Grace asked as they walked down the hall into the kitchen.

'No, not while the kids are alive,' she said matter of factly.

'Don't talk like that, Chloe,' Grace sat down at the table, hanging her large, distressed leather handbag on the back of her chair.

'I'm sorry for texting you yesterday,' Chloe said dully.

'I'm glad you did – that's what friends are for.'

'You were busy.'

'I was in a Deanery meeting – not that busy,' Grace sighed wistfully, wishing such meetings were more productive.

Chloe turned her back on Grace, put the kettle on, opened an overhead cupboard and lifted down two big mugs. As she raised her arms, her sweater rode up, revealing a roll of flesh sitting on top of her jeans. Grace was surprised. Chloe usually lost weight under stress. 'So what's happening?' Grace asked, averting her eyes.

'Not sure. I keep changing my mind. I don't know what's best. Part of me just wants to end it. I'm too tired … it's too much … I don't want any more drama.'

Grace frowned, tentatively floating a question, 'Do you still love him?'

'I'd had quite a bit to drink the night I saw what he was looking at,' she poured coffee into their mugs. 'After all Melanie'd been through – to find him looking at that … I mean … it beggars belief. He'd been going on about how he'd have "bloody well killed them",' she made speech marks with her fingers in the air, 'if it had been him that found them. And then he was going on about how hard he was working, how I was too wrapped up in my work and in Melanie to notice or care about him … I couldn't bear it … the deception … and a second time at that! And he didn't answer me when I asked if he was involved with someone else.'

Grace listened. 'You didn't answer my question,' she said quietly.

'I know … how can seventeen years of choosing to love someone suddenly end?' Chloe searched Grace's blue eyes for her answer. 'Were we naive before to think that he could be free of it? I mean it's a multi-billion dollar global business. It's what men want … maybe even what they need? He's not unusual. Is it unrealistic of the church to teach abstinence from sexual immorality? Why set a standard that no one seems to be able to reach?'

Grace said nothing. She just drank her coffee and kept on listening.

Chloe took a gulp from her mug, 'But if there's nothing wrong with it, why do I feel so ... so ... oh, I don't know!' She paused, 'And all those girls are somebody's daughters – like Melanie is mine! Would any good mother dream of a future like that for their daughter?'

Grace leant forward and reached over the table to squeeze Chloe's hand. As she did she caught a whiff of wine on Chloe's breath. 'Have you been drinking – in the morning?' Grace blurted out

Chloe withdrew her hand and pulled her sweater down unnecessarily. 'No, why?' she asked leaning back in her chair and crossing her arms.

'I just got a strong whiff of wine on your breath – is that from last night?'

'Yeah, probably ... I have been going a bit OTT on the old self-medication lately,' she crossed her legs and flicked her hair back off her shoulders.

'Chloe ... that's not going to make things any better ...'

'It's a quick fix for high levels of anxiety ... It makes me feel better!'

'Be careful, babe. How much are you drinking a week?'

'You're not my doctor!' Chloe's hackles were up.

'Well ... we've been friends for a long time ... if you can't tell me, who can you tell?' Grace pierced her with her disconcerting stare.

Chloe glared at her, 'A couple of bottles,' she lied.

'How many?' Grace didn't budge.

'It's fine. It's only a few a week. Don't worry – you're such a worrier,' Chloe's tone changed from self-defensiveness to dismissiveness.

Same thing, thought Grace eyeing her friend, 'You'll get fat ...'

'It's a pain isn't it?' Chloe pinched the roll of fat above her jeans, 'Hate this!' she said jiggling it. 'My arms are getting fatter too,' she pinched under her upper arm. 'I never used to have these. Ah the joys of growing older,' she returned to her coffee, looking pleased with herself for circumnavigating the issue.

Grace let it go for now.

※   ※   ※

She was still thinking about Chloe as she returned to the vicarage, but noticed that there seemed to be a lot of people in the office next door.

She made her way round the back of My Sister's House to find out what was going on.

'Mo's engaged! Show her the ring!' Val shouted over the music that blared out of the kitchen stereo.

'Congratulations!' Grace said as loudly as she could, reaching out to hug Mo through the crowd of women. The house was at full capacity, all eight beds taken.

'That man won't know what's hit him!' Grace laughed, repeating something she'd said to her a long time ago.

Mo nodded, 'Oh, yes!' and gulped back a glass of something sparkling.

'I hope that's not alcoholic?' Grace asked.

'No – just elderflower. Couldn't wait – he just proposed – had to come round here with something!'

Grace enjoyed watching Mo's euphoria, 'Let's see the ring?'

Mo held out her hand for inspection.

'Lovely!' It was five small diamonds in a row in white gold.

'Thanks … Sean and I chose it a few weeks ago … can you believe I kept it a secret that long?'

Grace shook her unruly curls and laughed.

'Like the hair,' Mo added.

'Thanks,' Grace tried to tame it with her hands, to no avail, noticing Rose was sitting by the window, detached from the festivities. They'd heard that week that she'd finally been granted asylum. Grace moved round the room to her side.

'Hi, Rose,' she shouted.

Rose looked up and smiled showing her beautiful, even, white teeth. But there was no matching smile in her almond eyes.

Grace sat down on the floor beside her chair, 'You got asylum!'

'Yes,' Rose replied, nodding once.

'That's good?' it came out as a question.

'Yes,' Rose said again.

'Why so sad?' Grace asked.

Rose looked down into Grace's upturned face. 'I don't want to leave. This is my home … with all of you. I don't want to live alone. They showed me the council flat yesterday. I … I am afraid.'

Grace rocked back against the wall. They'd been so fixated on getting her asylum and finding the money to keep funding her at My Sister's House, that she hadn't thought about how Rose might be feeling about leaving. She sent an arrow prayer shooting out into the stratosphere, *Is there another way, Lord?*

※   ※   ※

She'd written her sermon and was tweaking the All Saints' Day service. When Chloe wasn't, Rose kept appearing on the screen of her mind. She closed her laptop and her eyes, rubbing them with her fingers. *Lord, I don't want Rose to end up like Anja. You've said we weren't meant to live alone. Please show me if there is another way?*

She worshipped and waited in reverent silence. Gwen's face came to her mind.

She lives alone too … has done for years … so many lonely people, Lord … it must be the biggest blight on the human race … maybe Gwen could help Rose? Would she let her live with her? Ex-headmistress and ex-prostitute? Grace smiled.

She opened her eyes and reached for her phone, 'Hello, Gwen? Have you got a minute? Could you pop round to mine? Thanks, it won't take long.'

※   ※   ※

'Well,' Gwen took in a shaky breath after listening to Grace's suggestion, 'I'd have to think about it. I like my routines you see,' she straightened a pleat in her tartan skirt.

'I know … it wouldn't be for long, maybe a couple of months or something – be like a bridge for her into independent living, you know what I mean? Possibly living alone so suddenly is too brutal? Maybe we need to have halfway houses for short periods of time too?'

'Let me get back to you on it,' Gwen would not be rushed.

'When?' Grace asked stubbornly.

'I'll get back to you tomorrow,' Gwen said irritably.

Afflict the comfortable and comfort the afflicted … Grace thought. *Where did I last hear that?* She waited for her brain to locate its origin … *Bishop*

Duncan at my priesting! She noticed that at the thought of him, her body didn't react as it had done before. She felt pleased and gave thanks.

❈   ❈   ❈

Peter came to the All Saints' Day service. Grace's mum had come over to mind Zack, so both of them could focus on what they each wanted to do. Grace smiled at him across the candlelit congregation from her place at the front. He sat six rows back, leaning up against the wall. The pews were full and there was only standing room at the back.

St Stephen's was a more beautiful church than St Matt's, in Grace's opinion. It was older and more ornate. Evangelicalism had not been allowed to strip it of its images and symbols. When Grace had taken up her post as incumbent, she had revelled in the oasis it was to her senses. The only thing that marred it was the smell of mould. But it looked like the PCC were going to agree a refurb within the next year, so she refused to let the smell bother her. Instead she had introduced the idea of burning incense throughout all times that the church was open. She'd gone into London and trawled Camden Market for a scent that was not too intrusive or too Eastern. She'd settled on one that smelt of cinnamon and apples. It worked quite well, she thought as she breathed in through her nose and opened her service sheet.

❈   ❈   ❈

The candlelight had the effect of making Grace's hair look like a halo around her face. Peter watched as she opened the service with a prayer. He found himself being thankful, *to whom?* he asked, as he enjoyed the rise and fall of her voice and the movement of her lips as she spoke.

He became aware of a warm sensation in his chest as the service continued. It grew so warm, it was almost hot. He found he wanted to take his overcoat off, but couldn't for fear of disturbing the person next to him. As Grace spoke simply of the love of God being like an ocean – vast, unmeasured, boundless, free – he found he wanted to kneel. He got down onto the kneeler, leaning his elbows on the shelf in front of him and put his head in his hands.

He was vaguely aware of the congregation standing for the gospel reading, but hadn't the strength the rise with them. He was so overcome that he began to cry. For a man who had not shed a tear for many years, this was a particularly strange experience.

Thank you … thank you … thank you … he whispered again and again. An image of Helen laughing filled his mind. It was a memory that pre-dated her suffering with cancer. He hadn't thought of his first wife like that for years. He found he was smiling through his tears.

She prayed for me, came the revelation. *Grace has prayed for me too … all these years … thank you …* he felt a bubbling sensation in his chest that rose to his throat and then his mouth. He heard himself whispering in a language he'd never heard before.

He felt suddenly ashamed of the scornful attitude he'd had towards Grace's description of speaking in tongues. He was overwhelmed with conviction for thinking she was mad to pray, mad to think God spoke to her, mad to expect Him to answer prayer. He thought of how he'd tried to deter Zack from believing as he so naturally wanted to. *Forgive me … I didn't know … I'm so sorry for thinking I knew better, for patronising her faith … Oh, God …* His shoulders shook.

People were going up with their tea lights and placing them around the cross on the altar. Summoning all his composure, he pulled himself together and tried to stand up. He felt so heavy that he couldn't do it. He tried again after a few minutes. Again he felt as if his body was weighed down with liquid gold.

Maybe it's the glory of God? he thought and decided not to fight it. *I am yours, to do with as you please,* he whispered. *Take me, all of me … cleanse me from my unbelief, all my resistance to your will. Heal me …* he felt surprised at this last request. He hadn't thought he needed healing. With that he suddenly knew he could stand.

He was one of the last to come forward with his candle.

❈ ❈ ❈

It was St Matt's Holy Spirit weekend. They had gone away to a retreat house. Trevor had finished the second teaching session. He had invited people to come forward to receive prayer to be filled with the Holy Spirit.

James and Marie Martin were the first to approach the front. They asked if they could be prayed for together as Marie was slightly nervous. Trevor agreed.

He placed his hands on both their heads and invited the Holy Spirit to come. He remembered Whitsun when Grace had prayed a similar prayer. He smiled as he thought of himself flat out in the choir stalls.

He opened his eyes to observe the Martins' response to whatever the Holy Spirit might do. He kept praying quietly as he waited. He could feel a pressure building up inside him and with surprise, realised that James might be feeling the same sensation.

He asked him, 'James, are you feeling any physical sensations?'

James kept his eyes shut as he replied, 'Yes … I feel a building pressure in my chest … I don't know what it is?'

Trevor prayed, 'Lord, please show us what this is?' he then waited.

James opened his eyes and turned to Marie, 'I know what it is … I need to ask you to forgive me … I have done some terrible things … it's like a dam that's blocking the way … I want it to burst … but I'm scared.'

She looked up at him tenderly and said, 'James, the Lord has told me to cover over your sins with love. I forgive you and have prayed for you all our married life that God would set you free from the things that drive you. You don't need to be afraid …'

James's handsome features crumpled. He pulled her to him, holding her tightly as silent sobs racked his body. Eventually they disentangled themselves from each other. Trevor reached up and signed James with the sign of the cross with some oil on his forehead as he said, 'Your sins are forgiven, in Jesus' name, in whom no secrets are hid.'

James bowed his head and raised his hands as did Marie. Trevor continued to bless them as they swayed gently like long grass in a summer breeze. Then James began to shake. He shook and shook so much that Trevor wondered how his body could sustain it. Eventually he became still, much to Trevor's relief.

Others had come forward to receive prayer while all this had been going on. The ministry team Grace had trained did their work well. Many were set free that day.

Trevor's mind was racing as he thought about how to take these people forward after the Alpha course was finished.

❋   ❋   ❋

'Who's that?' Chloe looked at Melanie across the table.

'Dunno … it's too late for cold callers or Jehovah's Witnesses,' Melanie checked her watch.

Chloe stood up and went to the front door. James Martin stood on the drive, looking like an advert for Mediterranean living. 'Hi, James. This is a surprise,' she held the door open.

'Yes – sorry not to ring in advance. I was wondering if Mark was in?'

'Yes, I think he's in his study. I'll just get him. Do you want to come in?' she offered uncertainly.

'No. I'll wait here. Don't want to intrude,' his white teeth flashed in his tanned face.

Chloe knocked on the study door, 'Mark, there's someone here to see you. James Martin, from church?'

Mark opened the study door. Chloe averted her eyes not wanting to look at his computer screen. Mark saw and said under his breath, 'Don't worry, there's nothing there.'

Chloe rolled her eyes behind his back as she turned to go back to the kitchen.

'Hello – James?'

'Yes – we've not really spoken much at church. Sorry to just turn up. Feel a bit of a fool now, to be honest,' James shook Mark's outstretched hand.

'What can I do for you? Do you want to come in?'

'No – no – I don't want to intrude. I just wanted to give you something. It's a course I've just done in North London. I found it very helpful. I was praying today and you came strongly to my mind. I felt that I was to let you know about it …' he withdrew a box set of CDs from his jacket pocket along with a leaflet. 'I know it must sound crazy, but I've been practising being obedient every time I think I've heard instruction from the Big Man …' he looked heavenward, 'so if I've got it wrong, please don't hold it against a novice,' he held out the box.

Mark took it and the leaflet, 'Thanks,' he said non-committally.

'I put my mobile number on the back of the leaflet. Let me know …' James said as he turned and walked to his Mercedes parked on the road. He waved as he got into the driver's seat.

Mark watched him drive away as he opened the box and began flipping through the CDs. 'Healing Prayer School?' He closed the front door and returned to his study.

Half-an-hour later he was standing in the kitchen doorway glaring at Chloe, 'Melanie, could I have a word with your mother in private please?'

'Sure,' Melanie looked at him nervously. She collected up her AS books and headed for her room.

When he was sure she was out of earshot, he came and sat down opposite Chloe. 'I've just listened to the first one – it's all about sex addictions and how they're the result of sexualised childhood anxieties. So who've you been talking to?' he asked.

'No one,' Chloe replied.

'No one?' he glared at her.

'Well only Grace ... she knows everything about us 'cuz I know she loves us both.'

'I expected that. But have you told Trevor or my prayer partners?'

'No ... why would I? That's a matter for you to decide.'

'Does Grace know James?' he persisted.

'Yeah – don't think she likes him though. What did he want?'

Mark threw the CDs in front of her in frustration.

She opened the box and read through the titles on the CDs it contained, then picked up the leaflet and began to read. 'Mmmm ... sounds good,' she said, forcing herself to remain calm as she stood up and went to the fridge, bringing back a bottle of wine. 'Do you want a glass?'

'No,' he replied.

She filled her glass three-quarters full and took her first sip.

'How did he know? He said he'd been praying ... but someone must have said something.'

'Mark ... if the guy said he was praying then take it at face value. Maybe this has been sent to help you ... God hasn't given up on you, even if the rest of us have,' she took another gulp of wine, regretting the last bit of what she'd said.

The hurt was evident in his eyes, 'Look, Chloe – I hate myself enough without your help.'

She didn't reply. He rose from the table, taking the CDs and leaflet with him, leaving her alone. She gazed after him, gulping down more of the

French countryside. It wasn't until the second glass that she felt the first hit of alcohol on her system and began to relax.

❋　❋　❋

Chloe went upstairs to check on Melanie. She knocked on her bedroom door and waited for the 'Come in' she was hoping for.

'Hi, Mel, sorry about that. He's in a bit of a grump over something to do with work. You okay?'

'Yeah … Just struggling with psychology. So many terms to remember.'

Chloe nodded and stepped into her room, 'I know – it's a pretty tough subject to study … but it's fascinating.'

'I'm just getting bored now. I want A-levels to be over so I can get on with my life.'

'They'll help you get on with your life. Just take them a step at a time. You did so well in GCSEs. I'm sure you'll sail through these,' Chloe reassured her, coming to sit on the end of her bed.

'But I want to help people like Rose now! She doesn't want to live on her own … she's really scared about next week.'

'I know. I think Grace has something in mind to help her.'

'Really? What?'

'She hasn't said what yet …'

'Oh …' Melanie doodled on her note pad.

'How was your session today at the therapy centre?'

'Yeah, it was cool. We're learning about mindfulness – being present in the moment. It was good.'

'Do you feel it's helping you with … with everything?'

'Grace helped a lot and this is helping in a different way. It's kind of like a practical toolkit you get with a car for when you get a flat tyre or something.'

Chloe smiled, 'That's a good analogy. Reminds me – we need to book you some driving lessons.'

'Yeah … Mum?'

'Yes?'

'How would you feel if I started going to St Stephen's instead of St Matt's?'

Chloe was surprised, 'It's pretty high church you know,' she warned.

'I know – but Grace is so great and I don't really get anything out of St Matt's youth group any more ... well ... I don't go that much ... hate them all knowing about what happened to me.'

Chloe nodded. 'I don't mind darling. It's wonderful you still want to go to church. Most teenagers have long gone by now.'

'Thanks ... can I tell Grace tomorrow?'

'Sure ... what about Sean and Trevor?'

'Can you tell them?'

'Okay ... yes, I'll do that tomorrow too,' Chloe felt the urge for another drink. She leant over and kissed Melanie on the cheek and then left.

She knocked on Charlie's door as she went past, 'You guys all right in there?'

'Yes, Mum,' came Charlie's muffled voice.

'Can I come in?' she heard them scrambling around as she opened the door. 'Look boys, it's getting late. You need to go to sleep or you'll never wake up for school tomorrow.'

'Sorry, Mum,' Charlie piped up from under his duvet. 'We were playing a game. We'll stop now.'

'Okay – night Jules, night Charlie,' the only ground she gave her unease was to leave the door ajar.

※　　※　　※

'So I was wondering if I could get confirmed at St Stephen's?' Melanie asked Grace, sitting in 'My Sister's House' office.

'That would be great!' Grace replied, adding, 'You'd need to check with your parents and with Trevor and Sean first. Hey, did you know he and Mo got engaged?'

'Yeah – it's so sweet! They're all loved up! Yeah, Mum's talking to Trevor and Sean today. She's happy for me to come to your church – I'm sure she'll be even more happy about me getting confirmed.'

Grace smiled affectionately at Melanie, 'You're doing so well, Mel.'

'I know!' she beamed, 'the therapy centre's been really good for me.'

'You can tell. How's it going with food?'

'You wouldn't believe it but I had gravy on mashed potatoes last night.'

'Wow! That is awesome! Oh, I wanted to tell you that Rose is moving in with Gwen for a while before going to live independently.'

'With Gwen? But she's so old!'

'But she's lived alone all her life … she'll be able to help Rose prepare for it. It'll bridge the gap between living in a shared house to living alone. I think it'll be great.'

Melanie didn't look convinced, 'It is a good idea to have halfway houses between a safe house and independent living … but Gwen? She's so fusty!'

Grace chuckled, 'Underneath that school-marm exterior, lies a very compassionate heart.'

'Maybe that could be something I work on? I could develop ideas for halfway houses.'

'That would be great, Mel – get to work,' she brought her index finger down on the desk between them overdramatically.

'I will,' Melanie swivelled away spiritedly to her computer. 'Can I ask you something?'

'Sure,' Grace replied.

'Do you know what's going on with mum and dad? The atmosphere is pretty bad at home. They're not sharing a bed anymore either.'

Grace looked at her, 'You'll need to ask your mum and dad, Melanie.'

❋ ❋ ❋

'I think it's a brothel,' James said to Sean under his breath. They were scouting out that part of town, prior to their Street Pastors shift. They stood across the road from the Indian restaurant where Grace had found Melanie.

'It can't be,' Sean shook his head, 'the police were all over it after Melanie's rescue.'

'But what better place than one that everyone thinks has been searched and sorted?'

'I'm confused,' Sean muttered.

'Just watch,' James said, pretending to look at his phone. 'I think they've built onto the back as well – so the kitchen is tiny, and there's another couple of rooms back there that they're using as well as the flat above.'

'How do you know?'

'Look … how many men have you seen going in there in the last hour? Have you been keeping count?'

'Ten ... maybe twelve?' Sean's scalp reflected the orange street light overhead, through a number two hair cut.

'I've counted fifteen going in and only three have come out in the last hour.'

'So they're waiting for their orders,' Sean turned his collar up as it began to rain.

James crushed his impatience with the youngster and gritted his teeth, 'Look in the window – there's only standing room in there. No tables and chairs. There's only five men waiting.'

The lights were dim, but as Sean looked he realised James was right. 'What are we gonna do?' Sean asked uncertainly.

'Why don't we go in like clients and bust the thing wide open?'

'Clients?' Sean's usual laid-back voice suddenly sounded staccato. 'I can't be seen to be going into a brothel. I'd lose my CRB and risk my job – everything!'

'I'll go in then,' James said. 'You call the police when I give you the signal. Don't call them before I'm sure I'm right.'

'Okay ...' Sean was not convinced. 'I don't remember any Street Pastor training about this kind of op?' he squinted into the rain as he looked at James.

'Well maybe we'll have to add it to the training,' James grinned. 'Right, I'm off.'

Before Sean could argue, James was running across the street, dodging the puddles in his Italian leather shoes. He pushed open the door, noting that the man behind the counter scrutinised him carefully. He'd been to outfits like this in the past – there would be some kind of secret code he'd need to use to communicate what he wanted. He scanned the menu on the wall after making polite conversation about the disgusting weather. He noticed that at the end of the menu there were three kinds of rice offered. In bold type: *White, brown or wild*. There were two numbers beside each.

He went with his gut instinct and read out the two numbers beside the wild rice. The shop keeper narrowed his eyes slightly as he looked at him and said, 'That's a number 36 and a 12 and wild rice?'

'Yes please,' he replied confidently.

'I'm afraid you'll have to wait upstairs for that order, sir. The stairs are just here,' he waggled his head from side to side as he smiled slyly, 'You pay there.'

'Okay …' James said moving towards the door at the side of the counter.

He heard one of the customers say, 'This is the weirdest take away I've ever been to.'

James clenched his jaw muscles grimly and took the stairs two at a time as he heard the shop owner proceeding to go into an elaborate explanation to the waiting customers of why they had their take away restaurant functioning on two levels.

Sure enough when he reached the top, there was another set of stairs going down to the back of the premises. James texted Sean – *Call them now*, stuffing his phone back into his jacket pocket as he entered the black and white living room. There were two bored looking, skimpily clad girls sitting on the sofa watching the Jeremy Kyle show. One was black and one was oriental, possibly Indonesian or Vietnamese, James tried to guess.

On the other side of the room sat a fat, Asian man. He had several gold chains round his neck one of which had a large Islamic moon and star hanging from it. A thick gold bracelet adorned his wrist, with arabic writing running round it. James grinned at him, 'Business must be good?', he said eyeing the gold jewellery.

The man looked up at him one eye moving slower than the other, 'You wanted wild? You wait ten minutes more only … then yours.'

James raised an eyebrow questioningly, 'Where can I wait?'

'Sit here,' the man motioned with his hand to a black leather chair with a pile of newspapers on it. 'Throw them there,' he pointed at the glass coffee table. James noticed a dusting of white powder on the glass surface that flew into the air as the newspapers landed.

'You got any more?' James tapped his nose.

'Yes,' the man waggled his head from side to side '… good quality … how much you want?'

'May I see?' James asked leaning forward. He sensed the girls on the sofa lean forward too as the man pulled out a bag full of smaller sachets of white powder.

Now would be a really good time, he thought, glancing at the window.

He took one of the sachets and shook it, holding it up to the light.

'Is very good,' the man insisted.

'Can I taste?' James knew he was pushing it.

The man looked uncertain.

They heard a shout from below and the sound of booted feet on the stairs. The girls screamed as armed police burst into the room. James stood up and grinned broadly at them, holding up the sachet in front of him. 'They're all yours,' he spread his hands magnanimously.

The Asian man stood up and said, 'We find them for you!' wrapping an arm around James's shoulder. James looked at him and saw desperation in his eyes. He wrestled with how to react for a split second and then decided.

'Yeah, Omar here plays a blinder stooge!' James slapped the man's back and clamped his hand down on his shoulder in a vice-like grip.

The officer facing them wasn't buying it. James tried harder, 'He's with me, mate. We were in the sting together.'

'Together,' the man echoed, his voice rising with pain as James's grip tightened.

'Why's he not wearing Street Pastor stuff?' the officer asked moving towards 'Omar'.

'Undercover!' James tried.

Disregarding him, the officer pushed 'Omar' up against the wall and began handcuffing him.

Chaos, shouting and screaming could be heard coming from the other rooms.

In the end eight girls were rescued, the youngest a twelve year old.

※ ※ ※

'They kill me ... my wife, my children ... all die,'

'Who will kill you?' James asked as they waited in the alleyway to be questioned by the police.

'I come Pakistan – here – he pay – I work for him. Now girls gone, he kill me ... my family.'

'Not if we bring him in,' James said.

The man looked terrified.

'Where's your family?'

The man was shivering in the rain, wearing only a thin shirt. He didn't answer James.

'Look – I'll go get them – your family – I'll bring them to police station together. You give them the names of the traffickers – then they'll protect you. You see?'

'I don't know names,' he answered, wild-eyed.

'Sure you do!'

❈　❈　❈

'I'm really struggling, Peter.'

'What's up?' he put down his book and took his reading glasses off.

She finished brushing her hair at her dressing table and then turned and climbed into bed beside him, her dressing gown still wrapped round her. The high ceilinged rooms of the vicarage were hard to warm in winter.

'Trevor's asked James to be a trustee of My Sister's House and he's said yes.'

'Trevor knows how you feel?'

'Yep. We had some pretty fierce discussions about it. Short of telling them all the real reason I don't want him involved, I didn't really have a leg to stand on. We've been looking for someone with business acumen for a while … and he's been doing some great work with the Street Pastors as well – he's perfect for the role.'

Peter listened thoughtfully. Then much to Grace's surprise Peter asked her if he could pray. Grace listened in wonder at first, her ear pressed up to his chest. The undulating sound of his voice speaking to the Great Unseen in a rather stilted, yet conversational manner; the rise and fall in time to the beat of his heart was the most soothing thing she thought she'd ever heard. She felt her whole body relaxing.

The next thing she knew her alarm was going – it was five thirty am.

Zack usually woke at six thirty and Peter left the house at seven thirty. She looked over at Peter. His face seemed younger in sleep, like when they'd first met, except for the grey around his temples. A surge of love for him swept through her as she quietly got up, slipped on her slippers and tightly wrapped her dressing gown round her. She managed to avoid all the creaky floorboards as she crept downstairs.

Before she settled herself at her desk to pray she found the story from Acts chapter sixteen and read it through. She opened her laptop and found her story file. 'Even the jailer was set free ...' she said to herself, thinking of James Martin, wondering if he really could be trusted.

She began to write, and later after the interruption of the school run, returned to it:

❀   ❀   ❀

They arrived as others were gathering in the entrance courtyard of John-Mark's home. It was lavish, like that of a High Priest's. Situated near the Temple, it enjoyed one of the best locations in Jerusalem. Lila marvelled at the ornate mosaic tiled courtyard and the elegant fountain that tinkled at its centre. Servants made their way through the guests carrying bronze trays of sweetmeats and pastries.

Eventually Mary, John-Mark's mother stood at the top of the flight of stairs that led from the courtyard into her home, and called for people's attention. A hush descended as she introduced her guest of honour.

'Brothers and sisters, as some of you may know the apostles here in Jerusalem and the elders in Antioch have commissioned a record of the things that our Lord Jesus did and taught until the day he was taken up to heaven as well as a record of what has happened among us since. I want to introduce the dear friend and brother who is doing this work – Doctor Luke,' she stepped back as the doctor stepped forward.

'Thank you, Mary, for your warm welcome. Thank you all for gathering here tonight,' he spoke Aramaic well, his Syrian accent a pleasant distraction. 'As you have heard I am an itinerant doctor by trade. I have travelled much, but hail from Syria. It was through our brother Saul that I first believed in our Lord Jesus Christ, here in this very city,' he smiled through his black, glossy beard. 'I had returned from a season of work in Philippi and Troas and was visiting friends here in Jerusalem. A devout proselyte, I enjoyed spending time in debate and discussion with my educated friends among the Pharisees and the Sanhedrin.

'Saul had been sent from the Sanhedrin to Damascus, with authority to take prisoner all followers of The Way. While I was staying with my friend Aaron, Saul returned from his mission a changed man. He spoke of having an encounter with the risen Lord Jesus Christ on the road to Damascus, of being blinded and instructed to wait for a man named Ananias to come and pray for his sight to be restored.'

Lila felt her nerves jolt at the mention of Aaron's name. No matter how many years went by, he would not remain buried in the past. She shivered. She looked up at Jair anxiously, and was reassured by his calm expression and responded tentatively to his smile, thinking fondly of Ananias.

'He received his sight when Ananias laid hands upon him in the name of Jesus, repented of persecuting His followers and was baptised. He spent time in Damascus learning from the believers there. On threat to his life he escaped to Jerusalem. He sought out Aaron in particular because, I believe, he has great influence in the Sanhedrin. He wanted to convince him of the truth he now understood. Sadly Aaron was not persuaded.'

Lila and Jair exchanged another look.

'But I was,' he laughed joyfully. The listening crowd erupted into shouts of 'Amen' and 'Hallelujah!'

'I parted company with Aaron and spent some time with Saul, returning with him to his home in Tarsus. When Barnabas came and sought him out, I went with them to my home city of Antioch and have been involved in the growing church there ever since.

'Saul now uses his Roman name Paul as he spends much of his time ministering to Gentiles. We call him the apostle to the Gentiles!' he chuckled. 'He has travelled with Barnabas to Salamis and Paphos in Cyprus, then on to the mainland, to Artalia, Perga, Iconium, Lystra and Derbe, preaching the good news of our Lord Jesus Christ in all the synagogues, leading both Jews and God-fearing Gentiles to faith in our precious Messiah.

'John-Mark,' he turned to his hostess's son who stood to one side with his mother, 'you travelled with them as their helper for a time … I'm sure you have shared the many stories of the Lord's hand working powerfully with you as you proclaimed the gospel in Cyprus?'

John-Mark nodded seriously. Lila knew there'd been a falling out of some sort with Paul, but had only heard snippets. She studied John-Mark's young face as Doctor Luke paused, She thought she saw traces of hurt in his eyes, but couldn't be sure. She knew John-Mark loved the Lord Jesus, but she didn't know why he had left Paul and Barnabas in Perga. No one really knew.

Doctor Luke resumed his address, 'Paul and Barnabas returned to Antioch and continued to strengthen the church there. Paul came as part of the Council that met here in Jerusalem. Along with Barnabas and brother Peter, he has enabled all of us to come to a clear understanding that the Lord Jesus accepts the Gentile as well as the Jew who trusts in him, to be part of his chosen people. He freely gives them the gift of the Holy Spirit, regardless of circumcision.'

Again a few 'Amen's went up from among the listeners.

'Paul was eager to revisit all those to whom they had first preached the Word of God. He also wished to deliver the decisions reached by the apostles and elders in the Jerusalem Council, so that all the churches throughout the world would understand and know God's will. Barnabas wished to take you, John-Mark,' he turned to the young man, whose head was down, 'but I hear you and Barnabas are to return to Cyprus?'

John-Mark nodded, raising his eyes briefly to Luke's.

'And Paul chose brother Silas to go with him through Phrygia and Galatia. They left some time ago and in Lystra they have been joined by a brother named Timothy. I am on my way to meet them. I would greatly value your prayers for my journey and for whatever lies ahead of us as we go further in our mission to preach the gospel to all creation.

'As many of you know Paul and Barnabas suffered opposition in Paphos, expulsion from Pisidian Antioch, threats of ill-treatment in Iconium. They were mistaken as gods in Lystra because the Lord healed the feet of a lame man through Paul. Then the people were persuaded to oppose their teaching by some Jews from Antioch, and Paul was stoned and dragged out of the city, being left for dead. But the believers gathered round him and prayed for him and he was restored.'

A pregnant silence hung in the air as everyone thought of those they remembered and loved who had been treated in a similar way by Paul; Lila thought of Stephen.

'I am under no illusions,' Luke spread his hands, 'I know allegiance to the gospel may require our very lives,' he looked across his audience, his eyes soft with lamplight and affection. 'The church continues to grow across the world, despite opposition. As long as we hold on to the truth that our lives are hidden with Christ in God, we will not fail.

'I travel to Caesarea in a few days' time and then on to Troas. Please ... I welcome your prayers,' he beckoned them. Many surged forward, stretching their hands out towards the doctor. He disappeared from view under a forest of arms and hands. Lila turned to Jair.

'Are you thinking what I'm thinking?' he asked her.

'Let's speak with him after this,' she clasped his hand in hers.

※　※　※

Lila could hardly believe that they had managed to pack up their home in so short a time. They had left it to the church to use or to sell as they saw fit. Despite the years they had spent there, it was not hard to do. It had been used to strengthen the church while they lived in it, and it seemed fitting that it would continue to be used as such as they left it behind.

As they approached Caesarea, the smell of the sea reminded her of when she had discovered she was pregnant with Joshua. Those days of following Jesus were the sweetest she'd ever known. She looked at the back of her son's head as he walked between his father and Doctor Luke. She gave thanks again for his life as her eye followed the line of his neck into his dark curls. He was rapt in discussion with them, revelling in being a man amongst men. He had inherited Jair's studious nature and could always be found engrossed in a scroll, even when working with Jair in his workshop.

Anna walked tall – taller than her mother. There was no denying that she was a striking young woman. Lila had been aware of men looking at her as they'd journeyed along the road from Jerusalem. Her dread of arranging a marriage for her firstborn stung her. She swatted the thought like an insect, turning to rummage in one of the food bags for some dried figs.

'Do you want one?' she offered an open handful to Anna.

'No thank you, Mama. It won't be long now. I can smell the sea. Where are we staying?'

'With some friends of Luke's. Apparantly they are leaders in the church that meets there. They opened their home to him some years ago and he has stayed with them ever since.'

They eventually came to the house. Luke knocked on the outer door. It was late afternoon, past the time of rest. They heard the sound of girls' laughter and then the door was flung open by not one, but three girls of varying heights.

'Uncle Luke!' shouted the oldest one, throwing her arms round his waist. The other two followed so that he was encircled by a chain of arms and long, shiny plaits.

'Is that you, Luke?' came a male voice.

'Philip?' Jair and Lila said at once, recognising his voice.

On seeing them he shouted loudly, 'Mary! Mary! Come and see who is here.'

Lila looked up at Jair in disbelief. Could it be? The sound of light, running, bare feet were heard and then there she was, a baby in her arms.

'Mary!' Lila exclaimed, overjoyed.

※　※　※

They stayed several days with Mary and Philip. Martha and Lazarus came that first evening for a meal. Everyone talked over one another excitedly, reminiscing and retelling story upon story.

Mary's girls listened wide-eyed. They sat as close as they could to Anna and Joshua, thrilled at discovering they had extended family.

Lila and Mary sat arm in arm that first night, vascillating between laughter and tears. When Lila held Mary's youngest in her arms she could not stop crying, 'We thought you would never have children ...'

'I know!' Mary smiled, fondling the tiny foot that stuck out under Lila's arm. 'Junia became part of our family before I married Philip. She was ten when she came to us from Tabitha. She has been the greatest blessing. The Lord's hand is powerfully with her.'

'I've been wondering about that – trying to work out the timescale and Junia's age!' Lila laughed, 'Who's Tabitha?' she asked.

'She is a disciple who cares for widows and orphans in their distress down in Joppa. It was through her that I was delivered of the despair that held me prisoner for so long after Stephen's death.'

'What happened?'

'I think we had been here two or three years ... I can never be sure. The entire time I was locked in an emotional darkness. Tabitha became ill. Martha and Lazarus brought me to her, hoping she could help me come out of mourning, even on her sick bed, but by the time we arrived she had died. Peter came and as he prayed for her to live again, I too found myself being called back to life. You could say we were both resurrected that day.'

'Incredible!' Lila whispered, gently stroking the baby's tiny hand.

'We kept our connection with Tabitha and the sisters who have gathered to her. They do so much good. Tabitha had rescued Junia from a brothel. She'd been sold into slavery by her relatives after her mother died giving birth to her.'

'A child in a brothel?' Lila felt sick as dormant childhood memories of her father's drunken visits in the night suddenly sprang to life.

'I think Tabitha found her when she was five ... I know,' she said, watching Lila's expression. 'She prayed for her daily ... the child was tormented. She raised her as her own and to know the Lord. However, when she was ten God spoke to Tabitha in a vision, telling her he wished to instruct Junia further and to send her to us. Junia had the same instruction in a dream and so, along with some other sisters, came here. They helped us begin our work among the prostitutes near the harbour.'

'So four daughters! Four!' Lila silently committed the old feelings that had been stirred to God.

'I know!' Mary said again and smiled across the table at Philip.

'The Lord has restored the years the locusts have eaten,' Lila looked into Mary's eyes as they both thought of the four tiny babies that Mary had buried under bitter herbs all those years ago. 'May we bless them?' Lila asked.

'That would be wonderful,' Mary responded. 'Girls, come, come over here – sit between your uncle Jair and aunt Lila.'

Her daughters obeyed.

'Come, help us,' Lila beckoned her children.

They rose and came to stand behind Mary's girls.

'Let's bless these wonderful young miracles,' Lila smiled at Anna and Joshua, who placed their hands on the girls' shoulders as their parents rested their hands upon their heads in turn.

'Lord, we thank you for each one of these precious girls,' Jair prayed.

'Yes, Lord God, bless them with wisdom and insight. Fill them with your Spirit. May they declare your praises all the days of their lives,' Lila prayed as she laid her hands on Junia, pouring all the love she could muster upon her.

'May they have their minds fixed on you and speak forth your thoughts,' Anna prayed.

'May they be bold and very courageous,' Joshua prayed.

'So we bless you Junia, Esther, Phoebe ...you haven't told us your youngest's name?' Lila asked. 'Have you named her yet?'

'No, we hadn't. But when you arrived we both instantly knew her name – it's Lila!' Mary declared.

'After me?' Lila asked incredulous.

'No after Luke!' Philip roared with laughter.

※　※　※

As the wind caught the single rectangular sail of the ship, Lila wiped away the tears that persistently blurred her vision. She waved at the precious little group dwarfed by the temple to Caesar that Herod had built opposite the north-facing harbour-mouth. Mary, Philip, their girls, the elderly Martha and Lazarus clustered together blowing kisses and waving.

'Oh, Jair ... are we doing the right thing?' she leaned into him, resting her head on his chest.

His only answer was a tight hug.

'It was wonderful to see her again ... so happy ... a mother of children ... four girls!' she laughed through her tears.

'I know ... and with Philip! The Lord surely works in mysterious ways,' Jair laughed as a blast of wind whipped one of his ringlets into his face.

'Yes,' Lila sighed. She clutched the side of the ship as they hit deep water. Never having been at sea before, she panicked, 'Where are Anna and Joshua?' she turned from watching the diminishing harbour to frantically searching the deck of the ship.

'Don't worry. They are fine. They are with Doctor Luke. Look,' he pointed to the bow of the ship. The three of them stood, peering out to sea, the wind tearing at their hair, 'They will learn much from him,' Jair smiled.

Lila felt somewhat redundant and uncertain. She turned back to look at the harbour. The six colossal statues that stood either side of its mouth, were no bigger than her little finger now. She looked down at the greeny-blue depths beneath her and then back at the coast. She felt as small and insignifcant as the statues now appeared. Realisation dawned that this new phase of her life would require greater faith than she'd ever had before. She turned to Jair, 'Pray with me,' she gripped his arms, overwhelmed by the fear of the unknown.

There on the deck they knelt and prayed. They gave thanks for Mary and Philip and for Martha and Lazarus; they celebrated the miracle of their four children; they asked for comfort for their grief at leaving all that was familiar to them, for safety, for provision, for guidance, but most of all for the faith they would need to face whatever lay ahead.

※　※　※

Paul, Silas and Timothy met them at Troas harbour. After days and nights being driven by a strong wind, Lila yearned for solid ground beneath her feet. Sights, sounds and smells overwhelmed the senses as they entered the bustling Roman port. The smells of herbs and spices, rotting fish and rubbish had the greatest effect on Lila. Somehow their earthiness comforted her. She had hated being at sea: the monotony of it and the terrifying lack of stability had worked on her mind, causing her to seriously doubt they had done the right thing by embarking on this journey. But now, as they docked and ropes were flung over the bulwarks, her muddled emotions and thoughts began to rally.

Paul was the first to embrace each of them, showing no surprise that Luke had brought travelling companions with him, but rejoicing in being reunited with those who first shared the gospel with him. He introduced Silas and Timothy to them as they waited for their belongings to be unloaded. Lila was so thrilled to be on land again, that she almost missed the glint of interest that sparked in her daughter's eyes when young Timothy was presented to them. He was very serious and quiet and showed no obvious reciprocal interest that Lila could detect.

But it was later when they lay down to sleep that night that Jair whispered, 'Did you see the way Timothy looked at Anna when he thought no one was watching?'

※　※　※

'He said, "Come over to Macedonia and help us,"' Paul said as he scooped the gritty sweetness of a fig out of its skin and into his mouth.

The others ate their breakfast thoughtfully.

Silas was the first to speak, 'We must never ignore such specific dreams. It would be good to pray together and seek the Lord. The Spirit will give us discernment. Jair, I don't know what your plans are, but if you and your family would like to join us in prayer, you would be most welcome.'

Jair replied, 'We have come to join you in spreading the gospel,' he looked from Silas to Paul. 'As we prayed about what the Lord would have us do, we felt he did not wish us to remain in Jerusalem. It is becoming increasingly dangerous there, though that is not to say it will be any more safe here. But when we heard

Luke speak, we came to him and asked if we could join him to meet you ... and here we are,' he ended abruptly, unsure of where to go from there.

'Do you know of the troubles we have faced?' Paul asked, looking at Lila, Anna and Joshua.

'Yes,' Jair replied. 'But we have all sensed the Lord call us here to help you in any way we can.'

Paul smiled kindly at Lila and Anna, 'I would spare you the trials we may face.'

Anna spoke up, 'Brother Paul,' she smiled shyly, 'May I speak?'

'Certainly sister, speak your heart,' he returned the smile with a slight nod of his head. Lila's heart skipped a beat as she noted Timothy's expression.

'We love our Lord Jesus with all our hearts. We have known him and followed him ever since I can remember. Each one of us has entrusted our lives into his loving hands. We will go wherever he leads.'

Joshua nodded his head beside her, 'That's right, isn't it, brother Luke?' he turned to the doctor, who was wiping his mouth and beard with a napkin.

'You will not find a more committed family,' Luke said to Paul. 'They have impressed me beyond measure in their dedication and devotion to the Lord.'

Paul gazed at each of them, 'Well then, let us turn to prayer,' he said simply.

※　※　※

After Paul had seen the vision, we got ready at once to leave for Macedonia, concluding that God had called us to preach the gospel to them. From Troas we put out to sea and sailed straight for Samothrace, and the next day we went on to Neapolis. From there we traveled to Philippi, a Roman colony and the leading city of that district of Macedonia. And we stayed there several days.

Luke put his reed pen down beside the sheet of papyrus. The four stones at each corner held it still, despite the light breeze.

They were staying in a guesthouse on the edge of Philippi, a city which its inhabitants claimed was the leading Roman city in Macedonia. The next day was the Sabbath, yet they had not been able to locate a synagogue in the city.

'What shall we do on the Sabbath?' Luke asked Paul when he found him. He was sitting in the courtyard of the guesthouse, leaning against a wall with his face turned towards the sun.

Paul lifted his head off the wall and opened his eyes, squinting and lifting his hand for shade, 'There must be a house of prayer down near the river, outside the city. Shall we go and explore?'

'Yes ... I have found it is common practice for you Jews to build synagogues outside the city near sea or a river to facilitate your ritual washing,' Luke nodded his agreement.

The next day they rose early and together made their way down to the stream that flowed a short distance away from the city's west gate. Sure enough they found a small synagogue nestled among the Cyprus trees that grew close along its banks. Lila was surprised that there were only women gathered there, but Paul was not deterred and began to speak to them about Jesus, as was his custom.

Lila felt the old excitement she'd had when following Jesus. As she watched the women's faces, one in particular kept drawing her eye back again and again. She was a little older, Lila guessed, than herself. She did not cover her head, but in Macedonian style her greying hair was on display, piled up in several plaits. As she listened to Paul, an intelligent expression in her eyes, Lila knew she would believe.

As their time together drew to a close, Lila rose and approached her, 'My name is Lila,' she said. 'It is good to meet today and worship the one true God.'

The woman got to her feet as well and smiled, 'My name is Lydia. I have been a worshipper for many years now, but I have never heard the things that your companion spoke of today. I am fascinated. Did you know this Jesus?'

'Yes. He saved me in every way possible,' she pressed her hand to her chest, remembering the first time she'd become aware of the bubbling sensation that was the spring of eternal life welling up within her.

'I want what you obviously have,' she said candidly. 'My heart feels like it has been ripped open as I've listened. I want to respond in some way ... but I'm not sure how?'

Lila took her arm and said, 'Come,' leading her over to Paul.

They spoke for some time. He eventually called those who were waiting for her outside to come back into the synagogue. Lila exulted as Lydia and the members of her household believed. Paul then led them down to the river to baptise them. As they went under the crystal clear water of the stream with Paul and Silas, Lila knew then, without a doubt that there was no better way to live than to follow the Holy Spirit wherever he led.

As they dried themselves with their cloaks that they'd disguarded on the mossy banks, Lydia wanted to know where they were staying. When she heard they were in a guesthouse, she said, 'If you consider me a believer in the Lord, come and stay at my house.'

'But will you have enough room for all of us?' Lila asked. 'There are eight of us!'

'I deal in purple cloth in the city of Thyatira. There is plenty of room in my home for all of you.'

※　※　※

Lila whispered, 'Purple cloth pays for all of this?' to Jair as they entered the outer courtyard to Lydia's home through thick, iron clad doors. High walls surrounded them, blocking out much of the noise that came from the city. A pillared gazebo stood to the left and a fountain to the right. As they walked through the formal garden towards the ornate, panelled, wooden doors of the house, Lila caught the scents of mint, rosemary and basil.

Anna, who was all eyes and open mouth, leaned in to her mother and asked, 'Is she a queen?'

Lydia opened the doors of her villa wide for them all to come in. She led them into the cool, mosaic entrance hall with a shallow pool at its centre. Directly above this was an open section of roof, letting the Mediterranean sunlight flood in. There were twelve doors off the hall. Lydia opened six of them, one after the other, revealing beautifully hand-painted frescoes on the walls of each room. She took Lila by the hand first and led her, followed closely by Jair into the biggest room. A double bed, swathed in rich fabric stood at its centre. Lila had never seen anything like it.

'For us?' she whispered, hardly daring to believe it.

'Yes – for you,' Lydia laughed. She showed the others to their rooms, giving Anna and Joshua the smallest single rooms. Paul and Silas shared a larger room, as did Timothy and Luke. When everyone had settled, Lydia returned and invited them for a tour of the rest of the house.

She led them into a pillared courtyard, that was open to the sky, with another formal garden at its centre. All the walls were covered in hand-painted frescoes. Joshua ran his fingers along the intricate patterns made with tiny tiles that framed each fresco.

She showed them several tiled bathrooms, all with running water, something Lila had only heard of, but never seen. She showed them the kitchen where several newly baptised servants worked methodically, preparing food for later that evening. Lila felt her mouth water at the tantalising smells.

The last room she showed them was a large pillared space, with elegant couches and chairs scattered in a circle at its centre. Bowls of fire burned beside every pillar, lighting the room. There were small arched windows high in the walls that also gave light, but Lila preferred the warm, comforting glow of the fires. Even though it was unbearably hot outside, the thick walls of the villa and the tiled floors made the interior cool. The fires did not seem to warm the room too much, only lighting it perfectly.

'My husband was a general in the army. We retired here, but he became ill and died two years ago,' she said it quickly, as if she wanted to hurry past it. 'He left me and the children well cared for,' she smiled sadly.

No one said anything in reply. There was nothing to say.

Eventually Paul spoke, 'Lydia, thank you for your hospitality. You have a very beautiful home.'

She nodded her head, 'Please treat it as your own home. Now

before I go for a siesta I wanted to ask you whether you would be willing to teach us more this evening?'

'It would be my great pleasure,' Paul bowed his head.

❉ ❉ ❉

Over the weeks Lydia invited all her friends to come to her home and hear Paul and Silas speak. Many more believed and were baptised.

One sabbath as they were on their way through Philippi's crowded streets to the place of prayer, they were followed by a girl who kept shouting in a strange voice, 'These men are servants of the Most High God, who are telling you the way to be saved.'

They continued on their way, ignoring her harrassment as best they could. 'Why was she doing that?' Anna asked Lydia as they left the city behind.

'She is a slave. She is a fortune teller for her masters and earns them much money because of her accuracy. I believe she used to be a Pythia at one time.'

'What's that?' Anna asked.

Lydia explained, 'A priestess of Apollo at the Delphi sanctuary, north of Athens. The Pythia – the priestess – descends into the oracle grotto there, to seek inspiration from the god by allowing herself to be possessed by the python spirit that guards the entrance to the underworld. Then she utters the instruction of the god to the inquirer – first in an ecstatic, gibberish and then intelligibly. We call them "belly talkers", because of the sound of their voices when the spirit speaks through them.'

'That's so horrible,' Anna said, her face infused with compassion. 'She is a slave two times over.'

'What do you mean?' Lydia asked. 'We think the python spirit is good and helpful.'

'But she's been abused and used by her owners to make money for them and she's been abused and used by this python spirit. She is not free to be her true self.'

'Huh!' Lydia exclaimed, pondering this alien world view as she entered the synagogue.

'Knowing what's ahead may seem helpful and good at the time, but the end does not justify the means,' Anna concluded.

Lydia looked at her with fresh respect. This girl had a wisdom that was rare in the young. Paul followed on from what Anna had been saying in his teaching that day. He spoke of the freedom that came from the Holy Spirit, promised by Jesus to all who would believe in his name.

After that sabbath, the slave girl seemed to find them wherever they were in the city. She kept shouting at them for many days until Paul became so troubled by it that he turned round and said to the python spirit in her, 'In the name of Jesus Christ I command you to come out of her!' She collapsed on the ground instantly. Lila and Anna ran to her, cradling her head between them. When she came round she looked at them in bewilderment, asking them who they were and what had happened.

Lila's heart went out to her. She remembered how she had been set free from Aaron's control; how Mary had been set free from the unclean spirits that had infested her life through the abuse and slavery she had suffered. She was starting to explain all this to the girl, when her owners found them.

They pulled the girl roughly to her feet and when, bewildered, she spoke in a normal voice they realised that their hope of making money through her was gone. They were furious and on enquiring from several bystanders as to whose fault this was, they seized Paul and Silas. Timothy, Luke and Jair tried to stop them, but to no avail. They were dragged into the marketplace to face the authorities.

The commotion had caused quite a scene and the crowd grew quickly. Jair and the others were forced back by anti-semitic abuse as the slave owners brought them before the magistrates, seated high up on a platform that overlooked the market-place.

'These men are Jews, and are throwing our city into an uproar by advocating customs unlawful for us Romans to accept or practice,' they complained. The crowd joined in the attack on Paul and Silas, until the magistrates ordered them to be stripped and beaten.

Lila and Jair and the others watched helplessly as their brothers were flogged right there before their eyes. Anna and Joshua had never seen such ruthless cruelty and Lila feared that the shock and trauma would be too much for their young minds and hearts to bear. She wrapped her arms around them both and prayed for them in the language she had received at Pentecost. She prayed for their faith to grow in the face of oppostion. She prayed for the comforting presence of the Holy Spirit to soothe the trauma and enable them to endure.

They followed as Paul and Silas were dragged to the prison and handed over to the jailer who was commanded to guard them carefully. They stood for some time outside the jail at a loss as to know what to do next. The jailer would not let them in to bathe their brothers' wounds. He waved his hand at them dismissively from behind the locked gate. Luke and Timothy were distraught.

Anna came alongside Timothy as they despondently made their way back to Lydia's home, 'I know you feel terrible because you were not also beaten.'

Timothy looked at her, anger and confusion in his eyes.

'You have to trust that in all these things God will work for the good of those who love him and are called according to his purposes,' she quoted something Paul had taught her.

He stared into her dark eyes, framed by thick lashes. He marvelled that such beauty, composure and wisdom could all reside in one person. 'We must turn to prayer,' was all he said.

When they got back to the villa they gathered everyone in the luxurious main living room and together they lifted their voices in prayer for their brothers who were bound in agony in Philippi's squalid jail.

※ ※ ※

The stocks cut into their ankles. The inner cell was so small that they could not sit up straight, but had to keep their heads bowed. Leaning against the wall was agony. The deep lacerations oozed and wept blood and plasma down the wall and onto the floor, drying and sticking there. Every time they moved, they came unstuck from the wall and it felt like being whipped all over again.

About midnight Paul and Silas were praying and singing hymns, and the other prisoners were incredulously listening. Suddenly there was such a violent earthquake, as there often was in that area, that the foundations of the prison were shaken. Unusually though, all the prison doors flew open, and everyone's chains came loose.

The jailer woke up and when he saw the prison doors open, he drew his sword and was about to kill himself because he thought the prisoners had escaped. But Paul shouted, 'Don't harm yourself! We are all here!'

The jailer called for lights, rushed in and fell trembling before Paul and Silas. He then brought them out and asked, 'Sirs, what must I do to be saved?'

Paul gingerly straightened up and replied, 'Believe in the Lord Jesus, and you will be saved – you and your household.' Despite their pain and discomfort, they spoke the word of the Lord to him and to all the others in his house.

At that hour of the night the jailer took them and washed their wounds; then immediately he and his entire household were baptised in the large bathing pool he had in his courtyard. The jailer brought them into his home and had a meal prepared for them; he was filled with joy because he had come to believe in God – he and his whole household.

When it was daylight, the magistrates sent their officers to the jailer with the order: 'Release those men.'

The jailer told Paul, 'The magistrates have ordered that you and Silas be released. Now you can leave. Go in peace.'

But Paul said to the officers: 'They beat us publicly without a trial, even though we are Roman citizens, and threw us into prison. And now do they want to get rid of us quietly? No! Let them come themselves and escort us out.'

The officers reported this to the magistrates, and when they heard that Paul and Silas were Roman citizens, they were alarmed. They came to appease them and escorted them from the prison, requesting them to leave the city.

After Paul and Silas came out of the prison, they returned to Lydia's house, where they met with their brothers and sisters and encouraged them in the freedom they all shared in Christ.

It took them several weeks to heal. Lila wished she had Mary's oils with her to speed up the healing process. She remembered how they had prayed healing on the apostles when they'd been beaten after Pentecost. But the healing that came then, did not come in answer to their prayers this time.

She didn't understand, but Jair said, 'You cannot tell the Lord what to do, Lila. It is he who chooses to heal. It is our job to pray. If he does not heal, then we trust he has good reason for it. Perhaps we needed to stay here longer in order to establish the church that now meets in Lydia's home? See how the jailer and his household gather here regularly for teaching and to worship? Would this have happened if we had left this place earlier? Whatever the reason, we must trust even when we do not understand.'

One thing Lila did understand: the whole traumatic event had brought a deeper bond between them. Particularly between Anna and Timothy.

7. SOUL

Acts 17 The women with soul

It was raining again. It had held off for most of the Olympics, but the amount of precipitation that had fallen across the country was beyond belief. Grace was glad the vicarage and church were on a rise. She stared absently through the rivulets running down the large pane of her sash window.

Rain triggered memories of monotonous Sunday afternoons in boarding school. Her need for comfort back then was so great, so unmet, that it sent her off into another world suspended in time, an imagined world where she escaped to, in order to survive. She dragged herself back from there to the present with an effort and looked at her computer screen.

Life was good now … she tried to shake off the sad, lonely childhood feelings with a shudder. It didn't work. She turned to prayer, laying her hands on her stomach where she felt the emptiness most strongly.

Lord, please heal me. Thank you that you always loved me, even when I didn't know you.

The love of God … the love of God … the love of God … She ministered to herself.

She was twelve again, yearning to be comforted with a mother's hug.

Like a mother hen gathering her chicks under her wings I have longed to gather you … came words Jesus had spoken over Jerusalem. She imagined something like soft downy feathers encompassing her. An enormous soothing wave of love washed through her being.

Thank you, she prayed.

Her mind turned from being twelve, to focus in on her mother's face.

242

She traced her features slowly, seeing so much of herself there.

What do you want me to do? – she asked.

Forgive, came the simple reply.

Okay ... she thought and began to formulate a prayer.

I forgive you, mum, for not being there for me in the way I needed. I'm sorry I've held unforgiveness towards you. I release you to God. I know I shut down on you and refused the love you did have to offer ... I forgive you for all your failures, your absences and for abandoning me in boarding school ... For not standing with me when you found out about Dad ... I forgive you for not having me as the focus of your maternal love.

Lord, I turn to you for comfort and healing from the grief I feel at the loss of nurture and touch. Meet me in my longing for attachment, I pray.

She waited.

Enlarge my capacity to receive from you Lord. Fill me with your security. Rest in me as I rest in you.

She must have dozed off, because when the phone rang she jumped and wondered where she was a for a moment. It was James Martin.

'Hi, your Reverence,' he joked.

'Hello, James,' she knew the irritation was poorly concealed in her voice.

'Disturbed you, have I?' she could hear the Cheshire-cat grin in his mid-Atlantic accent.

'No ... no ...' she pulled herself together, wondering what his mother was like.

'Just need some help here. Don't know if you know, but we broke up a trafficking ring the other week,' he paused.

'Yes, Trevor said – quite something – well done.'

'Well ... it was amazing ... but anyway ... um ... the thing is that one of the guys has started coming to Alpha at St Matt's and he now wants his whole family to come. There's about thirty of them in all.'

'Oh?' Grace was genuinely surprised.

'The thing is, they're Muslim and the women in the family aren't allowed to, or aren't used to meeting with men outside their family. Trevor and I were wondering if you would be willing to meet with the women with the help of an interpreter? You know, run through the Alpha material with them?'

'With an interpreter?'

'Yeah – they only speak Urdu.'

'Are they recent arrivals in the country?'

'No … been here for years, I think. Omar says they don't need to learn English because they rarely leave the home and aren't educated anyway.'

Grace shook her head in disbelief.

'Grace? You still there?'

'Yep. Sorry … can I get back to you?'

'Sure. Don't leave it too long though. Don't want them to have a chance to go off the idea.'

'Okay. I'll call you back tomorrow.'

'Thanks, Rev,' he hung up.

❈　❈　❈

'Hi, Mum,' Grace said warmly as she met her at the door.

'Hello, dear,' she replied in her usual composed manner.

They kissed on either cheek. Grace breathed in her expensive scent. She liked it better than she could remember liking it before. 'How's the weekend been?' she asked, as they moved into the hall.

'Oh you know – quiet.'

Grace noticed that underneath the composure and aloofness she had always taken at face value, lay deep insecurity. She was surprised by this insight and realised she was staring. 'Can I take your coat?' she asked.

'That would be lovely dear,' she undid the two elegant buttons on the cream, cashmere fabric. She shrugged it off as Grace carefully helped her and then hung it on the coat stand near the door.

'Come on in. We're in for a treat today – Peter's done us a duck.'

'Fabulous!' she said checking herself in the hall mirror as she went past it. Even in her sixties she was a beautiful woman. Her platinum blonde hair was twisted up behind her head in a French pleat, showing off her long neck to perfection. Grace guessed she'd regularly had botox and probably had at least one stint under the surgeon's knife, but had never dared to ask. Her mother had always kept herself in good condition, eating little and exercising vigorously. She'd modelled with Twiggy back in the day and Grace thought she still competed with her now.

As they sat down to Sunday lunch, Peter winked at Grace. She wondered why. Zack chatted animatedly throughout to everyone. There seemed to be more to laugh about together than felt normal. Grace realised as she brought in a syrup sponge pudding with custard, that this was the most fun they'd ever had altogether. She felt emotional as she scooped steaming stickiness into everyone's bowls. When she poured custard on her mother's small portion, their eyes met and for the first time in her life Grace felt connected to her. They both started to laugh for no apparent reason. Zack joined in unquestioningly and Peter followed.

※　※　※

'Tell them to come forward for prayer whenever they want,' Grace addressed her interpreter. Monica was an elderly ex-missionary, who'd lived in Pakistan for many years, working as a nurse in a desert hospital. She'd returned several years previously to care for her dying mother. A regular communicant at St Matt's, Trevor had asked her if she spoke any Pakistani languages. Yes, she said, she was fluent in Urdu and a bit of Sindhi and yes, she would be more than delighted to help Grace lead an Alpha course for Muslim women.

Monica turned to Grace and said quietly, 'They won't come forward, you know. In Islamic thought, God is so holy that he would never come near a human being, let alone a woman. You see they don't believe they have souls. In the afterlife they only get into Paradise if a man wants them there for his pleasure, a bit like some of us think of our pets. God would certainly not come and live inside them as you have been teaching. They just have no expectation of it.'

'So what do you suggest?' Grace asked.

'Maybe if we offer to come to each of them and lay our hands upon them. Maybe if we talk in terms of experimentation ... you know ... let's just see what happens, then maybe they'll relax enough – be curious enough to let the Holy Spirit work in them.'

'Okay ... we'll take our lead from you, Monica.'

Grace had involved Melanie, Rose and another rescued girl named Silvi in helping lead the group. Having received prayer ministry from Grace along with Chloe's skilled psychotherapy, they had experienced levels of healing that had grown deeper and deeper over time. They were shining examples of souls in the process of being made whole. She wanted these women to be set free in the same way that the girls had experienced.

Monica proceeded to explain to the women what they wanted to do. There was some debate, but eventually the eldest among them made the unilateral decision to let the strange English women proceed with their experiment.

There were eight women altogether. Grace, Monica, Melanie, Silvi and Rose gathered round the eldest first, as a guinea pig for the other seven women to observe. They gently laid their hands on her shoulder and head, after Monica had asked her permission. She explained to the others what they were doing and translated each prayer, each visual image, each piece of scripture and each word of knowledge.

The woman's name was Miriam.

As they prayed Miriam became unnaturally still. When they'd finished praying and removed their hands, she remained still, eyes closed, lips slightly parted. She remained like this for about fifteen minutes, during which time the team prayed for two others, both of whom wept uncontrollably.

When at last she opened her eyes she called Monica over.

'She's asking "What was that?"' Monica interpreted.

'Tell her it was God's Holy Spirit. Tell her he loves her very much and will live with her forever. Tell her He has restored her soul, brought her to life inside. Tell her that one day, when she dies she will rise again like Jesus did. Tell her … oh, tell her …' Grace struggled to find the words, '…oh … you know what to tell her …' she laughed.

Monica did.

※　※　※

Melanie got confirmed at the same service Omar's whole family were baptised. It was held at St Stephen's, but churches from all over the Deanery were represented. Bishop Duncan led the service, preaching powerfully about the reality of the Holy Spirit's work in human bodies, minds and souls, no matter what your gender, religion or cultural background. Grace listened to him and watched his hands as they moved expressively. He was still very attractive to her, but she felt no draw towards him, no need of his focus or attention. She celebrated her freedom from the yearning she'd experienced that rooted from childhood loneliness.

She worshipped like she never had before through the Anglo-Catholic service, especially the dousing she gave the whole congregation with holy water, reaffirming their baptismal vows. The ritual, liturgy, symbolism, music and presence of the Holy Spirit felt like nourishing soul food.

As they hugged, Melanie asked, 'Can I become a server at Holy Communion?'

'Yes! That would be wonderful!' Grace responded feeling sad that Mark had not come to the service.

When Miriam hugged Grace, she squeezed her so tightly, Grace thought she was going to crack her ribs.

※ ※ ※

The trustees sat round Grace's kitchen table, drinking coffee and reminiscing.

They'd finished My Sister's House business, yet no one seemed to want to leave. Grace was aware that she didn't even mind James Martin sitting next to her. She pondered this every now and then while listening to others sharing their reflections on recent events round the table.

Eventually James got to his feet, 'Right, I better get home, or Marie will think I've run off with another woman,' he laughed too loudly. It grated on Grace's nerves.

She rose to escort him to the door as the others picked up their papers and collected their coats.

'You've done an incredible thing with those women,' James said as he followed her down the hall. 'That service was just fantastic! Their faces … they were so alive … so full of joy … Grace, you really are a gift … you honour people's humanity, you set them free in ways I've never seen before. I thank God for your ministry.'

Grace questioned the truth of that last statement sceptically, but thanked him nonetheless. Normally she just said goodbye to him and kept a safe distance between them, but tonight he suddenly reached over and hugged her. She stood frozen in his embrace at a loss to know how to react.

'Thanks, Grace – thanks for everything,' he said letting her go and stepping out into the night. 'Oh – by the way – I'm hoping to take Mark on that healing course I did in North London. They're holding one nearer us at a church in Chiswick. I'm gonna speak to him this week about it,' he grinned broadly.

'That's good,' Grace said lamely. She stood staring at him as he got into his sleek car and drove off.

'Grace? Grace? Are you all right?' Gwen was asking in her querulous voice.

'Sorry, Gwen … yes … I'm fine. How's Rose getting on? I've been meaning to ask you?' Grace focused hard on Gwen, putting her emotional turmoil to one side.

'She's doing very well with her business course. Came top of her class this term! And she's a great companion. Do you know she has the most beautiful voice? She sings all round the house. I shall miss her terribly when she moves out,' she sighed.

Grace thought of Rose singing to Jesus while cruel men used her to sate their perverse addictions. 'Maybe she could stay?' she suggested quietly.

Gwen looked at her oddly. 'Do you know — as I was praying this morning, that very thought came to my mind.'

'Well, you know, if the Lord repeats himself at least three times, you'd better listen,' she smiled, forcing James Martin to the back of her mind.

'Humph!' muttered the elderly woman as she made her way out the door.

※　※　※

'Aren't you going to church?' Mark asked.

'No,' came the muffled reply from under the duvet.

He stood in the doorway of what used to be their shared room.

'That's not like you,' he said.

'Isn't it? How would you know?'

'What?' he took a tentative step into the room.

Chloe rolled over, flipping the duvet off her face and glared at him, 'How would you know? We don't know each other at all,' she turned her back on him again, pulling the duvet back over her head.

Mark stared at the padded shape of her and in a low voice said, 'I've been waiting for the right time to say this … but I guess there is no right time. You're right – we don't know each other. I don't want to go on any more. I want a divorce.'

She stopped breathing, but didn't turn.

He waited a minute and then asked, 'Did you hear me?'

'Yes,' she replied, letting her breath out slowly like a deflating tire.

'Is that all?'

'I'm too tired right now, Mark,' she said in a dull monotone. 'If you hadn't said it I would have, sooner or later. I'm relieved it's out in the open. We'll talk later,' she pulled the duvet higher over her head.

He withdrew and slowly made his way down the stairs to Josh who was waiting in his football kit by the front door.

He closed it quietly.

※ ※ ※

'Mark wants a divorce.'

'Oh ...' Grace's chest constricted.

'So do I ... he just said it first. It's over ... been over way longer than either of us would admit.'

Grace searched Chloe's eyes, 'Do the children know?'

'Not yet. They know things have been bad between us for a while. It'll probably be a relief to all of them. I have to say I feel glad now that it's out in the open.'

'Has he got a lawyer? What grounds is he citing?'

'Don't know about a lawyer ... I guess irreconcilable differences? He's moving out next week after we tell the kids. He's already rented a flat.'

'Do you think he's got someone else?' Grace frowned.

'Don't know ... he hasn't said.'

'Are you going to ask?'

'I did, but he didn't say. Maybe ... Grace, I'm just too tired of it all. Love has grown cold in a whimpering, pathetic heap at the bottom of an impassable wall between us. He says when he's with me he feels bad about himself. He just wants to be accepted as he is and doesn't need any more talk about sin or repentance or healing ... Maybe he's shacking up with a porn star? That would be perfect!' she smiled mirthlessly. 'I feel so tired and sad ... I have no energy left. If he doesn't want me or us ... I can't make him.'

Grace knew there was nothing more to say. The weight of grief for her friends crushed her chest, 'I'm so sorry, Chloe … I don't know what else to say.'

'There is nothing else to say.'

Grace took hold of her friend's hand, 'You don't deserve any of this. You've poured your life out helping the girls here … you deserve to be rewarded with a husband who loves and honours you and wants you; a happy home life and security. None of this makes any sense.'

'No. It's a mad world.'

Grace nodded sadly, 'Thanks for telling me.'

'I know you love both of us. I know you won't hate him … I don't want people taking sides and judging. I just want to be supported as we go forward.'

'Yep … I know,' she reached over and hugged her. As they held on to each other they both began to cry.

Eventually Grace let her go and stood up, 'I need to go,' she said wiping her eyes.

'Yeah – life goes on. Thanks for listening,' Chloe responded. 'It's gonna take a while for it to really sink in.'

'Yeah,' Grace kissed her on the cheek, 'I love you.'

'Too bad we're not lesbians … and you're not single,' Chloe tried to smile.

When Grace got into her study, she fell down on her knees and burst into tears. *Oh God … what's going on? Heal her of trauma and disillusionment … keep her soul alive. Keep Mark's soul alive … oh God, he's been taken out … please … please …* She didn't know what else to pray.

After a while of holding Chloe and Mark before the Great Unseen in silent prayer, she went to the bathroom to wash her face. Returning to her desk she opened her Bible to Acts 17. She read through the chapter and then slowly ploughed through several commentaries, trying to keep her mind focused.

They're yours …

Help me focus on what you ask of me.

She began to write, losing herself to the story and the flow of imagination, leaving behind the devastation of her best friend's world:

Paul wanted to go on to Thessalonica, the major city in Macedonia. He felt it would be a strategic place from which the gospel would spread further throughout the Roman empire.

As they gathered with Lydia and others who were emerging leaders within the growing Philippian church, they came to the conclusion that Luke, Jair, Lila and the children would stay in Philippi a little longer to continue to support and enable Lydia's leadership.

Luke had begun running a medical practice from her home. The sick had heard via word of mouth and made their way in a steady stream to her door. Joshua was fascinated by all Doctor Luke did and said. He shadowed him constantly, mimicking him in every way. As Jair and Lila watched they knew their son would one day follow in his footsteps.

After they left Anna pined for Timothy like a wave reaching for shore. Lila knew she was losing weight because of him. She eventually spoke candidly with her.

'You miss him very much, don't you?'

Anna looked guarded, 'Who do you mean?'

'You know very well who I mean,' she frowned as she wrung out a tunic of Jair's before she hung it up to dry.

Anna sighed deeply.

'You think I can't see? You think I don't know your heart, my love?' Lila raised her daughter's chin with a finger.

Anna's eyes welled with tears.

'You love him, don't you?'

'Yes, Mama,' Anna whispered.

'Do you know if he feels the same about you?'

'No – I only know my own heart,' she replied simply.

'Perhaps when we meet with them again Papa could raise the subject with brother Paul?'

Anna looked surprised, 'He would do that? I thought traditionally the man had to initiate such things?'

'We'll see, shall we?' Lila smiled and hugged her.

✶ ✶ ✶

A fever broke out in Philippi. Lila, Jair and the children assisted Luke in treating as many as they could. That is, until Joshua began to shiver and sweat.

'Wash that arm. I've done this one,' Lila instructed Jair.

'His skin dries almost instantly,' Jair whispered.

'I know,' Lila replied as she wrung out the cloth and began wiping his chest again. His breathing was shallow, his skin like that of a drum stretched over bones.

There was a soft knock on the door. Lila turned to see Luke, 'May I come in?'

'Yes ... please ... how are you? What news from the city?' Lila asked, desperate for some hope.

'I am tired beyond belief,' he said, 'but it seems the epidemic is on the wane now. Five to ten days and those that survive it begin to recover.'

'This is the sixth day,' Lila whispered.

'I know,' Luke replied helplessly. 'May I see?' he asked.

Lila stepped back from Joshua's bedside. She watched the doctor as he held her son's wrist in the strange way that he did. Her eyes followed his elegant hand as it tenderly touched his forehead. They returned to his face to try and read what information he had gained. All she saw were tears welling in his eyes. No ... no ... don't give up ... not you ... you must know something ... must have some skill that will help?

'Is there nothing else we can do Luke?' Jair put voice to her question.

'We can pray ...' he said simply.

But Heaven is not listening ... He has hidden Himself in clouds so that our prayers do not reach Him – she thought.

Luke turned to her, 'He is listening, Lila.'

She was momentarily surprised out of dispair, 'How did you know what I was thinking?'

'I sensed it, somehow,' he smiled. 'Have faith sister, the Lord has purposes for your son that Satan does not want to be fulfilled. As we pray the angels are strengthened to fight on his behalf. So let us not give up. Our ancestor Daniel prayed for twelve days until the angel of the Lord came to him. He was told that his prayer had been answered immediately, but it had taken twelve days for the angel to overcome the Prince of Persia.

Lila nodded, remembering the story of Daniel's intercession. She felt her faith fuelled by it and began to pray aloud, 'Lord God, forgive my unbelief, help me ... help us,' she reached out to Anna and Jair on either side of her.

They prayed for some time and Luke anointed Joshua with oil on his forehead. Then the ritual of washing began all over again. Luke sent Jair to rest as he had been awake throughout the watches of the night, even though Luke had not rested for several days himself.

News filtered through the courtyard and thick walls of Lydia's home that many had died in the city. Lila prayed until her eyes closed and continued praying the moment they opened again. She could not eat as she watched the life drain from her beloved son. She thought about Jesus' mother Mary. How had she survived watching her son die on the cross? She prayed for strength to bear whatever was ahead. She prayed for humility to bow to the will of the Almighty.

Lila suddenly woke from her stupor, jerking her head up off her chest. She inwardly berated herself for falling asleep. Luke was on his knees near Joshua's head. A steady flow of tears fell into her boy's dark curls as the doctor prayed earnestly. It dawned on Lila that Luke's love for her son was very deep. If his prayers are not effective then whose will be?

She noticed that Joshua's breathing seemed more steady. She doubted herself and reached over, placing her hand on his chest. 'Luke ... his breathing has slowed ... it's more even ... his skin is not so hot to the touch ... feel ...'

The doctor's wet eyelashes parted stickily. He reached over and placed his hand beside Lila's. 'You're right ... the fever has broken!' he exclaimed.

'Thank you, thank you ...' Lila burst into relieved tears.

※　※　※

It took several weeks for Joshua to recover some of his strength.

A letter had arrived from Paul telling them of the oppostion he had faced in Thessalonica and Berea. Apparantly some of the Jewish leaders in Thessalonica had been jealous of Paul's influence over God-fearing Greeks. Many prominent women and men had believed his message. The troublemakers had followed him to Berea and stirred up opposition there too. He had left Timothy and Silas in Berea to strengthen the newly planted church, while some of the brothers had escorted him to Athens. He was asking if they would meet him there.

'Joshua cannot travel,' Jair said. 'He is still too weak. He needs to completely recuperate. We cannot leave.'

Luke stroked his beard thoughtfully, 'I believe the Lord wants me to stay and serve the city through this crisis. Would you consider leaving him here with me and Lydia while you, Lila and Anna travel to meet brother Paul? We will follow you when I think Joshua is able.'

Jair frowned, his brows becoming one across his eyes, 'We must pray about this together,' Jair said, 'I doubt Lila will easily come to such a conclusion.'

He was right. Lila did not like the suggestion at all. She had nearly lost him once ... she did not want to lose him again.

One morning it was Lila's turn to read the scriptures for the gathering of Lydia's household. She opened the scroll that was handed to her and began to read. It was the story of Abraham being asked to sacrifice his son Isaac. Her voice broke when she came to the part where Abraham raised the knife to plunge it into his son's chest. She handed the scroll to Jair and ran to their room in tears. She remained there for the duration of the day, not eating or drinking.

As the sun was setting she came out into Lydia's central courtyard and found Jair seated there with Anna. 'I think the Lord wants us to go to Athens,' she said. 'I think we are to leave Joshua here with Luke.'

Jair looked up into her face that he loved so dearly and nodded, 'He is a man now, Lila. Like Hannah did with Samuel, we will entrust him to the Lord's purposes.'

Anna reached up and clasped her mother's hand and smiled.

Lila thought, A man? He is my boy ...

❊ ❊ ❊

Paul met them in Athens harbour. The sea journey from Neapolis had been much less loathesome, as there was always coast to see, either of the mainland or of islands.

During the sea voyage Lila had begun to understand that her role with her children was fast changing. She needed to flow with the current of it or it would overwhelm and sweep her away. She daily committed them both to God. As they neared Athens she knew that soon she would have to let Anna go too. She watched as her daughter strained daily over the bow of the ship longing to take hold of what the future held for her.

When they arrived Paul embraced each of them with great affection, 'It is so good to have you with me again. I have never felt so distressed in a city before,' he shook his head as he explained. 'Athens is full of idols.' He went into detail of all that he'd seen as they made their way through the bustling harbour streets. 'I have been reasoning in the synagogues and market places with Jews and God-fearing Greeks alike. Tomorrow I am to speak to a gathering of Epicurean and Stoic philosophers in the Areopagus. It will be good to have you with me.'

'What are Epicureans and Stoics and what's an Areopagus?' Anna asked.

Paul laughed, 'You'll see.'

❊ ❊ ❊

Damaris waited patiently for her servant to dress her. It was not an unpleasant part of her daily routine, but it was sometimes tedious. The young girl was new and nervous of making mistakes. She was taking far longer than was necessary.

'That will be all,' she waved her hand impatiently in the servant girl's face, 'I will finish it.'

The girl looked distraught.

'Don't fret. It's all right. I know you're nervous. I just need to be at the Areopagus before the day is out,' Damaris tried to catch her eye, but was unsuccessful.

The slave girl retreated from her chambers. 'Foolish girl,' she said to her reflection in the polished mirror. I must try and teach her to live in accordance with nature. It pains me to be in her presence – she is so out of step – so unbalanced.

Damaris finished plaiting her hair and pinned it to her head. Then she went in search of her husband to bid him farewell for the day.

'Who are you going to listen to? Have I heard of him?' her husband looked up from studying his architectural drawings.

'He's a Roman citizen named Paul. He originates from Cilicia, having Jewish roots. He has brought some new ideas to our attention and we have invited him to speak at the Areopagus today. I doubt you will have heard of him.'

'No, I can't say I have. What's he advocating?'

'I'm not sure yet. I think he was suggesting we worship foreign gods. He also spoke of resurrection after death both for the soul and the body,' Damaris leant over her husband's shoulder and perused his drawings. 'Is that for Dimitrius?'

'Yes. He's been a good friend over the years – I'm designing this garden temple for him as a gift for his birthday.'

'It's beautiful – perfectly aligned,' she ran her forefinger along a series of pillars.

He smiled and patted her hand that rested on his shoulder. 'Now be careful with this chap. You know how persuasive Jewish orators can be. As for resurrection? That's ridiculous. Don't let him upset you. Everyone knows the soul and body are corporeal and that at death they both disintegrate.'

'I know, dear,' she said submissively. 'Dionysius was eager to have him speak at greater length with us. I am going only because I am curious,' she bent and kissed his head, hiding well the grief that often rose like a bubble though the depths of her being.

She looked forward to her weekly philosophical meetings and

this one was of particular interest to her. The question of what happens when you die had always concerned her since the death of their baby girl five years ago. Becoming an Epicurean had helped her handle the anxiety she felt around the subject. If there was no feeling in death … then it should be nothing. Her daughter had felt nothing; her baby had known no pain.

When she finally made it to the top of the hill where the Areopagus was located, Damaris knew she had missed the beginning of the presentation. Again she felt irritated by those that served her, but said nothing to the four sweating litter-bearers. She looked across the ravine to the Acropolis and took a moment to breathe deeply, attempting to align herself with nature. As she made her way through the pillared halls of Athen's ruling council, she could hear Paul was already speaking to the gathered philosophers. As she scanned the great hall the only seat that was easily accessible to her was next to a striking mother and daughter who wore the traditional Jewish head covering. They must have come in support of Paul. She made her way to take her seat beside them, acknowledging them with a nod.

'I have observed that many of you revere the gods and fear offending them. However I have found that there is one you honour that is unknown to you, whom I am here to proclaim,' Paul was saying.

'I know this God personally, for he has revealed himself. He has made us in his image and calls us to repent of idolatry and to worship him alone. If we bear his divine likeness, it is inconsistent for us to create inanimate objects as representations to worship.

'Neither do I believe in the fatalism of you Stoics or the impersonal view of you Epicureans. I am here to tell you that there is a God above all God's who rules over the course of history and cares for his creation.'

Damaris became aware of a warm sensation spreading through her torso. She took out her hand-carved ivory fan and began gently wafting air around her face. Paul was quoting from a Stoic philosopher. The heat intensified and seemed to focus around her abdomen.

'The living and true God I am proclaiming to you will eventually bring history to a conclusion and there will be a time of judgement by the resurrected Lord Jesus Christ,' Paul's eyes pierced Damaris's as he looked across his audience, attempting to make connection with them.

'Why be joined again to the physical body after death? What a repugnant idea!' she heard the person behind her whisper to their neighbour.

Dionysius stood to invite people for midday refreshments and to discuss amongst themselves the things they'd been hearing. Paul came and stood near Lila, Anna and Jair.

As they made their way to the refreshments Lila turned to Damaris, 'My name is Lila. I had a strong urge to pray for you during Paul's speech.'

'My name is Damaris. Thank you for your prayers. I'm sure they will have been a blessing to me,' she smiled politely.

'May I ask you something?'

'Certainly,' Damaris replied politely. 'The thing that kept coming to my mind was the word "soul". Is that of any significance to you?' Lila persisted.

Damaris was slightly taken aback, but quickly recovered and proceeded to explain her Epicurean view that both the soul and body were made of mortal material and would separate and disintegrate at death.

Lila frowned, 'How sad,' she said.

It was Damaris' turn to frown, 'Sad?'

'We have a joyful hope – we believe we will live for ever. That our earthly bodies will be transformed to be like Jesus' glorious resurrected body. Our soul will live on in a new body that will know no more sadness or crying or death,' she smiled.

At the word death, Lila saw that she had hit something of significance to Damaris. She silently asked for discernment and waited for it briefly. 'I have the sense that someone very dear to you has died. You have turned to Epicurean philosophy to find comfort for your grief. Is this true?'

Damaris stared at Lila, 'My daughter died five years ago. She was a baby. We found her one morning – there was nothing we could do.'

'Oh,' Lila's hand flew to her lips, 'how terrible. I didn't realise ...'

'How could you have known? As for comfort,' Lila heard the pain in her voice, 'we Epicureans value the feeling of pleasure when we are aligned to nature. When the body dies, there is no feeling and therefore death is nothing to us. My daughter knew neither pain nor pleasure. It is a sadness for me, but it is nothing really.'

Lila stared at her intuitively knowing that the true Damaris lay protected behind the smoke screen of philosophy. 'Damaris, may I ask you another question?'

'Yes,' she replied more cautiously.

'If our souls and bodies are not meant to live on why is death a sadness? Surely we would intuit that death is the way it's meant to be and our deep souls would happily accept this?' she paused and searched Damaris' eyes. 'I sense that your true self yearns for everlasting life; that you naturally believe that you should be reunited with your daughter and that death is not how it was meant to be. Your philosophy is a beautiful façade constructed to cover the sufferings you carry within you.'

Damaris was struggling to hold the shield of her well-argued belief system in the face of Lila's challenge. Dionysius was calling for everyone's attention, and Damaris thankfully retreated to her seat, having only eaten a few pieces of fruit and still shakily holding her drink in her hand.

Paul continued his presentation, only this time it was interspersed with debate. As the afternoon wore on it was clear that he had not won over his audience. The idea of resurrection seemed to be the greatest stumbling block to most.

Damaris overheard Dionysius and a few of his colleagues asking to meet privately with Paul afterwards. She asked if she could come too.

Lila prayed fervently for her.

※　※　※

'I met him myself on my way to Damascus, where I planned to take prisoner all those who believed in his name.'

'What do you mean – you met him?' Dionysius asked, frowning hard to comprehend what Paul was saying.

'I had been given authority by the Sanhedrin in Jerusalem to take captive all who believed in Jesus of Nazareth. We were vehemently opposed to the story purported by his disciples of his resurrection. We wanted to crush the movement as quickly as we could.

'As I neared Damascus, I was blinded by a bright light and heard a voice asking, "Saul, Saul why do you persecute me?"

'I fell to the ground and cried, "Who are you Lord?"

'The answer came – "I am Jesus whom you are persecuting. Now get up and go into the city and you will be told what you must do."

'The men with me heard the sound but did not see the flash of light. They were speechless and when they realised I was suddenly blind, they had to lead me by the hand into the city. For three days I could not see, neither eating nor drinking. As I waited and prayed the Lord told me that a man named Ananias would come and pray for my sight to be restored. He was this man's uncle,' he indicated Jair, who nodded his affirmation of the fact.

'It was through them,' again he indicated Jair and Lila, that I came to understand that this Jesus I preach to you now, is the Son of God, the exact representation of the Almighty Creator of all things. For centuries we had waited for the one promised through the prophets and when he came we rejected him, crucifying him like a common criminal,' at this Paul pressed his clenched fist to his chest with feeling.

He took a moment to control his emotions and then continued, 'But he confounded us and rose again from the dead. His tomb was empty, the seal broken on the tombstone, the soldiers guarding it terrified. The Sanhedrin paid for the story to go throughout Jerusalem that his disciples had stolen the body. But I assure you there is nowhere you will find his human remains.

'Over five hundred witnesses saw him over a forty day period. The eleven he had chosen saw him ascend into heaven, disappearing from their sight. He commanded them to preach this gospel to all creation starting at Jerusalem. They obeyed him and I was among those who sought to stop them. But on the road to Damascus I discovered I was fighting the very One I thought I was serving.'

He suddenly turned to Damaris, 'Dear woman, I sense you have a deep pain in your heart. Is this true?'

Damaris was holding herself together as best she could. She couldn't speak, the emotion was too raw. Lila reached over and squeezed her hand. Damaris nodded to her, wiping a tear that had escaped from her eye, giving her permission to speak on her behalf. 'Damaris lost a daughter – her baby girl – some years ago. All she has known is the Epicurean belief that at death the soul and the body separate and disintegrate. She has only known of impersonal gods that need to be respected and appeased, but nothing of a personal God who loves and knows her and her little girl.'

Moved with compassion, Paul walked over to Damaris, 'May we pray for you Damaris? May we ask God to minister His great love to you?'

Again Damaris could only nod her head as the tears flowed down her cheeks.

Paul joined Lila, by placing a hand gently on her shoulder. They began to pray quietly. Then Paul prayed, 'Lord God, reveal your great love to your daughter. May she know that she is known and loved and precious in your sight. Thank you Lord Jesus that as you hung on the cross and died you thought of Damaris. Thank you that you came to carry her sorrows, that you are familiar with her suffering.' He waited for the Holy Spirit to do His work.

Damaris broke down into sobs. She cried and cried as if she were being turned inside out. Lila held her in her arms and rocked her gently. Eventually she became quiet. Dionysius and his friends had gathered round her. Slowly Damaris raised her head, eyes still closed, a soft smile forming on her lips.

'What is happening?' Paul asked.

'I see a man full of light – is it Him?' she whispered. 'I am overwhelmed with ... with ... love,' she was surprised. 'The void that has always been within me, is gone. I see my daughter – she is older than she was when she ... she's holding His hand. Can it be?' her eyes flew open, searching Paul's.

'It can,' Paul affirmed simply. 'He is not limited by time or space. Salvation works backwards and forwards throughout the lives of those who call on His name.'

As they continued to pray each one experienced the power of the Holy Spirit at work in their hearts, minds and bodies. It wasn't many, but as Paul watched them and gave thanks for them, he knew in his spirit that from here would grow a church that would stand firm throughout the ages. He watched Dionysius particularly, sensing that he would be a mighty leader.

As they parted company, Damaris embraced Lila and thanked her for her prayers and understanding. Lila loved her like a sister. As they left the Areopagus she found herself praising God for this Greek woman and all the other spiritual sisters she had found over the years, from all walks of life, but especially for Mary. She wished she could go and see her and tell her about Damaris. She thought how significant Mary's testimony would have been for Damaris to hear, having lost four babies herself. She prayed God would grant Damaris the same merciful blessing of children.

8. PART

Acts 18–20 The women who let go and let God

Chloe listened at the kitchen door as Mark spoke to James Martin on the door step.

'No, James, it's not for me. Think you may have got your wires crossed,' she imagined him smiling winsomely.

'Oh … okay,' said James, '… sorry about that … Like I said, I'm a bit of a novice at this sort of thing. You sure you don't want to keep them?'

'No thanks, mate. Haven't got the time to listen to them, even if I wanted to.'

'Right,' Chloe could hear the disappointment in James' voice. 'Well, you know where they are if you change your mind. Sorry to have bothered you,' she heard the crunch of his foot on the gravel drive. 'See you Sunday?'

'Not sure … pretty busy with work at the minute and Josh's football is on a Sunday. He's really committed – like to support him, you know,' Mark responded coolly, sounding like the perfect father.

She heard him close the door and begin walking down the hall towards the kitchen. She quickly returned to her seat at the table and picked up her book. He came in nonchalantly and turned the kettle on.

'James Martin – like a dog with a bone,' he said as he unhooked a mug from the mug tree next to the kettle, 'Do you want a coffee?'

'No thanks,' she said, despite wanting one.

'Right we need to talk,' he said after making his coffee and pulling out a chair.

'Yes …' she laid her book down and folded her hands resolutely.

He seemed so calm, like he was about to discuss the end of a work project, not the end of their life's commitment. 'I've been thinking about it, and it seems to me the best way to handle this is to be very practical and down to earth about it with the kids.'

Chloe gazed at him, wondering how he could deceive himself so completely. 'So what do you want to say to them?'

'I think we need to lay it out simply. Say: we've tried working things out between us in our marriage over the years, but have come to the realisation that we can't do any more and it's over. We don't hate each other, we've just come to the end of the road. We need to emphasise that we love them – they will always be our priority. We'll do everything to help them adjust to the changes.'

Chloe sighed, shaking her head.

'You don't agree?' he frowned.

'It all sounds so sensible when you say it like that. What's worrying is I think you actually believe it is sensible.'

Mark glared at her and was about to speak, but then thought better of it. He composed his features, his lips forming a thin line. 'Look Chloe, that's how I see it … really. I don't want to argue about it with you. I just want to do this with as little stress and emotional fallout as possible.'

Chloe ran a finger across the table top, tracing the grain of wood thoughtfully. She reflected on the passion they'd shared on its surface all those years ago. As much as she stirred the ashes of the memory, she couldn't find one ember of desire now.

'Yes … love has grown cold … time to clean the hearth, sweep up the ashes and throw them away,' she said quietly. 'Can I ask you something?'

'What?' he looked pensive.

'I asked you before, but you didn't answer – Is there someone else?' she didn't look at him.

He didn't reply straight away. She looked up slowly, fresh pain coursing through her nervous system.

'We're friends. But once I move out … yeah … I think so …'

'Who is she?' Chloe looked back down at the table. *I did the same thing to him … I have no right to be angry or hurt …*

'Someone from work,'

'Work,' Chloe nodded. 'What's her name?'

'I'd rather not say at the minute. We're just friends,' Mark reiterated.

'Yeah, you said.' Another thought hit her, 'How old is she?'

'Why does that matter?'

'How old is she?' Chloe asked doggedly, fearing what she knew was coming.

Mark folded his arms, 'Twenty one,' he pursed his lips.

At this Chloe looked at him and laughed cynically. Searing memories of her father leaving for a girl not much older than herself leapt to life, licking round her like flames – the hellfire of a woman scorned.

'She accepts me the way I am,' he said, 'I don't feel bad when I'm with her.'

'She doesn't happen to be a lapdancer in her spare time, does she?' Chloe flung the words at him.

The look on his face was all the answer she needed.

※ ※ ※

'Twenty-one?'

'Yep,' Chloe replied, 'not much older than Melanie.'

Grace didn't know what to say. She shook her head and leaned back into the comfort of the new cushions the pub owner had scattered on the seating of their favourite alcove.

After a long silence Chloe continued, 'We didn't tell the kids … that bit of info can wait a while … just that he was leaving.'

'How are they?'

'Devastated. Like I was when my dad left – but I'm not going into a depression like mum; I will not disintegrate,' desperation crackled round the edges of her voice, 'I've got to hold it together for them,' her hand shook a little as she stirred her coffee.

'Where's he gone?'

'He's rented a flat down near the train station. I think he's hoping we'll sell the house eventually. He'll be waiting a long time for that, I can tell you,' her soft lips pursed tightly.

'Have you talked money?'

'Yeah – but I don't trust him, not now that he's going to have to play sugar daddy to a twenty one year old. I've got a meeting with a lawyer tomorrow.'

'Good,' Grace frowned, 'how're you paying for that?'

'Not sure yet …' she looked at her watch, 'I better go. Charlie's got a life drawing class after school today.'

'Life drawing?'

'Down at the college. I sit in – it's quite soothing really.'

'Are they nude models?'

'Yeah – mainly middle-aged women. There's something quite comforting about it.'

Grace questioned the wisdom of such a thing for a pubescent boy, but then shrugged it off, doubting her own opinion. She changed the subject, 'Melanie's enjoying learning the ropes at St Stephen's.'

'She's told me. I'm glad she wants to keep going to church. I guess perhaps it gives her the stability she craves – the high church stuff gives strong boundaries, where there are none in her life.'

'Mmmm … she does seem to really love God too, you know.'

Chloe shrugged at this dismissively.

'Are Charlie and Josh still going to St Matt's?'

'No – none of us have been for months now. Trevor came to see me and Sean came to see the boys. I just can't Grace … I just can't …' her eyes welled up.

'Don't,' Grace said reaching over and rubbing her arm, 'I know …' was all she could say. She studied her friend's ravaged face. It was too much …

'I think Josh wants to live with his dad. He's not said anything, but I just know. What if Mark doesn't want him? Oh God …'

'Let's take one step at a time Chloe. You'll have enough light for each step,' Grace soothed.

Chloe wiped her eyes with the backs of her hands.

'Do you want some time off My Sister's House?'

'No … don't take that away from me too. It's what's keeping me going. I need something to get me out of my head.'

Grace nodded, 'Okay. But you must tell me if you're not coping.'

※　※　※

To her surprise one Sunday she saw Bishop Duncan sitting at the back of church in the new family service she had recently begun. She tried not to let his presence distract her, but lost her place in the liturgy, despite her efforts. Afterwards he made his way slowly through the congregation towards Grace, chatting amiably with everyone he met.

'Hello, Grace, that was wonderful!' he said.

She looked into his eyes and saw warm appreciation and affection. She felt relieved at the absence of the other thing she dreaded and returned his smile, 'Thank you. It's great to have you with us. Why didn't you say you were coming? I would have told people.'

'Exactly!' he grinned.

Peter joined them. Grace felt the territorial energy exuding from him. 'Bishop Duncan, this is Peter, my husband.'

'Hello, Peter. We've met once before at one of the wonderful meals Wendy puts on for our clergy and their other halves. I think we had a conversation about Degas?'

'Well remembered,' Peter said shaking him by the hand and liking him, despite himself, 'It's good to see you again.'

'Yes, likewise. I came because I've been hearing such good things about what's going on here. I wanted to see it with my own eyes.'

'She's doing a great job,' Peter placed his hand on the small of Grace's back, 'You should promote her!' he grinned.

Bishop Duncan laughed, 'You don't know the Church of England very well, do you? There's not really much in the way of promotion with us. You can be an Area Dean – get lots more responsibility for a mere extra grand per year and then there's the role of Archdeacon – but those don't come up very often and there's only one or two per diocese. And finally there's Bishop and Archbishop. And at present, sadly, Grace is excluded from the last two.'

Peter shook his head, 'Hope women have your vote at Synod next week?'

'They most certainly do,' Bishop Duncan replied.

'Being a new convert, I'm struggling to understand what the fuss is about. I know I need to go off and do a lot more reading ... but I partly can't be bothered and partly think I won't need to hopefully.'

'Mmmm ... we'll have to wait and see on that one. Let's keep praying,' he smiled and then turned to Grace. 'Would it be all right if I had a brief word with you now, Grace, regarding a particular matter?'

'Sure, Bishop Duncan. Let me just go and change out of my alb. Peter could you show him where the coffee's being served?'

She found them after changing, surrounded by Zack and a group of his friends. As she approached, she enjoyed watching the way both men interacted with the children. She found herself comparing the two of them and realised that there was a lot of similarity between them. Peter was much better looking, but they both had a relaxed, engaging, natural manner. She could tell that Peter liked the Bishop.

'Okay, boys … I've got to talk with Grace for a minute. Would you excuse me?' he gently disentangled a young boy from around his legs.

'Come on, boys,' Peter said, 'Let's go out in the gardens and play football,' a loud cheer went up from the six or seven lads.

As they ran out followed by Peter, Bishop Duncan turned to Grace, 'He's a good man,' he smiled.

'Yes – he is,' she smiled back, 'a bit like yourself,' she felt heat rising up her neck and regretted saying it.

Brushing the uncomfortable moment aside graciously, Bishop Duncan said, 'Grace, I wanted to ask you whether you would consider taking on the job of Area Dean for this Deanery? St Stephen's has grown exponentially since you came. It is very rare for churches of this tradition to grow like this. I think the other churches in the Deanery of similar pursuasion, would benefit greatly from your leadership.'

'Oh!' she was quite taken aback, 'Oh,' she said again '… I wasn't expecting that.'

'Would you have a look at the job spec and talk to the other Area Deans about what you could expect? You'll need to discuss it with Peter, of course.'

She was so thrown, that she didn't have a reply. She just looked at him.

Bishop Duncan chuckled, 'Let me know,' he said, 'I'd better go. Wendy has all the grandchildren coming for lunch, and I daren't be late.'

'What's the occasion?' she asked.

'Oh, it's our thirtieth wedding anniversary,' as he said it, Grace saw the loneliness in his eyes for a split second and then it was gone.

❋ ❋ ❋

'I don't think I could do it and St Stephen's and My Sister's House,' Grace was thinking out loud with Peter as they lay in bed together.

'No ... you spend so much time next door talking and praying with the girls and overseeing the running of the whole project ... there wouldn't be enough hours in the day. But it was your vision, babe. You founded it ... What's He,' he raised his eyes heavenward, 'saying?'

'I don't know ... can we pray about it?'

'Sure,' he smiled, catching her fingers between his and pulling them to his lips. 'Can I ravish you afterwards?'

'Why does praying together make you so horny?' she queried with a grin.

'Who says I wasn't horny before praying? But yeah – it's the intimacy of it.'

She thought of that first prayer time with Bishop Duncan and the image she'd seen of their spirits entwining, which had so shocked her. 'Hey – maybe we could write a book about it? Call it something like *Entwined in Prayer*?'

'That's a bit boring ... why not something like *It's Rising Up*?'

'Peter!' she slapped his arm as they laughed together over the the title of the charismatic song the choir had attempted to sing that morning.

'I wonder if Rose would help the choir?' she mused.

'Stop it now ... all this church talk is turning me off ... prayer is one thing, but church business is a totally different matter. Come on – pray,' he pulled her to him and she began praying for the Holy Spirit to give them wisdom and insight.

※　※　※

'I'll still be the chair of trustees,' Grace said to Chloe, sitting in the office of My Sister's House, 'but would you be willing to take charge of the day-to-day oversight of the project?'

'Wow,' Chloe smiled, 'You still trust me with it, after everything?'

'What do you mean?'

'I thought you were doubting my ability to work here when you suggested I had a break. I know I'm a bit wobbly at the minute, but I will be okay. If nothing else, I am a survivor.'

Grace reached across her desk and took hold of her hand, 'I'd trust you with my life, Chloe. You're my best friend! You've had such a rough hand of cards dealt you. I think you're amazing! I was just worried for you … just wanted you to know that it was okay to take a break if you wanted to.'

Chloe's eyes glistened, 'I guess I've been doubting myself. Being rejected by Mark has made me doubt everything. I thought maybe you were thinking there might be good reason for why he's left me.'

'Chloe,' she looked her in the eye, 'I trust you. I respect you. You are a compassionate, wise, intelligent woman. In the name of Jesus, I wipe rejection off you,' she suddenly leant forward and swept the palm of her hand across Chloe's forehead. 'I affirm that the Lord receives you – he has not rejected you,' she made the sign of the cross with her fingertip on Chloe's surprised brow, which crumpled into grief. Grace got up, came round the desk and knelt down beside her, wrapping her arms around her friend. They clung together for a long time.

※　※　※

'Do you think I could work here with you full time once I finish uni?'

'I don't see why not,' Chloe smiled at Melanie. 'We could start fundraising for it now. I was going to ask Val if she would be willing to take on a bit more of that kind of work. I was also wondering if St Stephen's would consider funding a role here. I was going to talk to Grace about it. I know James Martin's support has grown, but that's just covering full time salaries for Val and me. Now that Dad has gone, I need it to pay the mortgage …'

Chloe saw the pain in her daughter's eyes at the mention of her father and stopped.

'It's okay, Mum,'

'How is your dad?'

'He's … he's … I met his girlfriend for the first time this week,' Melanie blurted it out. She couldn't hold it in any longer.

'Oh,' Chloe felt her heart knot.

'She can't be much older than me.'

'No …' was all Chloe could say.

'Did you know?' Melanie leant forward trying to catch her mother's eye.

'Yes ... yes, I did. I didn't want you to know straightaway. How was it?'

'Very weird! I'm sorry, Mum, but Dad is pretty pathetic ...' the anger surfaced in her voice.

Chloe said nothing, just listened to her daughter as the tirade of hurt, disgust and rage came tumbling out. Eventually Chloe asked, 'How was Josh?'

'Oh, he wants to live with them! But you should've seen her face when he came out with it,' Melanie frowned.

Chloe's stomach churned, thinking of how hurt Josh would be. 'I better speak to him about it,' she said picturing her eldest son's handsome face.

'I don't blame Charlie for not seeing Dad. I think he's right – I don't want to see him now.'

'No ... maybe a break would be good?'

'I know I need to forgive him and all that, but right now I just hate him,' Melanie confided.

'I know,' Chloe responded. 'Forgiveness is a process, Melanie. And if it's going to be real, it's going to be very difficult and costly, so don't rush it, honey.'

'Every time I go for communion I bring him and the pain he's caused our family to Jesus. But I don't feel any different yet.'

'No,' was all Chloe could say.

'Why don't you come to St Stephen's, Mum?'

Chloe took in a deep breath, 'I just can't at the minute, Melanie. I don't want to discourage you from going, but it's not for me right now. Who knows, maybe faith hasn't been snuffed out altogether ... maybe there is still a smouldering wick in there somewhere. But right now, just keeping the family together and running this place is taking all the energy I have.'

'But if you came, maybe Josh and Charlie would come? Maybe it would help them cope? They're both so hurt and angry.'

'Maybe ...' Chloe stared at her hands.

※　※　※

Synod had come and gone. There would be no women bishops.

Bishop Duncan watched the rain spattering against his train window and wondered how God could bear it. It had been a debate littered with landmines and in the end it was a small vocal minority in the House of Laity that held sway, by only a few votes.

If only they could see Grace! Intelligent, beautiful, Anglo-Catholic charismatic. She's like Esther … being prepared for the right time. When will that be? He turned dismally to scan *The Times* on the journey back home.

When he opened the front door, he felt the heaviness increase. *Lord, fill me with your love for Wendy … forgive my lovelessness … expand my heart.*

On hearing the heavy door close solidly behind him, Wendy came into the large entrance hall, drying her hands on her apron. 'Hello, darling,' she greeted him.

'Hello,' he smiled. Her cheeks were flushed from cooking, wisps of hair had come loose from her usually well groomed coiffeur. He kept looking and praying to see her as her Creator must. She approached him tentatively. He opened his arms and she pressed her ample bosom to his chest. He held her, breathing in the smells of the kitchen that clung to her.

'I've missed you,' she said as she kissed him on the cheek.

'What have you been cooking? Smells wonderful,' he said kissing her back perfunctorily.

'Pheasant,' she beamed.

'Wonderful!' he replied. They walked awkwardly, arm and arm into the kitchen as she asked him about Synod.

'Well there will be no women bishops, not for a while anyway,' he sighed.

'I didn't think there would be – sorry my dear – but it just isn't right. I know we'll have to agree to disagree,' Wendy disengaged from him and returned to the chopping board where potatoes and vegetables lay scattered around it. 'But I know how disappointed you must be. You're so good speaking up for those poor women,' she peeled a large potato, skillfully keeping the peel in one piece.

Bishop Duncan swallowed hard, fighting the anger that sprung unbidden to his mouth. 'I know many feel as you do dear,' he said in a controlled voice, 'so I suppose we'll all have to find a way of muddling through together.'

'Yes … just what the Church of England does best,' she smiled, making her plump, rosy cheeks bulge. 'At least I can rest easy knowing I'm never going to have to kiss the ring of a woman bishop,' she wiped a wisp of hair off her forehead with the back of her hand and looked up at him.

'No,' he said, suppressing a desire to laugh derisively at the double meaning, of which she was oblivious.

I'm just going to change. What time's dinner?' he asked, silently reprimanding himself for thinking of such a crude thing.

'Seven. I've invited Colin and his wife and the Braithwaites.'

'Oh ... I thought it was just you and me?'

'No,' she looked pleased with herself.

'Oh ... all right. I'll be down in a bit then. Any chores for me to do?'

'Yes ... could you set up the drinks tray and get the nibbles out when you come back down?'

'Certainly,' he said humbly as he made his way back out of the kitchen. He climbed the broad staircase, feeling a creeping sadness pulling him down like gravity. *It's too late ... we're stuck in ruts of isolation. Parallel lines ... not one ...* the loneliness he was so familiar with intensified to the point that he felt he could weep. Almost, but not quite. That too had been taken from him in boarding school all those years ago. *Stiff upper lip, old man. Pull yourself up by your bootstraps,* he commanded. *Colin! Oh, God ... really? We won't be able to shut him up once he's had a few glasses. He'll be dancing a jig about the vote.*

Bishop Duncan prepared for a long, interminable evening.

❊　❊　❊

'Are Josh and Charlie talking to anyone about how they're feeling?'

'Not really ... you know what boys are like. You're welcome to have a try with them if you want. You were so helpful to Melanie ... maybe if she encouraged them?'

'Maybe ... they really need a man to talk to ... I wonder whether they might open up to Peter?'

'That's a thought. Ask him ...'

'Okay, I will. Listen Chloe ... I was thinking today ...'

'Careful ... sounds dangerous ...'

Grace could hear the smile in her friend's voice. She laughed, 'This is not it.'

'What do you mean?'

'I mean ... marriage is a practicality for now ... it's not the end goal.

The end goal is that we will be like the angels … there will be no giving or taking in marriage in the age to come.'

'You're getting a bit deep for me, Grace,' Chloe sounded tired.

'I just mean … there's always Plan A with God … just because these dreams have been smashed on the floor, doesn't mean all dreams should be discarded. Don't give up on who you know you really are and on the dreams that come from the core of you. The enemy may have won this battle, but it's not over. Good will triumph over evil and everything will be well one day.'

'Grace … have you been drinking?' Chloe sighed.

'I've had a couple of glasses with Peter. But that's not why I'm saying this.'

'It's just a bit too ethereal – spiritual for me. I just wish I could make it all better for my kids in the here and now … I wish I could stop the pain … take it all back. But I can't and I just have to endure.'

'I guess I was trying to give you something to help you endure the now until the not-yet comes to be.'

'There you go again, sweetie … I know you mean well, but I'm too tired to think straight. I might follow your example and go find a bottle of wine myself.'

'I love you …' Grace said feeling a complete failure.

'I know. I love you too,' Chloe replied. 'I'll see you on Monday.'

Grace hung up the phone and opened her bible to Acts chapter eighteen. She hadn't written anything for a while, as work at St Stephen's had taken over. She read a couple of chapters and then pulled out several commentaries. It was midnight before she knew it. Peter came into her study and kissed her goodnight, warning her not to stay up too late as Sunday morning was looming.

But once she started writing she couldn't stop. It was 5 a.m. when she stopped:

'I thought Timothy would be here,' Anna said mournfully.

'I know my love,' Lila soothed her as she plaited her hair.

'Why did brother Paul leave him in Berea?'

'We are going to Corinth – perhaps he will join us there? Papa is going to speak with brother Paul about the matter.'

'Is he? When?' Anna's plait whipped round, thudding against Lila's chest. 'Oh sorry!' Anna reached out and pressed her hand where she'd hurt her mother.

'Now listen to me Anna. You need to be patient. These things take time and besides, once you are married, you can never go back to the carefree days of your youth.'

'I despise the days of my youth!' declared Anna passionately.

Lila stifled a giggle, 'Oh, come now, they're not so bad ... you have me and Papa for company ... are we so very dull?'

'But you have each other! That's what I want ... someone just for me. Most girls get married much younger than me. I've waited, hoping for the right man ... and I'm sure he is ... of course I'll miss you when I'm married, Mama ... I really will, but it's not the same, is it?'

Lila smiled and pulled her daughter to herself, hugging her tightly, 'Marriage is wonderful and if the two people are continually filled with the Holy Spirit, it can be incredible. But it's also very hard work, you know. Brother Paul is right: married people are preoccupied with trying to please each other – on earthly things. If you're single like him, you can focus on what pleases God.'

'I want to do both!' Anna said.

'I know ... just be patient darling. All things come in their proper season. Here, will you help me with cutting this fabric for brother Paul? He needs it by tomorrow morning.' *That will keep her occupied for a while!*

She watched her daughter resign herself to the mundanity of their task, when all the while her heart was yearning for romance and passion. She smiled to herself, remembering how bored she had been with the drudgery of marriage before ... before ... her mind came to a halt at the thought of Aaron. She had never told Anna of her true origin. She never would. She started cutting along the line Paul had drawn.

※　※　※

As they journeyed from Athens to Corinth Jair finally broached the subject with Paul. 'Brother Paul, may I speak with you regarding a personal matter?'

'Speak, Jair, you know you always have my ear and my heart,' Paul smiled and squinted against the bright morning light.

'It's regarding Timothy.'

'Oh?' Paul scrutinised Jair's face.

'I know he is a son to you,' Jair ventured.

'Yes, he is,' Paul nodded.

'Have you had any thoughts regarding marriage for him?' Jair asked.

'I have hoped he would remain as I am, as marriage brings with it many distractions and burdens as well as blessings,' Paul paused and looked at Jair again. 'Are you thinking of Anna as a match for him?'

'Yes ... we were.'

'She is a credit to you both, Jair. Timothy would be very blessed to have her as a wife. But we would need to talk with him and see what he thinks. As far as I know his heart has been set on serving the Lord with me. It is no life for a wife and possible mother to travel all over the world as we do.'

'No ... I know ... when is Timothy joining us?'

'He is on his way with Silas, having returned from Berea to Philippi for a brief visit. I think they will sail from there to the harbour at Cenchrea. We should soon see it,' he added, shielding his eyes and looking up ahead. 'It will be good to receive news of the church and of Luke and Joshua. I'm sure it will not be long.'

They fell into silence for a while, then Paul said, 'We must pray about this matter, Jair. Timothy is very dear to me. I would not want him to make a mistake.'

'Nor would we wish that for Anna,' Jair agreed. 'Shall we speak again about it in a few days' time?'

'That seems right to me brother,' Paul affirmed with a nod of his head.

It wasn't long before they saw the harbour of Cenchrea reaching out into the mixed blue-green waters of the Mediterranean and

Aegean seas. They didn't go down into the town, but kept on the Lechaeon, the Roman road headed for Corinth. Acrocorinth, the 1900 foot mountain cast its looming shadow across the landscape south of Corinth, dominating the horizon. As the sun went down behind it the detail of the famous temple to Aphrodite became more stark against the brilliance of orange and gold sky.

Paul had been given the address of a synagogue. He led the small party directly to it. The synagogue ruler, a man named Crispus greeted them. He gladly offered them hospitality that night in his beautiful home. The next day was the Sabbath and Paul asked Crispus if he might speak to the synagogue. It was packed with many Jews who had fled Rome since Emperor Claudius had ordered all Jews to leave Italy. There was a smattering of God-fearing Greeks assembled as well. Paul preached persuasively, but few responded at first. A man named Aquilla approached him afterwards and invited him to come to his home for a meal the following day to discuss his ideas further.

They were warmly welcomed by Aquilla who quickly introduced them to his wife, Priscilla. She washed their feet and anointed their heads with oil, serving them a wonderful meal. It transpired that they were tent makers, as Paul was. They quickly bonded over their shared knowledge of leather and woven goods. They invited Paul to join them in their workshop. Business was booming as most sailors lived in tents. With two harbours serving Corinth, there was never a shortage of work.

As the evening wore on, the conversation returned to Paul's message that he'd preached in the synagogue. Priscilla was full of questions that Aquilla had been unable to answer. Paul, Jair and Lila happily debated with them long into the night. Anna fell asleep, her head on Lila's lap.

They were intelligent people, Jews originally from Pontus along the Black Sea – an area Paul had not visited on his journeys. Their hearts and minds were very open.

Realising the time, they invited them to stay the night. In the morning, at their request, Paul baptised them in their bath. The others had gathered round to pray for them to be filled with the

Holy Spirit. Priscilla came out of the water, her stocky frame trembling. She was speaking in tongues even before they laid their hands upon her.

At their request, Paul, Jair, Lila and Anna moved into their home. It wasn't palatial, but there were four guest rooms around a simple courtyard. It was comfortable enough for them all, with a room to spare when Silas and Timothy came.

Priscilla picked wild flowers and put them in jugs in each of their rooms on a daily basis. She welcomed Lila and Anna's help with cooking and cleaning. When she discovered that Lila was a seamstress she asked her to help with detailed pieces of stitching. Anna joined in, learning skills from her that she'd not known before.

Priscilla immediately began studying the scriptures, under Paul's direction. She had a hunger for knowledge that far exceeded Aquilla's. He was content to listen to Paul in the synagogue and to discuss matters with Jair in private. But Priscilla could always be found with a scroll beside her even when she was working on a piece of leather or fabric long into the night.

Paul and Jair worked with them in the mornings and then during the time of rest went to the synagogue to proclaim the gospel. Jair accompanied him most days, but occasionally stayed with Lila, to sleep in the heat of the day.

Finally the glorious day came when Timothy and Silas found them, having been to the synagogue first to ask directions. Lila had hoped that Luke and Joshua may have come with them as a surprise, but they had not. She recovered from her disappointment quickly enough to start asking a myriad of questions regarding her young son.

Joshua was fully recovered from his illness, Timothy said, and was working with Luke in his practice daily. Luke wanted them to know that his protégé was a gifted student and growing in the skillful art of caring for the sick. They told of several instances when, faced with a patient they could not treat, Luke and Joshua had laid hands upon and prayed for the sufferer, who had subsequently been healed. Lila shed tears of mingled pride and yearning for her son.

Anna barely contained her excitement, fidgeting restlessly

as she listened to the conversation. Lila found it hard to gauge Timothy's reaction to Anna. He was an introvert and of a rather timid disposition, and she wondered what her daughter saw in him. But once they'd been shown their room and had time to refresh themselves before the evening meal, Lila admitted there was no denying the light in his eyes whenever he looked her daughter's way. As they spoke of their time in Berea, Thessalonica and latterly Philippi, Lila warmed to Timothy. Within the introversion lay a quiet confidence. Lila realised that to her extrovert daughter, these hidden depths were very intriguing.

They had brought a generous gift from the church that met in Lydia's home. The letter that accompanied it was from Lydia herself, asking that Paul use the gift to live on so as to focus completely on preaching the gospel. Paul was moved to tears as he read the letter. Being a businesswoman, Lydia understood how frustrating it was to seek to earn a living as well as minister. In order to be successful in business, she wrote, one must be very focused. We pray that this gift will enable you to have great success in Corinth as you focus solely on proclaiming the good news of Jesus Christ.

※ ※ ※

'Brother Paul, may I speak with you regarding a personal matter?'

Paul smiled to himself, realising what was coming, 'Certainly Timothy, my son.'

'During the time we have been ministering in Macedonia, I have been much in prayer regarding a matter of the heart.'

'Tell me,' Paul encouraged, crossing his legs on his bed and pushing himself up against the wall.

'I have been willing to be celibate, as you are, for the sake of the gospel. But I am not sure I am gifted for it.'

'Go on,' Paul said quietly.

'When we first met Jair and his family I had feelings for his daughter Anna, but I discounted them as being a distraction from my calling. However, during the time we've been apart I have not been able to put her out of my mind. As I have prayed, I have found that instead of diminishing, my feelings have grown stronger. When we met again today ... my whole heart and body yearned for her,' he looked embarrassed.

'There is nothing to be ashamed of in this, Timothy. It sounds to me that God may be calling you to the dual roles of marriage and ministry. It may please you to know that Jair has spoken to me regarding this matter already. I believe your sentiments are reciprocated.'

Timothy's young face lit up, 'Really?' he asked.

Paul nodded, 'She is a godly young woman. Her parents have modelled to her the life of grace and mercy. She is intelligent and knows much of the scriptures and of the ways of the the Holy Spirit. If you were to marry her, she will be a great asset to you.'

Timothy was beaming, like a child receiving a gift he hadn't expected. 'But please know this, my son, with the joy of marriage comes many responsibilities. Your life is no longer your own. You cannot focus solely on the ministry of the gospel, you must also focus on pleasing your wife and caring for any children you may have.'

Timothy blushed, 'Will you pray with me? I ... I do not want to make a mistake.'

And so they turned to prayer.

❋ ❋ ❋

'Hurry Anna, their ship may well be in port already,' Lila urged impatiently.

'Coming, Mama,' Anna called from her room. She came out into the early morning sunlight with a bundle in her arms.

'What is that?' Lila asked.

'It's something I've been making for Joshua,' she smiled secretively.

'Oh ... that's so lovely!' Lila exclaimed, then in a bossier voice, 'Jair, what are you doing?'

'I'm coming, I'm coming ...' he said walking out into the courtyard, still tying his belt around his waist, 'The ship won't have come in yet!'

They made the journey to Cenchrea in record time with Lila setting the pace. As they descended into the town, scanning the sea and harbour, Lila suddenly pointed, shouting, 'That's it – look – there!'

'How can you be sure, Lila?' Jair asked.

'I don't know ... I just know!' she declared.

Jair shook his head at his impetuous wife as he followed down behind her. He looked over at Anna walking beside him and smiled, wondering if Timothy had any idea what he was letting himself in for.

Lila had been right. They watched the ship come into harbour and it was she who first caught sight of their son. She began shouting and waving excitedly. Despite his embarrassment at his wife's exuberance, he found himself laughing and waving too.

When Joshua and Luke disembarked Jair was struck by how much older his son seemed even though they had not been parted for that long. Lila laughed and cried, kissing him on both cheeks several times. Jair embraced him too and Anna hugged her brother furiously.

'I can't believe you're getting married!' Joshua said, 'And to Timothy! He's a dark horse! He never said anything to me when he came to Philippi.'

Lila had to restrain herself, letting her children walk ahead, lost in conversation. Jair whispered in her ear, 'Don't worry, my love, you will have your turn. He will seek you out later, when it's quiet. You'll see,' he squeezed her hand. She blinked back the tears and made herself focus on brother Luke as Jair asked him about Lydia, the jailer, the Philippian church and his practice.

To her delight, he did seek her out in the evening. They sat and talked for several hours in Lila's room. Jair joined them after a while. When Joshua eventually left them for the tent they'd constructed in the courtyard, both parents marvelled at how much their son had grown. They gave thanks for him together before they drifted off to sleep in each others' arms.

※　※　※

Paul paid for the fabric for both Anna's dress and a suit for Timothy. Lila made both. Titius Justus, a worshipper of God, otherwise known to the believers as Gaius, who lived next door to the synagogue, offered his home to be the venue for the wedding. It was a lavish Roman villa with a huge central courtyard garden. He and his whole family had believed Paul's message along with a few others and had been baptised in the Gulf of Corinth, two miles north at Lechaeum.

Timothy and Anna stood under their wedding canopy surrounded by both Jewish and Gentile believers – their family – friends – the baby church. He placed the ring on her finger and declared his love for her. Lila wept; Joshua and Jair laughed; Paul was the first to start the dancing. Later when Jair sat with Paul gasping for breath from their exertion and sharing a goblet of wine, Jair sensed a sadness underlying the joy.

'Brother Paul, you have not lost a son, but you have gained a daughter,' he smiled affectionately at the apostle.

'I know, Jair, but that is not the cause of the sadness I know you sense in me.'

'What is?' Jair asked.

'It's the resistance to the gospel here. So few have believed from among our Jewish brethren. I don't know how much longer we will be welcome in the synagogue.'

Jair said nothing. He listened to his heart rate slowing and his breathing returning to normal. He prayed for wisdom.

'And this city … the temple to Aphrodite with its two thousand prostitutes …' Paul's voice faded to a whisper, 'It breaks my heart.'

Jair looked at his brother's face, feeling convicted, 'I confess I have been so preoccupied with family matters, that I have not paid much attention to the effect of the cult of Aphrodite upon the city.'

Paul nodded, 'It is right that you have been focused upon your family, Jair. They need your wisdom and care. I, however, am responsible before God for all those He sends me to. These people in this city are so far from Him. The Jews entrenched in tradition, clinging to the identity that religious practice brings, while the people of Corinth are dying in the darkness of their lasciviousness.

Sometimes the sorrow I feel overwhelms me and I fear I cannot go on much longer.'

Jair felt alarmed. He'd always thought of Paul as being so strong and definite. He felt honoured that Paul was confiding his weakness to him. 'I will pray for you brother. The Lord will strengthen you,' he clasped his arm in a firm grip.

'Thank you, Jair,' Paul smiled. 'Will you give my apologies to Lila, but I wish to retire now to pray.'

'Certainly,' Jair stood and helped the apostle to his feet. They embraced before Jair saw him to the outer courtyard door of Gaius's home.

The following sabbath the opposition to Paul and his message became abusive in the synagogue. Paul dramatically shook out his clothes in protest saying, 'Your blood be on your own heads! I am clear of my responsibility. From now on I will go to the Gentiles.'

The church began to meet in Gaius's home from then on. Crispus, the synagogue ruler, and his whole family left the synagogue too that day. Nothing anyone could say or do lifted Paul's mood. Despair seemed to have him by the throat. Jair, Silas, Luke, Timothy and Joshua took turns praying over him through the night.

At breakfast the next morning Paul seemed brighter – more himself. He told them he'd had a vision in which the Lord had spoken to him, saying: 'Do not be afraid; keep on speaking, do not be silent. For I am with you, and no one is going to attack and harm you, because I have many people in this city.'

They spent that morning praying in the courage and boldness only the Holy Spirit could bring.

※　※　※

Timothy and Anna had moved out into rented accommodation not far from Priscilla and Aquilla's home. Paul had encouraged them to spend their first year of marriage focusing on each other, as had been the practice of their ancestor David with his army. Paul continued to teach from Gaius's home and over the next year and a half many more were added to their number. The opposition from the synagogue next door continued to smoulder, despite many of them seeking the ministrations of Luke's medical practice that he set up with the help of his young apprentice.

Eventually a united attack from leading Jews in the city brought Paul to court before Gallio, the Roman Proconsul of Achaia. 'This man is persuading the people to worship God in ways contrary to our law,' they accused.

However Gallio had little respect for Judaism, following the racist example of Emperor Claudius. His response was, 'If you Jews were making a complaint about some misdemeanour or serious crime, it would be reasonable for me to listen to you. But since it involves questions about words and names and your own law – settle the matter yourselves. I will not be a judge of these things.'

So he had them ejected from the court. When a riot broke out and Sosthenes, the synagogue ruler, was beaten in front of the court within an inch of his life, Gallio showed no concern at all.

※　※　※

In the early Spring of '52 Paul decided to leave Corinth. Priscilla and Aquilla had grown so close to him by this stage that they too decided to leave too, planning on starting their business afresh in Ephesus.

Paul wanted to get to Jerusalem for the festival of Passover and Pentecost and then to visit his home church in Antioch. It was agreed between them that Silas and Timothy would stay on in Corinth to provide leadership for the growing church that met in Gaius's home. Anna was glad not to be moving.

Lila wanted to stay near her children but Jair was not sure. They argued about it for several days, until Paul spoke to them both.

'You must seek the Lord together. What is His will for you?' Paul challenged them. The hope of possible grandchildren distracted Lila. She wasn't sure she wanted to listen for the Lord's instructions. But as they began a three day fast she started realising that if she stayed and it was not the Lord's will for her to do so, she would be unhappy, grandchildren or no grandchildren.

When Lila and Jair broke their fast that evening Lila's mind was settled. She smiled at Jair and said, 'Let's go to Ephesus.'

※　※　※

Before sailing from Cenchrea, Paul took a thirty day Nazirite vow. They were staying with a disciple named Phoebe until they could board a ship. She had begun a church in her home after visiting Corinth. She'd heard and believed Paul's message in the synagogue and been baptised along with Crispus and Gaius's families. She gladly cut off his hair for him as part of the vow he had made. It was an expression of faith, commitment to the Lord, thanksgiving for God's blessing and strength he'd received to continue ministering despite the fierce opposition he'd faced in Corinth.

Lila embraced both her children without shedding a tear. She was convinced she would see them again soon.

※　※　※

Paul parted company with them in Ephesus, leaving them to the business of finding accommodation and networking to establish their business. They had no idea when they would see him again, but as they all embraced and prayed for one another, Lila grew in her understanding that parting did not have to be the dreaded painful thing she had once thought it would be.

Finding the synagogue in Ephesus Paul experienced a warm reception to his message. They were eager for him to stay on, but he declined, promising them he would return if it was the Lord's will. For now, he was set on Jerusalem and Antioch.

Lila, Jair, Priscilla and Aquilla all attended the local synagogue regularly after that. It didn't take long for them to become well established in their community. They opened their home for meals and discussions following Paul's initial visit.

It was Priscilla who began teaching those who were interested. It was clear she was gifted in this area. The home being the woman's domain had enabled many gifted women to lead the growing church. Aquilla strongly supported her in the ministry, but there was no doubt in anyone's mind that Priscilla was their leader. Aquilla's gifts lay more in pastoral care, and many came to their home for instruction, comfort and encouragement. Jair and Lila assisted them so that together they strengthened all those coming to faith in Jesus.

A Jewish itinerant teacher named Apollos, from Alexandria in Egypt, came to Ephesus. He was an incredibly capable speaker. But as Apollos spoke it became clear that he had not heard the full extent of Jesus' teachings, of Jesus' resurrection or experienced the empowering work of the Holy Spirit himself. His openness to Jesus excited Priscilla and Aquilla. They invited him to their home in order to explain more fully the account of Jesus' death on the cross, his resurrection and the events that followed Pentecost. Priscilla went into great depth as she explained the nature of Jesus' atoning sacrifice. Jair expounded the passages in Isaiah that were so dear to his heart. Apollos responded and was filled with the Holy Spirit when they all laid their hands upon him.

He stayed in Ephesus for a time, enjoying fellowship and instruction in their home. As they spoke of their time in Corinth with him, he became convinced that he was to go there to vigorously refute the Jewish leaders in public debate and to prove to them from the scriptures that Jesus was the Christ.

When they accompanied him down to the harbour, Lila gave him several presents and two long letters to give to Anna and Joshua.

※　※　※

It wasn't long before Lila got a reply from both her children in one letter, informing her that they would be joining them shortly in Ephesus. Luke wanted to meet with Paul again to continue writing his record of his missionary journeys and Anna and Timothy had felt for some time that the Lord was calling them to support the work in Ephesus.

Lila danced around her courtyard, clutching the letter to her heart and singing loudly. Jair joined her when he discovered that their little family would soon be reunited.

Paul returned to Ephesus and to the synagogue, but after three months of preaching to them, he was wearied by the obstinate refusal of many to believe. He also discovered that some were maligning The Way, so he left them.

Paul accompanied Jair and Lila to the harbour to meet the group arriving from Corinth. Jair could tell he was frustrated and uncertain as to what to do next. As they walked they talked and prayed about what the Lord would have them do.

When they saw their loved ones waving on the ship's deck, they all felt their hearts lift. 'Perhaps they have come at the perfect time!' Paul said, grinning broadly at Timothy and the others. Jair nodded his head in agreement, giving thanks to God for his timing.

The wonderful thing about partings are the reunions, thought Lila. She was so excited she flung herself into Joshua's arms, embracing him tightly and crying with joy. Anna had kept one thing secret in her letter. As she stepped off the ship last, helped by an attentive Timothy, Lila screamed with delight: there was no mistaking her pregnant belly. The laughter and tears flowed freely all the way through the city back to their home. There was so much to share, so many stories to tell.

It was late before they tore themselves away from each other and went to bed. The next day Paul returned and took the men with him.

'Where are you going?' Lila wanted to know.

'We are going to hire a lecture hall. It was Timothy's idea last night. Why didn't I think of it?' he laughed, clapping his son on the back.

With all of their help Paul began to teach those who gathered to him at the lecture hall of Tyrannus, both Jews and Greeks. Twelve disciples whom he had baptised on returning to Ephesus also helped.

He worked with Priscilla and Aquilla in the mornings in their tent-making workshop and then in the afternoons he taught intensively. In the evenings he took one or two of the others with him and spent time with believers in their homes, instructing and encouraging them.

Anna gave birth to a boy several weeks after arriving. Lila, Jair and Timothy waited with her through the watches of the night. He was born peacefully just before dawn. They named him Solomon, which means peaceful.

※　※　※

Paul wanted to return to Jerusalem with the gift he'd been collecting from all the Gentile churches. On his last visit he'd seen the devastation caused by a famine in Judea and Jerusalem and had promised to return with a gift to help the believers. He wanted to go back through Macedonia and Achaia in order to strengthen and encourage the churches, but also to collect a gift from each of them for the brethren in Israel.

He asked Timothy and another brother named Erastus, if they would go ahead of him to prepare the way. Initially Anna was cross with Paul for making such a request when they had just had their first child, but as she talked with her mother about it she began to see that perhaps now was a good time for Timothy to travel.

'Sol is so tiny right now … fathers aren't really needed for at least the first six months. And you now have your family here to support you.'

'You're right … but I'll miss him so much!'

'I know my love,' Lila soothed, smiling at her daughter's passion, 'but it won't be for long.'

※　※　※

A riot broke out in Ephesus. A silversmith named Demetrius, who made silver shrines of the goddess Artemis, brought in a lot of business for the craftsmen there. He called them together, along with the workers in related trades, and stirred them up. So many people had come to faith in Jesus, causing the numbers of worshippers of Artemis to diminish significantly, that it wasn't long before the whole city was in an uproar. Paul wanted to appear before the crowd, but the disciples would not let him. Even some of the officials of the province, friends of Paul, sent him a message begging him not to venture into the theatre where they had gathered. The city clerk quieted the crowd and eventually was able to dismiss the assembly. After this Paul set out for Macedonia.

❉   ❉   ❉

Months went by. Word finally came from Timothy: Come to Miletus. Paul sails for Caesarea from here. He is loathe to come to Ephesus, as he would be expected to spend much time with people, dealing with problems and issues in the church. As it is the twenty-fifth Pentecost since the Holy Spirit was poured out upon us, Paul feels it is significant and symbolic to bring the gift from the Gentile churches to the Jewish church on that great day. He is eager to see you all but also to reach Jerusalem in time.

He ended the letter with a personal note to Anna, I miss you my love and cannot wait to hold you and our son in my arms again.

It was only a thirty-mile, two-day journey south from Ephesus to Miletus. The elders of the church and their wives and families embarked on the journey early the next morning.

❉   ❉   ❉

When they arrived, there was a noisy and emotional reunion. Eventually Paul motioned for them to be quiet and Luke unrolled a scroll and readied his pen to take notes.

Paul motioned with his hands for them to be quiet. 'Keep watch over yourselves and all the flock of which the Holy Spirit has made you overseers. Be shepherds of the church of God, which he bought with his own blood. I know that after I leave, savage wolves will come in among you and will not spare the flock. Even from your own number men will arise and distort the truth in order to draw away disciples after them. So be on your guard! Remember that for three years I never stopped warning each of you night and day with tears.

'Now I commit you to God ...'

When Paul had finished speaking, he knelt down with all of them and prayed.

9. SHINE

Acts 21 The women who shine

Chloe held the letter in her hands as radio soundwaves wallpapered round her. *This is it then … it's over …* she tried to focus on the words printed on the headed paper but her eyes wouldn't focus. Instead they zoned in on the woodgrain of the table beneath it, following the lines to the edge, then into space.

She heard the word 'women' and was pulled back into the present by the radio: *'The Church of England has "lost a measure of credibility" after rejecting the introduction of women bishops, the Archbishop of Canterbury has said. The Most Reverend Rowan Williams told the ruling General Synod that the Church could be seen as "willfully blind"'* … she stopped listening, sighing deeply.

She let the letter fall to the table and slowly twisted off her engagement and wedding rings, placing them on the centerfold of the letter. She took off her diamond stud earrings and placed them inside the rings as the news continued on the radio.

Willfully blind … that's it, isn't it?

Who am I asking? …

Vows made before whom?

Rings – symbols of what?

Promises given, but never fulfilled …

No one is so blind as he who will not see …

All this time … all this time I thought I knew him … thought he loved me … only that he was weak … but he didn't … and the children? Despair viciously fed on the edges of the raw hole in the middle of her chest.

I tried ... I loved him ... I chose him again when I could have walked ... but he was blind and didn't want to see ... the real me ... didn't want to know me ... be intimate ... the craving to play on the surface won ... to play on baby-oiled nubile skin ... skin deep ... delivering so little ... so blind ...

Her mind turned slowly, like a mortally wounded beast facing its hunters. She thought of Grace and how the decision made by the Church today would affect her.

Even in the Church, they hunt you down and kill you with their "holy" kisses – misogyny disguised as love in platitudes and distortions of truth. Same thing really ... willful blindness ... They don't want to see real women ... just the stereotypes that soothe and reassure: Submissive women, obedient women, passive women, eager-to-please women, women whose beauty they bask in, whom they can control, women to blame, to carry their shame, to wash their stains. Mothers, wives, sisters, daughters: as long as they're not women fiercely facing the edge of darkness and continuing to shine.

And while they persist in their pathetic discussions round coffee and cake, thousands upon thousands of women will suffer like Anja did – like Grace did – like Melanie did – like Rose did – they are the ones who see the horror of the unmasked face of misogyny, while wolves in sheep's clothing seduce and deceive.

Wolves in sheep's clothing ... she thought of Mark, jerking her hands off the table. *Sell it on eBay ...* she decided.

She went to the tap and washed her hands, drying them on a tea towel and then opened the 'messy' drawer and pulled out an envelope. She wrapped the rings and earrings in kitchen roll and slipped them into it, sealing it and then writing Mark's new address on the front. Then she picked up the letter she'd left on the table and put it in a file marked 'Divorce', and slid it into the drawer.

The phone rang jarring her out of her reverie. She looked at the number, not really wanting to speak to anyone. It was Grace, 'Hi, Grace,' she said hesitantly into the receiver.

'Hi, babe, how you doing?'

'I was just thinking of you listening to the news.'

'What's the decision? I've been stuck in a meeting all day – I'm driving back now.'

'It didn't go through.'

'What?' there was a stunned silence.

Chloe could hear the sound of cars driving past. 'Hope you're on hands free?'

'I'm pulling over … hang on.'

'Where are you?'

'The A3 coming out of London – it's a nightmare. I'm trying to find a news programme on the radio … what happened?'

'They didn't pass it … no to women bishops. I think they needed five or seven more votes in favour in the House of Laity … something like that. It was close.'

'I don't believe it! Not after the new Archbishop's appointment and everything …' Again there was a crackling silence. 'Not that I've ever wanted to be a bishop … it's just the mentality of it. It beggars belief!'

'I know … I'm so sorry …' Chloe said lamely.

'It's certainly not your fault!' Grace responded. 'Hey, maybe you and me should get ourselves voted onto Synod?'

'I was thinking that … we could raise issues related to trafficked women too?'

'Yes … unbelievable … why is there still so much theological error around? I was writing about Paul's final words to the leaders in Ephesus last night … he warned them about people who would distort the truth in order to draw people after them.'

Chloe didn't reply.

'How are you? You didn't say? I was thinking about you on and off all day for some reason.'

'I got the letter from Mark's solicitors today filing for divorce.'

'Oh … oh, Chloe … I'm so sorry … what are you doing tonight? Shall I come round?'

'Yeah – okay. That would be nice,' she smiled.

'I'll be there after half eight. Zack'll be in bed by then.'

'Okay.'

'I better go if I'm gonna get back in time to pick him up. I'll see you later.'

'Bye,' Chloe hung up, curling her hair behind her ear and feeling the empty, soft lobe where Mark's tenth wedding anniversary present had been.

I will not feel sorry for myself … she chanted the phrase in her head, which had become her mantra.

❋   ❋   ❋

'We need you to come and speak to the women about their role in the church. They come with the men now to the Urdu service, which is quite a feat in itself, but they don't seem to engage. It's like they don't think it's for them ... I don't know.' Trevor paused shaking his head.

They were at the Deanery chapter meeting, sitting round a table in St Stephen's hall, sharing stories from their various parishes of encouragement and struggle over a selection of supermarket sandwiches. It still smelt of mould in the hall, which irritated Grace, if she let it. Getting decisions made in PCC meetings was like turning the wheel on the Titanic. Refurbishment had been on the agenda for several months now, with hope of decisive action on the horizon. She sniffed, lightly brushing her nose with the back of her hand.

'I'd be glad to come and speak to them. But sadly any authority I have, has been devalued by the decision Synod has just made. What message does it send to women like them?'

'What do you mean?' Trevor asked, exchanging a confused look with a few others.

Grace breathed deeply, 'Well ... we've taught them about a loving Father in heaven, who sends His Holy Spirit to bring life in all its fullness to all those who believe in His Son's name – both men and women made in His image, right?'

Trevor nodded.

'We've taught them that when the Holy Spirit lives in them He will enable them to prophesy – to speak forth God's word, right?'

'Right,' several people chorused.

'We've told them how precious they are to God, that He loved them so much that He sent His Son to die for them, so that they could know His love and call Him Father, right?'

'Yes,' Trevor was beginning to look irritated.

'But the decision this week tells them that nothing's changed ... they may as well have stuck with what they'd been taught before. There really isn't any difference for women, whatever your religion or culture. Women are always marginalised!'

'Now, Grace, you know that's not true. Look at you – you're a vicar and the Area Dean … that's why I want you to come and speak to them.'

'But don't you get it?' Grace looked exasperated. 'You're giving with one hand and taking away with the other! You're saying, "Yes – come – God loves you – His Spirit will enable you to do all things through Christ who strengthens you – BUT – you have to stay over there and be quiet – you cannot lead – you are not the head – you need the 'covering' of a man." – Or according to Forward in Faith – "you can't represent Jesus to the world because you've only got breasts and a vagina and not a penis!"'

'There's no need to be crude, Grace,' Trevor retorted.

'Surely we are all feminine in contrast to the masculinity of God? After all, aren't we – both men and women in the church – called the bride of Christ?' Grace broke the tension with a laugh. 'It makes a farce of the gospel. It's not good news for women! It's the same old, same old,' she looked round the group of clergy, knowing that she'd probably offended about thirty per cent of them.

Confirming that thought a young clergyman on the far side of the table said, 'I feel quite offended, Area Dean, that you have dismissed the theology of Headship and Covering out of hand. I happen to hold both very dear.'

'And I'm sure it suits you very well, but I think you'll find, if you want to, Graham, that there is very little in scripture to substantiate both ideas. There are two Greek words used for the word we have translated as "Head", one of which no one knows the meaning of … therefore to build a whole theology and practice on such shaky foundations is preposterous.

'The meaning of the word we do know is: "source of a river – the head of a stream". It speaks more of the Genesis concept of creation and not about hierarchical positions of authority and submission.'

Graham cut in, 'You can't seriously believe that in the context of the social order of Ephesus, Paul is teaching a reciprocal mutual submission between children, parents, slaves, masters as well as wives and husbands?'

'Yes I do. If not, the gospel isn't really good news, is it? And as for "Covering" you can only find the idea in the book of Ruth, where she offers herself on a plate to Boaz on the threshing floor and asks him to commit to care for her in exchange by the symbolic act of 'covering' her with the corner of his garment. He tells her to stay the night, and I'm sure I don't need to tell you that there's some debate as to whether he had his way with her or not that night, before he married her. But that's by the by.'

'I don't know what theologians you've been reading …' Graham glared angrily at Grace, his arms folded tightly across his chest.

Grace didn't falter, 'The fact remains, Graham, these things cannot be the basis on which we build a theology and practice. Women don't need to be "Covered" by a man's "Headship". Most women will tell you they have never experienced such a thing even from those who promote the idea. There are very few men selfless and loving enough to even do the job moderately well! Ask your wife!' Graham's face went white.

'Anyway,' Grace went on, even though she could feel she was running out of steam, 'Isn't Jesus big enough and able enough to be the head and covering over us women as well as you men? Was His death on the cross not enough for us? Or are women so terrible that they need men to do it too?

'What about women who have no husbands or fathers? What about all the women who have been abused by men, the millions of women enslaved in the sex trade world wide, and closer to home the women left as single mums to run the family?

'This is all the stuff of the curse. I don't know about you, but I'm dealing in the stuff of the cross, where Jesus became a curse for us, pouring out his fullness of life in exchange,' she looked fiercely round the stunned room. 'I'm sick of pandering to theological error and deception,' she said flatly. 'Enough's enough! So if you still want me to come and speak to your Urdu speaking congregation, I'd be happy to,' she looked fiercely at Trevor and then Graham.

Graham stood up, muttering under his breath and walked out. Several others excused themselves, while those who remained all started talking at once. Trevor sat back looking at Grace, twiddling his pen between finger and thumb. Eventually he cleared his throat, 'Can I have your attention please?' he called the meeting to order. 'Grace, I still want you to come and teach our women in the Urdu speaking service. I don't agree with everything you've said, but I certainly think your ministry with them will be invaluable.'

✳ ✳ ✳

Chloe and Charlie sat next to Grace and Peter at Zack's school recital. He was playing a piece he had composed himself.

Chloe leaned over and whispered, 'I had no idea he was so brilliant!'

Grace smiled, 'He's blown us away … you should hear his teacher gush about him.'

Charlie leaned forward and grinned at Grace, giving her two thumbs up. As he sat back she noticed the way he smoothed the scarf round his neck. He'd grown so tall, yet still seemed very young; his fifteen year old face, still innocent and beautiful. His GCSE year was looming for him as Melanie was finishing her degree. Grace wondered how Chloe managed all the tension around exams for all three of them, as Josh was doing his A-levels too, on top of the emotional fall out from Mark's departure.

She looked back at her son, marvelling at the skill with which he performed his piece. She squeezed Peter's hand. He reciprocated.

After the applause died down they made their way to Zack's side. His teacher was eager to speak with them, 'You do realise that your son has quite a unique gift, don't you?'

'Neither of us are that musical,' Peter replied, 'so we're amazed and thrilled.'

'In all my years of teaching, I've not come across a student at this age with the depth of understanding and skill Zack is displaying. Have you considered his future?'

'Well, he's still young …' Grace said defensively.

'Yes, but there are schools he could go to where he could focus on his gifting far more. Here we're only able to give him the minimum amount of support. As much as I'd hate to lose him,' she smiled at Zack, 'I think you need to think seriously about it.'

Grace exchanged a look with Peter and then put her arm around Zack's shoulders. 'Thank you so much for all you're doing with him,' she smiled at the teacher, turning to go.

Charlie came bounding exuberantly up to Zack, 'Wow, Zack, that was amazing!'

'Thanks, Charlie,' Zack looked admiringly up at his childhood hero. 'How's your art going?'

'Oh it's full on. Takes more time than any of my other work.'

Grace watched them as they walked ahead of her out to the car park. It surprised her to notice that Charlie's mannerisms were more affected than usual. There was no denying that neither were the most masculine of young men. They were both creative and expressive and had always been. But she wondered if insecurity and anxiety, since his parents split, were taking their toll on Charlie. She pushed the sadness back that she always felt when she thought of Mark. 'Has he seen his dad since the split?' Peter asked.

'No – they weren't close before, so you can imagine what it's like now,' said Chloe.

'But Mel and Josh have?' Grace asked.

'Yeah – they've stayed with him some weekends. It took a while for Mark to accept that they didn't want to see his girlfriend, but eventually it got sorted. She goes to her parents when they stay over.'

There was silence as the friends grieved again over the situation.

'Oh … Charlie wanted to know if Zack could come for his fifteenth birthday? We're planning on going to Paris for the weekend with a few of his friends. There's a John Galliano fashion show he wants to go to. It'll cost a bit mind …'

'That's no problem,' Grace said, 'is it?' she leaned forward to look at Peter for confirmation as they reached their cars.

'No – just let us know how much, closer to the time,' Peter said as he unlocked the car.

'Thanks for coming, Chloe.'

'I wouldn't have missed it for the world!' Chloe responded as she hugged her friend.

❊　❊　❊

'I need to,' Chloe was saying.

'But how will you do that and My Sister's House?' Grace asked.

'I don't know, but it's got to be done if we want to keep the house.'

'Isn't Mark giving you enough money?'

'Not always and until the court rules how much, I haven't got a leg to stand on. I think being a sugar daddy is proving expensive!' she laughed drily. 'Anyway, maybe circumstance is forcing me into something I'll actually love,' Chloe tucked her hair behind her ears.

'Oh – you're not wearing your diamonds,' Grace observed.

'No – I gave them back to him. Don't want anything connected with broken promises. Our kitchen table's sold on eBay too.'

'You should have sold the earrings,' Grace said pragmatically.

'It would have been dirty money.'

'All money is dirty,' Grace retorted.

Chloe shrugged, 'Suppose so …'

'So where will you run your private practice from?'

'From Mark's old study – it's right at the front of the house. Clients could come and go without invading the rest of my home.'

'Sounds like you've thought it out pretty well.'

'Yep. Do you want a couple of my business cards to hand out to anyone you think might benefit from my services?'

'Sure,' Grace smiled, taking the cards Chloe held out across her desk.

'I was thinking it would be good to give Val more responsibility? After Melanie's finished her degree, we could raise the funds for her to work full time too, what do you think?' Chloe asked.

'I'll raise it at the next Trustee's meeting,' Grace agreed. 'What I want to do is for us to develop a training presentation to take out round the Deanery, while I'm Area Dean. I want to see if we could get several more safe houses going. We're the prototype …'

'Sounds exciting but do you really think sleepy suburban parishes will get the vision? I mean look at St Stephen's and St Matt's – only a few people have really got it.'

'Better a few excellent people than a hoard of mediocre ones,' Grace stretched her arms over her head in several different directions. 'I need to go for a run!'

'I need a drink!' Chloe laughed.

'Running's better for you,' Grace chided patronisingly.

'Each to her own,' Chloe retorted irritably.

'I know you're not going to like what I'm about to say – but I'm gonna say it anyway,' Grace stood up eyeing her friend, 'You have got a bit chunky lately.'

'Oh, just *shut up*!' Chloe exploded, glaring up at her shocked, tall, willowy friend. 'We can't all be Nordic goddesses.'

'But you've always been so petite … don't let yourself go just 'cuz of …'

'Of what?' Chloe stood up in a rage, 'Of the trauma of having my daughter kidnapped and abused? Of finding out my husband, whom I thought I knew, was secretly as bad as the men that took her? Of being rejected in exchange for a twenty one year old? Of coping with three hurt teenagers?' she paused for breath, boring holes through Grace's skull. 'You know sometimes you're such a blunt instrument! I can't believe you!'

'All I was saying was …' Grace's mouth wouldn't shut up.

'If you say one more condescending thing … so help me, Grace…' Chloe's fists were clenched at her sides, her eyes wild with fury.

'I'm …'

'I can't bear to be with you right now!' Chloe grabbed her coat and bag off the back of her chair and stormed past Grace out of My Sister's House office.

✖   ✖   ✖

'Are you okay, Mum?' Melanie asked. Rose stood beside her putting spaghetti into a saucepan of boiling water in Chloe's kitchen. Both girls looked at one another and then back at Chloe. She was sitting at the new kitchen table, her head resting in her hands. She didn't reply.

'Mum?' Melanie tentatively approached her. The surface of the table was splattered with tears. 'Oh, Mum …' Melanie sat down in the chair next to her and put her arm around her shoulders.

Chloe shook her head, unable to speak.

Rose approached them and came to sit on the other side of her. She took one of her small hands between her long elegant ones. They sat like that for a time until the spaghetti started bubbling over. Melanie quickly jumped up and lowered the flame underneath it. She grabbed the kitchen roll and brought it back with her, tearing off several squares and putting them in her mother's hand.

Chloe covered her face and blew her nose loudly.

'Good one,' Melanie said.

Chloe laughed and then hiccupped. She tore more kitchen roll off and wiped her eyes and cheeks and then the table. 'Sorry,' she said, squeezing both girls' hands.

'For what?' Rose asked. 'You have done this for us many times. I am proud to be here for you now.'

Chloe burst into fresh tears. 'Don't be nice to me … I don't want to cry any more,' they all laughed a little at that.

'May we pray with you?' Rose asked politely.

'I don't know if I believe it works any more,' Chloe's voice was muffled by the kitchen roll squares she had over her mouth and nose.

'Doesn't matter ... as long as somebody does ...' Rose replied in her dignified manner.

Chloe nodded as more sobs lurched out of her, shaking her body as they did.

Melanie looked uncertain, but followed her friend's lead. She laid one hand on her mum's back and kept hold of the other one as Rose began to pray.

'Lord, you do not snuff out a smouldering wick or break a bruised reed. Thank you that you used Chloe to help me when my light had nearly gone out. Please use me to do the same for her now,' she paused.

'And me, God,' Melanie added.

'Lord, the storm has been fierce, but you are in the boat with Chloe. Your enemy – her enemy – would love to swamp her and drown her, but as long as you are with her she will not be swept away. Please speak to the wind and the waves and tell them to be still.'

Chloe remembered when her girlfriends had brought champagne and prayed for her after she'd moved house. She felt remorse for getting so angry at Grace as the same sensation of peace descended on her nervous system.

'I have a bible reference ... I don't know what it is? I'll just go get my bible,' Melanie jumped up and ran from the kitchen, returning immediately with the one Grace had given her when she was confirmed. 'It's Hebrews twelve, verses two and three,' she opened it and found the passage and began to read, ' "Let us fix our eyes on Jesus, the author and perfecter of our faith, who for the joy set before him endured the cross, scorning its shame, and sat down at the right hand of the throne of God. Consider him who endured such opposition from sinful men, so that you will not grow weary and lose heart." '

Chloe had stopped crying, 'Well – that's pretty pertinent,' she said looking at her daughter.

'Amazing! I didn't know what it was ... ' she said wide-eyed.

'Look at you prophesying over your old mum,' Chloe smiled through puffy lips.

'Oh, the spaghetti!' Rose stood up.

They had to throw it away and start again.

❋ ❋ ❋

Dear Grace,

I am deeply saddened by the recent vote in Synod and cannot believe it has happened. I feel acutely for you and all members of the church who believe this should take place to the Glory of God. My prayers are with Archbishop Rowan. This is one more huge disappointment for him as he passes the baton on to +Justin.

The next few years will be busy!

With that in mind I am writing to ask if you would consider speaking at our next diocesan conference? The theme is, 'For a time such as this.'

To find consolation in these dark days I have been reading Julian of Norwich. I leave you with this quote:

"He did not say, 'You shall not be tempest-tossed, you shall not be weary, you shall not be discomforted.' But He said, 'You shall not be overcome.'" Trust in His promises. Amen. Trust in deed in His calling for you, His promises of love, and nothing on this earth, no powers nor heights, nor depths, no pain nor disappointment, no weariness or discomfort can separate us from the love of Christ Jesus our Lord.

Yours,

+Duncan

Grace read the email several times over. She critically observed the huge pleasure she felt at his request. She looked at her diary for the date of the conference; it was several months away in the New Year. She sat back and looked up at her blue and gold icon of Jesus.

Do you want me to do it? She waited.

'For a time such as this?' I'm not ambitious ... *well, other than to bind up the broken hearted. I don't want to be seduced by power and prestige.*

She closed her eyes and prayed, her spirit babbling like a brook.

Seek first the Kingdom ... yes ... I am ... take up your cross and follow me.

She was stumped. Her eyes flew open.

Dear Bishop Duncan, she wrote,

Thank you for your email.

The vote does beggar belief. It must have been tough for all of you at Synod who had voted otherwise. I hope you know we at St Stephen's have had you in our prayers.

Thank you too for your kind invitation. I would be honoured to speak at the next diocesan conference, as long as you don't mind me offending a few people.

Yours,

Grace

An email came back immediately.

I've heard from a few clergy whom you offended at your last Deanery meeting, hence the invitation.

+Duncan

Grace smiled.

※　　※　　※

It was a freezing night. The rain was sheeting down, blown by a northerly wind of gale force proportions. James Martin, Sean and Omar, whose nickname had stuck, were walking the streets, their collars up, their Street Pastor hats pulled down low on their foreheads.

The weather ensured it was quiet in terms of human chaos. A few committed revellers huddled in groups under coats and umbrellas, protruding bare legs and stilettoes the only give away as to the gender make up of each group.

'What time do you think we should call it a night?' Sean asked, thoughts of his new bride asleep in their warm bed beckoning him.

'It's two now … give it another hour? What do you think, Omar?' James asked.

'The clubs close at three … better wait until then,' he replied, his voice muffled by his scarf.

'One more hour, Sean … not long,' James' teeth reflected the headlights of a taxi as it passed them.

A woman's scream assaulted their ears, above the sound of the wind and rain. They all started running as one man in the direction it had come from, round a sharp corner and down an alleyway. Ahead they saw a group of men. They all started shouting at once, hoping to frighten and disperse the group. Sean and Omar slowed their pace, obeying the Street Pastor policy of not getting involved. But James barrelled his way into the centre of the group. There on the rubbish strewn wet cobbles lay a young girl, her excuse for a skirt around her waist, her panties torn and ragged around one leg. Out of the periphery of his vision, crouched to his left, one of the men had just withdrawn from her and was on his hands and knees like an animal.

'Call the police!' James shouted to Sean as he lunged to his left, grabbing the man by his throat. He was shocked at the strength that met his hands. He'd thought perhaps the man was drunk – that they were all drunk – but too late he realised that was not the case. This man was sober, his senses finely tuned, his reflexes alert and keen. James had landed among a pack of wolves.

As they flashed their torches on the savage fight between James and the ringleader, Omar recognised the tattoo that curled its way up the neck of the man James was fighting. It was then that he turned and ran for his life, with Sean in hot pursuit. From the safety of the lit pavement they waited breathlessly for the police.

It was all over in a matter of minutes, but to James it seemed an eternity. He'd never encountered such vicious strength. He held his own at first, throwing punches when he could, but then there was a searing pain in his back. The rest of the gang, tired of watching, had begun kicking him and stamping on him. He felt his strength ebb, his grasp loosen, the cold of the cobbles on his face and the shock of each kick until mercifully everything went black.

※　※　※

'Hi, Trevor, how are you?' Grace was sitting at her desk, having just read Acts 20 again and Acts 21–24.

'I'm fine, Grace, but I've got some bad news.'

'What?' Grace held her breath.

'James Martin was attacked last night and is in intensive care,' he paused. 'He, Sean and Omar were doing their Street Pastor shift when they intervened in a rape attack. James got too involved and it doesn't look like he's going to make it. Marie's with him and I think Sean and Omar are at the hospital too. I just thought you would want to know. I'm going down there later on this morning.'

Grace felt herself detach, and listened to herself calmly say, 'Thanks for ringing Trevor. I'll go now.'

'I'm sure Marie would value your support.'

'Yes,' she said in a strangled voice. She hung up.

She stared at her print of Jesus knocking at the door. She reached for her keys and stood up, her heart pounding. As she left the house her thoughts began to come into focus. *So many times I've wished him dead … I've never really forgiven him for what he did to me … just kept him at a distance … never really cared about him or Marie … I'm getting what I wished for … he's dying … for intervening in a rape …*

The word ricocheted inside her head like a bullet.

She drove to intensive care in a daze, parked up and went in. She asked at the reception desk and followed directions. She waited at the double doors after pressing the button. A nurse opened it and told her to wait as no more than two people were allowed at the bedside at a time.

She sat down heavily in a plastic chair.

Marie came out with Sean, their faces ashen. Grace rose to her feet unsteadily. 'Marie, I came as soon as Trevor phoned. How is he?'

'He's still unconscious. They're doing everything they can for him.'

'He's in the right place,' Grace thought how lame she sounded but could think of nothing else to say.

'I'm going to go, Marie,' Sean said, touching her elbow. 'I'll pick the kids up from school for you and take them back to yours.'

'Thanks, Sean,' she smiled wanly at him. 'Oh, can you ring his mother? He hasn't seen her in years … and he'd kill me if he heard me now, but I think she should know.'

'Sure ... what's her number?' Sean waited while she fished out her mobile phone from her handbag and then read out the number.

'She might be a bit abrupt at first, but persevere,' she said and then waved him goodbye.

'You ready?' she turned to Grace.

It occurred to Grace that beneath the fine bones and delicate skin, the expensive clothes and jewellery lay a woman of steel. She had never taken any time to engage with Marie and suddenly regretted it, 'Yes,' she answered.

The nurse let them past several other unconscious patients to his bed. James was unrecognisable. His whole head was swollen. There were tubes everywhere and several monitors flashed and beeped round him. Marie went to his side immediately and took hold of his hand. It was bandaged, with only the fingers protruding covered in dried blood. Grace stood at the end of the bed feeling sick at heart.

Marie began speaking so quietly that Grace had to lean forward to hear what she was saying, 'So many times I wanted to kill him. I even thought about hiring a hit man once, you know ...' she didn't look up and Grace didn't interrupt. 'I knew he was a bit wild when I married him, but I had no idea really ... His mum was an alcoholic – had beaten him within an inch of his life a good few times. He'd just scraped by under the radar of the social services all the years he was growing up – I felt sorry for him ... wanted to mother him ... give him everything he'd never had ... why do women think they can save their men?' Grace didn't answer, but stepped round the other side of the bed, so she could hear better.

'The first time I found him with two prostitutes was in his office. He promised he'd never do it again – that it was a once off thing because of stress with the business ... I believed him. Naive I know ... the second time was in our home. I knew then I was seeing only the tip of the iceberg. That's when I began imagining doing things to him like those men did last night,' she started to cry, her small frame shaking like a leaf. 'In desperation I found a church ... I needed help ... I've been praying for him ever since.'

'Marie ...' Grace started to speak, unsure of what to say.

'I feel like this is my fault ... like what I wished for all those years ago has finally come true.'

'Oh no, Marie … no … this is not your fault. You saved him …'

Marie wept silently. Grace reached across the bed and rested her hand on top of hers, 'Could we pray for him together?'

'The doctors told me he wasn't going to make it. It's only a matter of hours,' Marie whispered.

'Let's pray anyway, Marie …'

'Okay.'

'Lord, thank you that you live in James, that you are the hope of glory in his life. Please may he live out his full number of days that you have ordained for him. May he know your presence with him. And Lord, please wrap your arms around Marie and the children. Please hold them close.'

'Lord, thank you for him,' Marie prayed, 'for his love for me and the kids, for his desire to make amends for the past, for how he's been able to forgive his mother recently. Thank you … Please bring him back …' she started to cry again.

They stood for a time in silence, but for the beeping of the machines. 'When do you have to go?' Marie asked.

'I can stay for a while … Trevor will be in later.'

'Can you stay while I go to the loo?'

'Of course,' Grace smiled. 'Have you eaten anything? Maybe go get yourself a drink or something?'

'I'm not hungry … but maybe a hot, sweet drink?'

'Good idea – I'll have a coffee,' Grace watched her leave and then looked back down at what was left of James. She pulled up a chair and sat on the edge of it. 'I'm sorry,' she whispered, 'sorry for never forgiving you … not really … for never caring for you or your family …' she sighed, her sick heart constricted her breathing.

'That's okay,' his voice rasped over swollen, cut lips, like sawdust. Grace jumped, looking up at his face. Nothing had changed. His eyes were still closed. She looked at the machines to see if they were indicating any change. They didn't seem to be. She wondered whether she'd imagined it.

'James?'

'Mmm.'

'Can you hear me?'

'Mmm.'

She stood up to look for his nurse, but heard him say, 'No ... don't ... please.'

Grace stood still, uncertain of what to do.

'I know ...' he said.

'What?' her chest hurt.

'I know it was you ... what I did to you ...'

'Oh, God,' she gasped, her hand flying to cover her mouth.

'I tried to take it back ... the girl ... is she okay?'

Grace wasn't sure what he meant at first and then realised he was concerned about the rape victim, 'She's alive ... she's in hospital.'

'Good ... I'm so sorry ... so sorry ... Marie ... Marie ... can you see him?' The heart monitor started beeping and flashing faster, 'Oh ... he's like you said ...' his surprised voice faded into a long sigh. The heart monitor began to beep madly.

'Nurse!' Grace shouted. The white uniformed man was already running from his computer to the bedside as others joined him, pushing Grace out of the way. She stood frozen, watching the team frantically fight for life.

She walked slowly out to the corridor and waited. When Marie came out of the lift and saw her, she dropped both coffee cups, splattering brown liquid across the white linoleum and walls. She began running towards her, alarm distorting her features. Grace caught her in her arms and held her tightly. They stood like that for ages.

Eventually they disentangled and Marie mechanically pressed the call button and watched through the section of glass in the double doors for the nurse. He came quickly, quietly explaining that James had slipped in to a coma. Marie approached his bedside slowly, then reached out and stroked his swollen face. Grace eyed the heart monitor, uncertain whether to trust it again. She stood behind Marie and silently prayed. She had no words.

❋ ❋ ❋

Grace couldn't sleep. She left the warmth of Peter's embrace and tiptoed downstairs to her study. She hadn't written anything for several weeks since that first day in intensive care. She'd been regularly with Marie who sat helplessly beside his inert body, hoping for change, but there was none. As Grace opened her bible she realised everything in her life had become suspended in time. She'd been going through the motions of her daily responsibilities as if she were in a dream. Tonight she felt like she was waking up. She'd taken notes on Acts twenty one to twenty four before James had been attacked, ready to finish her story, but every time she'd tried since then, she'd ended up deleting all her attempts.

She opened her notebook and read over her notes. She read the chapters again. She opened her laptop and her story file, reading over the end of what she'd last written.

She put thoughts of James and Marie to one side and threw herself into the first century:

On seeing Paul sitting with Luke, Joshua and Jair, he came over to him. A stunned silence fell as he took Paul's belt from around his waist and began tying his own hands and feet with it.

'The Holy Spirit says,' his voice rang out above the noisy time of fellowship, '"In this way the Jews of Jerusalem will bind the owner of this belt and will hand him over to the Gentiles."'

Paul stared at him. Luke leaned forward and grasped his arm, 'Paul, I'm pleading with you, don't go to Jerusalem.'

Joshua wept, knowing full well that Paul would not change his mind. Others stood and gathered round Paul, begging him to change his plans.

Eventually Paul stood up and motioned for the church to be quiet, 'Why are you weeping? You're beating my heart like women pound on cloths with stones as they wash them to get them clean. Please ... I can't bear it! Listen to me – I am ready not only to be bound, but also to die in Jerusalem for the name of the Lord Jesus.'

When he would not be dissuaded, they gave up and Philip echoed what many were thinking, 'The Lord's will be done,' he sighed, bringing the meeting to a close.

That afternoon Paul began preparing to leave. He purchased horses, saddling and packing. The gift he had collected from the Gentile churches was spread across all the packs. Early the next morning he was ready to go. Jair and Lila embraced him and kissed him as did Philip and Mary. As she held Joshua to her, he whispered, 'I will come back after Jerusalem. Wait for me.'

She pulled back from him and searched his eyes, 'Truly?' she asked.

'Truly,' he smiled.

She covered her mouth with her hand and prayed it would be so as she watched him take his horse by the reigns and lead it out onto the street. Eight others already waited out on the cobbles. Paul waved a final farewell as he said, 'Now to fulfil my vow in the temple and for all that will bring glory to the Lord. Pray for me,' he smiled, squinting in the morning sunlight.

They waved farewell until they disappeared from sight.

❋ ❋ ❋

It wasn't long before they received a letter from Luke and Joshua. It was a weighty scroll, written in Luke's fine hand. They sent messengers to gather the church and Jair sat to read it to them all:

Greetings,

We arrived safely and were warmly welcomed by James and all the elders in the city. Paul reported in detail of what God had done among the Gentiles through his ministry. When they heard this they praised God.

But they told us that many believing Jews had been informed that Paul had been teaching the Jews living among the Gentiles to turn away from Moses, telling them not to circumcise their children or live according to Jewish custom. They therefore instructed him to make a vow with four of us, joining in purification rights. They believed then that everyone would know there was no truth in the reports they had heard.

So we purified ourselves with him and then went to the temple to give notice of the date when the days of purification would end and the offering would be made for each of us. When the seven days were nearly over, some Jews from the province of Asia saw Paul at the temple. They stirred up the whole crowd and seized him. They had previously seen Trophimus the Ephesian in the city with Paul and assumed that Paul had brought him into the temple. The whole city was aroused, and the people came running from all directions.

Seizing Paul, they dragged him from the temple, and immediately the gates were shut. While they were trying to kill him, news reached the commander of the Roman troops that the whole city of Jerusalem was in an uproar. Thankfully when the commander and his soldiers arrived, they stopped beating Paul.

Paul was arrested and bound with two chains, much like the prophet Agabus predicted. The violence of the mob was so great Paul had to be carried by the soldiers. The crowd that followed kept shouting, 'Get rid of him!'

The commander wanted to find out why Paul was being accused by the Jews. So the next day he released him and ordered the chief priests and all the members of the Sanhedrin to assemble. Then he brought Paul and stood him before them.

Paul looked straight at the Sanhedrin and said, 'My brothers, I have fulfilled my duty to God in all good conscience to this day.'

At this the high priest Ananias ordered Aaron, the man standing near Paul to strike him on the mouth. Aaron struck him violently. Then Paul said to him, 'God will strike you, you whitewashed wall! You sit there to judge me according to the law, yet you yourself violate the law by commanding that I be struck!'

Then Aaron said to Paul, 'How dare you insult God's high priest!'

Paul replied contritely, 'Brother, I did not realise that he was the high priest; for it is written: "Do not speak evil about the ruler of your people."'

Then Paul, knowing that some of them were Sadducees and the others Pharisees, called out in the Sanhedrin, 'My brothers, I am a Pharisee, descended from Pharisees. I stand on trial because of the hope of the resurrection of the dead.' When he said this, a dispute broke out between the Pharisees and the Sadducees, and the assembly was divided.

There was a great uproar, and some of the teachers of the law who were Pharisees stood up and argued vigorously. 'We find nothing wrong with this man,' they said. 'What if a spirit or an angel has spoken to him?' The dispute became so violent that the commander was afraid that they would tear Paul to pieces. He ordered the troops to go down and take him away from them by force and bring him into the barracks.

The following night the Lord stood near Paul and said, 'Take courage! As you have testified about me in Jerusalem, so you must also testify in Rome.'

The next morning some Jews bound themselves with an oath to kill Paul. More than forty men were involved in this plot. They went to the chief priests and the elders and said, 'We have taken a solemn oath not to eat anything until we have killed Paul. Now then, you and the Sanhedrin petition the commander to bring him before you on the pretext of wanting more accurate information about his case. We are ready to kill him before he gets here.'

But when the son of Paul's sister, a servant to the chief priest, heard of this plot, he went into the barracks and told Paul who called one of the centurions and said, 'Take this young man to the commander; he has something to tell him.'

Dear brothers and sisters, soldiers will be bringing Paul with them during the night as far as Antipatris. The next day the cavalry will go on with him, while they return to the barracks. When the cavalry arrives in Caesarea, they will deliver the letter to the governor and hand Paul over to him. We will be following. Prepare to meet us. His accusers will follow shortly to present their case against him to Governor Felix.

❈   ❈   ❈

The church began to pray in earnest for Paul's safe arrival and for those returning behind him. They lamented the hardness of their fellow Jews' hearts and cried out to God for mercy. The time of prayer carried on into the early evening, before people began to disperse.

Lila and Mary were the first to see him. They had been watching and waiting on the main road into Caesarea, despite the burning heat of the midday sun. It was the light in their eyes that fuelled Paul's heart as he passed them in the street before entering Herod's palace under guard.

As they made their way back to Mary's home, they saw Luke and Joshua approaching the house from the other direction. Lila broke into a run and gasping, hurled herself into her son's arms. 'Oh Joshua, it is so good to see you. I have feared for your life too.'

They brought them in, washed their feet and anointed their

heads with oil. Then went to prepare them food as they had not eaten since leaving Jerusalem. Jair embraced his son and then Luke as if he had not seen them for years, instead of twelve days.

As they watched and waited over the next few days, word came to them that the high priest, Ananias, and Aaron, along with other elders and a lawyer named Tertullus had finally arrived to present their case before the governor in Caesarea. News filtered out through the network of believers that Felix had adjourned the proceedings having heard from both sides. He'd given permission for Paul's friends to visit him and care for his needs.

Lila and Jair, Mary and Philip came straightaway with Luke and Joshua. They brought food and drink, but most of all they brought the comfort and consolation of fellowship and deep affection. Several days went by and Felix called Paul before him again, this time with his wife, Drusilla, a Jewess. But Felix became afraid as Paul spoke of the judgement to come and sent him away again.

The community of believers adjusted to the regular trips they all took in turns to visit Paul in prison. Meanwhile the lack of action fuelled opposition to the church among the Sanhedrin. Many believers were beaten and imprisoned, their possessions taken from them and their homes burned.

Despite those dark days, the community of faith celebrated the marriage of Junia and Andronicus. Philip and Mary's household was turned upside down with the preparations, but Mary loved every minute, having thought at one stage that all her daughters would remain celibate.

Then disaster struck again. Not long after their wedding, Junia and Andronicus were caught in a raid of churches where they were teaching in Sebaste. They were brought before Felix and imprisoned with Paul.

As Mary visited them, she marvelled how God could take something meant for harm and turn it for good. Her eldest daughter and husband were able to minister to Paul during some of his darkest days.

Lila and Mary sat cross-legged with Junia and Andronicus on their cell floor. Paul leaned against the prison bars that separated their cells as they talked. Junia said to her mother, 'God is using this for good, Mama. We are here to comfort brother Paul. Don't cry, please don't cry ... the light Tabitha and you tended in me will not be snuffed out. I will shine in here until Jesus returns or calls me home. You should be proud that I have been called for a time such as this. It is a credit to you.'

Paul wiped a tear that trickled down one of the crow's-feet edging his eyes as he adressed Mary, 'They are outstanding among the apostles,' he said, a wobbly smile on his lips as he looked from Junia to Andronicus. 'They have been such a comfort to me here.'

Mary reached through the bars and held his chained hand for a time.

As she left Herod's palace, she remembered how she had wept at Jesus' feet, pouring out perfume worth a year's salary. 'I too was extravagant ... why should I expect anything less from my daughter?' she smiled sadly at Lila.

'Oh, Mary ...' Lila linked arms with her as they made their way home in the gathering dusk, 'the light shines in the darkness, but the darkness has not overcome it.'

They picked their way slowly through the littered street in the gathering dusk.

'I'm glad she's so deeply grateful to God ... but I don't want her to suffer.'

'No ... you'd be a strange mother if you did,' Lila frowned in the darkness, thinking of Anna and Sol so far away.

'Love for God leads us in paths that we would never naturally choose ...' Mary mused.

'Yes,' Lila agreed, 'into darkness we'd rather avoid.'

'But the whole point is to dissipate the darkness with light.'

'Yes ...'

They squeezed each others' hands resolutely. Relief and grief vied for dominance as they neared the comfort of Mary's home. How could they be glad to be back in safety when they'd left Junia, Andronicus and Paul in chains?

Grace stared at her computer screen for some time, the cursor blinking silently at her. She'd read in a commentary the other day that the phrase, 'To love' in Hebrew was the same as 'To show gratitude.'

How grateful am I?

Suddenly her mail icon started bouncing at the bottom of her computer screen. She clicked on it and saw an email from Chloe. She opened it bracing herself for what it might contain.

Hi Grace,

Long time no hear or see ...
I know you were giving me space after our last conversation.
Then I felt I should give you space as I've heard how involved you are in supporting Marie with James in intensive care.

I just wanted to say that I love you very much and am sorry I stormed out on you.

Hope to hear from you soon.

X Chloe

Grace wrote back immediately:

Hi Chloe,

What you doing up at this time of night?

I don't blame you for storming out – saved you from hitting me probably?

I'm sorry I was so insensitive ... and I love you too ... I've missed you these last few weeks, but I've been in a bit of a daze really.

Do you fancy lunch tomorrow at the pub ... say 1.00?

X G

Chloe replied: See you at 1.00

Grace got up, pulling her dressing gown round her, thankful for the comfort of Chloe's reconciliation and returned to her writing folder. She pressed 'save' and closed her laptop. As she climbed the stairs slowly back to bed, she heard the first voice of the morning chorus pierce the darkness.

I am so grateful … I will do anything for You … knowing that my sisters – Your sisters – are out there imprisoned in brothels, in abusive relationships, suffering as a result of misogynistic systems of belief … Help me set up more safe houses … help me raise a voice for the voiceless … be an Esther … a Julian of Norwich … a Hildegard von Bingen … For a time such as this … for You.

After Chloe's face, Anja's came before her. She smiled affectionately. *And for you, Anja.*

Anja smiled back.

It occurred to Grace that she'd never seen her smile like that in real life. She wondered how her imagination knew to put Anja's face together so beautifully.

Real life … she pondered the concept, wondering which was 'realer': this one or the next?

She reached the top of the stairs and gazed out the uncurtained landing window. It looked out on St Stephen's spire, a half moon hanging low just above the roof.

Her eyes blurred making the moon swim, as she tried to remember when Anja's aniversary was. *I'll look at last year's diary tomorrow,* she thought as she crept into bed, tucking herself close to Peter's back and wrapping her arm around him.

He murmured something incomprehensible in his sleep.

BABE'S BIBLE III
LOVE LETTER

Mark's eyes followed Charmaine's slender leg as it wound itself around the stainless steel pole. Her glittering thong nestling between perfectly sculpted cheeks, almost disappeared into her flesh as she stretched her leg above her head, parallel with the pole. She caught his eye through the heat-haze of lust, but his gaze quickly slid to the small triangle of cloth between her legs, as his burning loins dictated to him, pulsing in time with the music.

As her act ended she bent to pick up a few stray notes that had fallen from the nest of her thong, her young breasts swinging freely and her long blonde hair tumbling forward. Mark knew exactly how he wanted to have her this time. He rose and followed her purposefully, as she swayed down the narrow catwalk to the stage curtain. The bouncer acknowledged him with a grunt and a nod as he made his way past him into the bowels of the club.

Some time later he emerged from the neon-lit entrance onto the street, shrugging himself into his coat. Her shift would finish at 3.00 am. He couldn't wait for her tonight, he had a big presentation at work on Monday and needed the weekend to prepare for it, plus Josh was coming over for lunch and to watch the game. It would take half an hour to get back to the flat by tube and he needed his sleep. Despite his reservations at leaving her to get a taxi home, he squared his shoulders against the cold and started walking towards the tube station.

He watched a group of Street Pastors on the other side of the road helping two drunk women up off the pavement. As he kept walking, he inwardly sneered at the stupidity of all concerned in the struggling cluster of humanity. Why bother with drunk slags when they'll be out here again next weekend doing the same thing? Touchy-feely-heal-me crap, he smirked dismissively, returning his attention to thoughts of the pleasure he'd just enjoyed and reminding himself to put a Red Bull on his bedside cabinet for when she got home.

❋ ❋ ❋

Charmaine waited for her taxi outside the club. It was 3.15 a.m. A group of men stumbled out and stood near her, fumbling with their jackets and lighters. One of them sidled over, asking her for a light.

'I don't smoke,' she said, not taking her eyes off her phone screen and pressing the call button for the taxi again.

'You all alone?' he asked leaning in towards her.

She pulled away from him as the taxi service answered her call. She gave him a look filled with loathing, and then spoke into her phone. 'Where's my taxi?' keeping her voice as level as possible.

He reached out and grabbed her wrist. She instantly reacted twisting 360 degrees, breaking his grip. The sudden movement drew the other men's attention. As they crowded in behind him he reached for her again, but this time she was ready. She grabbed a can of hairspray from her bag, pointing it in his face.

'Look', she said, swearing again, 'I don't want to hurt you. You're pathetic.'

Bawdy laughter oozed from them. 'But I'd like to hurt you,' he grinned and then spat.

Charmaine pressed the nozzle of the hairspray as he lunged for her. 'Argh!' he screamed.

'Is everything okay here?' a Street Pastor shouted as he and his team approached the group outside the gentlemen's club.

Charmaine's admirer had her up against the wall, his full weight pressed against her and one hand round her throat, while he furiously rubbed his eyes with the other. She took advantage of the distraction afforded by the Street Pastor and pulled out of his grasp, coughing, spewing obscentities at him and rubbing her neck.

A taxi pulled up to the kerb and Charmaine ran to it. Eyes streaming, the man lunged after her and caught her coat as she opened the passenger door. She struggled out of it, got in and slammed the door shut, leaving him with the fake fur dangling limply in his hands. She was laughing and holding up her middle fingers at the window as the taxi pulled away into the night.

'That's that then, lads. Best just get home now, don't you think?' the leader of the Street Pastors' team said aimiably, only to be met with a barrage of verbal abuse. 'Yeah, yeah ...' he said, 'Go on home ... it's cold out here ... go sleep it off.'

❋ ❋ ❋

Zack's thumbs moved like a hummingbirds' wings across the keyboard of his Nintendo DS. Grace eyed the wobbly character apparently incapable of driving the car he was in. As he lurched over hilly graphics, capturing stars along his way, she couldn't help cringing every time he was thrown out of the car and crumpled in a heap on the primary coloured, digital background. Feeling irritated she got up and went to the magazine rack, pulling out a glossy magazine. She idly began flipping through it as they waited for Zack's name to be called.

She came to an article entitled 'Your man's new top fantasy' and began reading, wondering whether it would give her insight into Peter. She felt even more irritated as she skipped down to the advice of the writer. Grace couldn't read any more. She looked at the back of Zack's bowed head, engrossed in his game. How much do they pay these people to write such crap?

Closing the magazine she let it slide off her lap onto the seat beside her. Old memories scuttled across her mind of declining requests from clients for their darkest fantasies, often with some force. At least back then she was allowed to decide what she would and wouldn't do. Trafficked women had no such privilege. She shivered involuntarily.

'Zack Hutchinson,' the receptionist called.

'Yes,' Grace replied and nudged Zack out of his digital world.

They both made their way out of the waiting room and down a corridor.

'Just a check up is it, Mrs Hutchinson?'

'Yes ... don't think you've got any problems with your teeth, have you Zack?'

'No,' he replied as he settled himself in the dentist's chair and stared up into the light.

※　※　※

'What do you want to do for your fourteenth birthday?' Grace asked as they drove away from the surgery.

'I'd love to go to a Take That concert, if there was one.'

'Well, is there one on?' she asked as they turned into the drive of his music teacher's home, for his Monday lesson..

'Not on my birthday, but yeah there's one planned for the summer. Tickets should be coming out soon.'

'Can you show me the right website later? I'd love to see them too!'

'Yeah – can I invite Charlie and Jules?'

'Of course ... do you think they'd come? They're a bit old now.'

'Course they will – they love Take That – and anyway, Charlie promised me he'd come to my fourteenth.'

'Okay … I guess they'll be back from uni in May. Anyone else?'

'No – my other friends don't like them.'

'Like who … Charlie and Jules?'

'No, Mum,' Zack laughed, 'Take That!'

'Oh right …' she replied. 'We could go out for a meal and a film on your actual birthday? You know just us and Grandma?'

'Yeah – that would be cool.'

'Okay, love. I'll see you later … you happy to walk home after your lesson?'

'Yep,' he leaned over and kissed her on the cheek. Grace wondered how much longer she could enjoy such a precious pleasure.

Grace drove the short distance back home, then popped round to My Sister's House office to check on things with Melanie who was in charge that day.

After they'd made a cup of coffee and touched base on a few admin issues, the conversation turned to what she'd read in the magazine article at the dentist.

'Is that true?' she asked Melanie.

'Yeah … that's what Yusuf and Sony were trying to do that night … that's why it got so violent … I fought them, even though I knew I didn't stand a chance … I'd have rather died fighting than give into that.'

Grace was silent.

'Most of my friends at uni tried everything … literally no holds barred, excuse the pun. That's what you do when your head's full of porn, I guess. We're the digital generation. We've seen porn since we were young. I think the first time I saw it was sitting in the back of the school bus on someone's phone. It's like you were saying in your sermon last Sunday, "Sheep without a shepherd".'

Grace looked steadily at Melanie and listened.

'There is no right or wrong, just preference. Violence is an acceptable way of showing desire now – like – "I hurt you cos I feel that passionately about you". It's mad!'

Grace looked at her nails and then back at Melanie, shaking her head, 'How are the new girls?'

'One's only ten. She's from Ireland. Trafficked by her family. She's having to have an op tomorrow.'

Grace nodded. 'How's it going tracking the family down?'

'Oh we already have. They're known by the Garda over there. When she's recovered from her op, we'll record her testimony if she'll let us. She's terrified of them. It'll take some time before I think she'll feel safe and dare to talk.'

'Yep,' Grace held her breath and then let out a sigh. 'But they will get prosecuted in the end,' she paused, savouring the thought. 'How are you doing?'

'I'm okay – excited about the number of halfway houses we've got now. Rose is so great to work with and Val is fantastic at all the admin. Mum and I share the psychotherapy sessions pretty well ...'

'But how are you ... you personally?'

'Oh,' Melanie laughed shyly. 'I'm not bad. I had a blip there recently with food. I think it was because of stuff that came up for me out of hearing one of the girls' stories. I've been working on it with my supervisor.'

'That's good,' Grace smiled encouragingly. 'Have you got a social life outside of here?' she pressed gently.

Melanie looked down at her computer keyboard and wiped an invisible speck of dust away, 'No ... not really ... me and Rose go to the cinema together sometimes. I'm not really interested in anything else at the minute.'

Grace studied her young face and decided not to push any further. 'Well, you sound like me! Peter's taking me out for our aniversary tonight and I realised I haven't got anything nice to wear that isn't at least ten years old. I'm going shopping now ... you don't fancy coming with me, do you? I could do with a second opinion.'

Melanie looked at Grace, trying to gauge whether the offer was genuine or out of pity.

'Honestly, Mel, I really feel nervous about going clothes shopping. It's been so long – I'm really out of touch. Come with me, please?'

'Okay,' the twenty-four year old smiled. 'I'll ring Gwen and see if she can cover for me here.'

To be continued ...

Babe's Bible: Gorgeous Grace – available now

Babe's Bible: Love Letter – coming soon!